Nikolay Gavrilovich Chernyshevsky was born in 1828, and as one of the leaders of the Russian radical intelligentsia, wrote on politics, economics and literature. In 1862, a year after Tsar Alexander had emancipated the serfs, Chernyshevsky was sentenced to life imprisonment for his revolutionary writings and activities. A year later he smuggled his only novel, *What is To Be Done? Tales about New People* out of St Petersburg's Fortress of Peter and Paul. Soon after, he was exiled to Siberia where he spent most of the rest of his life. He died in 1889.

What is To Be Done? had an immediate success for it appealed to all those aspiring to a new life: to socialists wanting to throw off the yoke of autocracy, to women ruled by fathers and husbands, to a peasantry newly freed, but still bound by poverty. And offering as it did a model to the people for the ways they could work together in the future, they enthusiastically read passages aloud to each other. (Ten years after its publication, hundreds of these radicals had been rounded up for the show trials of the 1870s.)

Lenin carried a copy of the novel into exile with him; Alexandra Kollontai found it a source of inspiration for her ideas on sexual revolution; and today it is a popular classic in the Soviet Union.

For this new edition, Cathy Porter, author of *Alexandra Kollontai*, has translated passages censored from the original translation – passages which were considered too subversive in their sustained vision of socialism.

WHAT IS TO BE DONE ?

TALES ABOUT NEW PEOPLE

N. G. CHERNYSHEVSKY

Published by VIRAGO PRESS LIMITED 1982
Ely House, 37 Dover Street, London W1X 4HS

New Preface Copyright © Cathy Porter 1982

Original translation by Benjamin R. Tucker,
expanded by Cathy Porter

British Library Cataloguing in Publication Data
Chernyshevshiĭ,N.G.
  What is to be done? — (Virago Russian classics)
  I. Title   II. Porter, Cathy
  891.73'3 [F]   PG3321.C6C5
  ISBN 0–86068–336–2

Contents

Publisher's Note

Some unevenness in the printing of this book has been unavoidable, as we wanted to include the restored material in its correct place in the novel.

New Preface

1982

It was in 1862, a year after Tsar Alexander had emancipated the serfs, that thirty-four-year-old Chernyshevsky was sentenced to life imprisonment for his revolutionary writings and activities. The following year his first and only novel was smuggled out of St Petersburg's foul Peter and Paul fortress, while he was waiting to be deported to Siberia. *What is To Be Done? Tales About New People* was closely based on the triangular relationship between three of his friends, Maria Bokova, a pioneering medical student, her husband Pyotr, and their friend Mikhail Sechenov. But it spoke for a great many others too: for every young woman stifling at home with her parents; for thousands of women flocking into the cities after the emancipation to find independence; for all the socialist discussion groups and self-education circles in which women played such an important part; and for those in Land and Liberty, Russia's first revolutionary party.

Women who became revolutionaries in this and later generations would refer admiringly to the novel, and the impact its daring and revolutionary exploration of the 'woman question' had on them. For in Chernyshevsky's Véra Pávlovna they at last found a heroine they could positively identify with and learn from, a woman who had learnt from hard experience that she could no more deny her need for work than her need for love; that hard physical work could both bring economic and emotional independence from husbands and fathers, and increase the pleasures of love.

The emancipation of the serfs was the ruin of many aristocratic families. But for unmarried daughters, thrown out into the world either to find a rich husband (like Véra Pávlovna) or support themselves, this was the start of their own emancipation. Throughout the 1860s and '70s, women of all classes left their families to look for work and education in the cities. The problems they faced there gave Chernyshevsky his title. His story concerns just one such woman, her dreams of work and love. And it is through her that he challenges the new men and women of the 1860s to bring socialist principles to life.

To women imprisoned in authoritarian families the novel suggested platonic 'fictitious marriages' of convenience, in which a man would undertake to deliver a woman from her family, provide her with the passport she needed to work and travel in Russia, then set her free to follow her own desires. Many fictitious couples might prefer to stay together of course, like Véra Pávlovna and her first husband Lopukhin. To many of them this sort of platonic arrangement appeared as one way out of the old marriage, a partial solution to problems of jealousy and possessiveness, and the first step to sexual revolution.

But Chernyshevsky was also describing women's struggle for economic liberation. Véra Pávlovna's sewing collective shows that despite prejudice, despite lack of training and confidence, women are capable of creating their own employment and organising their lives collectively to suit their needs. It shows that such collectives could work happily and profitably, and that even the weak could become strong through cooperation. It became a highly popular model for new socialist work relations; hundreds of real-life workshops took their inspiration from Véra Pávlovna's example, and it was common for groups of people embarking on such projects to read appropriate passages of the novel aloud to one another.

It was a classic of this first phase of the revolution, and for later revolutionaries too; the Marxists of the 1890s grew up with it. Lenin first read it as a boy, carried it with him into exile, and acknowledged his debt to it when he used its title in 1902 for his pamphlet on party organisation. Alexandra Kollontai's imagination was immediately fired by it when she first read it at the age of fifteen, and she came back to it again and again as her ideas on sexual revolution matured. And when, again and again, she confronted her fellow Bolsheviks to demand that they listen to women, she was also reminding them of that first optimistic phase of the revolution, with its inspiring solutions to the problems of personal life. For she, like so many others, was transformed by this novel and its description of feelings in revolution.

What is To Be Done? was immediately, intensely popular. But Chernyshevsky was already popular for his literary criticism. In countless articles he had analysed the great works of Russian literature to expose the autocracy, and the way society split people's consciousness. And since women suffered especially harshly under tsarism, he argued, men must be prepared to 'bend the stick the other way'. For radical students like Peter Kropotkin in St Petersburg, for instance, this meant that:

> the young man who wouldn't lift a finger to serve a woman with a cup of tea would freely give to the young woman who came to study in Moscow or St Petersburg the only lesson he had, which brought him his daily bread, simply saying: "It's easier for a man to find work than it is for a woman. There's no attempt at chivalry in my offer, it's simply a matter of equality."

Ten years after the publication of *What is To Be Done?* hundreds of radicals had been rounded up and arrested, to appear in the two great show-trials fo the 1870s, the Trial of the 193 and the Trial of the Moscow Women. Those still free went underground, hardened their organisation to counter repression, and learnt to live lives of personal renunciation, with desperate acts of violence and endlessly deferred pleasure. Yet from prison and exile, at a distance from the struggle, Chernyshevsky continued to speak to them of the better lives they could lead in the present. With imagination and courage, he says, we can bring the future into the present. "Love it and work for it," he says, "for the closer you bring it, the brighter, richer and happier life will be!"

In prison, dreams of release, unhampered by the need for underground concealment, mingle with memories of love and freedom. For Véra Pávlovna happiness is the purpose of life – glimpsed in four dreams of almost hot-house intensity: of release from her parents, of indepen-dent work, of erotic pleasure, and finally her fourth dream, a triumphant, transcendent vision of joy. This dream, censored from the original translation, is the fulfilment of all the others, an extraordinary sustained vision of socialism. In it she looks to the past, when woman was slave, courtesan and nun, and to the present, when people will be freed from drudgery to work without compulsion and love without possessiveness. The other censored passages are equally subversive: Chernyshevsky's diatribe against blue-stockings, the great majority of whom are men; and a long and moving passage in which Nastasya Kryukova, a consumptive ex-prostitute working in the collective, tells Véra Pávlovna of the first man she ever loved sexually – the man who will soon be Véra Pávlovna's second husband.

For all who read *What Is To Be Done?*, then and later, it came as an exhortation to enjoy life, a manual of hope in depressing times. It is still a popular classic in the Soviet Union, read by every schoolchild. For us too, despite the occasional awkwardness of its construction and the dated ring of the original translation, I think it is a classic waiting to be rediscovered. And I don't think it is as humourless, high-minded or didactic as E.H. Carr suggests in his otherwise perceptive introduction; I find it funny, hopeful and erotic. It appeals to our capacity for pleasure, and to instincts frozen by cold-war propaganda and fears of war. It appeals for hope at a time when despair is engineered as a way of killing initiative and depriving us of the right to work, love and live in peace. "Rise up out of your hovel my friends, rise up!" he says. "It's not so hard! Go out into the bright free world. It's splendid to live there. Desire only to be happy!"

CATHY PORTER

Introduction

1960

The author of *What Is To Be Done?*, Nikolai Gavrilovich
Chernyshevsky, was a typical member—one might even
say, *the* typical member—of the Russian revolutionary intelligentsia of the second half of the nineteenth century. He
was dogmatic and self-assured, self-sacrificing to the point
of Quixotry, earnest to the point of humorlessness, a fervent believer in the power of reason and of ideas, but also
prepared for any action, however reckless and far-reaching,
which seemed rationally designed to promote the great
cause of progress. He was the son of a priest—this also
was a characteristic trait—and was born in 1828 in the
Volga town of Saratov. At the age of eighteen he found his
way to the University of Petersburg, and there he witnessed
from afar the European revolutions of 1848, which were the
turning-point in his life and in his beliefs. From then on,
he became a dedicated radical and revolutionary.

After a brief period as a teacher Chernyshevsky turned
to a literary career, and from 1854 onward was one of the
regular and most effective contributors to the progressive
journal *Sovremennik* (*The Contemporary*), Belinsky's old
organ. The moment was propitious. The death of Nicholas
I in 1855 and the relaxation of censorship and repression
which marked the first years of Alexander II enabled Chernyshevsky to abandon the literary and aesthetic essays,
which were the first cloak for his advanced opinions, for
the open discussion of the crucial problems of agrarian pol-

icy and of the peasant commune. Presently he became involved in the organization of underground activities. In the fresh wave of reaction which followed the proclamation of the emancipation of the serfs he was arrested in 1862. For more than eighteen months he remained in the Peter-and-Paul fortress; and it was here that he wrote *What Is To Be Done?* In 1864—the year in which the novel was published—he was sent to hard labor in Siberia, where he remained till 1883. Then he was allowed to live in Astrakhan, and eventually—a few months before his death in 1889—to return to his native town of Saratov. During this long postscript to his active political life he continued to record his impressions in letters and diaries, and even occasionally for publication. But the important part of his literary career is concentrated in the years 1854 to 1862, with *What Is To Be Done?* as its culminating point.

Chernyshevsky marked the transition from the group known in nineteenth-century Russian intellectual history as "the men of the forties" to "the men of the sixties," of whom he could claim to have been the first. "The men of the forties"—Bakunin, Herzen, Ogarev, Turgenev, Belinsky, with all their differences, all belonged to this group—were in essence members of the last generation of the Romantics. Politically, they were reared in the tradition of constitutional western liberalism; philosophically, in the tradition of the German idealists, mainly Fichte, Schelling, and Hegel. Reacting against the backwardness, the harshness, and the obscurantism of the Russia of the Tsars, finding their lodestar in an idealized picture of the liberty, equality, and fraternity of the West, they failed to evolve any concrete program, whether of reform or of revolution, for their own country. They often seemed to be concerned more with individual self-improvement than with the reconstruction of Russian society, which was abandoned or neglected as a hopeless task. The derisive label applied to them by "the men of the sixties" which stuck most closely was "the cult of the beautiful soul."

The European revolutions of 1848-9 were the dividing-line between the two Russian generations. Except for Belinsky, who died in Russia in 1847, all the important "men of the forties" had gone to western Europe as temporary or permanent *émigrés*. Bakunin, arrested in Saxony, spent more than ten vital years in the dungeons of three countries

and in Siberia, and reappeared in western Europe only after
the new lines of demarcation had been drawn. Only Herzen
and Turgenev remained to defend in their different ways
the outmoded tradition of the forties against the challenge
of the younger generation.

Chernyshevsky had begun his public career as an ardent
admirer and disciple of Herzen. At the end of the 1850's
when Herzen accepted at its face value the "thaw" of the
first years of Alexander's reign and seemed ready to come to
terms with the reforming autocrat, the breach occurred between Herzen and Chernyshevsky which marked the opening of hostilities between the generations. Herzen in a
famous article of 1859 in his London journal *The Bell*,
under the title (in English) "Very Dangerous!!," branded
the intransigent radicalism of Chernyshevsky and his friends
in Russia. A visit by Chernyshevsky to Herzen in London
only hardened the antipathy between them. Nor did it improve matters when, after the emancipation of the serfs in
1861 and the Polish insurrection two years later, Herzen
was forced to admit that the reforming zeal of Alexander II
had been skin-deep and had only skimmed the surface of
the autocracy. By this time the rift between the cautious
liberals of the forties and the angry young radicals of the
sixties was too deep to be bridged.

The men of the sixties proudly thought of themselves as
rejecting sentimental romanticism for hard-headed realism,
philosophical idealism for materialism, metaphysics for science. Though the ideas of the western European "Enlightenment" had penetrated Russian court circles under Cath-
erine the Great, they had made little impact on Russian life
or on Russian politics; and the cult of reason which played
so fundamental a role in Chernyshevsky's thinking was in
some respects only a belated afterglow of the vision which
had dawned on France and western Europe in the eight-
eenth century. Helvétius, Diderot, and Rousseau—the Rousseau of *Emile* and *La Nouvelle Héloïse* rather than of the
Confessions and the *Social Contract*—were among Chernyshevsky's early gods. The intellectual movement of the
1860's had some claim to be called Russia's Age of Reason.

But it was Reason cast in a new mold. This was pre-
eminently the age of the supreme cult of science. Chernyshevsky had been an early Russian devotee of Feuerbach
(*"man ist was man isst"*). But it was that once famous bible

of materialism, Büchner's *Kraft und Stoff,* published in Germany in 1855 and quickly circulated in Russia in illicit translations, which satisfied the young Russians of the 1860's that human life and human behavior were to be explained in material and physiological terms, and that the reform of society was in the strictest sense a scientific problem. Rather surprisingly, Chernyshevsky dismissed Comte as superficial, and was shocked by the deductions which some social thinkers were beginning to draw from Darwin's survival of the fittest. But this was because he felt himself to possess a simpler and more direct key to the problems of society. The question of morality seemed to him to have been solved once for all by the English Utilitarians, known to him principally through John Stuart Mill, whom he translated. Nothing else could be expected, and nothing else was needed, than the pursuit by every individual of his rational and enlightened self-interest. Like Buckle, Chernyshevsky attributed misconduct to ignorance.

The use of fiction for the discussion and dissemination of social ideas was already a Russian nineteenth-century tradition. Herzen in the forties, before his departure from Russia, had written a short and not very successful novel, *Who Is To Blame?,* which attempted to analyze the eternal triangle in the naïve terms of a rational morality. In 1862 Turgenev, quickly sensitive to the appearance on the scene of the young men of the sixties, had introduced a caricature of one of them, under the name Bazarov, into his novel *Fathers and Sons,* applying to him, and putting into popular circulation for the first time, the title of "nihilist." Bazarov is the classic example of the type: indeed, one may suspect that this is a case where a caricature of genius helped to create the type. Bazarov constantly insists on his mission: he is a man dedicated to a cause—"no ordinary man." His creed is science plus rational morality: he "does not believe in principles, but believes in frogs," and thinks that "a decent chemist is twenty times more useful than any poet." Chernyshevsky's *What Is To Be Done?* is not so much a retort to *Fathers and Sons* as a proud acceptance of it. His principal characters are reincarnations of Bazarov. Lopukhóv spurns "what are called lofty feelings, ideal impulses," and exalts "the striving of every man for his own advantage." Kirsánov (the very name is borrowed from Turgenev) treats "pompous words like honor" as "ambiguous and ob-

scure," and proclaims that "every man is an egoist." Rakhmétov, introduced in a chapter entitled "An Unusual Man,"
eats beef to make himself strong, sleeps on nails to harden
himself for the tasks ahead, and, like Bazarov, adopts a de-
liberately brusque manner of conversation lest he should
waste time unnecessarily on empty words and formalities.

Almost everything about *What Is To Be Done?* is disconcerting to the modern western reader. Its form is that of
a highly discursive Victorian English novel. Its original
subtitle, *Tales about New People,* should warn the reader
against expecting a single unitary plot. It wanders from
theme to theme, minor characters appear and disappear,
new major characters are suddenly introduced at the whim
of the author. The one character who runs throughout the
story, and round whom the action revolves, is the heroine,
Véra Pávlovna; but three quarters of the way through, a secondary heroine (with her attendant hero) appears in the
person of Katerína, and for some time occupies the center of
the stage. If symmetry and order were essential qualities
of art, *What Is To Be Done?* could not be ranked as a work
of art. The author holds conversations with the "perceptive
reader," buttonholing him in the distressingly arch manner
of Thackeray, whom he more than once quotes with admiration (an admiration tempered by the just criticism of same-
ness and lack of breadth—everything that he has to say is
in *Vanity Fair,* and the rest mere repetition). But he does
not even pick up the scattered threads of his story in the
last chapter with the formal tidiness of the Victorian novelist. (It ends in a bewildering and incomprehensible Wal-
purgis Night of Reason, with a nameless Woman in Black
leading the abstemious revels, and in the half-mocking
promise of a second part—which was, of course, never written. This material is omitted from the present edition.)

The other disconcerting factor for the contemporary
reader is Chernyshevsky's attitude to a question which has
become the predominant obsession of the mid-twentieth-
century western novelist. The Victorian novelist, like Victorian society, veiled the physical relations between the
sexes in a cloud of prudery. But neither he nor his reader
for a moment questioned their importance; they were
merely transposed by the convention of the period into a
sentimental key. The attitude of Chernyshevsky is quite
different. He does not mince his words when he brings onto

the stage a reformed prostitute or the mistress of a rich man. But in a book which is constantly—one might almost say, primarily—concerned with the relation, and specifically the marital relation, between men and women, he dismisses the physical aspect of that relation as unessential and not seriously worth discussion. He had already made his standpoint clear in a review of Turgenev's story "Asia":

> Away with erotic problems. The modern reader has no interest in them. He is concerned with the question of perfecting the administration and the judicial system, with financial questions, with the problem of liberating the peasant.

The descriptions of life in *What Is To Be Done?* lead us to suppose that Véra Pávlovna has no physical relations with her first husband, Lopukhóv, such relations being incompatible with their rational conception of human behavior. Certain passages might support the inference that she and her second husband, Kirsánov, conducted themselves more normally. But Chernyshevsky nowhere makes this point explicit, as he would have done if had thought it important; and it would be a complete anachronism to seek here an explanation of the breakdown of Véra's first marriage. Another strange feature of *What Is To Be Done?* comes into the picture at this point. In the endless discussions about marriage in which Véra Pávlovna and her two successive partners engage, no hint occurs anywhere that marriage commonly results in offspring or that this may be one of its functions. The leading characters of the novel have parents, but no children. In one place only, in reporting a conversation of the secondary heroine Katerína a few years after her marriage in which she casually mentions her son, the author adds, without further elaboration, in an almost comic parenthesis: "So she has a son." So passionate a believer as Chernyshevsky in the future of the human race must have wanted and expected children to be produced. But he would clearly have liked them to be produced in some way which impinged less disturbingly on the rational human personality. All this creates an embarrassing impression of lack not only of sophistication but also of common sense, especially when Chernyshevsky describes his characters diverting themselves in harmless merriment. Again and again the reader is tempted to exclaim in the language of Byron:

O Mirth and Innocence! O Milk and Water!

But the Russian revolutionaries were not innocents abroad, and were anything but milk-and-water characters. What was the inspiration which they found in *What Is To Be Done?* and what made it for more than fifty years a major revolutionary classic? It is not easy to label Chernyshevsky. A nihilist he was certainly not—except in the sense that every Russian radical and progressive believed automatically in the total destruction of the existing order of Russian society. Chernyshevsky is generally counted as a *narodnik* or "populist" (to use the conventional English equivalent); for that term covers a wealth of different ideas and a chaotic, amorphous movement of revolt. But Chernyshevsky lacked the idealization of the Russian peasant commune which was often regarded as the hallmark of "populism." He was more interested in the town than in the country; and this has helped to establish the picture of him in current Soviet tradition as an embryonic Russian Marxist. Nor does Chernyshevsky show anything of the common desire of the populists to glorify Russia at the expense of the bourgeois and decadent West. He had no Slavophile leanings and remained, in terms of Russian thought, an unrepentant westerner. The keynotes of all his writing, and what succeeding generations of revolutionaries above all found in him, were faith in socialism, faith in progress, and faith in reason.

Socialism was the term which all Russian radicals, from Herzen onward, applied to their vision of the society of the future. Negatively, it carried with it the firm rejection of western bourgeois democracy and western capitalism. Positively, early Russian socialism was nourished on the imaginary societies and commonwealths of the French utopians, of whom Fourier, with his "phalansteries" and his psychological speculations about the transformation of human nature, was the most popular and influential in Russia. In a country where any kind of political activity was taboo, socialism long remained in its utopian and purely imaginative stage. The economic background of *What Is To Be Done?* is provided by the co-operatives of seamstresses formed by the heroine and described in loving detail. From the socialist economy the features of profit, competition, and exploitation inherent in capitalism will disappear; and the welfare of the new community will be solidly built on equal co-operation and mutual aid among the workers engaged in production. Here Chernyshevsky provides an urban counterpart for the "going to the people" in the villages which was so characteristic a feature of the populist movement. Two generations of Chernyshevsky's readers were satisfied and inspired by this unsophisticated picture of selfless human endeavor.

Faith in progress and in the ultimate attainment of the goal is common to all the characters in *What Is To Be Done?* Here, too, Chernyshevsky harks back to the Enlightenment, and may be regarded as the disciple of Condorcet quite as much as of Darwin. Progress remains for him a basic assumption, an article of belief, rather than something that calls for scientific proof. A pathetic letter written to his wife from Siberia in 1871, after nine years of imprisonment and exile, attests both his faith in the future and his faith in his own mission:

> Poor Russian people, a miserable fate awaits it in this struggle. But the result will be favorable, and then, my dear, it will have need of truth. I am no longer a young man, but remember that our life is still ahead of us. . . . I can speak of historical events because I have learned and thought much. My turn will come. We will then see whether it is worth complaining about the fact that for so many years I have only been able to study and think. We will then see that this has been useful for our country.*

But, most of all, it is faith in human reason which served as the *leitmotif* of *What Is To Be Done?* and as the inspiration which drove men and women to do and to suffer in the sacred cause of the revolution. Reason had given man the power to master and transform his material environment: the wonders of science were unbounded. But reason, it now seemed clear, had also given man the power to transform himself and, in transforming himself, to transform

---

* Quoted from F. Venturi: *Roots of Revolution* (Alfred A. Knopf, Inc., 1960), p. 184. This work contains the best recent account of Chernyshevsky in English.

society. Like most Russians, Chernyshevsky was not an individualist in the sense of setting up any sharp opposition between society and the individual: to transform one meant to transform the other. When Chernyshevsky speaks of the "new men," he is thinking also of the new society which they will build.

The theme of the "new men" runs as a guiding thread through the pages of *What Is To Be Done?* Six years ago, remarks Chernyshevsky with odd precision, the new type of man did not yet exist. His predecessors (these are still "the men of the forties") "felt themselves alone, powerless, and were therefore inactive, or despondent, or exalted, or indulged in romanticism and fantasy." The new man is marked by "cold-blooded practicality, regular and calculating activity, active calculation." The characters in *What Is To Be Done?* are "new men" carried, as we have seen, to the extreme point of logical consistency. The heroine, Véra Pávlovna, is "one of the first women whose life has been ordered well." These people were the harbingers of the new society. At present there were still ten "antediluvians" to one modern man. But "the number of decent people grows every year," and soon "all people will be decent people."

The faith and optimism of Chernyshevsky are thus simpler, more direct, and more naïve than the faith and optimism of Marx. Marx believed in the forces of history working themselves out through the actions of men to a goal that could be foreseen. This, too, was belief in reason, but in a less personal reason than that which occupied the central place in Chernyshevsky's thought. For Chernyshevsky it was human ignorance rather than the interested resistance of those in possession which was the ultimate obstacle to progress. But this conviction also brought a message of hope. The task of the revolutionaries was to instruct and transform human beings, to make "decent people" of them, by persuading them to harken to the voice of reason.

There is no doubt about the potency of this message in the time and circumstances in which it was delivered. Even Turgenev, who complained that Chernyshevsky did not "understand poetry," admitted that he understood "the needs of real contemporary life." It was Chernyshevsky more than any other one man who shaped the moral attitudes of two generations of Russian revolutionaries. Lenin hailed him as "a great Russian socialist" (though still a "utopian socialist") and undoubtedly regarded him as one of the precursors of Bolshevism. Lenin's ideal revolutionary would have lived as Chernyshevsky's heroes and heroines lived. It should not be forgotten that Chernyshevsky's one novel was written in prison in the first year of his long martyrdom for his convictions. These grim surroundings were the birthplace not only of *What Is To Be Done?* but also of the whole revolutionary movement. It is neither accidental nor surprising that this gray, austere, humorless utopia—a reflection of these conditions—should have set the tone for the human and personal side of the revolution.

E. H. CARR

Translator's Preface

1883

This novel, the last work and only novel from Chernyshevsky's pen, originally appeared in 1863 in a St. Petersburg magazine, the author writing it at that time in a St. Petersburg dungeon, where he was confined for twenty-two months prior to being sent into exile in Siberia by the cruel Tsar who has since paid the penalty of this crime and many others. This martyr-hero of the modern Revolution still languishes in a remote corner of that cheerless country, his health ruined and—if report be true—his mind shattered by his long solitude and enforced abstention from literary and revolutionary work. The present Tsar, true son of his father, persistently refuses to mitigate his sentence, despite the petition for Chernyshevsky's freedom sent not long ago to Alexander III by the literary celebrities of the world gathered in international congress at Vienna.

The Russian Nihilists regard the present work as a faithful portraiture of themselves and their movement, and as such they contrast it with the celebrated *Fathers and Sons* of Turgenev, which they consider rather as a caricature. The fundamental idea of Chernyshevsky's work is that woman is a human being and not an animal created for man's benefit, and its chief purpose is to show the superiority of free unions between men and women over the indissoluble marriage sanctioned by Church and State. It may almost be considered a continuation of the great Herzen's novel, *Who Is To Blame?*, written fifteen years before on the same subject.

If the reader should find the work singular in form and sometimes obscure, he must remember that it was written under the eye of an autocrat who punished with terrific severity any one who wrote against "the doctrines of the Orthodox Church, its traditions and ceremonies, or the truths and dogmas of Christian faith in general," against "the inviolability of the Supreme Autocratic Power or the respect due to the Imperial Family," anything contrary to "the fundamental regulations of the State," or anything tending to "shock good morals and propriety."

As a work of art *What Is To Be Done?* speaks for itself. Nevertheless, the words of a European writer regarding it may not be amiss. "In the author's view the object of art is not to embellish and idealize nature, but to reproduce her interesting phases; and poetry—verse, the drama, the novel —should explain nature in reproducing her; the poet must pronounce sentence. He must represent human beings as they really are, and not incarnate in them an abstract principle, good or bad; that is why in this novel men indisputably good have faults, as reality shows them to us, while bad people possess at the same time some good qualities, as is almost always the case in real life."

Tyranny knows no better use for such an author than to exile him. But Liberty can still utilize his work. Tyranny, torture Truth's heralds as it may, cannot kill Truth itself— nay, can only add to its vitality. Chernyshevsky is in isolation, but his glad tidings to the poor and the oppressed are spreading among the peoples of the earth, and now in this translation for the first time find their way across the ocean to enlighten our New World.

BENJAMIN R. TUCKER

WHAT

IS TO BE DONE?

Véra Pávlovna Rozálsky (Vérka, Vérochka), heroine
Dmítry Sergéich Lopukhóv, Véra's first husband
Pável Konstantínych Rozálsky, Véra's father
Mária Alexévna Rozálsky, Véra's mother
Fédya Rozálsky, Véra's younger brother
Matryóna, Rozálsky's servant
Ánna Petróvna Storéshnikov, Rozálsky's employer
Mikhaíl Iványch Storéshnikov (Mísha, Michél), her son
Alexánder Matvéich Kirsánov (Sásha, Sáshenka), Véra's second husband
Rakhmétov (Nikítushka Lómov), the "unusual man," Lopukhóv's friend
Mítya Kirsánov, Véra's small son
Madame Mertzálov, Véra's friend and business associate
Sásha Pribýtkova, a working girl in Véra's factory
Nastásya Borísovna Kryúkov (Nastenka), a working girl, Kirsánov's friend
Julie Letellier ⎫
Serge ⎬ "fast set," friends of young Storéshnikov
Jean Solovtsóv ⎭
Katerína Vassílievna Pólozov (Kátya, Kátenka), Kirsánov's patient and Véra's friend
Pólozov, Kátya's father
Karl Fyódorych, one of the Pólozov doctors
Karl Yákovlich Beaumont, Kátya's husband
Some minor characters: Másha, Véra's maid; Stepán; Pyótr; servants

A FOOL

On the morning of the eleventh of July, 1856, the servants of one of the principal hotels in St. Petersburg, situated near the Moscow railway station, became greatly perplexed and even somewhat alarmed. The night before, after eight o'clock, a traveler had arrived, carrying a valise, who, after having given up his passport that it might be taken to the police to be visaed, had ordered a cutlet and some tea, and then, pleading fatigue and need of sleep as a pretext, had asked that he might be disturbed no further, notifying them at the same time to awaken him without fail at exactly eight o'clock in the morning, as he had pressing business.

As soon as he was alone, he had locked his door. For a while the noise of the knife, fork, and tea-service was heard, then all became silent again: the man doubtless had gone to sleep.

In the morning, at eight o'clock, the waiter did not fail to knock at the new-comer's door.

But the new-comer did not respond. The waiter knocked louder, and louder yet. Still the new-comer did not respond: he probably was very tired. The waiter waited a quarter of an hour, then began again to knock and call, but with no better success. Then he went to consult the other waiters and the butler.

"Could something have happened to the traveler?"

"We must burst open the door," he concluded.

"No," said another, "the door can be burst open only in the presence of the police."

They decided to try once more, and with greater energy, to awaken the obstinate traveler, and, in case they should not succeed, to send for the police.

Which they had to do. While waiting for the police, they looked at each other anxiously, saying: "What can have happened?"

Towards ten o'clock the commissioner of police arrived; he began by knocking at the door himself, and then ordered the waiters to knock a last time. The same success.

"There is nothing left but to burst open the door," said the official; "do so, my friends."

The door yielded; they entered; the room was empty.

"Look under the bed," said the official. At the same time, approaching the table, he saw a sheet of paper, unfolded, upon which were written these words:

"I leave at eleven o'clock in the evening and shall not return. I shall be heard on the Liteiny Bridge between two and three o'clock in the morning. Suspect no one."

"Ah! It's all clear now! at first we did not understand," said the official.

"What do you mean, Ivan Afanasyevich?" asked the butler.

"Give me some tea, and I will tell you."

The story of the commissioner of police was for a long time the subject of all sorts of conversations; as for the adventure itself, this was it: At half-past two in the morning, the night being extremely dark, something like a flash was seen on the Liteiny Bridge, and at the same time a pistol shot was heard. The bridge guard and the few people who were passing ran to the spot, but found nobody.

"It's not a murder; some one has blown his own brains out," they said; and some of the more generous offered to search the river. Hooks were brought and even a fisherman's net; but they pulled from the water only a few pieces of wood. Of the body no trace, and besides the night was very dark, and much time had elapsed: the body had had time to drift out to sea.

"Go on searching!" said a group of carpers, who maintained that there was no body and that some drunkard or practical joker had simply fired a shot and fled. "Perhaps he has even mingled with the crowd, and is laughing at the alarm which he has caused." These carpers were evidently *progressives.* But the majority, *conservative,* as it always is when it reasons prudently, held to the first explanation.

"A practical joker? Go to! Some one has really blown his brains out."

Being less numerous, the progressives were conquered. But the conquerors split at the very moment of victory.

He had blown his brains out, certainly, but why?

"He was drunk," said some.

"He had dissipated his fortune," thought others.

"Simply an imbecile!" observed somebody.

Upon this word *imbecile,* all agreed, even those who disputed suicide.

In short, whether it was a drunkard or a spendthrift who had blown his brains out or a practical joker who had made a pretense of killing himself (in the latter case the joke was a stupid one), he was an imbecile.

There ended the night's adventure. At the hotel was found the proof that it was no piece of nonsense, but a real suicide.

This conclusion satisfied the conservatives especially; for, said they, it proves that we are right. If it had been only a practical joker, we might have hesitated between the terms imbecile and insolent. But to blow one's brains out on a bridge! On a bridge, I ask you? Does one blow his brains out on a bridge? Why on a bridge? It would be stupid to do it on a bridge. Indisputably, then, he was a fool.

"Precisely," objected the progressives; "does one blow his brains out on a bridge?" And they in their turn disputed the reality of the suicide.

But that same evening the hotel personnel, being summoned to the police bureau to examine a cap pierced by a ball, which had been taken from the water, identified it as the actual cap worn by the traveler of the night before.

There had been a suicide, then, and the spirit of negation and progress was once more conquered.

Yes, it was really a fool; but suddenly a new thought struck them: to blow one's brains out on a bridge,—why, it is most clever! In that way one avoids long suffering in case of a simple wound. *He* calculated wisely; he was prudent.

Now the mystification was complete. A fool, and yet a prudent one!

FIRST CONSEQUENCE

OF THE

FOOLISH ACT

The same day, towards eleven o'clock in the morning, in a little country-house on Kamenny Island,* a young woman sat sewing and humming a singularly bold French song:

> *Sous nos guenilles, nous sommes*
> *De courageux travailleurs;*
> *Nous voulons pour tous les hommes*
> *Science et destins meilleurs,*
> *Etudions, travaillons,*
> *La force est à qui saura;*
> *Etudions, travaillons,*
> *L'abondance nous viendra!*
> *Ah! ça ira! ça ira! ça ira!*
> *Le peuple en ce jour répète!*
> *Ah! ça ira! ça ira! ça ira!*
> *Qui vivra verra!*

The melody of this audacious song was gay; there were two or three sad notes in it, but these entirely disappeared in the refrain and in the last couplet. But such was the condition of the mind of the songstress that these two or three sad notes sounded above the others in her song. She saw

* An island in the vicinity of St. Petersburg, full of country houses, where citizens of St. Petersburg used to go to spend their summers.

this herself, started, and tried to sustain the gay notes longer and glide over the others. Vain efforts! her thought dominated her in spite of herself, and the sad notes always prevailed over the others.

It was easy to see that the young woman was trying to repress the sadness which had taken possession of her, and when, from time to time, she succeeded and the song took its joyous pace, her work doubled in rapidity. She seemed to be an excellent seamstress. At this moment the maid, a young and pretty person, entered.

"See Másha," * the young lady said to her, "how well I sew! I have almost finished the ruffles which I am embroidering to wear at your wedding."

"Oh! there is less work in them than in the ones you wanted me to embroider."

"I readily believe it! Shouldn't the bride be more beautifully adorned than her guests?"

"I've brought you a letter, Véra Pávlovna."

Véra Pávlovna took the letter with an air of perplexity that showed in her face. The envelope bore the city stamp.

"So he's in Moscow!" she whispered,—and she hastily broke open the letter and turned pale.

"It isn't possible! . . . I did not read it right. . . . The letter cannot say that!" she cried, letting her arms fall by her sides.

Again she began to read. This time her eyes fixed themselves on the fatal paper, and those beautiful clear eyes became dimmer and dimmer. She let the letter fall upon her work-table, and, hiding her head in her hands, she burst into sobs.

"What have I done? What have I done?" she cried, despairingly. "Oh, what have I done?"

"Vérochka!" † suddenly exclaimed a young man, hurrying into the room; "Vérochka! What has happened to you? And why these tears?"

"Read this!" . . . She handed him the letter. Véra Pávlovna sobbed no longer, but remained motionless as if nailed to her seat, and scarcely breathing.

The young man took the letter; he grew pale, his hands trembled, and his eyes remained fixed for a long time upon the text, though it was brief. This letter read:

* Másha is the diminutive of Maria.
† Vérochka is the diminutive of Véra.

"I disturbed your tranquillity; I quit the scene.
Do not pity me. I love you both so much that I
am quite content in my resolution. Adieu."

Absorbed for a moment in his sadness, the young man
then came up to the young woman, who still was motionless, and took her hand:

"Vérochka! . . ."

But the young woman uttered a cry of terror, and, rising,
as if electrified, she convulsively repulsed the young man.

"Don't! Don't touch me! You're covered with blood!
Leave me!"

Suddenly she staggered and sank into an armchair, her
head in her hands.

"It's also on me, his blood! on me especially! You're not
guilty . . . it is I, I alone! What have I done? What have
I done?"

And her sobs increased.

"Vérochka," said the young man, timidly; "Vérochka, my
love!"

"No, leave me," she answered, with a trembling voice, as
soon as she could get breath. "Don't speak to me! In a moment you will find me calmer; leave me."

He went into his study, and sat down again at the writing-
table where a quarter of an hour before he had been so calm
and happy. He took up his pen and wrote: "It is in such
moments that one must retain self-possession. I have will
power, and this will all pass. But will *she* bear it? Oh! it is
horrible! Happiness is lost!"

"Shall we have a talk now, darling?" said an altered voice,
which tried to appear firm.

"We must separate," continued Véra Pávlovna, "We must
separate! I have decided upon it. It is frightful; but it would
be even more frightful to continue to live in each other's
sight. Am I not his murderer? Have I not killed him for
you?"

"But, Vérochka, it is not your fault."

"Do not try to justify me, unless you wish me to hate
you. I am guilty. Pardon me, my beloved, for taking a resolution so painful to you. To me also it is painful, but is the
only one that we can take. You will soon recognize it yourself. So be it, then! I wish first to fly from this city, which
would remind me too vividly of the past. The sale of my

effects will afford me some resources. I will go to Tver,
to Nizhni Novgorod, no matter where. I will give singing lessons; or else I will become a governess. I can
always earn what I need. If not, I will appeal to you. I
count on you; and let that prove to you that you are ever
dear to me. And now we must say goodbye . . . goodbye
forever! Go now; I shall be better alone; and tomorrow you
can come back, for I shall be here no longer. I will go to
Moscow; there I will find out what city is best adapted to
my purpose. I forbid your presence at the station at the
time of my departure. Goodbye, then, my love; give me
your hand for the last time."

He desired to embrace her; but she thrust him back forcibly, saying:

"No! that would be an outrage upon him. Give me your
hand; do you feel with what force I press it? Goodbye!"

He kept her hand in his till she withdrew it.

"Enough! Go!"

And with a look of ineffable tenderness, she retired with
a firm step, and without looking back.

He went about, dazed, like a drunken man, unable to find
his hat, though he held it in his hand without knowing it;
at last, however, he took his overcoat from the hall and
started off. But he had not yet reached the gateway when he
heard footsteps behind him. Doubtless it was Másha. Had
she vanished? He turned around; it was—Véra Pávlovna,
who threw herself into his arms and said ardently:

"I could not resist, dear friend; and now farewell forever!"

She ran rapidly away, threw herself upon her bed, and
burst into tears.

PREFACE

Love is the subject of this novel; a young woman is its principal character.

"So far so good, even though the novel should be bad," says the feminine reader; and she is right.

But the masculine reader does not praise so readily; thought in man being more intense and more developed than in woman. He says (what probably the feminine reader also thinks without considering it proper to say so, which excuses me from discussing the point with her),— the masculine reader says: "I know perfectly well that the man who is said to have blown his brains out is all right."

I attack him on this phrase *I know,* and say to him: "You *do not know it,* since it has not been told you. You know nothing, not even that by the way in which I have begun my novel I have made you my dupe. Didn't you know this? Really?"

Yes, the very first pages of the tale reveal that I have a very poor opinion of the public. I have employed the ordinary trick of novelists. I have begun with dramatic scenes, taken from the middle or the end of my story, and have taken care to confuse and obscure them.

Public, you are good-natured, very good-natured, and consequently you are neither quick to see nor difficult to please. One may be sure that you will not see from the first pages whether a novel is worthy of being read. Your scent is not keen, and to aid you in making up your mind, two things are necessary: the name of a known author and such a style of writing as will produce an effect.

This is the first novel that I offer you, and you have not yet made up your mind whether or not I have talent and art. My name does not yet attract you. I am obliged, therefore, to decoy you. Don't blame me for this. It is your own ingenuousness that compels me to stoop to this triviality. But now that I hold you in my hands, I can continue my story as I think proper—that is, without subterfuge. There will be no more mystery; you will be able to foresee twenty pages in advance the climax of each situation, and I will even tell you that all will end gaily amid wine and song.

The author needs no subterfuge, dear public, because he is ever concerned with the nonsense in your head, with the amount of unnecessary, yes, unnecessary suffering caused to each person by the wild muddle of your notions. I am sorry and amused looking at you. You are so helpless and so evil from the inordinate quantity of nonsense crammed into your poor head.

I am angry at you because you are so wicked towards people, that is towards yourselves! It is for that I am scolding you. You are wicked from intellectual impotence and, therefore, scolding you, I must help you. How, then, shall I start helping you? Well, let's begin with what you are thinking of right now— What sort of a writer is this fellow who dares to address me so insolently? I'll tell you.

I am an author without talent who doesn't even have a complete command of his own language. But it matters little. Read on at any rate, kind public. Truth is a good thing which compensates even for an author's faults. This reading will be useful to you, and you will experience no deception, since I have warned you that you will find in my novel neither talent nor art, only the truth.

For the rest, my kind public, regardless of how you may love to read between the lines, I prefer to tell you everything. Because I have confessed that I have no trace of talent and that my novel will be faulty in the telling, do not conclude that I am inferior to the story-tellers whom you accept and that this book is beneath their writings. That is not the purpose of my explanation. I merely mean that my story is very weak, so far as execution is concerned, in comparison with the works produced by real talent. But, as for the celebrated works of your favorite authors, you may, even in point of execution, put it on their level; you may even place it above them; for there is more art here than in the works aforesaid, you may be sure. And now, public, thank me! And since you love so well to bend the knee before him who disdains you, salute me!

Happily, scattered through your throngs, there exist, O public, persons, more and more numerous, whom I esteem. If I have just been impudent, it was because I spoke only to the vast majority of you. Before the persons to whom I have just referred, on the contrary, I shall be modest and even timid. Only, with them, long explanations are useless. I know in advance that we shall get along together. Men of research and justice, intelligence and goodness, it is but yesterday that you emerged among us; and already your number is great and becoming ever greater. If you were the whole public, I should not need to write; if you did not exist, I could not write. But you are a part of the public, without yet being the whole public; and that is why it is possible, that is why it is necessary, for me to write.

Chapter First

THE LIFE OF

VÉRA PÁVLOVNA

WITH HER PARENTS

: I :

The education of Véra Pávlovna was very ordinary, and there was nothing peculiar in her life until she made the acquaintance of Lopukhóv, the medical student.

Véra Pávlovna grew up in a fine house on Gorokhovaya Street, between Sadovaya Street and the Semenovsky Bridge. This house is now duly labelled with a number, but in 1852, when numbers were not in use to designate the houses of any given street, it bore this inscription:—

House of Ivan Zakharovich Storéshnikov, present Councillor of State.

So said the inscription, although Ivan Zakharovich Storéshnikov died in 1837. After that, according to the legal title-deeds, the owner of the house was his son, Mikhaíl Iványch. But the tenants knew that Mikhaíl Iványch was only the son of the mistress, and that the mistress of the house was Ánna Petróvna.

The house was what it still is, large, with two carriage-ways, four flights of steps from the street, and three interior courtyards.

Then (as is still the case today) the mistress of the house and her son lived on the first and naturally the principal floor. Ánna Petróvna has remained a beautiful lady, and Mikhaíl Iványch is today, as he was in 1852, an elegant and

handsome officer. Who lives now in the dirtiest of the innumerable flats of the first court, fifth door on the right? I
do not know. But in 1852 it was inhabited by the steward
of the house, Pável Konstantínych Rozálsky, a robust and
fine-looking man. His wife, Mária Alexévna, a slender person, tall and possessed of a strong constitution, his young
and beautiful daughter (Véra Pávlovna), and his son Fédia,
nine years old, made up the family.

Besides his position of steward, Pável Konstantínych was
employed as chief deputy in I know not which ministerial
bureau. As an employee he had no perquisites; his perquisites as steward were very moderate; for Pável Konstantínych, as he said to himself, had a conscience, which he valued at least as highly as the benevolence of the proprietor.
In short, the worthy steward had amassed in fourteen years
about 10,000 rubles, of which but 3,000 had come from the
proprietor's pocket. The rest was derived from a little business peculiarly his own: Pável Konstantínych combined
with his other functions that of a pawn-broker. Mária Alexévna also had her little capital: almost 5,000 rubles, she told
the gossips, but really much more. She had begun fifteen
years before by the sale of a fur-lined pelisse, a poor lot of
furniture, and an old coat left her by her brother, a deceased
government employee.

These brought her 150 rubles, which she lost no time in
lending on security. Much bolder than her husband, she
braved risks for the sake of greater gains. More than once
she had been caught. One day a sharper pawned to her for
five rubles a stolen passport, and Mária Alexévna not only
lost the five rubles, but had to pay fifteen to get out of the
scrape. Another time a swindler, in consideration of a loan of
twenty rubles, left her with a gold watch, the proceeds of
a murder followed by robbery, and Mária Alexévna had to
pay heavily this time to get clear. But if she suffered losses
which her more prudent husband had no occasion to fear,
on the other hand she saw her profits rolling up more
rapidly.

To make money she would stop at nothing.

One day—Véra Pávlovna was still small—a somewhat
strange event occurred. Vérochka, indeed, would not have
understood it, had not the cook, beaten by Mária Alexévna,
been eager to explain to the little girl, in a very intelligible
fashion, the matter in question.

A lady as beautiful as she was richly dressed stopped for some time at the house of Mária Alexévna.

This lady received the visits of a very fine-looking gentleman, who often gave bonbons to Vérochka and even made her a present of two illustrated books. The engravings in one of these books represented animals and cities; as for the other, Mária Alexévna took it away from her daughter as soon as the visitor had gone, and the only time that Vérochka saw the engravings was on the day when he showed them to her.

While the lady remained, an unusual tranquillity prevailed in the apartments of the pawnbrokers. Mária Alexévna neglected the closet (of which she always carried the key) in which the decanter of brandy was kept; she whipped neither Matryóna nor Vérochka, and even ceased her continual vociferations. But one night the little girl was awakened and frightened by the cries of the tenant and by a great stir and uproar going on in the house. In the morning, nevertheless, Mária Alexévna, in better humor than ever, opened the famous closet and said between two draughts of brandy:

"Thank God! all has gone well." Then she called Matryóna, and instead of abusing or beating her, as was generally the case when she had been drinking, she offered her a glass of brandy, saying:

"Go on! Drink! You too worked well."

After which she went to embrace her daughter and lie down. As for the tenant, she cried no more and did not even leave her room. She moved away soon after.

Two days after she had gone a captain of police, accompanied by two of his officers, came and roundly abused Mária Alexévna, who, it must be allowed, took no pains on her part, as the phrase goes, to keep her tongue in her pocket. Over and over again she repeated:

"I do not know what you mean. If you wish to find out, you will see by the books of the establishment that the woman who was here is named Sevastyanov, one of my acquaintances, engaged in business at Pskov. And that is all."

After having redoubled his abuse, the captain of police finally went away.

That is what Vérochka saw at the age of eight.

At the age of nine she received an explanation of the affair from Matryóna. For the rest, there had been but one case of the kind in the house. Sometimes other adventures of a different sort, but not very numerous.

One day, as Vérochka, then a girl of ten years, was accompanying her mother as usual to the old clothes shop, at the corner of Gorokhovaya Street and Sadovaya Street she was struck a blow on the neck, dealt her doubtless to make her heed this observation of her mother:

"Instead of sauntering, why don't you cross yourself as you go by the church? Don't you see that all respectable people do so?"

At twelve Vérochka was sent to boarding-school, and received in addition lessons in piano-playing from a teacher who, though a great drunkard, was a worthy man and an excellent pianist, but, on account of his drunkenness, had to content himself with a very moderate reward for his services.

At fourteen Vérochka did the sewing for the whole family, which, to be sure, was not a large one.

When she was fifteen, such remarks as this were daily addressed to her:

"Go wash your face cleaner! It is as black as a gypsy's. But you will wash it in vain; you have the face of a scarecrow; you are like nobody else."

The little girl, much mortified at her dark complexion, gradually came to consider herself very homely.

Nevertheless, her mother, who formerly had covered her with nothing but rags, began to dress her up. When Vérochka in fine array followed her mother to church, she said sadly to herself:

"Why this finery? For a gypsy's complexion like mine a dress of serge is as good as a dress of silk. This luxury would become others better. It must be very nice to be pretty! How I should like to be pretty!"

When she was sixteen, Vérochka stopped taking music lessons, and became a piano-teacher herself in a boarding-school. In a short time Mária Alexévna found her other lessons.

Soon Vérochka's mother stopped calling her gypsy and scarecrow; she dressed her even with greater care, and Matryóna told Vérochka that the chief of her father's bureau desired to ask her hand in marriage, and that this chief was a grave man, wearing a cross upon his neck.

In fact, the employees of the ministry had noticed the

advances of the chief of the department towards his subordinate. This chief said to one of his colleagues that he intended to marry and that the dowry was of little consequence, provided the woman was beautiful; he added that Pável Konstantínych was an excellent official.

What would have happened no one knows; but, while the chief of the department was in this frame of mind, an important event occurred:

The son of the mistress appeared at the steward's to say that his mother desired Pável Konstantínych to bring her several samples of wall paper, as she wished to newly furnish her apartments. Orders of this nature were generally transmitted by the major-domo. The intention was evident, and would have been to people of less experience than Vérochka's parents. Moreover, the son of the proprietor remained more than half an hour to take tea.

The next day Mária Alexévna gave her daughter a bracelet which had not been redeemed and ordered new dresses for her. Vérochka admired both the bracelet and the dresses, and was given further occasion to rejoice by her mother's purchase for her at last of some glossy boots of admirable elegance. These expenses were not lost, for Mikhaíl Iványch came every day to the steward's and found in Vérochka's conversation a peculiar charm, which was not displeasing to the steward and his wife. At least the latter gave her daughter long instructions which it is useless to detail.

"Dress yourself, Vérochka," she said to her one evening, on rising from the table; "I have prepared a surprise for you. We are going to the opera, and I have taken a box in the second tier, where there are none but generals. All this is for you, little stupid. For it I do not hesitate to spend my last copecks, and your father on his side scatters his substance in foolish expenditures for your sake. To the governess, to the boarding-school, to the piano-teacher, what a sum we have paid! You know nothing of all that, ingrate that you are! You have neither soul nor sensibilities."

Mária Alexévna said nothing further.

So they went to the opera. After the first act the son of the mistress came in, followed by two friends, one of whom, dressed as a civilian, was very thin and very polite, while the other, a soldier, inclined to stoutness and had simple manners. Mikhaíl Iványch, I say, came into the box occupied by Vérochka and her parents.

Without further ceremony, after the customary greetings, they sat down and began to converse in low tones in French, Mikhaíl Iványch and the civilian especially; the soldier talked little.

Mária Alexévna lent an attentive ear and tried to catch the conversation; but her knowledge of French was limited. However, she knew the meaning of certain words which perpetually recurred in the conversation: *beautiful, charming, love, happiness.*

Belle! charmante! Mária Alexévna has long heard those adjectives applied to her daughter. *Amour!* She clearly sees that Mikhaíl Iványch is madly in love. Where there is *amour* there is *bonheur.* It is complete; but when will he speak of marriage?

"You are very ungrateful, Vérochka," said Mária Alexévna in a low voice to her daughter; "why do you turn away your head? They certainly pay you enough attention, little stupid! Tell me the French for *engaged* and *marriage.* Have they said those words?"

"No, mamma."

"Perhaps you are not telling me the truth? Take care!"

"No; no such words have passed their lips. . . . Let us go; I can't stay here any longer!"

"Go! What do you say, wretch?" muttered Mária Alexévna, into whose eyes the blood shot.

"Yes, let's go! Do with me what you will; but I can't stay here any longer. Later I will tell you why. Mamma," continued the young girl, in a loud voice, "I have too severe a headache. Let's go, I beg of you."

And at the same time Vérochka rose.

"It is nothing," said Mária Alexévna, severely; "Take a walk in the corridor with Mikhaíl Iványch, and it will pass away."

"Mamma, I feel very ill; come quickly, I beg of you."

The young people hastened to open the door and offered their arms to Vérochka, who had the impoliteness to refuse. They placed the ladies in the carriage. Meanwhile Mária Alexévna looked upon the valets with an air which seemed to say: "See, rabble, how eager these fine gentlemen are in their attentions, and that one there will be my son-in-law, and soon I too shall have wretches like you at my bidding." Then mentally addressing her daughter:

"Must you be obstinate, stupid that you are! But I will

put you on your good behavior. . . . Stay, stay, my future
son-in-law is speaking to her; he arranges her in the carriage. Listen: *santé, savoir, visite.* Ah, *permettez* (he is asking her permission to call and inquire after her health)."
Without becoming any the less angry, Mária Alexévna took
into consideration the words she had just heard.

"What did he say on leaving you?" she asked, as soon as
the carriage had started.

"He told me that tomorrow morning he would come to
our house to ask after my health."

"You are not lying? He really said tomorrow?"

Vérochka said nothing.

"You're a lucky one," commented the mother, who could
not refrain from giving her hair a pull. "No, I'll not beat
you, but, mind you, be gay tomorrow! Sleep tonight, stupid,
and above all do not take it into your head to weep; for if
tomorrow morning you are pale, if your eyes are red, be-
ware! I shall be pitiless; your pretty face will be gone; but
I shall have asserted myself!"

"I long ago stopped crying, as you well know."

"That's right! But talk with him a little more."

"I'll try tomorrow."

"That's right! It's time to become reasonable. Fear God
and have a little pity for your mother, you brazen hussy!"

After a silence of ten minutes:

"Vérochka, don't be angry with me; it's through love for
you and for your good that I torment you. Children are so
dear to their mothers. I carried you for nine months in my
womb. I ask of you only gratitude and obedience. Do as I
tell you, and tomorrow he will propose."

"You are mistaken, mamma; he does not dream of it. If
you only knew of what they talked!"

"I know it. If he does not think of marriage, I know of
what he thinks. But he does not know the people with
whom he has to deal. We will reduce him to servile obedience, and, if necessary, I'll carry him to the altar in a sack,
or I will drag him there by the hair, and still he will be
content. Enough! I've already said too much; young girls
should not know so much. It's the business of their mothers.
The daughters have only to obey. Tomorrow you will speak
to him."

"Yes."

"And you, Pável Konstantínych? What are you sitting

there like a piece of wood for? Tell her, as a father, to obey her mother in everything."

"Mária Alexévna, you are a wise woman; but the affair is difficult, and even dangerous. Can you carry it through?"

"Imbecile! What a thing to say! And before Vérochka, too! Don't sit there speculating, just tell me, should a daughter obey her mother?"

"Certainly! Certainly! Mária Alexévna, of course she must."

"Well, then order her as a father."

"Vérochka, obey your mother, who is a wise woman, an experienced woman. She will not teach you to do evil. This obedience I urge you as a father."

On stepping from the carriage Vérochka said to her mother:

"Alright. I'll talk with him tomorrow. But I am very tired, and I need rest."

"Yes, go to bed. I won't disturb you. Sleep well; you need it for tomorrow."

In order to keep her promise Mária Alexévna entered the house without making a disturbance. How much that cost her! How much it cost her also to see Vérochka enter her room directly without stopping to take tea!

"Vérochka, come here!" she said to her, pleasantly.

The young girl obeyed.

"Bow your little head; I wish to bless you. There! May God bless you, Vérochka, as I bless you!"

Three times in succession she blessed her daughter, after which she offered her her hand to kiss.

"No, mamma. I told you long ago that I will not kiss your hand. Let me go now, for I really feel very ill."

How Mária Alexévna's eyes blazed with hatred! But she restrained herself, and gently said:

"Go! Take a rest."

Vérochka spent much time in undressing.

While taking off her dress and putting it in the closet, while taking off her bracelets and ear-rings, each of those simple operations was followed by a long reverie. It was some time before she remembered that she was very tired, and that she had sunk into an arm-chair, being unable even to stand up before the mirror. At last she realized it, and hastened to get into bed.

She had scarcely lain down when her mother entered, car-

rying on a tray a large cup of tea and a number of biscuits.
"Come, eat, Vérochka! It will do you good. See, your
mother didn't forget you. I said to myself: Why has my
daughter gone to bed without her tea? And I brought it to
you myself. Help yourself, dear."

This kind and gentle voice which Vérochka had never
heard surprised her very much. She glanced at her mother
in bewilderment and saw her cheeks inflamed and her eyes
disordered.

"Eat!" continued Mária Alexévna; "when you have finished, I will go for more."

The tea and cream which she had brought aroused Vérochka's appetite, and, raising herself on her elbow, she began to drink.

"Tea is really good when it is fresh and strong, with
plenty of sugar and cream. When I get rich, I shall always
drink it so; it is not like warmed-over, half-sweetened tea,
which is so unpalatable. Thank you, mamma."

"Do not go to sleep; I'll bring you another cup. Drink,"
she continued, as she came back bearing an excellent cup
of tea; "drink, my child; and I'll keep you company a bit."

She sat down, and, after a moment's silence, she began to
talk in a somewhat confused voice, now slowly, now rapidly.

"Vérochka, you just said 'Thank you' to me; it's a long
time since those words escaped your lips. You think me
wicked; well, yes, I am wicked! Can one help it?

"But, dear me! how weak I am! Three punches in succession—at my age! And then you vexed me; that is why I am
weak.

"My life has been a very hard one, my daughter! I do not
want you to live one like it. You shall live in luxury. How
many torments I have endured! Oh, yes! how many torments!

"You do not remember the life that we lived before
your father got his stewardship. We lived very poorly; I
was virtuous then, Vérochka. But I'm no longer so, and I'll
not burden my soul with a new sin by falsely telling you
that I am still virtuous. I have not been for a long time,
Vérochka. You are educated, I am not; but I know all that
is written in your books, and I know that it is written there
that no one should be treated as I have been. They reproach
me for not being virtuous, too! and your father the first, the
imbecile!

"My little Nadinka was born. He was not her father. Well, what of it! What harm did that do him? He reproached me, insulted me, yet wasn't it his fault as much as mine, and more? They took my child to put it with the foundlings, and I know not what became of her. Now I hardly care whether she is still living; but then I suffered much. I became wicked, and then all began to go well. I made your father chief deputy, I made him steward, and at last we were where we could live well. Now, how have I succeeded in doing that? By becoming dishonest; for it is written in your books, I know, Vérochka, that none but rascals make any figure in the world. Is it not true? Now your fool of a father has money, thanks to me. And I too have money! Perhaps more than he. It was I who made it all!

"Your fool of a father has come to esteem me, and I have made him walk straight. When I was virtuous, he ill-treated me without reason, and just because I was good. I had to become wicked.

"It is written in your books that we should be good; but how can one, the way things are? It is necessary to live. Why do they not make society anew, and in accordance with the beautiful order which exists only in your books? It would be better, I know, but the people are so stupid! What can be done with such people? Let us live, then, according to the old order. The old order, your books say, is built on robbery and falsehood. The new order does not exist. We must live according to the old. Steal and lie, daughter; it is through love of you . . . that I speak . . . and . . ."

Mária Alexévna's voice sputtered and turned into a snore.

: II :

Mária Alexévna, while she knew what had happened at the theatre, did not however know the sequel. While she was snoring on a chair, Storéshnikov, his two friends, and the officer's French mistress were finishing supper in one of the most fashionable restaurants.

"M'sieur Storéshnik!"—Storéshnikov beamed, this being the third time that the young Frenchwoman had addressed him since the beginning of the supper.—"M'sieur Storéshnik! let me call you so, it sounds better and is easier to pronounce; you did not tell me that I was to be the only lady in your society. I hoped to meet Adèle here; I should have been pleased, for I see her so rarely!"

"Unfortunately, we've had a fight."

The officer started as if to speak; then, changing his mind, kept silent. It was the civilian who said:

"Do not believe him, Mlle. Julie. He's afraid to tell you the truth and confess that he has abandoned this French-woman for a Russian."

"I do not clearly understand why we came here either," muttered the officer.

"But," replied Julie, "why not, Serge, since Jean invited us? I am very glad to make the acquaintance of M. Storésh-nik, though he has very bad taste, I admit. I should have nothing to say, M. Storéshnik, if you had abandoned Adèle for the beautiful Georgian whom you visited in her box, but to exchange a Frenchwoman for a Russian! I can fancy her pale cheeks,—no, I beg pardon, that is not exactly the word; peaches and cream, as you call it,—that is, a dish which only you Eskimos are able to relish.

"You have just said so many foolish things, Julie. She whom you call Georgian is precisely the Russian in ques-tion," said the officer.

"You are laughing at me."

"Not at all; she is a pure-blooded Russian."

"Impossible!"

"You are wrong in supposing, my dear Julie, that our country has but one type of beauty. Don't you have bru-nettes and blondes in France? As for us, we are a mixture of tribes including blondes like the Finns ("Finns! that is it! that is it!" exclaimed the Frenchwoman) and brunettes darker than the Italians, the Tartars, and the Mongolians. ("The Mongolians! very good!" again exclaimed the Frenchwoman.) These different types are mingled, and our blondes whom you so hate are but a local type, very nu-merous, but not exclusive."

"That is astonishing! But she is splendid! Why doesn't she become an actress? But mind, gentlemen, I speak only of what I have seen; there is still an important question to be settled,—her foot. Has not your great poet Karassin said that in all Russia there could not be found five pairs of dainty little feet?"

"Julie, it was not Karassin who said that. Karassin, whom you would do better to call Karamzine, is neither a Russian nor a poet; he is a Tartar historian. It was Pushkin who spoke of the little feet. That poet's verses, very popular in his day, have lost a little of their value. As for the Eskimos, they live in America."

"I thank you, Serge; Karamzine historian. Pushkin: . . . I know. The Eskimos in America. I shall remember, gentlemen. These things are useful to know in a conversation. Besides, I have a passion for knowledge; I was born to be a Staël. But that is another affair. Let us come back to the question—her foot?"

"If you'll allow me to call upon you to-morrow, Mlle. Julie, I shall have the honor to bring you her shoe."

"I hope so; I will try it on; that excites my curiosity."

Storéshnikov was enchanted. And how could he help it? Hitherto he had been the follower of Jean, who had been the follower of Serge, who had been the follower of Julie, one of the most elegant of the Frenchwomen in Serge's society. It was a great honor that they did him.

"The foot is satisfactory," said Jean; "I, as a positive man, am interested in that which is more essential; I looked at her bust."

"Her bust is very beautiful," answered Storéshnikov, flattered at the praises bestowed upon the object of his choice, and he added, to flatter Julie:

"Yes, ravishing! And I say it, though it be a sacrilege in this presence to praise the bust of another woman."

"Ha! Ha! Ha! He thinks to pay me a compliment! I am neither a hypocrite nor a liar, M. Storéshnik; I don't praise myself, nor do I suffer others to praise me where I am unworthy. I have plenty of other charms left, thank God! But my bosom! . . . Jean, tell him what it is. Give me your hand, M. Storéshnik, and feel here, and there. You see that I wear a false bosom, as I wear a dress, a petticoat, a chemise. Not that it pleases me; I do not like such hypocrisies; but it is admitted in society: a woman who has led the life that I've led—M. Storéshnik, I am now an anchorite in comparison with what I've been—such a woman cannot preserve the beauty of her bosom."

And Julie burst into tears, crying:

"O my youth! O my purity! O God! was it for this that I was born?

"You lie, gentlemen," she cried, rising suddenly in her seat and striking her hand upon the table; "you slander this

young girl; you are vile! She is not his mistress; I saw it all.
He wishes to buy her of her mother. I saw her turn her
back upon him, quivering with indignation. Your conduct
is abominable! She is a pure and noble girl!"

"Yes," said Jean, stretching himself languidly.

"You've been bragging, Storéshnikov. Your affair is far
from settled, and yet you claim that you're living with her
already. And to further convince us, you say that you and
Adèle have separated. You describe very well what you've
not seen. What does it matter, after all, when it is—a week
sooner or later. You won't be disappointed, and the reality
will exceed your imagination. I gave her a good once over
and I assure you—you'll be pleased."

Storéshnikov held back no longer:

"*Pardon,* Mlle. Julie, you are mistaken in your conclusions; she is really my mistress. It was a cloud caused by
jealousy. She had taken offence because during the first act
I had remained in Mlle. Mathilde's box. That was all."

"You are lying, my dear," said Jean, yawning.

"No, truly!"

"Prove it! I am positive, and do not believe without
proofs."

"What proof can I give you?"

"You yield already! What proof? This, for instance. Tomorrow we will take supper here again together. Mlle.
Julie shall bring Serge, I will bring my little Berthe, and
you shall bring the beauty in question. If you bring her, I
lose, and will pay for the supper; if you do not bring her,
we will banish you in shame from our circle."

While speaking Jean had rung, and a waiter had come.

"Simon," he said to him, "prepare a supper tomorrow
for six persons. A supper such as we had here at the time
of my marriage to Berthe. Do you remember it, before
Christmas? In the same room."

"Ah, sir, could one forget such a supper? You shall have
it."

"Abominable people!" resumed Julie; "do you not see
that he will set some trap for her? I have been plunged in
all the filth of Paris, and I never met three men like these!
In what society must I live? Why do I deserve such igno-
miny?"

And falling on her knees:

"My God! I was only a poor and weak woman! I endured

hunger and cold in Paris. But the cold was so intense, the temptations so irresistible. I wished to live; I wished to love! Was that, then, so great a crime that you punish me thus severely? Lift me from this mire! My old life in Paris! Rather that than to live among such people!"

She rose suddenly and ran to the officer:

"Serge, are you like these people? No, you are better."

"*Better,*" echoed the officer, phlegmatically.

"Is this not abominable?"

"Abominable! Julie."

"And you say nothing! You let them go on? You become an accomplice!"

"Come and sit on my knee, my girl." And he began to caress her until she grew calm:

"Come, now, you are a brave little woman; I adore you at such times. Why will you not marry me? I have asked you so often."

"Marriage! The Yoke! Prejudice! No, never! I have already forbidden you to talk to me of such nonsense. Do not vex me. But, my beloved Serge, defend her. He fears you; save her!"

"Calm down, Julie! This is impossible. If it isn't one, it'll be another. It's all the same. Look here—now. Jean's already angling to take her away from him. And people of his sort, you know, are to be found by the thousands. One cannot defend her against everybody, especially when the mother desires to put her daughter on the market. We are a wise people, Julie: see how calm my life is, because I know how to bow to fate, because I've accepted this Russian principle."

"That is not the way of wisdom. I, a Frenchwoman, struggle; I may succumb, but I struggle. I, for my part, will not tolerate this infamy! Do you know who this young girl is and where she lives?"

"Perfectly well."

"Well, let us go to her home; I will warn her."

"To her home! And past midnight! Let us rather go to bed. *Au revoir,* Jean; *au revoir,* Storéshnikov. You will not look for me at your supper tomorrow. Julie is going mad, and this affair doesn't please me either. *Au revoir.*"

"That Frenchwoman is a devil unchained," said Jean, yawning, when the officer and his mistress had gone. "She is very *piquant;* but she is getting stout already. Very agree-

able to the eye is a beautiful woman in anger! All the same,
I would not have lived with her four years, like Serge. Four
years! Not even a quarter of an hour! But, at any rate, this
little caprice shall not lose us our supper. Instead of them
I will bring Paul and Mathilde. Now it's time for home. I
am going to see Berthe a moment, and then to the little
Lotchen's, who is veritably charming."

: **III** :

"That's fine now, Véra. Your eyes aren't red. Obviously
you've finally come to realize that your mother speaks the
truth. You were so rebellious before!"

Vérochka made a gesture of impatience.

"Come! come!" continued the mother, "don't get impatient; I won't say anything. Last night I fell asleep in your
room; perhaps I said too much: but you see, I was drunk, so
do not believe anything I told you. Believe none of it.
Understand?"

The young girl had concluded the night before that, beneath her wild beast's aspect, her mother had preserved
some human feelings, and her hatred for her had changed
into pity; suddenly she saw the wild beast reappear, and felt
the hatred returning; but at least the pity remained.

"Dress yourself," resumed Mária Alexévna, "he will probably come soon." After a careful survey of her daughter's
preparations, she added:

"If you behave yourself well, I will give you those beautiful emerald earrings left with me as security for one hundred and fifty rubles. That is to say, they are worth two
hundred and fifty rubles, and cost over four hundred. Act
accordingly, then!"

Storéshnikov had pondered as to the method of winning
his wager and keeping his word, and for a long time sought
in vain. But at last, while walking home from the restau-
rant, he had hit upon it, and arrived home calm and pleased
with himself. Having inquired first as to the health of Véra
Pávlovna, who answered him with a brief "I am well,"
Storéshnikov said that youth and health should be made
the most of, and proposed to Véra Pávlovna and her mother
to take a sleigh-ride that very evening in the fine frosty
weather. Mária Alexévna agreed readily, adding that at this

moment she had to hustle and set up the coffee and refreshments. Vérochka, meanwhile, would sing something.

"Will you sing something, Vérochka?" she added.

Vérochka sang "Troïka," * which describes, as we know, a girl of charming beauty, all eyes to see an officer pass.

"Well, now, that's not so bad," murmured the old woman from the adjoining room. "When she likes, Vérka† can be very agreeable at least."

Soon Vérochka stopped singing and began to talk with Storéshnikov, but in French.

"What a fool I am!" thought the old woman; "to think that I should have forgotten to tell her to speak Russian! But she talks in a low voice, she smiles; it's going well! it's going well! Why does he make such big eyes! It is easy to see that he is an imbecile, and that is what we are after. Good! She is offering him her hand. Well, Vérka has come to her senses. I approve."

This is what Vérochka said to Storéshnikov:

"I must speak seriously, sir; last evening at the theatre you told your friends that I was your mistress. I will not tell you that this lie was cowardly; for, if you had understood the whole import of your words, I do not think that you would have uttered them. But I warn you that if, at the theatre or in the street, you ever approach me, I will slap you. I know that my mother will kill me with ill-treatment [it was here that Vérochka smiled], but what does that matter, since life is so little to me? This evening you will receive from my mother a note informing you that I am indisposed and unable to join you in the sleigh-ride."

He looked at her with big eyes, as Mária Alexévna had observed.

She resumed.

"I address you, sir, as a man of honor not yet utterly depraved. If I am right, I beg you to stop calling on us, while I, for my part, will pardon your insult. If you accept, give me your hand."

He shook her hand without knowing what he did.

"Thank you," she added; "and now go. You can give as a pretext the necessity for ordering the horses."

He stood as one stupefied, while she returned to singing "Troïka."

* A song by Nekrassov.
† Vérka is an ill-natured diminutive of Véra.

If connoisseurs had heard Vérochka, they would have been astonished at the extraordinary feeling which she put into her song. There was, perhaps, too much emotion in it for art.

Meanwhile Mária Alexévna was coming, followed by her cook carrying the coffee tray. But Storéshnikov, pretending that he had orders to give concerning the preparation of the horses, withdrew toward the door instead of approaching, and, before the steward's wife could protest, the young man went out.

Mária Alexévna, pale with rage and fists lifted in the air, rushed into the parlor, crying:

"What have you done? Damn you!"

But "damn Vérka" had already fled from the parlor. The mother dashed after her, but the door to Vérka's room was locked. Beside herself, she tried to break down the door, and struck it heavy blows.

"If you break down the door," cried the young girl, "I will break the windows and call for help; in any case, I warn you that you shall not take me alive."

The calm and decided tone with which these words were uttered did not fail to make an impression on the fuming mother, who contented herself with shouting and made no more attacks on the door.

At last she got tired of screaming and Vérochka said to her:

"Formerly I just didn't love you, but since yesterday I've come to pity you. You've had a lot of grief and this has made you what you are. Formerly I wouldn't talk to you, but now I would like to chat with you—however, only when you're not angry. Let's talk things over as we've never talked before."

These words did not go straight to the heart of Mária Alexévna, but her tired nerves demanded rest: she asked herself if, after all, it were not better to enter into negotiations. She will no longer obey, and yet she must be married to that fool of a Mishka.* And then, one cannot tell exactly what has happened; they shook hands . . . no, one cannot tell. She was still hesitating between stratagem and ferocity when a ring of the bell interrupted her reflections; it was Serge and Julie.

---

* Mishka is an ill-natured diminutive of Mikhaíl.

: I V :

"Serge, does her mother speak French?" had been Julie's first word on waking.

"I know nothing about it. What! have you still that idea?"

"Still. But I do not believe she speaks French: you shall be my interpreter."

Had Véra's mother been Cardinal Mezzofanti,* Serge would have consented to go to her with Julie.

But Julie had waked late and had stopped at four or five stores on the way, so that Storéshnikov had time to explain himself and Mária Alexévna to rage and calm down again before their arrival.

"What horrible stairs! I never saw anything like them in Paris. And, by the way, what shall be our excuse for calling?"

"It doesn't matter. The mother is a usurer; we will pawn your brooch. No, I have a better idea; the daughter gives piano lessons. We will say that you have a niece, etc."

At the sight of Serge's beautiful uniform and Julie's dazzling makeup, Matryóna blushed for the first time in her life; she had never seen such fine people. No less were the enthusiasm and awe of Mária Alexévna when Matryóna announced Colonel X. and his wife.

And his wife!

The scandals which Mária Alexévna started or heard of concerned nobody higher in station than counsellors. Consequently she did not suspect that Serge's marriage might be only one of those so-called *Parisian* marriages, in which legality goes for nothing. Besides, Serge was brilliant; he explained to her that he was fortunate in having met them at the theatre, that his wife had a niece, etc., and that, his wife not speaking Russian, he had come to act as an interpreter.

"Oh yes! I may thank heaven; my daughter is a very talented musician, and were she to be appreciated in a house like yours I should be extremely happy; only, she is not very well; I do not know whether she can leave her room."

* Who spoke sixty languages, it is said.

Mária Alexévna spoke purposely in a very loud voice in order that Vérochka might hear and understand that an armistice was proposed. At the same time she devoured her callers with her eyes.

"Vérochka, can you come, my dear?"

Why should she not go out? Her mother certainly would not dare to make a scene in public. So she opened her door; but at sight of Serge she blushed with shame and anger. This would have been noticed even by poor eyes, and Julie's eyes were very good; therefore, without indirection, she explained herself.

"My dear child, you are astonished and indignant at seeing here the man before whom last night you were so shamefully outraged. But though he be thoughtless, my husband at least is not wicked; he is better than the scamps who surround him. Forgive him for love of me; I have come with good intentions. This niece is but a pretext; but your mother must think it genuine. Play something, no matter what, provided it be very short, and then we will go to your room to talk."

Is this the Julie known to all the rakes of the aristocracy, and whose jokes have often caused even the libidinous to blush? One would say, rather, a princess whose ear has never been soiled.

Vérochka went to the piano; Julie sat near her, and Serge busied himself in sounding Mária Alexévna in order to ascertain the situation regarding Storéshnikov. A few minutes later Julie stopped Vérochka, and, taking her around the waist, led her to her room. Serge explained that his wife wished to talk a little longer with Vérochka in order to know her character, etc. Then he led the conversation back to Storéshnikov. All this might be charming; but Mária Alexévna, who was by no means innocent, began to cast suspicious looks about her. Meanwhile Julie went straight to the matter in hand.

"My dear child, your mother is certainly a very bad woman, but in order that I may know how to speak to you, tell me why you were taken to the theatre last evening. I know already from my husband; but I wish to get your view of the matter."

Vérochka needed no urging, and, when she had finished, Julie declared, "Yes, I can talk to you. You have character."

And in the most fitting and chaste language she told her

of the wager of the night before. To which Vérochka answered by informing her of the invitation to a sleigh-ride.

"Did he intend to deceive your mother? Or were they in conspiracy?"

"Oh!" quickly cried Vérochka, "my mother does not go as far as that."

"I shall know presently. Stay here; there you would be in the way."

Julie went back to the parlor.

"Serge," she said, "he has already invited this woman and her daughter to a sleigh-ride this evening. Tell her about the supper."

"Your daughter pleases my wife; it remains but to fix the price, and we shall be agreed. Let us come back to our mutual acquaintance, Storéshnikov. You praise him highly. Do you know what he says of his relations with your daughter? Do you know his object in inviting us into your box?"

Mária Alexévna's eyes flashed.

"I do not retail scandal, and seldom listen to it." she said, with restrained anger; "and besides," she added, while striving to appear humble, "the chatter of young people is of little consequence."

"Possibly! But what do you say to this?" And he told the story of the previous night's wager.

"Ah! the rascal, the wretch, the ruffian! That is why he desired to take us out of the city,—to get rid of me and dishonor my daughter."

Mária Alexévna continued a long time in this strain; then she thanked the colonel; she had seen clearly that the lessons sought were but a feint; she had suspected them of desiring to take Storéshnikov away from her; she had misjudged them; and humbly asked their pardon.

Julie, having heard all, hastened back to Vérochka, and told her that her mother was not guilty, that she was full of indignation against the impostor, but that her thirst for money would soon lead her to look for a new suitor, which would at once subject Vérochka to new annoyances. Then she asked her if she had relatives in St. Petersburg, and, being answered in the negative, Julie said further:

"That is a pity. Have you a lover?"

Vérochka opened her eyes wide. She simply didn't know what to answer.

"Forgive me, forgive me! That is understood. So much the worse. You are without protection. What's to be done? But wait, I am not what you think me; I am not his wife, but his mistress; I cannot ask you to my house, I am not married; all St. Petersburg knows me. Your reputation would be lost; it is enough already that I should have come here; to come a second time would be to ruin you. But I must see you once more, and still again perhaps,—that is, if you have confidence in me. Yes? Good! At what time shall you be free tomorrow?"

"At noon."

Noon was a little early for Julie; nevertheless she will arrange to be called and will meet Vérochka by the side of the Gostiny Dvor,* opposite the Nevsky.† There no one knows Julie.

"What a good idea!" continued the Frenchwoman. "Now give me some paper, and I'll write to M. Storéshnikov."

The note which she wrote read as follows:

> Monsieur, you are probably very much dis-
> turbed by your position. If you wish me to aid
> you, call on me this evening, at seven o'clock.
> Now, adieu.
> J. Letellier.

But instead of taking the hand which she extended, Vérochka threw herself upon her neck and wept as she kissed her. Julie, also much moved, likewise could not restrain her tears, and with an outburst of extreme tenderness she kissed the young girl several times, while making a thousand protests of affection.

"Dear child," she said at last, "you cannot understand my present feelings. For the first time in many years pure lips have touched mine. O my child, if you knew! . . . Never give a kiss without love! Choose death before such a calamity!"

* The Palais Royal of St. Petersburg (Leningrad).

† That is, the Nevsky Prospect, the finest street in St. Petersburg (Leningrad).

: V :

Storéshnikov's plan was not as black as Mária Alexévna had imagined, she having no reason to disbelieve in evil; but it was none the less infamous. They were to start off in a sleigh and get delayed in the evening; the ladies soon becoming cold and hungry, Storéshnikov was to offer them some tea; in the mother's cup he was to put a little opium; then, taking advantage of the young girl's anxiety and fright, he was to conduct her to the supper-room, and the wager was won. What would happen then chance was to decide; perhaps Vérochka, dazed and not clearly understanding, would remain a moment; if, on the contrary, she only entered and at once went out again, he would assert that it was the first time she had been out alone, and the wager would be won just the same. Later he would square everything with Mária Alexévna. After all, what else could she do . . . But now . . . he swore at his boastfulness before his friends, at his lack of resourcefulness in the face of Vérochka's resistance. He wished he could just fall through the earth!

It was in this frame of mind that he received Julie's letter; it was like a sovereign elixir to a sick man, a ray of light in utter darkness, firm ground under the feet of one sinking. Storéshnikov rose at a bound to the most sanguine hope.

"She will save me, this generous woman. She is so intelligent that she'll devise something. O noble Julie!"

At ten minutes before seven, he stood at her door.

"Madame is waiting for you; please come in."

Julie received him without rising. What majesty in her mien! What severity in her look!

"I am very glad to see you; be seated," she said to him in answer to his respectful greeting.

Not a muscle of his face moved; Storéshnikov was about to receive a stern reprimand. What matter, provided she would save him?

"Monsieur Storéshnikov," began Julie, in a cold, slow voice, "you know my opinion of the affair which occasions our interview; it is useless to recall the details. I have seen the person in question, and I know the proposition that you made to her this morning. Therefore I know all, and am

very glad to be relieved from questioning you. Your position is clear, to you and to me. ("God!" thought Storéshnikov, "I would rather be upbraided by far!") You can
escape only through me. If you have any reply to make, I am
waiting. . . . You do not reply? You believe, then, that I
alone can come to your aid. I will tell you what I can
do, and, if you deem it satisfactory, I will submit my conditions."

Storéshnikov having given sign of assent, she resumed:
"I have prepared here a letter for Jean, in which I tell
him that, since the scene of last night, I have changed my
mind, and that I will join in the supper, but not this
evening, being engaged elsewhere; so I beg him to induce
you to postpone the supper. I will make him understand
that, having won your wager, it will be hard for you to put
off your triumph. Does this letter suit you?"

"Perfectly."

"But I will send the letter only on two conditions. You
can refuse to accept them, and in that case I will burn the
letter.

"These two conditions," she continued, in a slow voice
which tortured Storéshnikov,—"these two conditions are as
follows:

"First, you shall stop persecuting this young person.

"Second, you shall never speak her name again in your
conversations."

"Is that all?"

"Yes."

A ray of joy illuminated Storéshnikov's countenance.
"Only *that?*" he thought. "It was hardly worth while to
frighten me so. God knows how ready I was to grant it."

But Julie continued with the same solemnity and delib-
eration:

"The first is necessary for her, the second for her also,
but still more for you; I will postpone the supper from
week to week until it has been forgotten. And you must
see that it will not be forgotten unless you speak the name
of this young person no more."

Then, in the same tone, she went into the details of
carrying out the plan. "Jean will receive the letter in time.
I have found out that he is to dine at Berthe's. He will go
to your house after smoking his cigar. We will send the
letter, then. Do you wish to read it? Here is the envelope.

I will ring . . . Pauline, you will take this letter. We have not seen each other today, Monsieur Storéshnikov. Do you understand?"

At last the letter is sent; Storéshnikov breathes more freely, but Julie continues,

"In a quarter of an hour you must be at home in order that Jean may find you there; you have a moment left, and I wish to take advantage of it to say a few words more. You may follow my advice, or not, as you please; but you must reflect upon it.

"I will not speak of the duties of an honest man toward a young girl whose reputation he has compromised. I know our worldly youth too well to think it useful to examine that side of the question. I think that marriage to this young person would be a good thing for you. I will explain myself with my usual frankness, and though some of the things that I am going to say may wound you. If I go too far, a word from you will stop me.

"You have a weak character, and, if you fall into the hands of a bad woman, you will be duped, deceived, and tortured into the bargain. *She* is good, and has a noble heart; in spite of her plebeian birth and poverty, she will aid you in your career.

"Introduced into the world by you, she will shine and wield an influence there. The advantages which such a situation procure for a husband are easy to see. Besides these external advantages, there are others more intimate and precious still. You need a peaceful home and even a little watchful care. All this she can give you. I speak in all seriousness; my observations of this morning tell me that she is perfection. Think of what I've said to you.

"If she accepts, which I very much doubt, I shall consider the acceptance a great piece of good fortune for you.

"I keep you no longer; it is time for you to go."

: VI :

Vérochka was left alone for the time being. Her mother could not in fairness be angry with her for having escaped a trap so basely laid; consequently she was free enough the next day to go to the Gostiny Dvor.

"It is very cold here, and I don't like the cold," said Julie, on arriving. She entered a store, where she bought Vérochka a very thick veil.

"Put that on! Now you may come with me without being recognized. Pauline is very discreet; yet I do not wish her to see you, so careful am I of your reputation; and, above all, do not lift your veil while we are together."

Julie was dressed in her servant's cloak and hat, and her face was hidden beneath a thick veil. First they were obliged to warm themselves; after which, being questioned by Julie, Vérochka gave her the latest details.

"Good, my dear child; now be sure that he asks your hand in marriage. My dear child, there's no question that he's going to propose. Men like him become madly amorous when their gallantries are received coldly. Do you know that you've treated him like an experienced flirt? Perhaps, too, my arguments will have some influence on him. But the principal thing is your firmness; however that may be, he is almost sure to propose, and I advise you to accept him."

"You! who told me yesterday that it was better to die than to give a kiss without love."

"My dear child, I said that in a moment of exaltation; it is right, but it is poetry, and life is made up of very prosaic interests."

"No! I will never marry him; he fills me with horror! I will never stoop to that! I would rather die, throw myself out of the window, beg! Yes, rather death than marry a man so debased!"

Julie began to explain the advantages of the marriage.

"You would be delivered from your mother's persecutions. You are threatened with the risk of being sold. As for him, he is rather stupid, but he is not a brute. A husband of that sort is what an intelligent woman like you needs; you would rule the household."

Then she described vividly to her the situation of actresses and dancers who do not submit to men, but dominate them instead.

"That is a fine position for a woman! and finer yet when she joins to such independence and power a legality of ties which commands the respect of society; That is, when the husband regards and treats his wife as an actress' lover treats his mistress."

The conversation grew more and more animated. Julie talked a great deal, and Vérochka finally replied:

"You call me whimsical, and you ask me what I seek in life. I wish neither to dominate nor be dominated. I wish neither to dissimulate nor deceive; nor do I wish to exert myself to acquire what I am told is necessary, but of which I do not feel the need. I do not desire wealth; why should I seek it? I've never moved in social circles and don't know what it means to be glamorous. I just have no interest in this sort of thing at all. Why should I sacrifice anything for a brilliant position only because someone else considers it desirable? I wish to be independent and live in my own fashion. What I need I feel that I have the strength to earn; what I do not need I do not desire. You say that I am young, inexperienced, and that I shall change with time; that remains to be seen. For the present I have no concern with the wealth and splendor of the world.

"You will ask me what I want. I do not know. Do I want to fall in love? I don't know. Did I know, yesterday morning, that I was going to love you? that my heart was going to be taken possession of by friendship a few hours later? Certainly not. No more can I know how I shall feel toward a man when I shall be in love with him. What I do know is that I wish to be free; that I do not wish to be under obligations to any one. I wish to act after my own fancy. Let others do the same. I respect the liberty of others, as I wish them to respect mine."

Julie listened, moved and thoughtful, and several times she blushed.

"Oh! my dear child, how thoroughly right you are!" she cried, in a broken voice. "Ah! if I were not so depraved! They call me an immoral woman, my body has been polluted, I have suffered so much,—but that is not what I consider my depravity. My depravity consists in being habituated to luxury and idleness; in not being able to live without others . . . .

"Wherever there is idleness, there is vice and abomination; wherever there is luxury there also is vice and abomination. Run! Go quickly!"

: VII :

More and more often Storéshnikov began to think: and
what if I really were to marry her! Under these circumstances there happened to him what happens, not only to
dependent men like him, but also to men of firmer character. Men drag themselves along in a beaten track simply
because they have been told to do so; but tell them in a
very loud voice to take another road, and, though they will
not hear you at first, they will soon throw themselves into
the new path with the same spirit. Storéshnikov had been
told that, with a great fortune, a young man has only to
choose among the poor the beauty whom he desires for a
mistress, and that is why he had thought of making a mistress of Vérochka. Now a new word had been thrown into
his head: *Marriage!* And he pondered over this question:
Shall I marry her? as before he had pondered over the
other: *Shall I make her my mistress?*

That is the common trait by which Storéshnikov represented very adequately nine-tenths of his fellow-citizens
of the world. Historians and psychologists tell us that in
each special fact the common fact is *individualized* by local,
temporary, individual elements, and that these particular
elements are precisely those of most importance. Let us
examine, then, our particular case. The main feature had
been pointed out by Julie (as if she had taken it from
Russian novels, which all speak of it): resistance excites
desire. Storéshnikov had become accustomed to dream
of the *possession* of Vérochka. Like Julie I call things by
their names, as, moreover, almost all of us do in current
conversation. For some time his imagination had represented Vérochka in poses each more voluptuous than the
previous one. These pictures had inflamed his mind, and,
when he believed himself on the point of their realization,
Vérochka had blown upon his dream, and all had vanished.
But if he could not have her as a mistress, he could have her
as a wife; and what does it matter after all, provided his
gross sensuality be satisfied, provided his wildest erotic
dreams be realized? O human degradation! Depravity! to
possess! Who dares possess a human being? One may possess a pair of slippers, a dressing-gown. But what am I
talking about? Each of us, men, *possesses* some one of you,

our sisters! Are you, then, our sisters? You are our servants. There are, I know, some women who subjugate some men; but what of that? Many valets rule their masters, but that does not prevent valets from being valets.

These amorous images had developed in Storéshnikov's mind after the interview at the theatre; he had found her a hundred times more beautiful than at first. And his filthy imagination was excited.

It is with beauty as with wit, as with all qualities; men value it by the judgment of general opinion. Every one sees that a beautiful face is beautiful, but how beautiful is it? It is at this point that the data of current opinion must be classified. As long as Vérochka sat in the galleries or in the back rows of the pit, she was not noticed; but when she appeared in one of the boxes of the second tier, several glasses were levelled at her; and many expressions of admiration were heard by Storéshnikov when he returned to the lobby after escorting her to the carriage.

"Serge," said Storéshnikov, "is a man of very fine taste! And Julie? how about her? But . . . when one has only to lay his hand on such a marvel, he does not ask himself by what title he shall *possess* her."

His ambition was aroused as well as his desires. Julie's phrase, "I doubt very much whether she accepts you," excited him still more. "What! she will not accept me, with such a uniform and such a house! I will prove to you, Frenchwoman, that she will accept me; yes, she shall accept me!"

There was still another influence that tended to inflame Storéshnikov's passion: his mother would certainly oppose the marriage, and in this she represented the opinion of society. Now, heretofore Storéshnikov had feared his mother; but evidently this dependence was a burden to him. And the thought, "I do not fear her, I have a character of my own," was very well calculated to flatter the ambition of a man as devoid of character as he.

He was also urged on by the desire to advance a little in his career through the influence of his wife.

And to all this it must be added that Storéshnikov could not present himself before Vérochka in his former *rôle,* and he desired so much to see her!

In short, he dreamed of the marriage more and more every day, and a week afterwards, on Sunday, while Mária

Alexévna, after attending mass, was considering how she could best coax him back, he presented himself and formulated his request. Since Vérochka remained in her room, he had to address himself to Mária Alexévna, who answered that for her part the marriage would be a great honor, but that as an affectionate mother she wished to consult her daughter, and that he might return the next morning for his answer.

"What an excellent daughter we have!" said Mária Alexévna to her husband a moment later. "How well she knew how to get him! I thought it a hopeless affair, but my Vérka did not spoil matters. She conducted them with perfect strategy. Good girl!"

"It is thus that the Lord inspires children," said Pável Konstantínych.

He rarely played a part in the family life. But Mária Alexévna was a strict observer of traditions, and in a case like this, of conveying to her daughter the proposition that had been made, she hastened to give her husband the *rôle* of honor which by right belongs to the head of the family and the master.

Pável Konstantínych and Mária Alexévna installed themselves upon the divan, the only place solemn enough for such a purpose, and sent Matryóna to ask Mademoiselle to be good enough to come to them.

"Véra," began Pável Konstantínych, "Mikhaíl Iványch does us a great honor: he asks for your hand. We have answered him that, as affectionate parents, we did not wish to coerce you, but that for our part we were pleased with his suit. Like the obedient and wise daughter that we have always found you to be, trust to our experience. We have never dared to ask of God such a suitor. Do you accept him, Véra?"

"No," said Vérochka.

"What did you say, Véra?" cried Pável Konstantínych (the matter was so clear that he could fall into a rage without asking his wife's advice).

"Are you mad or an idiot? Just dare to repeat what you said, you detestable creature!" cried Mária Alexévna, waving her fists at her daughter.

"Take care, Mamma," said Vérochka, rising also. "If you so much as touch me, I will leave the house; if you shut me up, I will throw myself out of the window. I knew how

you would receive my refusal, and have considered well all
that I have to do. Sit down and stay calm, or I go."

Mária Alexévna sat down again. "What stupidity!" she
thought; "we didn't lock the outer door. It takes but a second
to push the bolt back. This mad creature will go, as she
says, and no one will stop her."

"I will not be his wife," repeated the young girl, "and
without my consent the marriage cannot take place."

"Véra, you are mad," insisted the mother with a stifled
voice.

"Is it possible? What shall we say to him tomorrow?"
added the father.

"It is not your fault; it is I who refuse."

The scene lasted nearly two hours. Mária Alexévna, furious, cried, and twenty times raised her tightly clenched
fists: but at each outbreak Vérochka said:

"Do not rise, or I go."

Thus they argued without coming to any conclusion,
when the entrance of Matryóna to ask if it was time to
serve dinner—the cake having been in the oven too long
already—put an end to it all.

"Think about it until evening, Véra. There is still time.
Come to your senses, you fool!"

Then Mária Alexévna said something in Matryóna's ear.

"Mamma, you are trying to set some trap for me, to take
the key from the door of my room, or something of that
sort. Do nothing of the kind: it will be worse."

Again Mária Alexévna yielded.

"Don't do it," she said, turning to the cook. "The wench
is a wild beast. Oh! if it were not that he wants her for her
face, I would tear it to pieces. But if I touch her, she is
capable of self-mutilation. Oh, wretch! Oh, serpent! If I
could!"

They dined without saying a word. After dinner Vérochka
went back to her room. Pável Konstantínych lay down,
according to his habit, to sleep a little: but he did not
succeed, for hardly had he begun to doze when Matryóna
informed him that the servant of the mistress of the house
had come to summon him.

Matryóna trembled like a leaf.

Why?

: VIII :

And why shouldn't she tremble when she was the cause
of the mess? Hadn't she, without loss of a minute, told
the wife of the mistress's cook about Mikhaíl Iványch's
suit? The latter had complained to the second waiting-maid
of the secrets that were kept from her. The second servant
had protested her innocence. If she had known anything,
she would have said so, but she had no secrets. She told
everything. The cook's wife then made apologies; but the
second servant ran straight to the first servant and told her
the great news.

"Is it possible?" cried the latter. "As I did not know it,
then Madame does not; he has concealed his course from
his mother." And she ran to warn Ánna Petróvna.

See what a fuss Matryóna had caused.

"O my wicked tongue!" she thought. "Fine things are
going to happen to me now! Mária Alexévna will ask about
how all this happened.

But the affair took such a turn that Mária Alexévna
forgot to look for the origin of the indiscretion.

Ánna Petróvna sighed and groaned; twice she fainted
before her first waiting-maid. That showed she was deeply
afflicted. She sent in search of her son.

He came.

"Can what I have heard be true, Michél?" she said to
him—in French—in a tone of irate suffering.

"What have you heard, Mamma?"

"That you have made a proposition of marriage to that
. . . to that . . . to that . . . to the daughter of our
steward."

"It is true, Mamma."

"Without asking your mother's advice?"

"I intended to wait, before asking your consent, until
I had received hers."

"You ought to know, it seems to me, that it is easier to
obtain her consent than mine."

"Mamma, it is now proper to first ask the consent of the
young girl and then speak to the parents."

"That is proper, in your opinion? Perhaps for you it is
also proper that sons of good family should marry a . . .

one knows not what, and that mothers should give their consent!"

"Mamma, she is not a *one knows not what;* when you know her, you will approve my choice."

"When I know her! I shall never know her! Approve your choice! I forbid you to think of it any longer! I forbid you, do you understand?"

"Mamma, this parental absolutism is now somewhat out of date; I am not a little boy, to be led by the end of the nose. I know what I am about."

"Ah!" cried Ánna Petróvna, closing her eyes.

Though to Mária Alexévna, Julie, and Vérochka, Mikhaíl Iványch seemed stupid and irresolute, it was because they were women of mind and character: but here, so far as mind was concerned, the weapons were equal, and if, in point of character, the balance was in favor of the mother, the son had quite another advantage. Hitherto he had feared his mother from habit; but he had as good a memory as hers. They both knew that he, Mikhaíl Iványch, was the real owner of the establishment. This explains why Ánna Petróvna, instead of coming straight to the decisive words, *I forbid you,* availed herself of expedients and prolonged the conversation. But Mikhaíl Iványch had already gone so far that he could not recoil.

"I assure you, Mamma, that you could not have a better daughter."

"Monster! Do you want to kill your mother?"

"Mamma, let us talk calmly. Sooner or later I must marry; now, a married man has more expenses than a bachelor. I could, if I chose, marry such a woman that all the income of the house would hardly be enough for us. If, on the contrary, I marry this girl, you will have a dutiful daughter, and you can live with us as in the past."

"Monster! Murderer! Leave me!"

"Mamma, do not get angry. It is not my fault."

"You marry such trash, and it is not your fault!"

"Now, Mamma, I leave you, for I cannot permit her to be characterized like that in my presence."

"Go, assassin!"

Ánna Petróvna fainted, and Michél went out, quite content at having come off so well in this first skirmish, which in affairs of this sort is the most important.

When her son had gone, Ánna Petróvna hastened to come out of her fainting fit. The situation was serious; her son was escaping her. In reply to "I forbid you," he had explained that the house belonged to him. After calming herself a little, she called her servant and poured out her sorrow to her; the latter, who shared her mistress' contempt for the steward's daughter, advised her to send for her steward.

"Hitherto I have been very well satisfied with you, Pável Konstantínych, but intrigues, in which, I hope, you have no part, may set us seriously at odds."

"Your excellency, it is none of my doing. God is my witness!"

"I know that Michél has been paying court to your daughter. I did not prevent it, for a young man needs distraction. I am indulgent toward the follies of youth. But I will not allow the degradation of my family. How did your daughter come to entertain such hopes?"

"Your excellency, she has never entertained them. She is a respectful girl; we have brought her up in obedience."

"What do you mean by that?"

"She will never dare to thwart your will."

Ánna Petróvna could not believe her ears. Was it possible?

"Listen to my will. I cannot consent to so strange, I should say so unfitting, a marriage."

"We feel that, your excellency, and Vérochka feels it too. These are her own words: 'I dare not, for fear of offending her excellency.' "

"How did all this happen?"

"It happened in this wise, your excellency: Mikhaíl Iványch expressed his intentions to my wife, and my wife told him that she could not give him a reply before tomorrow morning. Now, my wife and I intended to speak to you first. But we did not dare to disturb your excellency at so late an hour. After Mikhaíl Iványch's departure, we said as much to Vérochka. She answered that she was of our opinion and that the thing was not to be thought of."

"Your daughter is, then, a prudent and honest girl?"

"Why, certainly, your excellency, she is a dutiful daughter!"

"I am very glad that we can remain friends. I wish to

reward you instantly. The large room on the second floor, facing on the street and now occupied by the tailor, will soon be vacant?"

"In three days, your excellency."

"Take it yourself, and you may spend up to a hundred rubles to put it in good order. Further, I add two hundred and forty rubles a year to your salary."

"Allow me to kiss your hand, your excellency."

"Good, good! Tatyana?" The servant came in.

"Bring me my blue velvet cloak. I make your wife a present of it. It cost one hundred and fifty rubles [it really cost only seventy-five], and I have worn it only twice [she had worn it more than twenty times]. This is for your daughter [Ánna Petróvna handed the steward a small watch such as ladies carry]; I paid three hundred rubles for it [she paid one hundred and twenty]. You see, I know how to reward, and I shall always remember you, always! Do not forget that I am indulgent toward the foibles of the young."

When the steward had gone, Ánna Petróvna again called Tatyana.

"Ask Mikhaíl Iványch to come and talk with me. . . . But no, I will go myself instead." She feared that the ambassadress would tell her son's servant, and the servant her son, what had happened. She wished to have the pleasure of crushing her son's spirit with this unexpected news. She found Mikhaíl Iványch lying down and twirling his moustache, not without some inward satisfaction.

"What brings her here? I have no smelling salts for fainting fits," thought he, on seeing his mother enter. But he saw on her face an expression of disdainful triumph.

She took a seat and said:

"Sit up, Mikhaíl Iványch, and we'll have a talk."

She looked at him a long time, with a smile upon her lips. At last she said slowly:

"I am very happy, Mikhaíl Iványch: guess at what."

"I do not know what to think, Mamma; your look is so strange."

"You will see that it is not strange at all; look closely and you will guess, perhaps."

A prolonged silence followed this fresh thrust of sarcasm. The son lost himself in conjectures; the mother delighted in her triumph.

"You cannot guess; I will tell you. It is very simple and very natural; if you had had a particle of elevated feeling, you would have guessed. Your mistress,"—in the previous conversation Anna Petrovna had manoeuvred; now it was no longer necessary, the enemy being disarmed,—"your mistress,—do not reply, Mikhaíl Iványch, you have loudly asserted on all sides yourself that she is your mistress,— your mistress, this creature of base extraction, base education, base conduct, this even contemptible creature . . . ."

"Mamma, my ear cannot tolerate such expressions applied to a young girl who is to be my wife."

"I would not have used them if I had had any idea that she could be your wife. I did so with the view of explaining to you that that will not occur and of telling you at the same time why it will not occur. Let me finish, then. Afterwards you can reproach me, if you like, for the expressions which I have used, supposing that you still believe them out of place. But meantime let me finish. I wish to say to you that your mistress, this creature without name or education, devoid of sentiment, has herself comprehended the utter impropriety of your designs. Is that not enough to cover you with shame?"

"What? What do you say? Finish!"

"You do not let me. I meant to say that even she—do you understand? even she!—understood and appreciated my feelings, and, after learning from her mother that you had made a proposition for her hand, she sent her father to tell me that she would never rise against my will and would not dishonor our family with her degraded name."

"Mamma, you deceive me."

"Fortunately for you and for me, I tell only the exact truth. She says that . . . ."

But Mikhaíl Iványch was no longer in the room; he was putting on his cloak to go out.

"Hold him, Pyótr, hold him!" cried Ánna Petróvna.

Pyótr opened his mouth wide at hearing so extraordinary an order. Meanwhile Mikhaíl Iványch sped down the staircase.

: IX :

"Well?" said Mária Alexévna, when her husband re-entered.

"Fine, Mother! She knew already, and said to me: 'How dare you?' and I told her; 'We do not dare, your excellency, and Vérochka has already refused him.'"

"What? What? You jackass! You blurted out just that?"

"Mária Alexévna . . ."

"Ass! Rascal! You've killed me, murdered me, you old fool! There's one for you! [the husband received a blow.] And there's another! [the husband received a blow on the other cheek]. Wait. I'll teach you, you old imbecile!" And she seized him by the hair and pulled him into the room. The lesson lasted sufficiently long, for Storéshnikov, reaching the room after the long pauses of his mother and the information which she gave him between them, found Mária Alexévna still actively engaged in her work of education.

"Why didn't you close the door, you imbecile? A pretty state we are found in! Aren't you ashamed, you old pig?" That was all that Mária Alexévna could say.

"Where is Véra Pávlovna? I wish to see her directly. Is it true that she refuses me?"

The circumstances were so embarrassing that Mária Alexévna could only wave her hand.

"Véra Pávlovna, is it true that you refuse me?"

"I leave it to you, could I do otherwise than refuse you?"

"Véra Pávlovna, I have outraged you in a cowardly manner; I am guilty; but your refusal kills me." And thus he continued.

Vérochka listened for some minutes; then, to end the painful interview, she said:

"Mikhaíl Iványch, your entreaties are useless. I cannot consent."

"At least grant me one favor. You still feel very keenly how deeply I outraged you. Don't give me your reply today. Let me have time to become worthy of your pardon! I seem to you despicable, but wait a little. I wish to become better and more worthy. Aid me, do not repel me, grant me time. I will obey you in all things! Perhaps at last you will find me worthy of pardon."

"I pity you; I see the sincerity of your love [it is not love, Vérochka; it is a mixture of something low with something painful; one may be very unhappy and deeply mortified by a woman's refusal without really loving her; love is quite another thing,—but Vérochka is still ignorant regarding these things, and she is moved],—you wish me to postpone my answer; so be it, then! But I warn you that the postponement will end in nothing; I shall never give you any other reply than that which I have given you to-day."

"I will become worthy of another answer; you save me!"

He seized her hand and began kissing it rapturously.

Mária Alexévna entered the room, and in her enthusiasm blessed her dear children without the traditional formalities,—that is, without Pável Konstantínych; then she called her husband to bless them once more with proper solemnity. But Storéshnikov dampened her enthusiasm by explaining to her that Véra Pávlovna, though she had not consented, at least had not definitely refused, and that she had postponed her answer.

This was not altogether glorious, but after all, compared with the situation of a moment before, it was a step taken.

Consequently Storéshnikov went back to his house with an air of triumph, and Ánna Petróvna had no resource left but fainting.

Mária Alexévna did not know exactly what to think of Vérochka, who talked and seemed to act exactly against her mother's intentions, and who, after all, surmounted difficulties before which Mária Alexévna herself was powerless. Judging from the progress of affairs, it was clear that Vérochka's wishes were the same as her mother's; only her plan of action was better laid and, above all, more effective. Yet, if this were the case, why did she not say to her mother: "Mamma, we have the same end in view; be calm." Was she so out of sorts with her mother that she wished to have nothing to do with her? This postponement, it was clear to Mária Alexévna, simply signified that her daughter wished to excite Storéshnikov's love and make it strong enough to break down the resistance of Ánna Petróvna.

"She is certainly even shrewder than I," concluded Mária Alexévna after much reflection. But all that she saw and heard tended to prove the contrary.

For the moment, at any rate, the only course was to wait, and so Mária Alexévna waited.

The suitor was as gentle as a lamb. His mother struggled for three weeks; then the son got the upper hand from the fact that he was the proprietor, and Ánna Petróvna began to grow docile; she expressed a desire to make Vérochka's acquaintance. The latter did not go to see her. Mária Alexévna thought at first that, in Vérochka's place, she would have acted more wisely by going; but after a little reflection she saw that it was better not to go. "Oh! she is a shrewd rogue!"

A fortnight later Ánna Petróvna came to the steward's herself, her pretext being to see if the new room was well arranged. Her manner was cold and her amiability biting; after enduring two or three of her caustic sentences, Vérochka went to her room. While her daughter remained, Mária Alexévna did not think she was pursuing the best course; she thought that sarcasm should have been answered with sarcasm; but when Vérochka withdrew, Mária Alexévna instantly concluded: "Yes, it was better to withdraw; leave her to her son, let him be the one to reprimand her; that is the best way."

Two weeks afterwards Ánna Pertóvna came again, this time without putting forward any pretext; she simply said that she had come to make a call; and nothing sarcastic did she say in Vérochka's presence.

Such was the situation. The suitor made presents to Vérochka through Mária Alexévna, and these presents very certainly remained in the latter's hands, as did Ánna Petróvna's watch, always excepting the gifts of little value, which Mária Alexévna faithfully delivered to her daughter as articles which had been deposited with her and not redeemed; for it was necessary that the suitor should see some of these articles on his sweetheart. And, indeed, he did see them, and was convinced that Vérochka was disposed to consent; otherwise she would not have accepted his gifts. Why, then, was she so slow about it? Perhaps she was waiting until Ánna Petróvna should be thoroughly softened; this thought was whispered in his ear by Mária Alexévna. And he continued to break in his mother, as he would a saddle-horse, an occupation which was not without charm for him. Thus Vérochka was left at rest, and everything was done to please her. This watch-dog kindness was repugnant to her;

she tried to be with her mother as little as possible. The mother, on the other hand, no longer dared to enter her daughter's room, and when Vérochka stayed there a large portion of the day, she was entirely undisturbed. Sometimes she allowed Mikhaíl Iványch to come and talk with her.

Then he was as obedient as a child. She commanded him to read and he read with much zeal, as if he were preparing for an examination. He did not reap much profit from his reading, but nevertheless he reaped a little. She tried to aid him by conversation, and conversation was much more intelligible to him than books. Thus he made some progress, slow, very slow, but real. He began by treating his mother a little better than before: instead of breaking her in like a saddle-horse, he preferred to hold her by the bridle.

Thus things went on for two or three months. All was quiet, but only because of a truce agreed upon, with the tempest liable to break forth again any day. Vérochka viewed the future with a shrinking heart: some day or other Mikhaíl Iványch or Mária Alexévna were going to press her to a decision. For their impatience would not put up long with this state of things.

Chapter Second

THE FIRST LOVE

AND LEGAL MARRIAGE

: I :

We know how in former times such situations were settled: a fine young girl in a despicable family is saddled
with a fiancé, whom she despises. He was trash to begin
with and the longer he lived the worse he became. But now,
through constant association with her, gradual subordina-
tion to her will, he gradually acquired some semblance of
humanity. He was neither good nor bad. At first the girl
would have nothing to do with him, but little by little she
became accustomed to having him under her thumb. Indeed, she even became convinced that he was really the
lesser of the two evils, that is, if one had to choose between
him and a family such as hers.

She made her fiancé "happy." At first it revolted her to
learn what it meant to "make a man happy" without love.
The husband, however, was tractable. To endure is to grow
fond of one another. Gradually she became an ordinary
good lady, that is, a woman who, in herself, is good but has
reconciled herself to banality and accommodated herself to
vegetative life. That is what became of young girls formerly.

It was almost the same with young men, who themselves
became as comfortable inhabitants of this world as stupidity, selfishness, and triviality could desire.

That is why so few really human men were to be found.

Now, one cannot live alone all his life without consuming himself by his own force; truly human men either wasted away or became reconciled to banality.

In our day it is no longer the same; the number of these human beings grows continually, and from year to year the increase is perceptible. As a result they become acquainted with each other, and their number increases further on this account.

In time they will be the majority. In time, even, they will be the totality: then all will be well in the world.

All is well for Vérochka even now. That is why (with her permission) I tell her story.

She, as I happen to know, is one of the first women whose life was thus well ordered.

Let us return to Véra Pávlovna. It was time for preparing Vérochka's little brother for school. Pável Konstantínych inquired among his colleagues to find an inexpensive tutor. They recommended a medical student Lopukhóv.

Lopukhóv came five or six times to give lessons to his new pupil before he met Vérochka. He stayed with Fédya at one end of the apartment, while she remained in her room at the other end. But as the examinations at the Medico-Surgical Academy were approaching and he had to study in the morning, he came to give his lessons in the evening. This time, on his arrival, he found the whole family at tea: the father and mother, Fédya, and an unknown person,—a young girl of large and beautiful figure, bronzed complexion, black hair, and black eyes.

Her hair was beautiful and thick: her eyes were beautiful, very beautiful indeed, and quite of a southern type, as if she came from southern Russia. One would have said even a Caucasian type rather; an admirable face, only too cold,— which is not a southern trait.

She seemed beaming with health; the redness of her cheeks was wholesome; there would be no need of so many doctors, were there many such constitutions as hers.

When she enters society, she will make an impression. But what's that to me? Such were Lopukhóv's reflections as he looked at her.

She, too, threw her eyes upon the teacher who had just entered. The student was no longer a youth; he was a man of a little above the average height, with hair of a deep chestnut color, regular and even handsome features, the whole relieved by a proud and fearless bearing. "He is not bad, and ought to be good; but he must be too serious." She did not add in her thought: "But what is that to me?" and for the very simple reason that it had not occurred to her that he could interest her. Besides, Fédya had said so much to her of his teacher that she could no longer hear him spoken of without impatience.

"He is very good, sister; only he is not a talker. And I told him, my dear sister, that you were a beauty in our house, and he answered: 'How does that concern me?' And I, my dear sister, replied: 'Why, everybody loves beauties,' and he said in return: 'All imbeciles love them,' and I said: 'And don't you love them, too?' And he answered me: 'I don't have the time.' And I said to him: 'So you do not wish to make Vérochka's acquaintance?' 'I have many acquaintances without her,' he answered me."

Such was Fédya's account. And it was not the only one; he told others of the same sort, such as this:

"I told him to-day, sister, that everybody looks at you when you pass, and he replied: 'So much the better.' I said to him: 'And don't you wish to see her?' He answered: 'There is time enough for that.'"

Willy nilly, the teacher had learned from Fédya all that he could tell him on the subject of "his dear sister"; he always stopped the little fellow whenever he began to babble about family affairs; but how prevent a child of nine years from telling you everything, especially if he loves you more than he fears you. Among the bits of information of all sorts upon family affairs, the teacher had heard such things as these:

"My sister has a wealthy suitor! But Mamma says that he is very stupid." "Mamma also pays court to the suitor; she says that my sister has trapped him very cleverly." "Mamma says: 'I am shrewd, but Vérochka is even shrewder than I!'" And so on. It was natural that, hearing such things about each other, the young people should not feel any desire to become more intimately acquainted.

But what was Lopukhóv really like? According to Fédya, a savage with head full of books and anatomical preparations,—all the things which make up the principal intellectual enjoyment of a good medical student. Or had Fédya slandered him?

: II :

No, Fédya was not telling tales on him. Lopukhóv was actually a student with a *head full of books,* and what books?
The bibliographical researches of Mária Alexévna will tell
us that in due time. Lopukhóv's head was also full of anatomical preparations, for he dreamed of a professorship.
But, just as the information communicated by Fédya to
Lopukhóv concerning Vérochka has given an imperfect
knowledge of the young girl, there is reason to believe that
the information imparted by the pupil as to his teacher
needs to be completed.

In money matters Lopukhóv belonged to that small minority of day students not supported by the crown, who suffer, nevertheless, neither from hunger nor cold. How and
whereby do the great majority of these students live? God
knows, of course; to men it is a mystery. But it is unpleasant
to think so much about people who die of hunger; therefore
we will only mention the period during which Lopukhóv
found himself also in this embarrassing situation, and which
lasted three years.

Before he entered the medical academy he ate in abundance. His father was a Ryazan bourgeois, and lived satisfactorily as bourgeois live, that is, his family had cabbage
soup with meat not only on Sundays, and drank tea every-
day. He managed to put his son through the gymnasium
somehow, but then starting at fifteen the son himself helped
him out by giving private lessons. The father's resources
weren't up to supporting the son in Petersburg.

Lopukhóv received, nevertheless, during the first two
years, thirty-five rubles per year, and he earned almost as
much more as a copyist in one of the quarters of the district
of Wyborg without being an office-holder.

If he suffered still, it was his own fault.

He had been offered support by the crown; but then had
gotten into some sort of a quarrel, which cost him dearly.
In his third year his affairs began to take a better turn: the
deputy head clerk of the police offered him a chance to give
lessons, and to these he added others, which for two years
had given him at least the necessaries of life.

He and his friend Kirsánov, a lucky fellow like himself,
occupied two adjacent rooms in one apartment. They were

fast friends. Early both friends had become accustomed to depending only on themselves; and in general they acted so much in concert that one meeting them separately would have taken them for men of the same character. But when one saw them together, it then became plain that, although both were very serious and very open people, Lopukhóv was a little more reserved, and his companion a little more expansive. For the present only Lopukhóv is before us; Kirsánov will appear much later.

All that may be said of Lopukhóv can be repeated of Kirsánov.

At the present stage of our story Lopukhóv was absorbed by this thought: How to arrange his life after ending his studies? It was time to think about that: there were but a few months left. Their plans for the future were identical.

Lopukhóv was sure of being received as a doctor in one of the military hospitals of St. Petersburg (that is considered real luck) and of obtaining a chair in the Academy of Medicine.

As for being simply a practitioner, he did not dream of it.

It is a very curious trait, this resolution of the medical students of these last ten years not to engage in practice. Even the best disdained this precious resource of the exercise of their art, which alone would have assured their existence, or accepted it only provisionally, being always ready to abandon medicine, as soon as possible, for some auxiliary science, like physiology, chemistry, or the like. Moreover, each of them knew that by practice he could have made a reputation at the age of thirty, assured himself a more than comfortable existence at the age of thirty-five, and attained wealth at forty-five.

But our young people reason otherwise. To them the medical art is in its infancy, and they busy themselves less with the art of attending the sick than with gathering scientific materials for future physicians. They busy themselves less with the practice of their art than with the program of beloved science.

They cry out against medicine, and devote all their powers to it. For it they renounce wealth and even comfort, and stay in the hospitals to make observations interesting to science. They cut up frogs; they dissect hundreds of bodies every year, and, as soon as possible, fit themselves out with chemical laboratories.

They think little of their own poverty. Only when their families are in straitened circumstances do they practice, and then just enough to afford them necessary aid without abandoning science; that is, they practice on a very small scale, and attend only such people as are really sick and as they can treat effectively in the present deplorable state of science, —not very profitable patients as a general thing. It was precisely to this class of students that Lopukhóv and Kirsánov belonged. As we know, they were to finish their studies in the current year, and were preparing to be examined for their degrees; they were at work upon their theses. For that purpose they had exterminated an enormous quantity of frogs.

Both had chosen the nervous system as a specialty. Properly speaking, they worked together, aiding each other. Each registered in the materials of his thesis the facts observed by both and relating to the question under consideration.

But it's time, at last, to speak of Lopukhóv alone.

There was a time when he caroused in his own way: this was when he didn't even have tea, or at other times when he had no boots. Such a time was most favorable for high living, not only from the point of view of disposition, but from the point of possibility. It is cheaper to drink than to eat and dress oneself. But carousing was the consequence of boredom, from unbearable poverty. Nothing more. Now things have changed. Now he led a life of exemplary sobriety and strictness.

Likewise he had had many gallant adventures. Once, for example, he became enamored of a dancing girl. What should he do? He reflected, reflected again, and for a long time reflected, and at last went to find the beauty at her house. "What do you want?" he was asked. "I am sent by Count X with a letter."

His student's costume was easily mistaken by the servant for that of an officer's attendant.

"Give me the letter. Will you wait for a reply?"

"Such was the Count's order."

The servant came back, and said to him with an astonished air:

"I am ordered to ask you to come in."

"Ah! is it you?" said the dancing girl; "you, my ardent applauder! I often hear your voice, even from my dressing

room. How many times have you been taken to the police
station for your excess of zeal in my honor?"

"Twice."

"That is not often. And why are you here?"

"To see you."

"Exactly; and what then?"

"I don't know."

"Well, I know what I want; I want some breakfast. See,
the table is laid. You sit down, too."

Another plate was brought. She laughed at him, and he
could not help following her example. But he was young,
good-looking, and had an air of intelligence; his bearing
was original; so many advantages conquered the dancing
girl, who for him was very willing to add another to her
list of adventures.

A fortnight later she said to him:

"Are you going now?"

"I was already thinking of doing so, but I didn't dare."

"Well, then, shall we part friends?"

Once more they embraced each other, and separated in
content.

But that was three years ago, and it was already two years
since Lopukhóv had entirely given up adventures of that
sort.

Except for his comrades, and two or three professors who
foresaw in him a true man of science, he saw no one outside
the families where he gave lessons. And among them with
what reserve! He avoided familiarity as he would the fire,
and was very dry and cold with all the members of these
families, his pupils of course excepted.

: I I I :

Thus, then, Lopukhóv entered the room where he found
at the tea-table a company of which Vérochka was one.

"Take a seat at the table, please," said Mária Alexévna;
"Matryóna, another cup."

"If it is for me, I do not care for anything, thank you."

"Matryóna, we do not want the cup. (What a well-
brought-up young man!) Why don't you take something?
It won't hurt you."

He looked at Mária Alexévna; but at the same moment, as if intentionally, his eyes fell on Vérochka, and indeed perhaps it was intentional. Perhaps even he noticed that she made a motion, which in Vérochka meant: Could he have seen me blush?

"Thank you, I take tea only at home," he answered.

At bottom he was not such a barbarian; he entered and bowed with ease.

"This girl's morality may be doubtful," thought Lopukhóv, "but she certainly blushed at her mother's lack of good-breeding."

Fédya finished his tea and went out with his tutor to take his lesson.

The chief result of this first interview was that Mária Alexévna formed a favorable opinion of the young man, seeing that her sugar-bowl probably would not suffer much by the change of lessons from morning to evening.

Two days later Lopukhóv again found the family at tea and again refused a cup, a resolution which drove the last trace of anxiety from Mária Alexévna's mind. But this time he saw at the table a new personage, an officer, in whose presence Mária Alexévna was very humble.

"Ah! this is the suitor!" thought he.

The suitor, as befit his station and house, deemed it necessary, not only to look at the student, but to examine him from head to toe with that slow and disdainful look which is prevalent in high society. But scarcely did he begin to take stock, when he was embarrassed by the fixed and penetrating gaze of the young tutor. Wholly disconcerted, he hastened to say:

"The medical profession is a difficult one, is it not, Monsieur Lopukhóv?"

"Very difficult, sir." And Lopukhóv continued to look the officer in the eye.

Storéshnikov, for some inexplicable reason, placed his hand on the second and third buttons from the top of his tunic, which meant that he was so confused that he knew no other way out of his embarrassment than to finish his cup of tea as quickly as possible in order to ask Mária Alexévna for another.

"You wear, if I'm not mistaken, the uniform of the S —— regiment?"

"Yes, I serve in that regiment," replies Mikhaíl Iványch.
"Have you served a long time?"
"Nine years."
"Did you enter the service in that same regiment?"
"The same."
"Have you a company yet, or not?"
"Not yet. (But he is putting me through an examination as if I were under orders.)"
"Do you hope to get a company soon?"
"Not yet."
"Hmm." Lopukhóv thought that enough for once, and left the suitor alone, after having looked him again in the eye.
"Curious," thought Vérochka; "Curious; yes, curious!"
This *curious* meant: "He behaves as Serge would behave, who once came here with the good Julie. Then he is not such a barbarian. But why does he talk so strangely of young girls? Why does he dare to say that none but imbeciles love them? And . . . why, when they speak to him of me, does he say: 'That does not interest me.'"
"Vérochka, will you go to the piano? Mikhaíl Iványch and I enjoy listening to you," said Mária Alexévna, after Vérochka had put her second cup back upon the table.
"Very well."
"I beg you to sing us something, Véra Pávlovna," added Mikhaíl Iványch, gently.
"Very well."
"This *very well* means: 'I will do it in order to be in peace,'" thought Lopukhóv.
He had been there five minutes, and, without looking at her, he knew that she had not cast a single glance at her suitor except when obliged to answer him. Moreover, this look was like those which she gave her father and mother, —cold and not at all cordial. Things were not entirely as Fédya had described them. "For the rest," said Lopukhóv to himself, "probably the young girl is really proud and cold; she wishes to enter fashionable society to rule and shine there; she is displeased at not finding for that purpose a suitor more agreeable to her; but, while despising the suitor, she accepts his hands, because there is no other way for her to go where she wants to go. Nevertheless she is interesting."

"Fédya, hurry and finish your tea," said the mother.

"Do not hurry him, Mária Alexévna; I would like to listen a little while, if Véra Pávlovna will permit."

Vérochka took the first book of music which fell under her hand, without even looking to see what it was, opened it at random, and began to play mechanically. Although she played thus mechanically and just to get rid as soon as possible of the attention of which she was the object, she performed the piece with singular art and perfect measure; before finishing she even put a little animation into her playing. As she rose, the officer said:

"But you promised to sing us something, Véra Pávlovna; if I dared, I would ask you to sing a motive from 'Rigoletto.'" That winter *la donna è mobile* was very popular.

"Very well," said Vérochka, and she sang *la donna è mobile,* after which she rose and went to her room.

"No, she is not a cold and insensible young girl. She is interesting."

"Perfect! wasn't it?" said Mikhaíl Iványch to the student, simply and without any look of disdain; ("it is better not to be on a bad footing with spirited fellows who question you so coolly. Talk amicably with him. Why not strike up a conversation with him without pretension, so that he doesn't take offence?")

"Perfect!" answered Lopukhóv.

"Are you a connoisseur of music?"

"Hm! Well enough."

"Are you a musician yourself?"

"So-so."

Mária Alexévna, who was listening to the conversation, had a happy thought.

"On what instrument do you play, Dmítry Sergéich?" she asked.

"The piano."

"Might we ask you to give us the pleasure?"

"Certainly."

He played a piece, and sufficiently well. After the lesson Mária Alexévna approached him, told him that they were to have a little party the following evening in honor of her daughter's birthday, and asked him to come.

"There are never very many at such parties," thought he; "there's usually a shortage of men at these parties, and that is why I am invited; all the same, I will go, if only to observe the young girl a little more closely. There is something in her, or out of her, that is interesting."

"I thank you," he answered, "I will be there."

But the student was mistaken as to the motive of this invitation: Mária Alexévna had an object much more important than he imagined.

Reader, you certainly know in advance that at this party there will be an "understanding" between Lopukhóv and Vérochka, and they will fall in love with each other. Of course; just as you suspected.

: IV :

Mária Alexévna wanted to make Vérochka's birthday a big affair, but Vérochka begged her to invite nobody. One wished to make a public show of the suitor; to the other such a show would have been distressing. It was agreed finally to give a small party and invite only a few intimate friends. They invited the colleagues of Pável Konstantínych (of course, older in rank and higher in position), two friends of Mária Alexévna, and the three young girls with whom Vérochka was most intimate.

Surveying the assembled guests, Lopukhóv saw that there were plenty of young people. For each lady there was a young man, a potential suitor or perhaps an actual suitor. Lopukhóv, then, had not been invited in order to get one more dancer. For what reason, then? After a little reflection, he remembered that the invitation had been preceded by a test of his skill with the piano. Consequently, he had been invited to save the expense of a pianist.

"I will upset your plan, Mária Alexévna," thought he; so approaching Pável Konstantínych, he said:

"Pável Konstantínych, how about getting up a game of cards; look how bored the old people are!"

"Of how many points?"

"As you prefer."

A game was immediately made up, in which Lopukhóv sat down to play.

The Academy in the district of Wyborg is an institution in which card-playing is a classic. In any of the rooms occupied by the crown students it is no rare thing to see thirty-six hours' continuous playing. It must be allowed that, although the sums which change hands over the cloth are much smaller than those staked in English club-rooms, the players are much more skilful. At the time when Lopukhóv was short of money, he played a great deal.

"Ladies, how shall we arrange ourselves?" said some one. "*Tour à tour* is good, but then there will be seven of us, and either one dancer will be lacking, or a lady for the quadrille."

They were finishing the first game when one young lady, bolder than the others, flew up to the student and said:

"Monsieur Lopukhóv, you must dance."

"On one condition," said he, rising and bowing.

"What is it?"

"That I may dance the first quadrille with you."

"Alas! I am engaged; I am yours for the second."

Lopukhóv bowed again. Two of the dancers played *tour à tour*. He danced the third quadrille with Vérochka.

He studied the young girl, and became thoroughly convinced that he had done wrong in believing her a heartless girl, marrying for selfish purposes a man whom she despised.

Yet he was in the presence of a very ordinary young girl who danced and laughed with zest. Yes, to Vérochka's shame it must be said that as yet she was only a young person fond of dancing. She had insisted that no party should be given, but, the party having been made,—a small party, without the public show which would have been repugnant to her,—she had forgotten her chagrin. Therefore, though Lopukhóv was now more favorably disposed toward her, he did not exactly understand why, and sought to explain to himself the strange being before him.

"Monsieur Lopukhóv, I should never have expected to see you dance."

"Why? Is it, then, so difficult to dance?"

"As a general thing, certainly not; for you evidently it is."

"Why is it difficult for me?"

"Because I know your secret, yours and Fédya's; you despise women."

"Fédya hasn't a very clear idea of my secret: I do not disdain women, but I avoid them; and do you know why? I have an extremely jealous sweetheart, who, in order to make me avoid them, has told me their secret."

"You have a sweetheart?"

"Yes."

"I should hardly have expected that! A student and already engaged! Is she pretty? Do you love her?"

"Yes, she is a beauty, and I love her much."

"Is she a brunette or a blonde?"

"I can't tell you. That is a secret."

"If it is a secret, keep it. But what is this secret of women, which she has betrayed to you, and which makes you shun their society?"

"She had noticed that I do not like to be in low spirits; now, since she told me their secret, I cannot see a woman without being cast down; that is why I shun women."

"You cannot see a woman without being cast down! I see you are not a master of the art of gallantry."

"What would you have me say? Is not a feeling of pity calculated to cast one down?"

"Are we, then, so much to be pitied?"

"Certainly. You are a woman: do you wish me to tell you the deepest wish of your soul?"

"Tell it, tell me!"

"It is this: 'How I wish I were a man!' I never met a woman who had not that desire planted deep within her. How could it be otherwise? There are the facts of life, bruising and crushing woman every hour because she is woman. Consequently, she only has to come to a struggle with life to have occasion to cry out: *Poor beings that we are, what a misfortune that we are women!* or else: *With man it is not the same as with woman,* or, very simply: 'Ah, why am I not a man!'"

Vérochka smiled: "That's true. You can hear this from any woman."

"See, then, how pitiful women are, since, if the profoundest desire of each of them were to be realized, there would not remain a single woman in the world."

"It seems to be so," said Vérochka.

In the same way, there would not remain a single poor person, if the profoundest desire of each poor person were to be realized. Women, therefore, are to be pitied as much as the poor, since they have similar desires; now, who can feel pleasure at the sight of the poor? It is quite as disagreeable to me to see women, now that I have learned their secret from my jealous sweetheart, who told me on the very day of our engagement. Till then I had been very fond of the society of women; but since then I have been cured of it. My sweetheart cured me."

"Your sweetheart is a kind and wise girl. Yes, we women are beings worthy of pity. But who, then, is your sweetheart? You speak so enigmatically."

"That is a secret which Fédya will not reveal to you. Do you know that I share absolutely the desire of the poor,—that there may be no more poverty, and someday this wish will come true. After all, sooner or later, we'll be able to arrange life so that there won't be any more poor people."

"There won't be any more poor people?" Vérochka interrupted. "I thought likewise, but I just couldn't figure out how it was possible. Tell me, how?"

"This I really can't say. Only my fiancée can tell you. I'm here alone, and without her I can only say that she is working on it. And she is strong. She is the most powerful thing on earth. But we're talking not about her, but about women. Though I share the hopes of the poor concerning the abolition of poverty, I cannot share the desire of women, which is not capable of realization, for I cannot admit that which cannot be realized. But I have another desire: I would like women to be bound in ties of friendship with my fiancée, who is concerned about them also, as she is concerned about many things, I might say, about all things. If women cultivated her acquaintance, I should no longer have to pity them, and their desire: 'Ah, why am I not a man!' would vanish. For, knowing her, women would not have a destiny worse than that of men."

"Monsieur Lopukhóv! another quadrille! I insist!"

"I'll praise you for it." And the student pressed the young girl's hand, but in a manner as calm and serious as if Vérochka had been his comrade or he her friend. "Which, then?" he added.

"The last one."

"Good."

Mária Alexévna scooted by them several times during this quadrille.

What idea would she have formed of their conversation, if she had heard it? We who have heard it from beginning to end will declare frankly that such a conversation is a very strange one to occur during a quadrille.

Finally came the last quadrille.

"So far we have talked only of myself," began Lopukhóv,

"but that is not at all gracious on my part. Now I wish to be gracious. Let's talk about you, Véra Pávlovna. Do you know that I had a still worse opinion of you than you had of me? But now . . . well, we will postpone that. Only there is one question I should like to put to you. Is your marriage to be soon?"

"Never!"

"I have thought so for the last three hours, ever since I left the game to dance with you. But why is he treated as your fiancé?"

"Why is he treated as my fiancé? Why? The first reason I cannot tell you, for it would give me pain. But I can tell you the second: I pity him. He loves me so dearly. You will say that I ought to tell him frankly what I think of our projected marriage; but when I do that, he answers: 'Oh! do not say so! That kills me; do not say so!' "

"The first reason, which you cannot tell me, I know; it is that your family relations are horrible."

"For the present they are endurable; no one torments me; they wait, and almost always leave me alone."

"But that cannot last long. Soon they will press you. And then?"

"Don't worry. I've thought of that and I've decided. Then I will not stay here. I will become an actress. What an enviable career. Independence! Independence!"

"And applause."

"Yes, and that gives pleasure too. But the principal thing is independence, to do what I want, live as I like, without asking any one's advice, without feeling the need of any one. That is how I should like to live!"

"That's it! Splendid . . . Now I have a favor to ask of you. I'll find out how it is to be done and to whom we should turn. All right?"

"Thank you," said Vérochka, pressing his hand. "Do so as quickly as possible. I so much wish to free myself from this humiliating and frightful situation. I said, indeed: 'I am calm, my situation is endurable'; but no, it is not so. Don't I see what they are doing with my name? Don't I know what those who are here think of me? An intriguer, schemer, greedy for wealth, she wishes to get into high society and shine there; her husband will be under her heel, she will turn him about at pleasure and deceive him. Yes, I know all that. I don't want to live this way! I don't want to . . . !" Suddenly she became thoughtful, and added: "Do not laugh at what I am going to say: I pity him much, for he loves me so dearly!"

"He loves you? Does he look at you, as I do, for instance? Tell me."

"You look at me in a frank and simple way. No, your look does not offend me."

"See, Véra Pávlovna, it is because . . . But never mind. . . . And does he look at you in that way?"

Vérochka blushed and said nothing.

"That means that he does not love you. That is not love, Véra Pávlovna."

"But . . ." Vérochka did not dare to finish.

"You intended to say: 'But what is it, then, if it is not love?' What is it? What you will. But that it is not love you will say yourself. Whom do you like best? I do not refer now to love, but friendship."

"Really? No one. Ah, yes, I did happen to meet not long ago a very strange woman. She talked to me very disparagingly of herself, and forbade me to continue in her society; we saw each other for a special purpose, and she told me that, when I should have no hope left but in death, I might come to her, but not otherwise. Her I like very much."

"Would you like to have her do something for you which would be disagreeable or injurious to her?"

Vérochka smiled. "Of course not."

"No. Well, suppose it were necessary, absolutely necessary to you that she should do something for you, and she should say to you: 'If I do that, I shall be very miserable myself.' Would you repeat your request? Would you insist?"

"I would die first."

"And you yourself say that that is love! Love! Such love is only a sentiment, not a passion. What distinguishes a passion from a simple sentiment? Intensity. Then, if a simple friendship makes you prefer to die rather than owe your life to troubles brought upon your friend,—if a simple friendship speaks thus, what, then, would passion say, which is a thousand times stronger? It would say: Rather die than owe happiness to the sorrow of the one I love! Rather die than cause her the slightest trouble or embarrass her in any way! A passion speaking thus would be true love. Otherwise, not. Now I must leave you, Véra Pávlovna; I have said all that I had to say."

Vérochka shook his hand. "Well, goodbye! You do not congratulate me? Today is my birthday."

"Perhaps, perhaps!" he said; "if you are not mistaken, so much the better for me!" Lopukhóv gave her a singular look.

: V :

"How quick! How unexpected all this was!" thought Vérochka, on finding herself alone in her room after the guests had gone. "We talked for the first time and became so close to each other. Half an hour ago we did not know each other, and now we are so close! How strange!" No, it is not strange at all, Vérochka. Men like Lopukhóv have magic words which draw to them every injured and outraged being. It is their *sweetheart* who whispers such words to them. And what is strange indeed, Vérochka, is that you should be so calm. Love is thought to be a startling feeling. Yet you will sleep as calmly and peacefully as a little child, and no painful dreams will trouble your slumbers; if you dream, it will be only of childish games or dances amid smiling faces.

To others it is strange; to me it is not. Trouble in love is not love itself; if there is trouble, that means that something is wrong; for love itself is gay and careless.

"Yes, it is very strange," still thought Vérochka; "about the poor, about women, about love, he told me what I had already thought, pondered and felt.

"Where did I find it? In books?

"No; for everything in them is expressed with so much doubt and reserve as if it were something extraordinary, improbable; as if they were dreams that could never come true! These things seem to me simple, ordinary, inevitable, in fact; it seems to me that without them life is impossible. Yet the best books present them as incapable of realization. Take Georges Sand, for instance; what goodness! what morality! but only dreams. Our novelists are such to offer nothing of the kind. Dickens, too, has these aspirations; but he does not seem to hope for their realization; being a good man, he desires it, but as one who knows that it cannot come to pass. Why do they not see that life cannot continue without this new justice, which will tolerate neither poverty nor wretchedness, and that it is towards such justice that we must march? They deplore the present, but they believe in its eternity, or little short of it. If they had said what I thought, I should have known then that the good and wise think so too, whereas I thought myself alone, a poor dreamer and inexperienced young girl, in thus thinking and hoping for a better order!

"He told me that his sweetheart inspires all who know her with these ideas and urges them to labor for their realization. This sweetheart is quite right; but who is she? I must know her; yes, I must know her.

"Certainly, it will be very fine when there shall be no more poor people, no more servitude, and when everybody shall be gay, good, learned, and happy."

It was amid these thoughts that Vérochka fell into a profound and dreamless sleep. No, it is not strange that you have conceived and cherished these sublime thoughts, good and inexperienced Vérochka, although you have never even heard pronounced the names of the men who first taught justice and proved that it must be realized and inevitably will be. If books have not presented these ideas with clearness, it is because they are written by men who caught glimpses of these thoughts when they were but marvellous and ravishing utopias; now it has been demonstrated that they can be realized, and other books are written by other men, who show that these thoughts are good, with nothing of the marvellous about them. These thoughts, Vérochka, float in the air, like the perfume in the fields when the flowers are in bloom; they penetrate everywhere, and you have even heard them from your drunken mother, telling you that one can live in this world only by falsehood and robbery; she meant to speak against your ideas, and, instead of that, she developed them; you have also heard them from the shameless and depraved Frenchwoman who drags her lover after her as if he were a servant, and does with him as she will. Yet, when she comes back to herself, she admits that she has no will of her own, that she has to indulge and restrain herself, and that such things are very painful. What more could she desire, living with her Serge, good, tender, and gentle? And yet she says: Even of me, unworthy as I am, such relations are unworthy. It is not difficult, Vérochka, to share your ideas. But others have not taken them to heart as you have. It is well, but not at all strange. What can there be strange, indeed, in your wish to be free and happy? That desire is not an extraordinary discovery; it is not an act of heroism; it is natural. But what is strange, Vérochka, is that there are men who have no such desire though they have all others, and who would, in fact, regard as strange the thoughts under the influence of which you fall asleep, my young friend, on the first evening of your love, and that, after questioning yourself as to him whom you love and as to your love itself, you think that all men should be happy and that we should aid them to become so as fast as possible. It is very natural, nevertheless; it is human; the simple words, "I wish joy and happiness," mean, "It would be pleasant to me if all men were joyous and happy"; yes, Vérochka, it is human; these two thoughts are but one.

Lopukhóv believes you a marvellous young girl. What is there astonishing in that? He loves you,—and that is not astonishing either. It is not astonishing that he loves you, for you are lovable, and if he loves you, he must necessarily believe you such.

: VI :

Mária Alexévna had hovered over Lopukhóv and Vérochka during their first quadrille; during the second she could not do as much, for she was entirely absorbed in the preparation of a *repas à la fourchette,* a sort of improvised supper. When she had finished, she looked about for the tutor, but he had gone. Two days later he returned to give his lesson. The *samovar* was brought, as always during the lesson. Mária Alexévna entered the room where the tutor was busy with Fédya to call the latter, a duty which had hitherto been Matryóna's; the tutor, who, as we know, did not take tea, wished to remain to correct Fédya's copy-book; but Mária Alexévna insisted that he come with them a moment, for she had something to say to him. He agreed, and Mária Alexévna plied him with questions concerning Fédya's talents and the school at which it would be best to place him. These were very natural questions, but were they not asked a little early? While putting them, she begged the tutor to take some tea, and this time with so much cordiality and affability that Lopukhóv consented to depart from his rule and took a cup. Vérochka had not arrived; at last she came; she and Lopukhóv greeted each other as if nothing had occurred between them, and Mária Alexévna continued to talk about Fédya. Then she suddenly turned the conversation to the subject of the tutor himself, and began to question him. Who was he? What was he? What were his parents. Were they wealthy? How did he live? What did he think of doing? The tutor answered briefly and vaguely: He had parents; they lived in the country; they were not rich; he lived by teaching; he should remain in St. Petersburg as a doctor. Nothing came of all that. Finding him so stubborn, Mária Alexévna went straight to business.

"You say that you will remain as a doctor (and doctors can live here, thank God!); do you not contemplate family life as yet? Or have you already a young girl in view?"

What should he say? Lopukhóv had almost forgotten already the sweetheart of his fancy, and came near replying, "I have no one in view," when he said to himself: "Ah! but she was listening, then." He laughed at himself, and was somewhat vexed at having employed so useless an allegory. And they say that propaganda is useless!

See what an effect propaganda had had upon this pure soul disposed so little to evil! She was listening! Had she heard? Well, it was of little consequence.

"Yes, I have one," answered Lopukhóv.

"And you are already engaged?"

"Yes."

"Formally? Or is it simply agreed upon between you?"

"Formally."

Poor Mária Alexévna! She had heard the words, "my sweetheart," "your sweetheart," "I love her much," "she is a beauty." She had heard them, and for the present was calm, believing that the tutor would not pay court to her daughter, and for this reason, the second quadrille not disturbing her, she had gone to prepare the supper. Nevertheless, she wanted to know more about this reassuring story and she cross examined Lopukhóv in detail regarding dowry, beauty, future plans and the like.

The tutor had pleased Mária Alexévna first by the fact that he did not take tea; he was a man of thoroughly good quality. He said little: hence he was not a giddy fellow. What he said, he said well, especially when money was in

question. But after she found out that it was absolutely impossible for him to pay court to the daughters of the families where he gave lessons, he became a godsend incapable
of over-estimation. Young people like him rarely have such
characteristics. Hence he was entirely satisfactory to her.
What a positive man! Far from boasting of having a rich
sweetheart, he allowed, on the contrary, every word to be
drawn from him as if by forceps. He had had to look long
for this rich sweetheart. And one can well imagine how he
had to court her. Yes, one may safely say that he knows how
to manage his affairs. And how he talks! He is a perfect
man.

Vérochka at first had difficulty in suppressing a smile, but
little by little it dawned upon her that Lopukhóv, although
replying to Mária Alexévna, was talking to her, and laughing
at her mother. Was this an illusion on Vérochka's part, or
was it really so? He knew, and she found out later. The
fact was that Vérochka, listening to Lopukhóv, began by
smiling, and then went seriously to thinking whether he was
talking not to Mária Alexévna, but to her, and whether, instead of joking, he was not telling the truth. Mária Alexévna, who had all the time listened seriously to Lopukhóv,
turned to Vérochka and said:

"Vérochka, are you going to sit there like a boor? Now
that you know Dmítry Sergéich, why don't you ask him
to accompany you while you sing?" These words meant:
We esteem you highly, Dmítry Sergéich, and we wish you
to be a close friend of our family; and you, Vérochka, do
not be afraid of Dmítry Sergéich; I will tell Mikhaíl Iványch that he already has a fiancée, and Mikhaíl Iványch
will not be jealous. That was the idea addressed to Vérochka and Dmítry Sergéich,—for already in Mária Alexévna's inner thoughts he was not *"the tutor,"* but Dmítry
Sergéich,—and to Mária Alexévna herself these words had
a third meaning, the most natural and real: We must be
agreeable with him; this acquaintance may be useful to us
in the future, when this rogue of a tutor shall be rich.

This was the general meaning of Mária Alexévna's words
but there was also a special one: After having flattered him,
I will tell him that it is a burden upon us, who are not rich,
to pay a ruble a lesson. Such are the different meanings
that the words of Mária Alexévna had.

Dmítry Sergéich answered that he was going to finish the

lesson and that afterward he would willingly play on the piano.

: VII :

Mária Alexévna's words had many meanings and they also had many results. As regards their special meaning,—that is, the reduction in the price of the lessons,—Mária Alexévna was more successful than she could hope; when, after two more lessons, she broached the subject of their poverty, Dmítry Sergéich haggled. He didn't want to give in and held out for three rubles (worth 75 copecks). Mária Alexévna hadn't even counted on a larger cut but against all expectations they settled on 60 kopeks a lesson. It must be allowed that this hope of reduction did not seem consistent with the opinion she had formed of Dmítry Sergéich as a crafty and avaricious fellow. A covetous individual does not yield so easily on money matters simply because the people with whom he is dealing are poor. Dmítry Sergéich had yielded; to be logical, then, she must disenchant herself and see in him nothing but an imprudent and consequently harmful man. Certainly she would have come to this conclusion in dealing with any one else. But the nature of man is such that it is very difficult to judge his conduct by any general rule: he is so fond of making exceptions in his own favor! Mária Alexévna was not exempt from this defect, which especially distinguishes base, crafty, and greedy individuals. This law admits exceptions, but only in two extreme cases,—either when the individual is a consummate scamp, a transcendental scamp or those whom a simple honesty of heart serves to protect. Ask the Vidocqs and Vanka Caïns of all sorts, and they will tell you that there is nothing more difficult than to deceive an honest and sincere man, provided he has intelligence and experience. Honest people who are not stupid cannot be seduced individually. But they have an equivalent defect,—that of being subject to seduction *en masse.* The knave cannot capture them individually, but collectively they are at his mercy. Knaves, on the contrary, so easy to deceive individually, cannot be duped as a body. That is the whole secret of universal history.

But this is not the place to make excursions into universal history. When one undertakes to write a romance, he must do that and nothing else.

The first result of Mária Alexévna's words was the reduction in the price of the lessons. The second result was that by this reduction Mária Alexévna was more than ever confirmed in her good opinion of Lopukhóv as a valuable man; she even thought that his conversations would be useful to Vérochka in urging her to consent to marry Mikhaíl Iványch; this deduction was too difficult for Mária Alexévna ever to have arrived at it herself, but a speaking fact occurred to convince her. What was this fact? We shall see presently.

The third result of Mária Alexévna's words was that Vérochka and Dmítry Sergéich began, with her permission and encouragement, to spend much time together. After finishing his lesson at about eight o'clock, Lopukhóv would stay with the Rozálskys two or three hours longer. He often played cards with the mother and father, talked with the suitor, or played Vérochka's accompaniments on the piano. At other times Vérochka played and he listened. Sometimes he simply talked with the young girl, and Mária Alexévna did not interfere with them or look at them askance, though keeping a strict watch over them nevertheless.

Certainly she watched them, although Dmítry Sergéich was a very good young man; for it is not for nothing that the proverb says: The occasion makes the thief. And Dmítry Sergéich was a thief,—not in the blameworthy, but the praiseworthy sense; else there would have been no reason for esteeming him and cultivating his acquaintance. Must one associate with imbeciles? Yes, when there is profit in it. Now, Dmítry Sergéich having nothing yet, association with him could be sought only for his qualities,— that is, for his wit, his tact, his address, and his calculating prudence.

If every man can plot harm, all the more a man so intelligent. It was necessary, then, to keep an eye on Dmítry Sergéich, and that is what Mária Alexévna did, after keen reflection. All her observations only tended to confirm the idea that Dmítry Sergéich was a positive man of good intentions.

He did not look too closely at Vérochka's bodice. There she is, playing; Dmítry Sergéich listens, and Mária Alexévna watches to see if he does not cast indiscreet glances.

No, he has not the least intention! He does not even look at Vérochka at all; he casts his eyes about at random, sometimes upon her, but then so simply, openly, and coldly.

How else can one detect the existence of love between young people? When they speak of love. Now they are never heard to speak of love; moreover, they talk very little with each other; he talks more with Mária Alexévna. Later Lopukhóv brought books for Vérochka.

One day, while Mikhaíl Iványch was there, Vérochka went to see one of her friends. Mária Alexévna showed the books to Mikhaíl Iványch.

"Look here, Mikhaíl Iványch, this one, in French, I have almost made out myself: 'Gostinaya.' * That means a manual of etiquette. And here is one in German; I cannot read it."

"No, Mária Alexévna, it is not 'Gostinaya'; it is 'Destinée.' " He said the word in Russian.

"What, then, is this destiny? Is it a novel, a ladies' oracle, or a dream-book?"

"Let's see." Mikhaíl Iványch turned over a few pages.

"It deals with series;† it is a book for a *savant*."

"Series? I understand. It treats of transfers of money."

"That's it."

"And this one in German?"

Mikhaíl Iványch read slowly: " 'On Religion,' by Ludwig Feuerbach"—that means: by Louis Fourteenth. This Louis XIV was a king of France, father of the king whom the present Napoleon succeeded."

"Then it is a pious book."

"Pious, Mária Alexévna, you have said it."

"Very well, Mikhaíl Iványch; although I know that Dmítry Sergéich is a good young man, I wish to see. One can't be too careful."

"Surely it is not love that is in his head. In any case I appreciate your vigilance."

"It could not be otherwise, Mikhaíl Iványch; to watch is the duty of a mother who wishes to preserve her daugh-

* *Gostinaya* is the Russian equivalent of the French word *salon*, meaning drawing-room primarily, and derivatively, fashionable society.

† Series-paper-money at interest. The book was Considérant's "Social Destiny."

ter's purity. That is what I think. But of what religion was the king of France?"

"He was a Catholic, naturally."

"But his book may convert to the religion of the Papists?"

"I do not think so. If a Catholic archbishop had written it, he would try to convert, it is unnecessary to say, to the religion of the Papists. But a king cares nothing about that; a king, as a prince and wise politician, wishes piety simply."

That was enough for the moment. Mária Alexévna could not help seeing that Mikhaíl Iványch, while having a narrow mind, had reasoned with much justice; nevertheless, she wished to clarify matters. Two or three days later she suddenly said to Lopukhóv, who was playing cards with her and Mikhaíl Iványch:

"Say, Dmítry Sergéich, I have a question that I wish to ask you: did the father of the last king of France, whom the present Napoleon succeeded, ordain baptism in the religion of the Papists?"

"Why, no, he did not ordain it, Mária Alexévna."

"And is the religion of the Papists good, Dmítry Sergéich?"

"No, Mária Alexévna, it is not good. I play the seven of diamonds."

"It was out of curiosity, Dmítry Sergéich, that I asked you that; though not an educated woman, I am interested just the same in knowing things. And how much have you abstracted from the stakes, Dmítry Sergéich?"

"Oh, that's all right, Mária Alexévna; we are taught that at the Academy. It's impossible for a doctor not to know how to play."

To Lopukhóv these questions remained an enigma. Why did Mária Alexévna want to know whether Philippe Egalité ordained baptism in the religion of the Papists? But Mária Alexévna had still another test.

: V I I I :

TEST À LA HAMLET

One day Mária Alexévna said, while taking tea, that she had a severe headache; after having drunk the tea and locked up the sugar-bowl, she went to lie down. Vérochka and Lopukhóv remained alone in the parlor, which adjoined Mária Alexévna's bedroom. A few moments later, the sick woman called Fédya.

"Tell your sister that their conversation prevents me from sleeping; let them go into another room; but say it politely, in order that Dmítry Sergéich is not offended. He takes such care of you!" Fédya did the errand.

"Let us go into my room, Dmítry Sergéich," said Véra Pávlovna, "it is away from the bedroom, and there we won't prevent Mamma from sleeping."

That was precisely what Mária Alexévna expected. A quarter of an hour later she approached with stealthy step the door of Vérochka's room. The door was partly open, and between it and the casing was a crack which left nothing to be desired. There Mária Alexévna applied her eyes and opened her ears.

And this is what she saw:

Vérochka's room had two windows; between the windows was a writing-table. Near one window, at one end of the table, sat Vérochka; she was knitting a worsted waistcoat for her father, thus strictly carrying out Mária Alexévna's recommendation. Near the other window, at the other end of the table, sat Lopukhóv: supporting one elbow on the table, he held a cigar in his hand, and had thrust the other hand into his pocket—between him and Vérochka was a distance of two *archines*,* if not more. Vérochka looked principally at her knitting, and Lopukhóv looked principally at his cigar. A satisfactory disposition of affairs.

And this is what she heard:

. . . "And is it thus, then, that life must be regarded?" Such were the first words that reached the ears of Mária Alexévna.

"Yes, Véra Pávlovna, precisely thus."

* Two and one-third feet.

"Practical and cold men are therefore right in saying that man is governed exclusively by self-interest?"

"They are right. What are called elevated sentiments, ideal aspirations,—all that, in the general course of affairs, is absolutely null, and is eclipsed by individual interest; these very sentiments are nothing but self-interest clearly understood."

"But you, for example,—are you too thus governed?"

"How else should I be, Véra Pávlovna? Just consider what is the essential motive of my whole life. The essential business of my life so far has consisted in study; I was preparing to be a doctor. Why did my father send me to school? Over and over again he said to me: 'Study, Mítya; then you will become an office-holder; you will support us, myself and your mother, and you will be comfortable yourself.' That, then, was why I studied; if they had not had that interest in view, my father would not have sent me to school: the family needed a laborer. Now, for my part, although science interests me now, I should not have spent so much time upon it if I had not thought that this expense would be largely rewarded. My studies at school were drawing to an end; I prevailed upon my father to allow me to enter the Academy of Medicine instead of becoming an office-holder. How did that happen? We saw, my father and I, that doctors live much better than government functionaries and heads of bureaus, above whom I could not expect to rise. That is the reason why I entered the Academy,—the hope of a bigger piece of bread. If I had not had that interest in view, I should not have entered."

"But you liked to study in college, and the medical sciences attracted you?"

"Yes. But that is ornamental; it helps in the achievement of success. But success is ordinarily achieved without it; never without interest as a motive. Love of science is only a result; the cause is self-interest."

"Supposing that you are right. All the actions, that I understand, can be explained by self-interest. But this theory seems to me very cold."

"Theory in itself should be cold. The mind should judge things coldly."

"But it is pitiless."

"For senseless and mischievous fancies."

"It is very prosaic."

"The poetic form is not suited to science."

"So this theory, which I do not see my way to accept, condemns men to a cold, pitiless, prosaic life?"

"No, Véra Pávlovna: this theory is cold, but it teaches man to procure warmth. Matches are cold, the side of the box against which we scratch them is cold, kindling is cold; but the fire which prepares warm nourishment for man and keeps him warm none the less springs from them; this theory is pitiless, but by following it men cease to be wretched objects of the compassion of the idle."

"Well, I too shall be pitiless, Dmítry Sergéich," said Vérochka, smiling; "do not flatter yourself with the idea that you have had in me an obstinate opponent of your theory of self-interest, and that now you have gained a new disciple. For my part, I thought so long before I ever heard of you or read your book. But I believed that these thoughts were my own, and that the wise and learned thought differently; that is why my mind hesitated. All that I read was contrary to what went on within me and made my thought the object of blame and sarcasm. Nature, life, intelligence lead one way; books lead another, saying: This is bad, that is base. Do you know, the objections which I have raised seemed to me a little ridiculous."

"They are indeed ridiculous, Véra Pávlovna."

"But," said she, laughing, "we are paying each other very pretty compliments!"

"Ah! Yes!" said he, smiling also, "we have no interest in being polite to each other, and so we are not."

"Good, Dmítry Sergéich; men are egoists, are they not? There, you have talked about yourself; now I wish to talk a little about myself."

"You are perfectly right; every one thinks of himself first."

"I have a rich suitor. I do not like him. Should I accept his proposal?"

"Calculate that which is the most useful to you."

"That which is the most useful to me? You know I am poor enough. On the one hand, lack of sympathy with the man; on the other, domination over him, an enviable position in society, money, a multitude of admirers."

"Weigh all considerations, and choose the course most advantageous for you."

"And if I should choose the husband's wealth and a multitude of adorers?"

"I shall say that you have chosen that which seemed to you most in harmony with your interests."

"But will not my choice deserve blame?"

"People who talk nonsense may say what they will; but people who have a correct idea of life will say that you have acted as you had to act. If your action is such and such, that means that you are such an individual that you could not act otherwise under the circumstances. They will say that your action was dictated by the force of events, and that you had no other choice."

"And no blame will be cast upon my actions?"

"Who has a right to blame the consequences of a fact, if the fact exists? Your person under given circumstances is a fact; your actions are the necessary consequences of this fact, consequences arising from the nature of things. You are not responsible for them; therefore, to blame them would be stupid."

"So you do not recoil from the consequences of your theory. Then, I shall not deserve your blame, if I accept my suitor's proposal?"

"I should be stupid to blame you."

"So I have permission, perhaps even sanction, perhaps even direct advice to take the action of which I speak?"

"The advice is always the same: figure out what's useful for you. If you follow this advice, you will have approval."

"I thank you. Now, my personal matters are settled. Let us return to the general question with which we started. We began with the proposition that man acts by the force of events, that his actions are determined by the influences under which they occur. If stronger influences overcome others, that shows that we have changed our reasoning; when the action is one of real importance, the motives are called interests and their play in man a combination or calculation of interests, and consequently man always acts by reason of his interest. Do I sum up your ideas correctly?"

"Yes."

"See what a good pupil I am. Now this particular question concerning actions of vital importance is settled. But as to the general question some difficulties yet remain. Your book says that man acts from necessity. But there are cases where it depends upon my good pleasure whether I act in one way or another. For example, in playing, I turn the leaves of my music book; sometimes I turn them with the left hand, sometimes with the right. Suppose, now, that I turn with the right hand; might I not have turned them with the left? Does not that depend on my good pleasure?"

"No, Véra Pávlovna; if you turn without thinking about it, you turn with the hand which it is more convenient for you to use. There is no good pleasure in that. But if you say: 'I am going to turn with the right hand,' you will turn with the right hand under the influence of that idea; now that idea sprang not from your good pleasure but necessarily from another thought."

Here Mária Alexévna stopped listening.

"Now they are going into learned questions; those are not what I am after, and furthermore I care nothing about them. What a wise, positive, I might say noble, young man! What prudent rules he instils in Vérochka's mind! That is what a learned man can do: when I say these things, she does not listen, she is offended; she is very obstinate with me, because I cannot speak in a learned way. But when he speaks in this way, she listens, sees that he is right, and admits it."

This conversation, to which Mária Alexévna had listened, produced in her then the definitive conviction that the interviews between the two young people were not only not dangerous to Vérochka (she had been of that opinion for some time), but that they would be even useful to her in inducing her to abandon, as her mother desired, the foolish ideas which she had adopted as an inexperienced girl, and in thus hastening her marriage to Mikhaíl Iványch.

: IX :

Mária Alexévna's attitude towards Lopukhóv is not without a certain comic side, and Mária Alexévna is represented here under a somewhat ridiculous light. But really it is against my will that things present themselves in this aspect. If I had seen fit to act in accordance with the rules of what we call art, I should have carefully glided over these incidents which give the romance a tinge of the *vaudeville*. To hide them would have been easy. The general progress of the story might well be explained without them. But I tell this story, not to win a reputation as a man of talent, but just as it happened. As a novelist, I am sorry to have written a few pages that touch the level of the comic.

My determination to tell things, not in the easiest way, but as they actually occurred, causes me still another embarrassment: I am not at all contented to have Mária Alexévna represented in a ridiculous light by her reflections upon the sweetheart which her fancy had pictured as Lopukhóv's; by her fantastic way of guessing the contents of the books given by Lopukhóv to Vérochka; by her questions about Philippe Egalité and his supposed Papist absolutism and about the works of Louis XIV. Every one is liable to make mistakes. The errors may be absurd, when one tries to judge in matters of which he is ignorant; but it would be unjust to infer from Mária Alexévna's blunders that these were the sole cause of her unfavorable attitude towards Lopukhóv. No, her queer ideas about the rich sweetheart and the piety of Philippe Egalité would not have obscured her good sense for a moment, if she had only noticed anything suspicious in Lopukhóv's acts and words. But he so conducted himself that really there was nothing to be said. Though naturally bold, he did not cast indiscreet glances at a very pretty young girl; he did not follow her assiduously; he sat down without ceremony to play cards with Mária Alexévna without betraying any sign that it would give him greater pleasure to be with Véra; when left with Véra, he held such conversations with her that Mária Alexévna regarded them as the expression of her own thought. Like her, he said that self-interest is the motive of human actions; that there is no sense in getting angry with a rascal and reminding him of the principles of honor, inasmuch as the rascal acts in accordance with the laws of his own nature under the pressure of circumstances; that, given his individuality, he could not help being a rascal, and that to pretend otherwise would be an absurdity. Yes, Mária Alexévna had reason to think that she had found in Lopukhóv a kindred spirit.

I realize how greatly Lopukhóv is compromised in the eyes of the enlightened public by Mária Alexévna's sympathy for his way of thinking. But I conceal nothing. In fact, I take it upon myself to explain that he really deserved Mária Alexévna's favor.

From Lopukhóv's conversation with Vérochka, it is plain that his way of looking at things might appear better to persons of Mária Alexévna's stamp than to those holding fine ideas; Lopukhóv saw things in the aspect which they present to the mass of mankind, minus those holding lofty ideas.

If Mária Alexévna could rejoice at the thoughts that he had voiced regarding Vérochka's projected marriage, he, on his side, could have written beneath the drunken usurer's confession: *This is true.* The resemblance in their actions is so great that enlightened novelists holding noble ideas, journalists, and other public teachers have long since proclaimed that individuals like Lopukhóv are in no wise distinguishable from individuals like Mária Alexévna. If writers so enlightened have thus viewed men like Lopukhóv, is it for us to blame Mária Alexévna for coming to the same conclusions about this Lopukhóv that our best writers, thinkers, and teachers have arrived at?

Certainly, if Mária Alexévna had known only half as much as our writers know, she would have had good sense enough to understand that Lopukhóv was no companion for her. But, besides her lack of knowledge, she had still another excuse: Lopukhóv, in his conversations, never pursued his reflections to their conclusions, not being of those amateurs who try very hard to inspire in Mária Alexévna the high thoughts in which they take delight themselves. He had good sense enough not to undertake to straighten a tree fifty years old. He and she understood facts in the same way and reasoned accordingly. If, for instance, in talking with Vérochka, he had undertaken to explain what he meant by "self-interest," Mária Alexévna probably could have seen that his idea of self-interest was not exactly the same as her own; but Lopukhóv did not explain himself on this point to the usurer, nor even to Vérochka, the latter knowing his meaning from the books which had occasioned their conversation. On the other hand, in writing "This is true" under the confession made by Mária Alexévna when drunk, Lopukhóv would have added: "But, whereas, by your own admission, the new order of things will be better than the old, we should not oppose those who joyfully and devotedly labor to establish it. As for the stupidity of the people, though it is indeed an obstacle, you will admit that men would soon become wise if they saw that it was for their advantage to become so, a fact which they have not yet been able to perceive; you will admit also that it has not been possible for them to learn to reason. Give them this possibility, and you will see that they will hasten to profit by it."

But the conversation with Mária Alexévna never reached that point, not from reserve, although he was reserved, but simply from good sense. He had good sense and delicacy enough not to torment people with discourse beyond their grasp.

I say all this only to justify Mária Alexévna's oversight in not understanding in time what sort of a man Lopukhóv was, and not at all to justify Lopukhóv himself. To justify Lopukhóv would not be a good thing. Why? That you shall see later, reader. Those who, without justifying him, would like, from motives of humanity, to excuse him, could not do so. For instance, they might say in his behalf that he was a doctor and an investigator of the natural sciences, circumstances which dispose one to accept the materialistic way of looking at things. But with me such an excuse is not a valid one. Many other sciences lead to materialism, as, for instance, the mathematical, historical, social, and, in short, all the sciences. Is that to say that all the geometers, astronomers, historians, economists, jurists, publicists, and other *savants* are materialists? Very far from that. Lopukhóv could not then be justified. The compassionate people who do not justify him might say further in his favor that he is not entirely without praiseworthy qualities. But to this latter excuse it would be necessary to reply that, generally speaking, there is no man entirely without good qualities, and that the materialists, whatever they may be, are always materialists, and are shown by that very fact to be low and immoral men who must never be excused, since to excuse them would be to compromise with materialism. So, not justifying Lopukhóv, we cannot excuse him.

: X :

The question as to what is the true way of looking at things certainly was not the principal object of Vérochka's interviews with Lopukhóv. As a general thing they talked very little with each other, and their long conversations, which occurred but rarely, turned on general questions alone. They knew further that they were watched by two very experienced eyes. Consequently they seldom exchanged words on the subject which most interested them, and, when they did, it was usually while turning the leaves of music books.

It should be said also that the subject which so preoccupied them and about which they had so little chance to talk was not, as may be supposed, the expression of their inmost feeling. Of this feeling they had not said a word since the vague phrases of their first interview, and they had no time to discuss it during the moments in which they could talk freely, and which were entirely devoted to Vérochka's situation. How could she escape from it? How could she get a foothold on the stage? They knew that the theatre presents many dangers for a young girl, but that these dangers might be avoided by Vérochka's firmness.

Nevertheless one day Lopukhóv said to Vérochka:

"I advise you to abandon the idea of becoming an actress."

"Why?"

"Because it would be better for you to marry your suitor." There the conversation stopped. These words were said at the moment when Vérochka and he were taking their music books, he to play, she to sing. Vérochka became very sad and more than once lost the time, although singing a very well known piece. While looking for another piece, Vérochka said: "I was so happy! It is very hard for me to learn that it is impossible. I will take another course; I will be a governess."

Two days later she said to him:

"I have found no one who can secure me a place as governess. Will you do it yourself, Dmítry Sergéich? I have only you to ask."

"It is very unfortunate that I have so few acquaintances to aid me. The families where I have given and still give lessons are all relatively poor, and the people of their acquaintance are almost as badly off. No matter, I will try."

"My friend, I take all your time, but what am I to do?"

"Véra Pávlovna, time is no consideration between friends."

Vérochka smiled and blushed; she had not noticed that her lips had substituted the name "My friend," for that of Dmítry Sergéich.

Lopukhóv smiled too.

"You did not intend to say that, Véra Pávlovna. With-draw the name if you regret having given it."

"It is too late—and then . . . I do not regret it," re-plied Vérochka, blushing scarlet.

"You shall see, if the opportunity offers, that I am a faithful friend."

They shook hands.

Such were their first two interviews after the famous *soirée*.

Two days afterwards there appeared in the "Journal of Police" an announcement that a noble young girl, speaking French and German, etc., wanted a place as governess, and that inquiries concerning her could be made of such a functionary at Kolomna, Rue N. N., house N. N.

Lopukhóv did indeed have to spend a lot of time on Vérochka's affairs. He went every morning, generally on foot, from Vyborg to Kolomna to see the friend whose address he was using. It was a long way, but Lopukhóv had no friends nearer to Vyborg. It was necessary that this friend should satisfy many conditions; among other things essen-tial were a decent house, a well-regulated household, and an air of respectability. A poor house would have presented the governess at a disadvantage. His own address? What would have been thought of a young girl who had no one to answer for her but a student! Therefore Lopukhóv had a great deal to do. After getting from his friend the ad-dresses of those who had come to find a governess, he started out to visit them. The clerk told them that he was a distant relative of the young person and only an inter-mediary, but that she had a nephew who would not fail to go in a carriage the next day to talk with them more fully. The nephew, instead of going in a carriage, went on foot, examined the people closely, and, as goes without say-ing, almost always found something which did not suit him. In this family they were too haughty; in another the mother was good, the father stupid; in a third it was just the reverse; in still another it would have been possible to live, but the conditions were above Vérochka's means; or else English was required, and she did not speak it; and so forth.

The advertisement was kept in the "Journal of Police," and applicants continued to call on the clerk. Lopukhóv did not lose hope. He spent a fortnight in his search. Coming home on the fifth day weary after his long tramp, Lopukhóv threw himself on the sofa, and Kirsánov said to him:

"Dmítry, you aren't working with me as you did before. You disappear every morning and one evening out of two. You must have found many pupils. But is this the time to take on so many? For my part, I'm trying to give up even those that I have. I have seventy rubles, which will last during the remaining three months of the term. And you have saved more than I,—one hundred rubles, I believe."

"Even more,—one hundred and fifty rubles; but it is not my pupils that keep me, for I have given them all up save one: I have business on hand. After I have finished it, you will have no more reason to complain that I lag behind you in my work."

"What, then, is the business?"

"This: in the family where I still give lessons, an excessively bad family, there is a very remarkable young girl. She wishes to become a governess and leave her parents, and I am searching for a place for her."

"Is she a fine girl?"

"Oh! yes!"

"Well, then. Keep looking."

And there the conversation ended.

Well, Kirsánov and Lopukhóv, though you're learned men, you've missed what is more remarkable. Why hadn't Kirsánov even thought to remark, "Say, brother, you aren't in love perchance? You're certainly doing a lot for her!" While Lopukhóv likewise didn't think to say, "Brother, am I keen on her!" Or if he didn't wish to say this, it hadn't even occurred to him to ward off such conjecture by saying, "Now, Alexánder, don't think that I've fallen in love." They both thought that, when the deliverance of a person from a dangerous situation was in question, it was of very little importance whether the person's face was beautiful, even though it was a girl's face, and still less whether one was in love or not. The idea that this was their opinion did not even occur to them; they were not aware of it, and that is precisely the best feature of it. For the rest, does this not prove to the class of penetrating readers—to which belong the majority of aesthetic *littérateurs,* who are endowed with exceptional penetration—does this not prove,

I say, that Kirsánov and Lopukhóv were dry people, absolutely without the "aesthetic streak"? That was the expression in vogue but a very short time since among the aesthetic and transcendental *littérateurs*. Perhaps they still use it. No longer associating with them, I cannot say. Is it natural that young people, so devoid of taste and heart, should interest themselves in a young girl? Certainly they are without the aesthetic sentiment. According to those who have studied the nature of man in circles endowed with the *aesthetic sentiment* even to a greater degree than our *normalien* aesthetic *littérateurs*, young people in such a case should speak of woman from a purely plastic standpoint. So it has been, and so, gentlemen, it still is.

: XI :

"Well, my friend, no job yet?"

"Not yet, Véra Pávlovna; but don't get discouraged. Chin up! We shall finally find a suitable place."

"Oh, if you knew, my friend, how hard it is for me to stay here! As long as I saw no possible way of deliverance from this perpetual humiliation, I forced myself into a sort of excessive insensibility. Now I stifle in this heavy and putrid atmosphere."

"Patience, Véra Pávlovna, we shall find something."

Such conversations as this occurred periodically for a week.

The following Thursday witnessed the test *à la Hamlet* according to Saxon, the Grammarian, after which Mária Alexévna relaxed her supervision a little.

Saturday, after tea, Mária Alexévna went to count the linen which the laundress had just brought.

"It looks, my friend, as if things are shaping up."

"Yes? Oh! so much the better! And let it be quickly. I'm afraid I'll die if this lasts much longer. But when and how?"

"All will be decided to-morrow. I am almost certain of it."

"Tell me about it, then."

"Be calm, my friend, you may be noticed. There you are, leaping with joy, and your mother's liable to come in at any moment!"

"But you yourself came in so radiant with joy that Mamma looked at you for a long time."

"Therefore I told her why I was gay; for I thought it would be better to tell her, and so I said to her: 'I have found an excellent job.'"

"You're insufferable! Here you stand with all sorts of advice to me and not a word about what really matters. Speak up! Will you?"

"This morning Kirsánov—that, you know, my friend, is my friend's name—"

"I know, I know; speak, speak quickly."

"You're interrupting me, my friend."

"Oh God! Still a lot of talk and no business! What shall I do with you? I would put you on your knees, if it were not impossible here. I order you to kneel when you get home, and Kirsánov shall report to me whether you have done proper penance."

"So be it, and I will keep silence until I have done my penance and been pardoned."

"Granted, but speak quickly, insufferable!"

"I thank you. You pardon me, Véra Pávlovna, when you yourself are the guilty one. You are constantly interrupting. This morning Kirsánov gave me the address of the lady who expects me to call tomorrow. I am not personally acquainted with her; but I have often heard her spoken of by our mutual friend, and again he has been the intermediary. The lady's husband I know personally, having met him several times at the house of the clerk in question. Judging from appearances, I am satisfied that the family is a good one. The lady said, when giving her address, that she was sure that we could agree upon terms. Therefore we may consider the matter practically settled."

"Oh! How wonderful!" repeated Vérochka. "But I must know immediately, as quickly as possible. You will come here right from their place?"

"No, my friend, that would arouse suspicion. I must come here only at lesson-time. This is what we will do. I will send a letter by city post to Mária Alexévna announcing that I cannot come on Tuesday to give the usual lesson, and will come on Wednesday instead. If I say Wednesday morning, that will mean that the affair has been settled; if Wednesday evening, that it has fallen through. But it is almost certain to be Wednesday morning. Mária Alexévna will tell Fédya, as well as yourself and Pável Konstantínych."

"When will the letter get here?"

"Tomorrow evening."

"So late! I simply can't wait. And what am I going to learn from the letter? A simple 'yes,' and then wait till Wednesday! It's torture! My friend, I am going to this lady's house. I want to know everything once and for all. But how shall we do that? Oh, I know; I will wait for you in the street, until you come away from her house."

"But, my friend, that would be even more imprudent than for me to come back here. I had better come here."

"No, we may not be able to talk here. And, in any case, Mamma would be suspicious. It is better to follow my suggestion. I have a veil so thick that no one will recognize me."

"Perhaps, indeed, it is possible. Let me think a little."

"There is no time to lose in long reflections. Mamma may enter at any moment. Where does this lady live?"

"Galernaya Street, near the bridge."

"When will you be there?"

"At noon; that is the hour she set."

"From noon onward I will be seated on the Boulevard Konno-Gvardeisky, on the last bench on the side near the bridge. I told you that I would wear a very thick veil. But here is a signal for you: I will have a music roll in my hand. If I am not there, it will be because I have been detained. No matter, sit down on the bench and wait. I may be late, but I will not fail to come. How good I feel! How grateful I am to you! How happy I shall be! How about your fiancée, Dmítry Sergéich? You have fallen from the title of 'friend' to that of 'Dmítry Sergéich.' Oh, I'm so happy!"

Vérochka ran to her piano, and began to play. "What a degradation of art, my friend! What has become of your taste? You abandon operas for gallops."

"Abandoned! Thrown to the winds!"

A few minutes later Mária Alexévna entered. Dmítry Sergéich played a game of cards with her; he began by winning; then allowed her to recover her losses, and finally he lost thirty-five copecks; it was the first time he had let her win, and when he went away, he left her well contented, not with the money, but with the triumph. There are joys purely ideal, even in hearts completely sunk in materialism, and this it is that proves the materialistic explanation of life unsatisfactory.

: XII :

VÉROCHKA'S FIRST DREAM

Vérochka dreamed that she was shut up in a dark and damp cellar. Suddenly the door opened, and she found herself at liberty in the country; she began to run about joyfully, saying to herself: "How did I manage to keep from dying in the cellar?" And again she ran about. But suddenly she felt a stroke of paralysis. "How is it that paralysis has fallen upon me?" thought she; "only old people are subject to that, old people and not young girls."

"Girls also are subject to it," cried a voice. "As for you, you will be well, if I but touch you with my hand. You see, there you are, cured; arise."

"Who speaks thus to me? And how well I feel! The illness has quite gone."

Vérochka arose; again she began to run about and play, saying to herself: "How was I able to endure the paralytic shock? Undoubtedly because I was born a paralytic, and did not know how to walk and run; if I had known how, I never could have endured to be without the power."

But she sees a young girl coming. How strange she is! her expression and manner are constantly changing; by turns she is English and French, then she becomes German, Polish, and finally Russian, then English again, German again, Russian again,—and yet why do her features always remain the same? An English girl does not resemble a French girl, nor a German a Russian. She is by turns imperious, docile, sad, gentle, angry. But she is always good, even when she is angry. That is not all; she suddenly begins to improve; her face takes on new charms with every moment, and, approaching Vérochka, she says to her: "Who are you?"

"Formerly he called me Véra Pávlovna; now he calls me 'my friend.'"

"Ah! it is you, the Vérochka who has formed an affection for me."

"Yes, I love you much. But who are you?"

"I am the fiancée of your sweetheart."

"Of which sweetheart?"

"I do not know. I am not acquainted with my sweethearts. They know me, but I cannot know them, for I have many. Choose one of them; never take one elsewhere."

"I have chosen" . . . .

"I have no need of his name; I do not know them. But I say to you again, choose only among them. I wish my sisters and my sweethearts to choose each other exclusively. Weren't you shut up in a cellar? Weren't you paralyzed?"

"Yes."

"And now, aren't you free?"

"Yes."

"It is I who delivered you, who cured you. Remember that there are many who are not yet delivered, who are not yet cured. Go, deliver them and cure them! Will you do it?"

"I will do so. But what is your name? I wish to know it."

"I have many names. I tell to each the name by which he is to know me. As for you, call me Love of Mankind. That is my real name; but there are not many people who know it; you, at least, shall call me so."

Then Vérochka found herself in the city; she saw a cellar where young girls were shut up. She touched the lock, the lock fell; she said to the young girls: "Go out!" and they went out. She saw then a room where young girls lay paralyzed. She said to them: "Arise!" They arose, and all ran into the country, light-hearted and laughing. Vérochka followed them, and in her happiness cried out:

"How pleasant it is to be with them! How sad it was to be alone! How pleasant it is to be with the free young girls who run in the fields, so lithe and joyous!"

: XIII :

Lopukhóv, overburdened with cares, had no longer any time to see his friends at the Academy. Kirsánov, who had not ceased to associate with them, was obliged to answer a hundred questions about Lopukhóv: he revealed the nature of the affair that occupied his friend, and thus it was that one of their mutual friends gave the address of the lady on whom Lopukhóv is about to call at this stage of our story. "How fortunate it will be, if this works!" thought he, as he walked along; "in two years, two and a half at most, I shall be a professor. Then we can live together. In the meantime she will live quietly with Madame B., provided Madame B. proves really to be a good person whom one can trust."

Lopukhóv found Madame B. to be an intelligent and good woman, without pretensions. The conditions were good, Vérochka would be well placed there. All was going on famously, then, and Lopukhóv's hopes had not been groundless.

Madame B., on her side, being satisfied with Lopukhóv's replies regarding Vérochka's character, said: "If my conditions suit your young aunt, I beg her to move here as soon as possible."

"She will be pleased. She has authorized me to act for her. But now that we have come to an agreement, I must tell you (what was needless to tell you before) that this girl is not my relative. She is the daughter of the functionary in whose family I give lessons. She had no one but me whom she could trust in this affair. But I am almost a stranger to her."

"I knew it, Monsieur Lopukhóv. You, Professor N. (the name of the friend who had given the address), and your comrade esteem yourselves so highly that one of you can form a friendship for a young girl without compromising her in the eyes of the two others. Now N. and I think the same, and, knowing that I was looking for a governess, he felt justified in telling me that this young girl is not related to you. Do not blame him for being indiscreet; he knows me very well. I believe myself also worthy of esteem, Monsieur Lopukhóv, and be sure that I well know who is worthy of being esteemed. I trust N. as I trust myself, and N. trusts you as he trusts himself. Let us say no more on that point, then. But N. did not know her name, and it will be necessary for me to know it, since she is to come into our family."

"Her name is Véra Pávlovna Rozálsky."

"Now, I have an explanation to make to you. It may seem strange to you that, careful as I am of my children, I have decided upon a governess for them whom I have not seen. But I made the bargain with you because I know well, very well indeed, the men who compose your circle, and I am convinced that, if one of you feels so keen an interest in a young person, this young person must be a veritable treasure to a mother who desires to see her daughter become worthy of the esteem of all. Consequently to make inquiries about her seemed to me a superfluous indelicacy. In saying this I compliment, not you, but myself."

"I am very glad for Mademoiselle Rozálsky. Life in her family was so painful to her that she would have been contented in any family at all endurable. But I never should have hoped to find her a home like yours."

"Yes, N. told me that her family life was very bad."

"Very bad indeed!" And Lopukhóv told Madame B. such facts as she would need to know in order to avoid, in her conversations with Vérochka, touching on subjects which would give her pain by reminding her of her former troubles.

Madame B. listened with much interest, and finally, grasping his hand, she said to him:

"Enough, Monsieur Lopukhóv; I shall have a nervous attack; and at my age of some forty years it would be ridiculous to show that I cannot yet listen in cold blood to a story of family tyranny, from which I suffered so much when I was young."

"Permit me to say another word; it is of so little importance that perhaps it is not necessary to speak of it. Nevertheless it is better that you should be informed. She is fleeing from a suitor whom her mother wishes to force upon her."

Madame B. became thoughtful, and Lopukhóv, looking at her, in his turn became thoughtful too. "This circumstance, if I'm not mistaken, seems of more importance to you than to me."

Madame B. seemed utterly disconcerted.

"Pardon me," he continued, seeing that she did not know what to say,—"pardon me, but I see that this presents difficulties."

"Yes, it is a very serious matter, Monsieur Lopukhóv. To leave the house of her parents against their will would alone be certain to cause a grave quarrel. But, as I have already told you, that might be overlooked. If she only ran away from their coarseness and tyranny, that could be settled with them in one way or another; in the last extremity a little money would set everything right. But when such a mother forces a marriage, it is evident that the suitor is rich, very rich in fact."

"Indeed," said Lopukhóv in a very sad tone.

"Of course! Monsieur Lopukhóv, he is rich, evidently; that is what has disconcerted me. Under such circumstances the mother could not be satisfied in any way whatever. Now, you know the rights of parents. They would halt at nothing; they would begin an action which they would push to the end."

Lopukhóv rose.

"There is nothing further to say except to ask you to forget all that I have said to you."

"No, no, stay. I wish first to justify myself in your eyes. Heavens, I must seem awful to you! What should command my sympathy and protection is just what holds me back. Believe me, I am much to be pitied. Oh, I am much to be pitied!"

She was not shamming. She was really much to be pitied. She felt keenly; for some time her speech was incoherent, she was so troubled and confused. Gradually, nevertheless, order was restored in her thoughts, but even then she had nothing new to say, and it was Lopukhóv's turn to be disconcerted. Consequently, after allowing Madame B. to finish, though not listening very closely to her explanations, he said:

"What you have just said in your justification was unnecessary. I remained in order that I might not seem impolite and that you might not think that I blame you or am offended. Oh! if I did not know that you are right! How I wish you were not right! Then I could tell her that we failed to come to an agreement, that you did not suit me. That would be nothing, and we should still retain the hope of finding another place and reaching the deliverance so long awaited. But now what shall I say to her?"

Madame B. wept.

"What shall I say to her?" repeated Lopukhóv, as he went down the stairs.

"What will she do? What will she do?" thought he, as he turned from Galernaya Street into the street leading to the Boulevard Konno-Gvardeisky.

It goes without saying that Madame B. was not as entirely right as the man who refuses the moon to a child. In view of her position in society and her husband's powerful connections, it was very likely, and even certain, that if she had really wished Vérochka to live with her, Mária Alexévna would have been unable to prevent it or even to cause any serious trouble either to herself or to her husband, who would have been officially responsible in the matter and for whom Madame B. was afraid. Madame B. would simply have been put to a little inconvenience, perhaps even to a disagreeable interview or two; it would have been necessary to demand such protection as people generally prefer to utilize in their own behalf. What prudent man would have taken any other course than Madame B.'s. We have no right to blame her. Nor, on the other hand, was Lopukhóv wrong in despairing of Vérochka's deliverance.

: X I V :

For a long time, a very long time, Vérochka sat on the bench at the place agreed upon, and many times had her heart begun to beat faster as she saw in the distance a military cap.

"At last! There he is! It is he! My friend!" She rose suddenly and ran to meet him. Perhaps he would have regained his courage by the time he reached the bench, but, being taken unawares, he could show only a gloomy countenance.

"Unsuccessful?"

"Yes, my friend."

"And it was so sure! How did it happen? For what reasons? Speak, my friend."

"Let us go to your house; I will escort you, and we will talk as we walk; presently I will tell you the whole story, but first let me collect my thoughts; it is necessary to devise some new plan and not lose courage."

Having said this, he took heart.

"Tell me directly. I can't bear to wait. Do I understand that it is necessary to devise some new plan and that your first plan is not at all feasible? Is it, then, impossible for me to be a governess? Oh! How unfortunate I am!"

"Why should I deceive you? Yes, impossible. That is what I intended to tell you, but patience, patience, my friend! Be firm. Whoever is firm always succeeds in the end."

"Yes, my friend, I am firm; but it is hard!"

They walked for some time without saying a word.

Lopukhóv saw that she had a bundle under her cloak.

"I beg you," said he, "my friend, allow me to carry that."

"No, no, it does not trouble me; it is not at all heavy."

Again they walked silently. Thus they walked for a long time.

"If you knew, my friend, that I have not slept for joy since two o'clock this morning. And when I slept, I had a marvellous dream. I dreamed that I had been delivered from a damp cellar, that I was paralyzed, that I was cured; then, that I ran gaily in the country with a multitude of young girls, who like me had come from dark cellars and been cured of paralysis, and we were so happy at being able to run freely in the fields! Alas! my dream is not realized. And I intended not to return home any more!"

"My friend, let me carry your bundle; you cannot keep its contents secret from me."

And once more they walked in silence.

"All was so arranged," said Lopukhóv, at last; "you cannot leave your parents against their will. It is impossible, impossible. . . . But give me your arm."

"No, don't bother. This veil stifles me, that is all."

She raised her veil.

"Ah! I am better now."

"How pale you are! My friend, do not look at things in the worst light; I didn't express myself correctly. We'll find a way out."

"How? You say that, my friend, to console me. There is nothing in it."

He did not answer.

How pale she is! How pale she is! "There is a way, my friend."

"What way?"

"I will tell you, when you are a little calmer. You will have to think it over coolly."

"Tell me directly. I shall not rest until I know."

"No, you are getting excited again; now you are in no condition to come to a serious decision. Some time later. Soon . . . Here are the steps. Good-bye, my friend. As soon as I find you in a condition to give me a cool answer, I will tell you the rest."

"When, then?"

"Day after to-morrow, at the lesson."

"That is too long."

"I will come to-morrow expressly."

"No, sooner."

"This evening."

"No, I will not let you. Come in with me. You say I am not calm enough, that I cannot form a well considered judgment. So be it; but dine with us, and you shall see that I am calm. After dinner mamma is going out, and we can talk."

"But how can I go in? If we enter together, your mother's suspicions will be aroused again."

"Suspicions! What does it matter? No, my friend, that is still another reason why you should go in. My veil is raised, and perhaps I have been seen."

"You are right."

: X V :

Mária Alexévna was much astonished at seeing her daughter and Lopukhóv come in together. She fixed her piercing eyes upon them.

"I have come, Mária Alexévna, to tell you that I shall be busy day after to-morrow, and will give my lesson to-morrow. Allow me to take a seat. I am very tired and weary. I should like to rest a little."

"Indeed! What is the trouble, Dmítry Sergéich? You are very sad." Have they come from a lovers' meeting, she continued to herself, or did they simply meet by chance? If they had come from a lovers' meeting, they would be gay. Nevertheless, if the difference in their characters had led them into any disagreement, they would have reason to be sad; but in that case they would have quarreled, and he would not have accompanied her home. On the other hand, she went straight to her room without so much as looking at him, ... and yet they did not seem to have quarreled. Yes, they must have met by chance. Curse it all. I've got to keep my eyes peeled.

"Don't trouble yourself on my account, Mária Alexévna," said Lopukhóv. "Don't you think that Véra Pávlovna looks a little pale?"

"Vérochka? She sometimes does."

"Perhaps it was only my imagination. My head whirls, I must confess, under so much anxiety."

"But what is the trouble, then, Dmítry Sergéich? Have you quarreled with your sweetheart?"

"No, Mária Alexévna, I am well satisfied with my sweetheart. It is with her parents that I wish to quarrel."

"Is it possible? Dmítry Sergéich, how can you quarrel with her parents? I had a better opinion of you."

"One can do nothing with such a family. They demand unheard-of impossibilities."

"That is another thing, Dmítry Sergéich. One cannot be generous with everybody; it is necessary to keep within bounds. If that is the case, and if it is a question of money, I cannot blame you."

"Pardon my importunity, Mária Alexévna, but I am turned so completely upside down that I need to rest in pleasant and agreeable society. Such society I find only here. Permit me to invite myself to dinner with you, and permit me also to send your Matryóna on a few errands. I believe Dencher's cellar is in this neighborhood, and that he keeps some very fair wines."

A scowl came over Mária Alexévna's countenance at the first word about dinner, but her face relaxed when she heard Matryóna's name and assumed an inquiring expression which seemed to ask: "Are you going to pay for your share of the dinner? At Dencher's! It must be something nice, then!" Lopukhóv, without even raising his eyes, drew from his pocket a cigar case, and, taking from it a piece of paper which it happened to contain, began to write upon it with a pencil.

"May I ask you what wine you prefer, Mária Alexévna?"

"To tell the truth, Dmítry Sergéich, I do not know much about wine, and seldom drink it: it is not becoming in women." (One readily sees from a glance at your face that you do not generally take it.)

"You are quite right, Mária Alexévna, but a little *maraschino* does no one any harm. It is a young ladies' wine. Permit me to order some."

"What sort of wine is that, Dmítry Sergéich?"

"Oh! it is not exactly wine, it is more of a syrup." Drawing a bill from his pocket, he continued: "I think that will be enough," and after having looked at the order, he added: "But, to make sure, here are five rubles more."

It was three weeks' income and a month's support. No mattter, there was nothing else to be done; Mária Alexévna must be dealt with generously.

Mária Alexévna's eyes glistened with excitement, and the gentlest of smiles unconsciously lighted up her face.

"Is there also a confectioner's near here? I do not know whether they keep walnut cake ready made,—in my opinion, that is the best kind of cake, Mária Alexévna,—but, if they do not keep it, we will take what they have. It will not do to be too particular."

He went into the kitchen, and sent Matryóna to make the purchases.

"We are going to feast to-day, Mária Alexévna. I want to drown in wine my quarrel with her parents. Why should we not feast? My sweetheart and I are getting on swimmingly together. Someday we shall no longer live in this way; we shall live gaily. Am I not right, Mária Alexévna?"

"You're quite right, Dmítry Sergéich. That is why you squander money,—something I never expected of you, as I thought you a selfish man. Perhaps you have received some money from your sweetheart?"

"No, I have received no money, Mária Alexévna, but if one has some money perchance, why should he not amuse himself?"

They passed the three-quarters of an hour which they had to wait for dinner in agreeable conversation on lofty matters only. Among other things Dmítry Sergéich, in an outburst of frankness, said that the preparations for his marriage had been progressing finely of late. And when would Véra Pávlovna's marriage take place?

On that point Mária Alexévna could say nothing, for she was far from forcing her daughter.

"That is right; but, if my observations are correct, she will soon make up her mind to marry. She has said nothing to me about it, but I have eyes in my head. We are a pair of old foxes, Mária Alexévna, not easily caught. Although I am still young, I am an old fox just the same. Am I not an old fox, Mária Alexévna?"

"That you are, old man. You are a cunning rogue."

This agreeable and effusive interview with Mária Alexévna thoroughly revived Lopukhóv. What had become of his sorrow? Mária Alexévna had never seen him in such a mood. Making a pretence of going to her room to get a pocket-handkerchief, she saw fine wines and liquors that had cost twelve rubles and fifty copecks. "We shall not drink more than a third of that at dinner," thought she. "And a ruble and a half for that cake? Truly, it is throwing money out of the window to buy such a cake as that! But it will keep; we can serve it instead of preserves to our cronies. This is all to the good."

: X V I :

Vérochka remained in her room.

"Did I do right in making him come in? Mamma looked at him so penetratingly!

"What a difficult position I have put him in! How can he stay to dinner?

"O my God, what is to become of me?

"There is a way, he told me; alas! no, dear friend, there is none.

"Yes! there is one: the window.

"If life should become too burdensome, I will throw myself out.

"That is an odd thing for me to say: if life should become too burdensome! And what is it now?

"To throw one's self out of the window! One falls so quickly! Yes, the fall is as rapid as flight; and to fall on the sidewalk, how hard and painful it must be!

"Perhaps there is only the shock, a second after which all is over, and before the fatal moment you are going through the air which opens softly beneath you like the finest down. Yes, it is a good way.

"But then? Everybody will rush to look at the broken head, the crushed face, bleeding and soiled. If, before leaping, you could only sprinkle the spot where you are to fall with the whitest and purest sand, all would be well.

"The face would not be crushed or soiled, nor would it wear a frightful aspect.

"Oh, I know; in Paris unfortunate young girls suffocate themselves with charcoal gas. That is good, very good. To throw yourself out of the window,—no, that is not fitting. But suffocation,—that's the thing, that's the thing.

"How they do talk! What are they saying? What a pity that I cannot tell what they're talking about!

"I will leave a note telling all.

"How sweet the memory of my birthday when I danced with him! I did not know what true life was.

"After all, the young girls of Paris are intelligent. Why should I not be as intelligent as they are? It will be comical: they will enter the room, they will be unable to see anything, the room will be full of charcoal gas, the air will be heavy; they will be frightened: 'What has happened? Where is Vérochka?' Mamma will scold Papa: 'What are you waiting for, imbecile? Break the windows!' They will break the windows, and they will see; I shall be seated near my dressing-table, my face buried in my hands. 'Vérochka! Vérochka!' I shall not reply.

" 'Vérochka, why don't you answer? Oh, God, she is suffocated.' And they will begin to cry, to weep. Oh, yes, that will be very comical, to see them weep, and Mamma will tell everybody how much she loved me.

"But he, he will pity me. Well, I will leave him a note.

"I will see, yes, I will see, and I shall die after the fashion of the poor girls of Paris. Yes, I will certainly do it, and I am not afraid.

"And what is there to be afraid of? I will only wait until he tells me about the way out that he mentioned. Ways! There are none. He said that simply to calm me.

"What is the use of calming people when there is nothing to be done? It is a great mistake; in spite of all his wisdom, he has acted as any other. Why? He was not obliged to.

"What is he saying? He speaks in a gay tone, and as if he were happy.

"Can he, indeed, have found a way out?

"It does not seem possible.

"But if he had nothing in view, would he be so gay?

"What can he have thought of?"

: X V I I :

"Vérochka, come to dinner!" cried Mária Alexévna.

Pável Konstantínych had just come in. The cake had been on the table for some time,—not the baker's but one of Matryóna's, a cake filled with meat, left over from the day before.

"Mária Alexévna, you have never tried taking a drop of brandy before dinner? It is very good, especially this brandy made from bitter orange. As a doctor, I advise you to take some. Taste of it, I beg of you."

"No, no, thank you."

"But if, as a doctor, I prescribe it for you?"

"The doctor must be obeyed, but only a small half-glass."

"A half-glass! It would not be worth while."

"And yourself, Dmítry Sergéich?"

"I? Old as I am? I have taken the pledge . . ."

"But it is very good! And how warming it is!"

"What did I tell you? Yes, indeed, it is warming."

("But he is very gay. Can there really be a way? How well he acts toward her, while he has not a glance for me! But it is all strategy just the same.")

They seated themselves at the table.

"Here, Pável Konstantínych and I are going to drink this ale, aren't we? Ale is something like beer. Taste it, Mária Alexévna."

"If you say that it is beer, why not taste it?"

("What a lot of bottles! Oh, I see now! How fertile friendship is in methods!")

("He does not drink, the cunning rogue. He only carries the glass to his lips. This ale, however, is very good; it has a taste of *kvass,* only it is too strong. After I have married Mísha to Vérka, I will abandon brandy, and drink only this ale. He will not get drunk; he does not even taste of it. So much the better for me! There will be the more left; for, had he wanted to, he could have emptied all the bottles.")

"But yourself, why don't you drink, Dmítry Sergéich?"

"Oh, I have drunk a great deal in my time, Mária Alexévna. And what I have drunk will last me a good while. When labor and money failed me, I drank; now that I have labor and money, I need wine no longer, and am gay without it."

The bought cake was brought in.

"Dear Matryóna Stepanovna, what is there to go with this?"

"Directly, Dmítry Sergéich, directly," and Matryóna returned with a bottle of champagne.

"Véra Pávlovna, you haven't had a sip. Neither have I. Now then let us drink too. To the health of your sweetheart and mine!"

"What is that? What can he mean?" thought Vérochka.

"May they both be happy, your sweetheart and Vérochka's!" said Mária Alexévna: "and, as we are growing old, may we witness Vérochka's marriage as soon as possible!"

"You'll witness it soon, Mária Alexévna. Won't she, Véra Pávlovna?"

"What does he really mean?" thought Vérochka.

"Come, then! Is it yes, Véra Pávlovna? Say yes, then."

"Yes," said Vérochka.

"Bravo! Véra Pávlovna, your mother was doubtful; you have said yes, and it is all settled. Another toast. To the earliest possible consummation of Véra Pávlovna's marriage! Drink, Véra Pávlovna! Don't be afraid. Let's touch glasses. To your speedy marriage!"

They touched glasses.

"Please God! Please God! I thank you, Vérochka. You comfort me, daughter, in my old age!" said Mária Alexévna, wiping away the tears. The English ale and the *maraschino* had quickened her emotions.

"Please God! Please God!" repeated Pável Konstantínych.

"How pleased we are with you, Dmítry Sergéich!" continued Mária Alexévna, getting up from the table; "yes, we are delighted with you! You have come to our house and you have given us a treat; in fact, we might say that you have given us a feast!" So spoke Mária Alexévna, and her moist and hazy eyes did not testify to sobriety.

Things always seem more necessary than they really are. Lopukhóv didn't expect to succeed so well; his object was simply to cajole Mária Alexévna that he might not lose her good will.

Mária Alexévna could not resist the brandy and other liquors with which she was familiar, and the ale, the *maraschino,* and the champagne having deceived her inexperience, she gradually grew weaker and weaker. For so sumptuous a repast she had ordered Matryóna to bring the *samovar* when dinner was over, but it was brought only for her and Lopukhóv.

Vérochka, pretending that she wanted no tea, had retired to her room. Pável Konstantínych, like an ill-bred person, had gone to lie down as soon as he had finished eating. Dmítry Sergéich drank slowly; he was at his second glass when Mária Alexévna, completely played out, pleaded an indisposition which she had felt since morning, and withdrew to go to sleep. Lopukhóv told her not to trouble her-self about him, and he remained alone and went to sleep in his arm-chair after drinking his third glass.

"He, too, like my treasure, has entered into the Lord's vineyard," observed Matryóna. Nevertheless her treasure snored loudly, and this snoring undoubtedly awakened Lopu-khóv, for he arose as soon as Matryóna, after clearing the table, had returned to the kitchen.

: XVIII :

"Pardon me, Véra Pávlovna," said Lopukhóv, on entering the girl's room,—and his voice, which at dinner had been so loud, was soft and timid, and he no longer said "My friend," but "Véra Pávlovna,"—"pardon my boldness. You remember our toasts; now, as husband and wife cannot be separated, you will be free."

"My dear friend, it was for joy that I wept when you entered."

He took her hand and covered it with kisses.

"You, then, are my deliverer from the cellar of my dream? Your goodness equals your intelligence. When did this thought occur to you?"

"When we danced together."

"And it was at the same moment that I too felt your goodness. You make me free. Now I am ready to suffer; hope has come back to me. I shall no longer stifle in the heavy atmosphere that has oppressed me; for I know that I am to leave it. But what shall we do?"

"It is already the end of April. At the beginning of July I shall have finished my studies; I must finish them in order that we may live. Then you shall leave your cellar. Be pa-tient for only three months more, and our life shall change. I will find employment in my profession, though it will not pay me much; but there will be time left to attend to pa-tients, and, taking all things together, we shall be able to live."

"Yes, dear friend, we shall need so little; only I do not wish to live by your labor. I have lessons, which I shall lose, for Mamma will go about telling everybody that I am a wretch. But I shall find others, and I too will live by my labor; isn't that fair? I should not live at your expense."

"Who told you that, dear Vérochka?"

"Oh! he asks who told me! Your books are full of such thoughts. A whole half of your books contains nothing but that."

"In my books? At any rate I never said such a thing to you. When, then, did I say so?"

"When? Haven't you always told me that everything rests on money?"

"Well?"

"And do you really consider me so stupid that I cannot understand books and draw conclusions from premises?"

"But again I ask you what conclusion. Really, my dear Vérochka, I do not understand you."

"Oh! the strategist! He too wants to be a despot and make me dependent upon him! No, that shall not be, Dmítry Sergéich; do you understand me now?"

"Speak, and I'll try to understand."

"Everything rests on money, you say, Dmítry Sergéich; consequently, whoever has money has power and freedom, say your books; then, as long as woman lives at man's expense, she will be dependent on him, will she not? You thought that I could not understand that, and would be your slave? No, Dmítry Sergéich, I will not suffer your despotism; I know that you intend to be a good and benevolent despot, but I do not intend that you should be a despot at all. And now this is what we will do. You shall cut off arms and legs and administer drugs; I, on the other hand, will give lessons on the piano. What further plans shall we make for our life?"

"Perfect, Vérochka! Let every woman maintain, with all her strength, her independence of every man, however great her love for and confidence in him. Will you succeed? I don't know, but it matters little: whoever arrives at such a decision is already almost proof against servitude; for, at the worst, he can always dispense with another. But how ridiculous we are, Vérochka! You say: 'I will not live at your expense,' and I praise you for it. How can we talk in this way?"

"Ridiculous or not, that doesn't matter, dear friend. We are going to live in our own way and as we deem most fitting. What further plans shall we make for our life?"

"I gave you my ideas, Véra Pávlovna, about one side of our life. You have seen fit to overturn them completely and substitute your own. You have called me tyrant, despot; be good enough therefore to make your own plans. What plans, then, would be your choice, my friend? I am sure that I shall have only congratulations to offer."

"What's this? Now you wish to pay me compliments! You wish to be gracious? You flatter yourself that you are going to rule, while appearing to submit? I know that trick, and I beg you to speak more plainly hereafter. You give me too much praise. I am confused. Do nothing of the kind; I shall grow too proud."

"Very well, Véra Pávlovna. I will be rude, if you prefer. Your nature has so little of the feminine element that you are undoubtedly about to put forth utterly masculine ideas."

"Tell me, dear friend, what is the feminine nature? Because woman's voice is generally clearer than man's, is it necessary to discuss the respective merits of the contralto and the baritone? We are always told to remain women. Isn't that nonsense?"

"Worse than that, Vérochka."

"Then, my dear, I am going to throw off this femininity and put forth utterly masculine ideas as to the way in which we shall live. We will be friends. Only I wish to be your first friend. Oh! I haven't told you yet how I detest your dear Kirsánov."

"Too bad, Vérochka. He is an excellent man."

"I detest him, and I shall forbid you to see him."

"A fine beginning! She is so afraid of despotism that she wants to make a doll of her husband. How am I to see no more of Kirsánov when we live together?"

"Are you always in each other's arms?"

"We are together at breakfast and dinner, but our arms are otherwise occupied."

"Then you are not together all day?"

"Very near together. He in his room, I in mine."

"Well, if that is the case, why not entirely cease to see each other?"

"But we are good friends; sometimes we feel like talking, and we talk as long as we care to."

"They are always together! They embrace and quarrel, embrace and quarrel again. I detest him!"

"But who tells you that we quarrel? That has never happened once. We live nearly separately; we are friends, it is true; but how can that concern you?"

"How nicely I have trapped him! You did not intend to tell me how we shall live, and yet you have told me all! Listen, then; we will act upon your own words. First, we will have two rooms, one for you and one for me, and a little parlor where we will take breakfast, dine, and receive our visitors,—those who come to see us both, not you or me alone. Second, I shall not dare to enter your room lest I bore you. Kirsánov does not dare to, and that is why you do not quarrel. Neither shall you dare to enter mine. So much for the second place. In the third—ah! my dear friend. I forgot to ask you whether Kirsánov meddles in your affairs and you in his. Have you a right to call one another to account for anything?"

"I see now why you ask this question. I will not answer."

"But really I detest him! Don't answer me; it is needless. I know how it is: you have no right to question each other about your personal affairs. Consequently I shall have no right to demand anything whatever of you. If you, dear friend, deem it useful to speak to me of your affairs, you will do so of your own accord, *vice versa*. There are three points settled. Are there any others?"

"The second rule requires some explanation, Vérochka. We see each other in the little parlor. We have breakfasted; I stay in my room, and do not dare to show myself in yours; then I shall not see you until dinner-time?"

"No."

"Precisely. But suppose a friend comes to see me, and tells me that another friend is coming at two o'clock. I must go out at one o'clock to attend to my affairs; shall I be allowed to ask you to give this friend who is to come at two o'clock the answer that he seeks,—can I ask you to do that, provided you intend to remain at home?"

"You can always ask that. Whether I consent or not is another question. If I do not consent, you will not ask the reason. But to ask whether I will consent to do you a service, that you can always do."

"Very well. But when we are at breakfast, I may not know that I need a service; now, I cannot enter your room. How shall I make my want known?"

"Oh, God! how simple he is! A real child! You go into the neutral room and say: 'Véra Pávlovna!' I answer from my room: 'What do you wish, Dmítry Sergéich?' You say: 'I must go out; Monsieur A. (giving the name of your friend) is coming. I have some information for him. Can I ask you, Véra Pávlovna, to deliver it to him?' If I say 'no,' our conversation is at an end. If I say 'yes,' I go into the neutral room, and you tell me what reply I am to make to your friend. *Now* do you know, my little child, how we must conduct ourselves?"

"But, seriously, my dear Vérochka, that is the best way of living together! Only where have you found such ideas? I know them, for my part, and I know where I have read them, but the books in which I have read them you have not seen. In those that I gave you there were no such particulars. From whom can you have heard them, for I believe I am the first new man* that you have met?"

"But is it, then, so hard to think in this way? I have seen the inner life of families; I do not refer to my own, that being too isolated a case; but I have friends, and I have been in their families; you cannot imagine how many quarrels there are between husbands and wives."

"Oh! I can easily imagine it."

"Do you know the conclusion that I have come to? That people should not live as they do now,—always together, always together. They should see each other only when they need or wish to. How many times I have asked myself this question: Why are we so careful with strangers? Why do we try to appear better in their presence than in our families'? And really we are better in the presence of strangers. Why is this? Why are we worse with our own, although we love them better? Do you know the request I have to make of you? Treat me always as you have done heretofore. Although you have never given me a rude reply or passed any censure upon me, that has not prevented you from loving me. People say: How can one be rude to a woman or girl whom he does not know, or how can he criticize her? Well, darling, here I am your fiancée and about to become your wife; treat me always as it is customary to treat strangers; that seems to me the best way of preserving harmony and love between us. Am I not right?"

"Truly, I don't know what to think of you, Vérochka; you are always astonishing me."

"Too much praise, my friend; it isn't so difficult to understand things. I am not alone in entertaining such thoughts:

---

* By "new man" the author means a man of advanced thought.

many young girls and women, quite as simple as myself, think as I do. Only they do not dare to say so to their suitors or their husbands. They know very well what would be thought of them: immoral woman! I have formed an affection for you precisely because you do not think as others do in this matter. I fell in love with you when, speaking to me for the first time on my birthday, you expressed pity for woman's lot and pictured for her a better future."

"And I,—when did I fall in love with you? On the same day, as I have already told you, but exactly at what moment?"

"But darling, you have almost told me yourself, so that one cannot help guessing, and, if I guess, you will begin praising me again."

"Guess, nevertheless."

"At what moment? When I asked you if it were true that we could so act as to make all men happy."

"For that I must kiss your hand again, Vérochka."

"But, dear, this kissing of women's hands is not exactly what I like."

"And why?"

"Oh! you know yourself; why ask me? Do not, then, ask me these questions, my darling."

"Yes, you are right; one should not ask such questions. It is a bad habit; hereafter I will question you only when I really do not know what you mean. Do you mean that we should kiss no person's hand?"

Vérochka began to laugh. "There, now, I pardon you, since I too have succeeded in catching you napping. You meant to put me through an examination, and you do not even know the reason of my repugnance. It is true that we should not kiss any one's hand, but I was not speaking from so general a standpoint: I meant simply that men should not kiss women's hands, since that ought to be offensive to women, for it means that men do not consider them as human beings like themselves, but believe that they can in no way lower their dignity before a woman, so inferior to them is she, and that no marks of affected respect for her can lessen their superiority. But such not being your view, my dear, why should you kiss my hand? Moreover, people would say, to see us, that we were betrothed."

"It does look a little that way, indeed, Vérochka; but what are we then?"

"I do not know exactly, darling, or rather it is as if we had already been married a long time."

"And that is the truth. We're friends; nothing is changed."

"Nothing changed but this, my dear friend,—that now I know I am to leave my cellar for liberty."

: XIX :

Such was their first talk,—a strange one, for lovers. They shook hands and Lopukhóv went to his home. Vérochka had to lock the outside door herself, for Matryóna, thinking that her *treasure* was still snoring, had not yet begun to think of returning from the *cabaret*. And indeed "her treasure" did sleep a number of hours.

Reaching home at six o'clock, Lopukhóv tried to go to work, but did not succeed. His mind was occupied, and with the same thought that had absorbed him when going from the Sémenovsky Bridge to the district of Vyborg. Were they dreams of love? Yes, in one sense. But the life of a man who has no sure means of existence has its prosaic interests; it was of his interests that Lopukhóv was thinking. What could you expect? Can a materialist think of anything but his interests? Our hero, then, thought of interests solely; instead of cherishing lofty and poetic dreams, he was absorbed by such dreams of love as are in harmony with the gross nature of materialism.

"Sacrifice! That is the word that I shall never get out of her head, and there is the difficulty; for, when one imagines himself under serious obligations to any one, relations are strained. She'll find out. My friends will tell her that for her sake I renounced a brilliant career, and if they do not tell her, she will easily see it herself. 'See, then, what you have renounced for my sake,' she will say to me. Pecuniary sacrifices it is pretty sure that neither she nor my comrades can impute to me. It is fortunate that at least she will not say: 'For my sake he remained in poverty, while without me he would have been rich.' But she will know that I aspired to scientific celebrity, and that that aspiration I have given up. Then will come her sorrow: 'Ah! what a sacrifice he has made for me!' That is something I have never dreamed of. Hitherto I have not been foolish enough to make sacrifices, and I hope that I never shall be. My interest, clearly understood, is the motive of my acts. I am not a man to make sacrifices. For that matter, no one makes them. But how can I explain that to her? In theory it is comprehensible; but when we see a fact before us, we are moved. 'You are my benefactor,' we say. The germ of this coming revolt has already made its appearance: 'You deliver me from my cellar.' 'How good you are to me!' she said to me. But are you under any obligations to me for that? If in so doing I labored for my own happiness, I delivered myself. And do you believe that I would do it if I did not prefer to? Yes, I have delivered myself; I wish to live, I wish to love, do you understand? It is in my own interest that I always act.

"What shall I do to extinguish in her this detrimental feeling of gratitude which will be a burden upon her? In whatever way I can I will do it; she is intelligent, she will understand that these are sentimental illusions.

"Things have not gone as I expected. If she had been able to get a place for two years, I could during that time have become a professor and earned some money. This postponement is no longer possible. Well, what great disadvantage shall I experience? Have I ever thought much of my pecuniary position? To a man that is of little consequence. The need of money is felt principally by woman. Boots, an overcoat not out at the elbows, soup on the table, a warm room, —what else do I need? But for a young and pretty woman that is not enough. She needs pleasure and social position. For that she will have no money. To be sure, she will not dwell upon this want; she is intelligent and honest; she will say: 'These are trifles, which I despise,' and indeed she will despise them. But because you do not feel what you lack, do you really lack nothing? The illusion does not last. Nature stifled by the will, by circumstances, by pride, is silent at first, but a silent life is torture. No, this is no way for a young woman, a beauty, to live. It is not right that she should not be dressed as well as others and should not shine for want of means. I pity you, my poor Vérochka; it would have been better could I have arranged my affairs first.

"For my part, I win by this haste: would she accept me two years hence? Now she accepts me."

"Dmítry, come to tea," said Kirsánov.

Lopukhóv started for Kirsánov's room, and on his way his thoughts continued thus: "With what did I begin? Sacrifice. What irony! Do I really renounce fame, a chair in the academy? What change will there be in my life? I shall work in the same way, I shall obtain the chair in the same way, and, finally, I shall serve medical science in the same way. From the objective standpoint it is curious to watch how selfishness mocks at our thoughts in practice."

I forewarn my reader of everything. Consequently I will tell him that he must not suppose that Lopukhóv's monologue contains any allusion to the nature of his future relations with Véra Pávlovna. The life of Véra Pávlovna will not be tormented by the impossibility of shining in society and dressing richly, and her relations with Lopukhóv will not be spoiled by the "detrimental feeling" of gratitude.

"From now on, Alexánder, you will have no reason to complain that I neglect my work; I am going to recover the lost time."

"Then you have finished your affair with this young girl?"

"Yes, I have finished."

"Is she going to be a governess at Madame B.'s?"

"No, she will not be a governess. The affair is arranged otherwise. Meantime she will lead an endurable life in her family."

"Very good. The life of a governess is really a very hard one. You know I have got through with the optic nerve; I am going to begin another subject. And where did you leave off?"

"I have still to finish my work upon . . ." and anatomical and physiological terms followed each other in profusion.

: X X :

That was Sunday evening. Monday came the lesson, changed from Tuesday.

"My friend, my darling, how happy I am to see you again even for so short a time! Do you know how much time I have yet to live in my cellar? Will your affairs be arranged by the tenth of July?"

"Certainly."

"Then there are but seventy-two days and this evening left. I have already scratched off one day, for I have prepared a calendar, as young boarding-school pupils do, and I scratch off the days. I simply adore to cross them off!"

"My darling Vérochka, you don't have long to suffer. Two

months and a half will pass by quickly, and then you will be free."

"Oh, what happiness! But, my darling, don't speak to me any more, and don't look at me; we must not play and sing together so frequently hereafter, nor must I leave my room every evening. But I can't help it! I will come out every day, just for a moment, and look at you with a cold eye. And now I am going straight back to my room. Till I see you again, my dear friend. When will it be?"

"On Thursday."

"Three days! How long that is! And then there will be but sixty-eight days left."

"Less than that: you shall leave here about the seventh of July."

"The seventh. Then there are but sixty-eight days left now? How you fill me with joy! Good-bye, my beloved!"

: XXI :

The marriage had been effected without very many difficulties, and yet not without some. During the first days that followed the engagement, Vérochka rejoiced at her approaching deliverance; the third day "the cellar," as she called it, seemed to her twice as intolerable as before; the fourth day she cried a little; the fifth she cried a little more than the fourth; the sixth she was already past crying, but she could not sleep, so deep and unintermittent was her anguish.

Then it was that Lopukhóv, seeing her red eyes, gave utterance to the monologue, "Hum, hum!" After seeing her again, he gave utterance to the other monologue, "Hum, hum! Yes! hum!" From the first monologue he had inferred something, though exactly what he did not know himself; but in the second monologue he explained to himself his inference from the first. "We ought not to leave in slavery one to whom we have shown liberty."

After that he reflected for two hours. The first quarter of an hour he said to himself: "All that is of little consequence; what great need is there that I should finish my studies? I shall not be ruined for having no diploma. By lessons and translations I shall earn as much as, and probably even more than, I should earn as a doctor."

He had no reason, therefore, to knit his brows; the problem had shown itself so easy to solve, at least partially, that since the last lesson he had felt a presentiment of a solution of this sort. He understood this now. And if any one could have reminded him of the reflections beginning with the word "sacrifice" and ending with the thoughts about the poor, he would have had to admit that at that time he foresaw such an arrangement. Otherwise the thought, "I renounce a career of learning," would have had no basis. It seemed to him then that he did not renounce, and yet instinct told him: "This is not a simple postponement. It is a renunciation." But, if Lopukhóv had been convicted, as a practical thinker, of violating logic, he would have triumphed as a theorist and would have said: "Here is a new instance of the sway of selfishness over our thoughts. I have left the young girl to suffer a week longer, when I should have foreseen and arranged everything on the spot."

But none of these thoughts came into his head, because, knitting his brows, he said to himself for seven quarters of an hour: "Who will marry us?" And the only reply that presented itself to his mind was this: "No one will marry us." But suddenly, instead of *no one,* his mind answered: "Mertzálov." Then it was that he struck his forehead and justly reproached himself for not having thought of Mertzálov at first. It is true that he was not accustomed to consider Mertzálov as one who marries.

In the Academy of Medicine there are all sorts of people, —among others, seminarists. These have acquaintances in the Theological Academy, and through these Lopukhóv had some there also.

A student in the Theological Academy, with whom he had no intimate acquaintance but was on friendly terms, had finished his studies the previous year, and was a priest in a certain edifice with endless corridors situated on Vassilievsky Island. Lopukhóv went to his house, and, in view of the extraordinary circumstances and the late hour, he even took a cab.

Mertzálov, whom he found at home alone, was reading some new work,—perhaps that of Louis XIV, perhaps one by some other member of the same dynasty.

"So that is what brings me here, Alexey Pétrovich! I know very well that it involves a great risk on your part. It will amount to nothing if the parents are reconciled; but, if they bring a suit, you may be ruined. In fact, you're sure to be, but . . ."

Lopukhóv could think of nothing with which to follow this "but." Indeed, how can one persuade a man to put his head in the noose for our sake?

Mertzálov reflected for a long time; he too was trying to find a "but" that would authorize him to run such a risk, but he too could find none.

"What's to be done? I should very much like . . . What you ask me to do now, I did a year ago; but now I am not free to do all that I would like to do. It is a case of conscience: it would be in accordance with my inclinations to help you. But when one has a wife, one fears to take a step without looking to see where it will lead him."

"Good evening, Alyosha.* My relatives send their regards to you. Good evening, Lopukhóv; we have not seen each other for a long time. What were you saying about wives? You men are always grumbling about your wives," said a pretty and vivacious blonde of seventeen years, just returning from a call upon her parents.

Mertzálov stated the situation to her. The young woman's eyes sparkled.

"But, Alyosha, they won't eat you!"

"There is danger, Natasha." †

"Yes, very great danger," added Lopukhóv.

"But what's to be done? Risk it, Alyosha, I beg of you."

"If you will not blame me, Natasha, for forgetting you in braving such a danger, our conversation is over. When do you wish to marry, Dmítry Sergéich?"

Then there was no further obstacle. Monday morning Lopukhóv said to Kirsánov:

"Alexánder, I am going to make you a present of my half of our labor. Take my papers and preparations, I leave them all. I am to leave the Academy; here is the petition. I am going to marry." And Lopukhóv told the story briefly.

"If you were not intelligent, or even if I were a booby, I should tell you, Dmítry, that none but fools act in this way. But I do nothing of the sort. You have probably thought more carefully than I upon all that could be said. And even though you had not thought upon it, what difference would it make? Whether you are acting foolishly or wisely I do

* Alyosha is the diminutive of Alexey.
† Natasha is the diminutive of Natalya.

not know; but I shall not be thoughtless enough to try to change your resolution, for I know that that would be in vain. Can I be useful to you in any way?"

"I must find some rooms in some quarter at a low price. I need three. I must make my application to the Academy to obtain my papers as soon as possible, tomorrow in fact. You must find rooms for me."

Tuesday Lopukhóv received his papers, went to Mertzálov, and told him that the marriage would take place the next day.

"What time will suit you best, Alexey Pétrovich?"

"It is all one to me; tomorrow I shall be at home all day."

"I expect, moreover, to have time to send Kirsánov to warn you."

Wednesday at eleven o'clock Lopukhóv waited for Vérochka on the boulevard for some time, and was beginning to grow anxious, when he saw her running.

"Vérochka, dearest, has anything happened to you?"

"No, my dear, I am late only because I slept too long."

"What time did you go to sleep, then?"

"I do not like to tell you. At seven o'clock, darling; no, at six; up to that time I was continually troubled by unpleasant dreams."

"I have a request to make of you, Vérochka dear; we must come to an understanding as quickly as possible."

"That is true, dearest."

"So, in four days, or in three . . ."

"Ah, how good that will be, darling!"

"In three days I probably shall have found some rooms; I shall have purchased everything needful for our household. Can we then begin to live together?"

"Certainly, my precious. Certainly."

"But first we must get married."

"Ah, I forgot; yes, we must first get married."

"We can do so at once."

"Well, let us do so, darling. But how have you managed to arrange everything so soon? How well you know how to do things!"

"I will tell you on the way; come, let us go."

On leaving the cab, they went through long corridors leading to the church. They found the doorkeeper, whom they sent to Mertzálov's, who lived in this same building with the interminable corridors.

"Now, Vérochka, I have another request to make of you. You know that in church they bid the newly-married to kiss each other."

"I know, dear, but how embarrassing it must be!"

"That we may be less confused when the time comes, let us kiss each other now."

"Very well, let us kiss each other, but can it not be dispensed with there?"

"At the church it is impossible to avoid it; therefore we had better prepare for it."

They kissed each other.

"Dearest, it's lucky we had time to prepare. There is the doorkeeper coming back already."

It was not the doorkeeper coming back,—he had gone to look for the sexton. It was Kirsánov who entered; he had been waiting for them at Mertzálov's.

"Vérochka, I introduce to you that Alexánder Matvéich Kirsánov, who you detest and wish to forbid me to see."

"Véra Pávlovna, why would you separate two such tender hearts?"

"Because they are tender," said Vérochka, extending her hand to Kirsánov. She became thoughtful, though continuing to smile. "Shall I love him as well as you do? For you love him much, don't you?" she added.

"I? I love no one but myself, Véra Pávlovna."

"And him also?"

"We have lived without quarreling, that is enough."

"And he loves you no more than that?"

"At least I have not noticed it. For that matter, let us ask him: do you love me, Dmítry?"

"I have no particular hatred for you."

"Well, if that is the case, Alexánder Matvéich, I will not forbid him to see you, and I will love you myself."

"That is much the better way, Véra Pávlovna."

Alexey Pétrovich came.

"Here I am; let us go to the church." Alexey Pétrovich was gay and even in a joking mood; but when he began the service, his voice became a little tremulous.

During the ceremony Natalya Andrevna, or Natasha, as Alexey Pétrovich called her, arrived. When all was over, she invited the newly-married couple to go home with her where she had prepared a little breakfast. They went, they laughed, they danced a couple of quadrilles, they even waltzed. Alexey Pétrovich, who did not know how to dance, played the violin. Two short hours passed quickly by. It was a gay wedding. Then Vérochka remembered that it was "time to go." "Now, my darling, I will be patient three, four days in my 'cellar' without fretting too much. I could even live there longer. Why should I be sorrowful? What have I to fear now? No, do not escort me; I will go alone; we might be seen."

"Oh, the devil! they will not eat me; do not be so anxious on my account," said Alexey Pétrovich, in seeing out Lopukhóv and Kirsánov, who remained a moment longer to give Vérochka time to go. "I am very glad that Natasha encouraged me."

After four days' search, they found satisfactory rooms at the end of the fifth line on Vassilievsky Island where they rented three furnished rooms with board from a *petit bourgeois* couple.

The *petit bourgeois* was an old man, passing his days peacefully beside a basket filled with buttons, ribbons, pins, etc., and placed against the wall of the little garden situated on the Central Prospect between the first and second lines, or in conversation with his wife, who passed her days in repairing all sorts of old clothes brought to her by the armful from the second-hand stores. The service was performed by the proprietors themselves.

The Lopukhóvs paid thirty rubles a month.

At that time life in St. Petersburg was still comparatively inexpensive. Under these circumstances the Lopukhóvs with their resources could live for three or even four months; ten rubles a month would pay for their food. Lopukhóv counted, in the course of these four months, on obtaining pupils, literary work, or occupation in some commercial house.

On Thursday, the day when the rooms were found, Lopukhóv, coming to give his lesson, said to Vérochka:

"Come tomorrow; here is the address. I will say no more now, lest they notice something."

"My darling, you have saved me!"

But how was she to get away from her parents? Should she tell them everything? So Vérochka thought for a moment; but her mother might shower blows upon her with her fists and lock her up. Vérochka decided to leave a letter in her room. But when Mária Alexévna manifested an intention of following her daughter to the Nevsky Prospect, the latter went back to her room and took the letter again; for it seemed to her that it would be better and more honest to tell her to her face what had been done. Would her mother come to blows with her in the street? It would be necessary only to keep a certain distance from her, then speak to her, jump into a cab, and start off before she could seize her by the sleeve.

And thus the separation was effected near Rousanóv's perfumery.

: XXII :

But we have witnessed only half of this scene.

For a minute Mária Alexévna, who was suspecting nothing of the sort, stood as if thunderstruck, trying to understand and yet not at all comprehending what her daughter said. What did all that mean? But her hesitation lasted only a minute, and even less. She suddenly began to hurl insults, but her daughter had already entered the Nevsky; Mária Alexévna hurried a few steps in that direction; it was necessary to take a cab.

"Coachman!"

"Where do you wish to go, Madam?"

Which way should she go? She thought she heard her daughter say Karavannaja Street but she had turned to the left along the Nevsky.

"Overtake that wretch!"

"Overtake, Madam? But tell me clearly where I am to go?"

Mária Alexévna, utterly beside herself, insulted the coachman.

"I see that you are drunk, lady," said he and drove off.

Mária Alexévna followed him with her insults, called other coachmen, and ran now one way, now another, brandishing her arms; at last she stopped under the colonnade, stamping with rage. A half-dozen young people, venders of all sorts, gathered around her, near the columns of the Gastiny Dvor. They gazed at her, exchanged more or less spicy remarks, and bestowed upon her praises, not without wit, and advice that testified to their good intentions. "Ah! what a lady! So early and drunk already! Quite a lady!"

"Madam, do you hear? Buy a half-dozen lemons from me. They are good things to eat after drinking, and I will sell them to you cheap."

"Don't listen to him, M'am; lemons will not help you any; you would do better to take a drink of something strong."

"Lady, what a powerful tongue you have! Are you willing to match it against mine on a wager?"

Mária Alexévna, now no longer knowing what she was about, slapped the face of one of her tormenters, a boy of about seventeen, who put his tongue out, not without some grace; the little merchant's cap rolled off into the dirt, and Mária Alexévna, thus enabled to get her hand into his hair, did not fail to grasp it by handfuls. The other scamps were seized with an indescribable enthusiasm:

"That's it! Hit him! Now then! Bravo, Madam!"

"Lick him, lick him, M'am!"

Others said: "Fedka,* defend yourself. Hit her back!"

But the majority were on Mária Alexévna's side.

"What can Fedka do against this jolly old girl? Lick him, lick him, girl! The scamp is getting no more than he deserves."

In addition to the speakers, many spectators had already gathered—coachmen, warehouse-men, and passers-by were approaching in crowds. Mária Alexévna seemed to come to her senses, and, after having by a last mechanical movement pushed away the unfortunate Fedka, she crossed the street. Enthusiastic tributes of praise followed her. She became conscious that she was going home when she had passed the carriage-way of the Corps des Pages; she took a cab, and reached the house in safety. On arriving she administered a few blows to Fédya, who opened the door; rushed to the brandy closet; administered a few blows to Matryóna, who had been attracted by the noise; made for the closet again; ran into Vérochka's room, and came back to the closet a third time; ran again into Vérochka's room, and stayed there a long time; and then began to walk up and down the rooms scolding and reviling: but whom should she hit now? Fédya had fled to the kitchen stairs; Matryóna, peeping through a crack into Vérochka's room and seeing Mária

* Fedka, a diminutive of Fyodor in popular usage.

Alexévna start in her direction, had precipitately fled toward the kitchen, but, not being able to reach it, had rushed into María Alexévna's bed-room and hidden under the bed, where she remained in safety awaiting a more peaceable summons.

It is impossible to say exactly, but for a long time María Alexévna ranted and walked up and down the empty rooms, since Pável Konstantínych, on his arrival, was also received with blows and insults. Nevertheless, as everything must end, María Alexévna cried at last: "Matryóna, get the dinner ready!" And Matryóna, seeing that the storm was over, came out from under the bed and set the table.

During dinner María Alexévna stopped scolding and contented herself with muttering, but without offensive intentions and simply for her own satisfaction. Then, instead of going to lie down, she took a seat and remained alone, now saying nothing, now muttering; then she stopped muttering, and shouted:

"Matryóna, wake your master, and tell him to come to me."

Matryóna, who, expecting orders, had not dared to go away, either to the *cabaret* or anywhere else outside of the house, hastened to obey.

Pável Konstantínych made his appearance.

"Go to the proprietor and tell her that your daughter, thanks to you, has married this blackguard. Say: 'I was opposed to my wife.' Say: 'I did it to please you, for I saw your consent was lacking.' Say: 'The fault was my wife's alone; I carried out your will.' Say: 'It was I who arranged this marriage.' Do you understand me?"

"I understand, María Alexévna; you reason very wisely."

"Well, get along! If she is at dinner, don't let that make any difference; have her called from the table. Hurry, while she still doesn't know."

The plausibility of the words of Pável Konstantínych was so evident that the proprietor would have believed the worthy steward, even if he had not been endowed with the faculty of presenting his ideas with humility, veneration, and in a persuasive and respectful manner; but this power of persuasion was so great that the proprietor would have pardoned Pável Konstantínych, even if she had not had palpable proofs of his misunderstanding with his wife.

Was it not evident that he had put his daughter in relations with Lopukhóv in order to avoid a marriage embarrassing to Mikhaíl Iványch?

"What were the terms of the marriage?"

Pável Konstantínych had spared nothing in order to give his daughter her marriage portion; he had given five thousand rubles to Lopukhóv, had paid the expenses of the wedding, and established the couple in housekeeping. It was he who had carried the notes from one to the other. At the house of his colleague, Filatiev, chief of the bureau and a married man, added Pável Konstantínych,—yes, it was at his house, your excellency, for although I am an humble man, your excellency, the virgin honor of my daughter is dear to me,—it was at his house, I say, that the meetings took place, in my presence; we were not rich enough to employ a teacher for an urchin like Fédya; no, that was only a pretext, your excellency, etc.

Then Pável Konstantínych painted in the blackest colors the character of his wife. How could one help believing and pardoning Pável Konstantínych? It was, moreover, a great and unexpected joy. Joy softens the heart. The proprietor began her notice of discharge by a long condemnation of Mária Alexévna's abominable plans and guilty conduct, and at first called on Pável Konstantínych to turn his wife out of doors. He begged her not to be so severe.

She spoke thus only for the sake of saying something. Finally they agreed on the following terms:

Pável Konstantínych held his stewardship; the apartments fronting on the street were taken away from him; the steward was to live in the rooms farthest in the rear; his wife was not to show herself about the front of the establishment where the proprietor's eye might fall upon her, and she was to go into the street only through the carriage-way, which was far from the proprietor's windows.

Of the twenty rubles a month formerly added to his pay fifteen were taken back and five left as a reward for the zeal shown by Pável Konstantínych in carrying out the proprietor's will and to make good the expenses occasioned by his daughter's marriage.

: XXIII :

Mária Alexévna had thought of several plans as to the way in which to deal with Lopukhóv when he should come in the evening. That nearest her heart consisted in hiding two man-servants in the kitchen who, at a given signal, should throw themselves upon and beat him unmercifully. The most pathetic consisted in hurling from her own lips and those of Pável Konstantínych the paternal and maternal curse on their rebellious daughter and the ruffian, her husband, insisting at the same time on the import of this curse, the earth itself rejecting, as is well known, the ashes of those whom their parents have cursed. But these were dreams, like those of the proprietor in wishing to separate Pável Konstantínych from his wife; such projects, like poetry in general, are destined less to be realized than to relieve the heart by serving as a basis for solitary reflections leading to no results and for explanations in future interviews: that is how I might have developed affairs, that is how I desired to develop them, but through goodness of heart I allowed myself to relent. The idea of beating Lopukhóv and cursing her daughter was the ideal side of Mária Alexévna's thoughts and feelings. The real side of her mind and soul had a tendency much less elevated and much more practical, —an inevitable difference, given the weakness of every human being. When Mária Alexévna came to her senses, near the carriage-way of the Corps des Pages, and comprehended that her daughter had actually disappeared, married, and escaped, this fact presented itself to her mind in the form of the following mental exclamation: "She has robbed me!" All the way home she did not cease to repeat to herself, and sometimes aloud: "She has robbed me!" Consequently, after delaying a few minutes through human weakness to tell her chagrin to Fédya and Matryóna,—every individual allows himself to be dragged by the expression of his feelings into forgetting in his fever the real interests of the moment,—Mária Alexévna ran into Vérochka's room. She rushed to the dressing-table and the wardrobe, which she reviewed with a hasty glance. "No," said she, "everything seems to be here." Then she proceeded to verify this first reassuring impression by a detailed examination. Everything, indeed, was really there, except a pair of very simple gold ear-rings, the old muslin dress, and the old sack that Vér-ochka had on when she went out. Regarding this real side of the affair, Mária Alexévna expected that Vérochka had given Lopukhóv a list of the things belonging to her which he would claim; she was fully determined to give up no article of gold or anything in that line, but only the four plainest dresses and the most worn linen: to give nothing was impossible; *noblesse oblige,*—an adage of which Mária Alexévna was a rigid observer.

Another question of real life was the relations with the proprietor; we have already seen that Mária Alexévna had succeeded in settling it satisfactorily.

There remained the third question: what was to be done with the guilty, that is, with her daughter and the son-in-law that had been thrust upon her? Curse them? Nothing easier, only such a curse must serve as a dessert to something more substantial. Now, this substantial something could take but one practical shape, that of presenting a petition, bringing a suit, and arraigning before a court of assizes. At first, in her fever, Mária Alexévna viewed this solution of the question from her ideal side, and from this point of view it seemed very seductive to her. But in proportion as her mind became calmer, the affair gradually assumed another aspect. No one knew better than Mária Alexévna that all lawsuits require money, much money, especially lawsuits like this, which pleased her by its ideal beauty, and that, after dragging for a long time and devouring much money, they end absolutely in nothing.

What, then, was to be done? She finally concluded that there were but two things to do,—give herself the satisfaction of abusing Lopukhóv as much as possible, and save Vérochka's things from his claims, to which end the presentation of a petition would serve as a means. But, at any rate, she must roundly abuse him, and thus derive all the satisfaction she could.

Even this last part of the plan was not to be realized.

Lopukhóv arrived, and began in this tone: "We beg you, my wife and I, to be kind enough, Mária Alexévna and Pável Konstantínych, to excuse us for having without your consent . . ."

At this point Mária Alexévna cried out:

"I will curse her, the good— . . . !" She could not finish

the epithet *good-for-nothing*. At the first syllable Lopukhóv
raised his voice:

"I have not come to listen to your insults, but to talk
business. And since you are angry and cannot talk calmly, I
will explain myself in a private interview with Pável Konstantínych; and you, Mária Alexévna, will send Fédya or
Matryóna to call us when you calm down."

As he spoke, he led Pável Konstantínych from the parlor
into the small room adjoining, and his voice was so strong
and positive that there was no way out. So she had to reserve
her remarks.

Having reached the parlor door with Pável Konstantínych, Lopukhóv stopped, turned back, and said: "I would
like nothing better than to make my explanation to you also,
Mária Alexévna, if you wish, but on one condition,—that
I may do so uninterrupted."

Again she began her abuse, but he interrupted her: "Well,
since you cannot converse calmly, we leave you."

"And you, imbecile, why do you go with him?"

"Why, he drags me after him."

"If Pável Konstantínych were not disposed to give me a
quiet hearing, I would go away, and that would be perhaps
the better course: what does it matter to me? But Pável
Konstantínych, why do you consent to be called such names?
Mária Alexévna knows nothing of affairs; she thinks perhaps that they can do, God knows what, with us; but you,
an officeholder, must know how things are done. Tell her,
therefore, that at this stage she can do nothing with Vérochka and still less with me."

"He knows, the rascal, that nothing can be done with
him," thought Mária Alexévna, and then she said to Lopukhóv that, though at first her mother's feelings had carried
her away, she was now in a condition to talk calmly.

Lopukhóv and Pável Konstantínych retraced their steps.
They sat down, and Lopukhóv begged her to listen patiently
until he had finished all that he had to say, after which she
might have the floor. Then he began, taking care to raise
his voice every time that Mária Alexévna tried to interrupt
him, which enabled him to carry his story to its conclusion.
He explained that it was impossible to unmarry them, that
there was no chance therefore for Storéshnikov, and that it
would be useless trouble, as they knew themselves, to begin

a suit. That for the rest they could do as they pleased, and that, if they had an abundance of money, he would even advise them to try the courts; but that, all things considered, there was no occasion for them to plunge into the depths of despair, since Vérochka had always rejected Storéshnikov's proposals and the match therefore had always been chimerical, as Mária Alexévna had seen for herself; that a young girl nevertheless must marry some time, which means as a general thing a series of expenses for the parents,—that is, the dowry first, and the wedding next, but especially the dowry.

Whereupon Lopukhóv concluded that Mária Alexévna and Pável Konstantínych ought to thank their daughter for having got married without occasioning them any expense.

Thus he spoke for a full half-hour.

When he had finished, Mária Alexévna saw that there was nothing to say to such a rascal and she placed herself first on the ground of sentiment, explaining that what had wounded her was precisely the fact that Vérochka had married without asking the consent of her parents, thus lacerating the maternal heart. The conversation, transferred thus to the subject of maternal feelings and wounds, naturally had for either party no more than a purely dialectical interest. They could not help going into it, the proprieties required it. So they satisfied the proprieties. They spoke: Mária Alexévna of how, as an affectionate mother, she had been wounded; Lopukhóv of how, as an affectionate mother, she need not have been wounded; when, finally, they had filled the measure of the proprieties by digressions of a proper length upon sentimental grounds, they approached another subject equally demanded by the proprieties,—that, on the one side, she had always desired her daughter's happiness, while he answered, on the other, that that was clearly indisputable; when the conversation on this point had likewise attained the proper length, they entered on the subject of farewells. Lopukhóv, comprehending the confusion into which the maternal heart had been thrown, did not beg Mária Alexévna for the present to give her daughter permission to see her, because that perhaps would add to the strain on the maternal heart. Mária Alexévna, however, would not be slow in finding out that Vérochka was happy, which of course was always Mária Alexévna's first desire, and then, the maternal heart having recovered its equanimity, would be in a position to see her daughter without having to suffer thereby. This agreed upon, they separated amicably.

"Oh, the rascal!" said Mária Alexévna, after having shown her son-in-law to the door.

That same night she had the following dream:

She was seated near a window, and she saw a carriage, a splendid carriage, passing in the street; this carriage stopped, and out of it came a beautiful lady followed by a gentleman, and they entered her room, and the lady said to her: "See, Mamma, how richly my husband dresses me!" This lady was Vérochka. Mária Alexévna looked at her: the material of Vérochka's dress was really of the most expensive sort. Vérochka said: "The material alone cost five hundred rubles, and that is a mere bagatelle, Mamma, for us; of such dresses I have a dozen! And here is something that cost still more, see my fingers!" And Mária Alexévna looked at Vérochka's fingers, and saw rings set with huge diamonds! "This ring, Mamma, cost two thousand rubles, and that one four thousand more; and just glance at my breast, Mamma; the price of this brooch was still greater; it cost ten thousand rubles!" And the gentleman added, the gentleman being Dmitry Sergéich: "All these things are just nothing at all for us, my dear Mamma, Mária Alexévna! The really precious stuff is in my pocket; here, dear Mamma, see this pocket-book, how it is swollen! It is full of hundred-ruble notes. Well, this pocket-book is yours, Mamma, for it is a small matter to us! Here is another more swollen still, dear Mamma, which I will not give you; it does not contain small currency, but large bank-bills and bills of exchange, and each of these bank-bills, each of these bills of exchange, is worth more than the whole pocket-book which I have given you, dear Mamma."

"You knew well, my dear son, Dmítry Sergéich, how to make my daughter and our whole family happy; but where do you get so much wealth?"

"I have bought the liquor-selling monopoly, Mamma!"

And, on waking, Mária Alexévna said to herself: "Truly, he must go into the liquor-selling business."

: X X I V :

EULOGY OF MÁRIA ALEXÉVNA

You now cease to be an important personage in Vérochka's life, Mária Alexévna, and in taking leave of you the author of this story begs you not to complain if he makes you quit the scene with a *dénoûement* not wholly to your advantage. Do not think yourself diminished in our eyes. You are a dupe, but that can in no degree change for the worse our opinion of your judgment, Mária Alexévna: your error does not testify against you. You have fallen in with individuals such as previously you had not been in the habit of meeting, and it is not your fault if you have made a mistake in judging things according to your experience. Your whole past life had led you to the conclusion that men are divided into two classes,—fools and knaves; whoever is not a fool is a knave, an absolute knave, you have supposed; not to be a knave is necessarily to be a fool. This way of looking at things was very just, Mária Alexévna, was perfectly just until these latter days. Your errors, Mária Alexévna, in no wise diminish my esteem for you as a prudent and reasonable woman. You have lifted your husband from his obscurity, you have provided for your old age,—good things not easily accomplished. Your methods were bad, but your surroundings offered you no others. Your methods belong to your surroundings, but not to your person; therefore the dishonor is not yours, but the honor is to your judgment and strength of character.

Are you content, Mária Alexévna, to see your good qualities recognized? You would have asked no other tribute than that which I have accorded you. But I can say in your honor one word more: of all the persons whom I do not like and with whom I should wish to have no dealings, you are among those whom I should like the best. To be sure, you are pitiless when your interest is at stake. But if you have no interest in doing evil to any one, you will not do it, having nothing in view but the satisfaction of your petty and stupid passions. You reason that it is not worth while to lose one's time, labor, and money for nothing. It is needless to say that you would have taken pleasure in roasting your daughter and her husband over a slow fire, but you succeeded in repressing the spirit of revenge that had taken possession of you and in reflecting coldly upon the matter, and you recognized that roasting was out of the question; now it is a great quality, Mária Alexévna, to be able to recognize the impossible. After recognizing this impossibility, you did not allow yourself to begin an action which would not have ruined the individuals who have offended you; you perceived that all the little annoyances which you might have caused them by such an action would have cost you many greater embarrassments and sacrifices, and so you did not bring an action. If one cannot conquer his enemy, if for the insignificant loss that one can inflict on him one must suffer a greater loss, there is no reason for beginning the struggle. Understanding that, you had good sense and valor enough to submit to the impossible without uselessly injuring yourself and others,—another great quality. Yes, Mária Alexévna, one may still have dealings with you, for your rule is not evil for evil even to your own injury, and that is an extremely rare quality, a very great quality! Millions of men are more dangerous than you, both to themselves and to others, although they may not have your surly countenance. You are among the best of those who are not good, because you are not unreasonable, because you are not stupid. I should have liked very well to reduce you to dust, but I esteem you; you interfere with nothing. Now you are engaged in bad business in accordance with the exigencies of your surroundings; but if other surroundings were given you, you would willingly cease to be dangerous, you would even become useful, because, when your interest is not at stake, you do not do evil, and are capable of doing anything that seems advantageous to you, even of acting decently and nobly. Yes, you are capable, Mária Alexévna, and it is not your fault if this capacity of yours is in a state of inertia, and if in its stead capacities of an opposite nature are at work; you none the less possess it, which cannot be said of everybody. Base people are capable of nothing good, but you, you are only bad, not base. Consequently you are above many men in point of morality!

"Are you content, Mária Alexévna?"

"Have I any reason to be content, my good sir, when my affairs are in such a bad way?"

"It is for the best, Mária Alexévna."

Chapter Third

MARRIAGE

AND SECOND LOVE

: I :

Three months had passed since the marriage. Lopukhóv's affairs were going on well. He had found some pupils, work at a book-publisher's, and, more than all, the task of translating a geographical treatise. Véra Pávlovna, too, had found two pupils; who, though they did not pay her much, were better than none. Together they were now earning eighty rubles a month. With this sum they could live only in a very moderate way, but they had at least the necessaries. Their means continuing to increase, they counted on being able in four months to furnish their rooms (and later that is what they did).

Their life was not arranged quite as Véra Pávlovna had planned it on the day of their betrothal, half in sport, half in earnest, but nevertheless it did not lack much of it.

Their aged landlady and her husband had a great deal to say about the strange way in which the newly-married couple lived,—as if they were not husband and wife at all, as if they were God knows not what!

"Therefore, according to what I see and what you say, Petróvna, they live—how shall I say—as if they were brother and sister."

"Nonsense! What a comparison! Between brother and sister there is no ceremony; is there none between them? He rises, puts on his coat, sits down, and waits until I bring the *samovar*. After having made the tea, he calls her; she too comes in all dressed. Is that the way brother and sister behave? This would be a better comparison: it sometimes happens that among people in moderate circumstances two families live for economy's sake in one and the same apartment. They resemble two such families."

"How is it, Petróvna, that the husband cannot enter his wife's room? She is not dressed. Do you see? How do you like that?

"And what is better yet, when they separate at night, she says: 'Good night, my darling; sleep well!' Then they go, he to his room, she to hers, and there they read old books, and sometimes he writes. Do you know what happened one night? She had gone to bed and was reading an old book; I suddenly heard through the partition—I was not asleep— I heard her rise. What do you think she did? I heard her place herself before her mirror to arrange her hair, understand? Just as if she were going to make a visit. Then I heard her start. I went out into the corridor, got up on a chair, and looked through the transom into her husband's room. On reaching the door she said:

" 'Can I come in, my darling?'

"And he answered: 'Presently, Vérochka; wait a moment.' He was in bed also; he made haste to dress. I thought he was going to put on his cravat next, but he didn't. After he had arranged everything, he said:

" 'Now you can come in, Vérochka.'

" 'I do not understand this book,' she said to him; 'explain this to me.'

"He explained it to her."

" 'Pardon me, darling, for having disturbed you.'

" 'Nothing at all, Vérochka. I wasn't busy; you did not disturb me.'

"And out she went."

"She simply went out?"

"She simply went out."

"And he did nothing?"

"And he did nothing. But that is not the most astonishing part of it. The most astonishing thing is that she should have dressed to go to his room and that he should have dressed to receive her. What does that mean?"

"I think, Petróvna, that this must be a sect; there are all sorts of sects, you know, in that line."

"So there are. You're probably right."

Another conversation.

"Danilych, I have asked them about their ways.

" 'Do not be offended,' I said, 'at what I am going to ask you, but of what faith are you?'

" 'Of the Russian faith. What a question!'

" 'And you belong to no sect?'

" 'To none; but what put that idea into your head?'

" 'This, Lady (I do not know whether I am to call you Madame or Mademoiselle),—do you live with Monsieur your husband?'

"She smiled: 'Certainly,' she said."

"She smiled?"

"She smiled, and answered: 'Certainly.'

" 'Why, then, this habit of never seeing him half dressed, as if you were not united?'

" 'In order,' she answered, 'not to exhibit ourselves in unbecoming garb. As for sect, there is none.'

" 'What, then, does this mean?'

" 'We act in this way in order that there may be more love and fewer quarrels.' "

"But that seems to be correct, Petróvna; they are very reserved toward each other."

"She further said to me: 'I do not wish others to see me too carelessly dressed; now, I love my husband more than I love others; therefore it is not fitting that I should appear before him without first washing myself.' "

"And that, too, has an air of truth, Petróvna; why do we covet our neighbors' wives? Because we always see them dressed up, while we see our own in careless array. So it is said in the proverbs of Solomon. He was a very wise king."

: II :

All went well, then, at the Lopukhóvs'. Véra Pávlovna was always gay. But one day—about five months after their marriage—Dmítry Sergéich, on returning from one of his pupils, found his wife in a somewhat inexplicable humor; her eyes shone with pride as well as joy. Then Dmítry Sergéich remembered that for some days past she had shown signs of an agreeable restlessness, a smiling thoughtfulness, a gentle pride.

"Something pleasant seems to have come to you, my friend; why don't you let me share it?"

"Indeed, I believe I have reason to be joyful, dear, but wait a little while: I will tell you about it as soon as I feel sure of it. It will be a great joy for us both, and will also please Kirsánov and the Mertzálovs."

"But what is it, then?"

"Have you forgotten our agreement, my darling? No questions. As soon as it is a sure thing, I will tell you."

A week passed.

"My darling, I am going to tell you my joy. I need only your advice: you are an expert in these things. For a long time I have wanted to do something useful, and I have conceived the plan of establishing a dressmaker's shop; is that a good idea?"

"It is agreed that I am not to kiss your hand, but that referred only to general situations; under such circumstances as the present no agreement holds. Your hand, Véra Pávlovna."

"Later, my darling, when I have succeeded."

"When you have succeeded, not to me alone will you give your hand to kiss. Kirsánov, Alexey Pétrovich, and everybody will demand the privilege. Now I am alone, and your intention of itself is worth the kiss."

"If you do me violence, I'll scream."

"Well, scream, then."

"You make me ashamed of myself, and I will have nothing more to say to you."

"Is it, then, very important?"

"Indeed it is, and that is why we talk all the time and do nothing."

"And you, who started out later than any of us, are the first to begin action."

Vérochka had hidden her face in her husband's breast.

"That's too much praise, my dear."

"No, you have a wise mind."

Her husband kissed her.

"Oh, stop! No one can say a word to you."

"Very well; speak, my good Vérochka."

"Do not call me that."

"Then I will say my wicked Vérochka."

"Oh, you! You're forever bothering! Sit quiet and listen

to me. The important thing here is that from the very first, in making a selection of a few, one be very circumspect. One must choose people who are honest, good and serious minded, steady, persistent and resilient, so that there shouldn't be any silly squabbles and that they know how to select others. Right?"

"Exactly so, my friend."

"I have found three young girls satisfying these conditions; but how I have had to search for the last three months! How I have been through the stores, making acquaintances, until at last I have found what I wanted and am sure of my choice!"

"They must also understand business management; the house must be self-sustaining and the business must be successful in a commercial sense."

"Not otherwise. That's understood."

"What else is there upon which advice is needed?"

"The details."

"What details? You probably have thought of everything already, and will adapt yourself to circumstances. The important thing now is the principle, character, and skill. Details settle themselves, in accordance with the conditions of each special case."

"I know it; nevertheless, I shall feel more confident having your approval."

They talked for a long time. Lopukhóv found nothing to correct in his wife's plan, but to herself the plan developed itself more clearly as she told it.

The next day Lopukhóv carried to the "Journal of Police" an advertisement announcing: *Véra Pávlovna Lopukhóv does sewing and laundry-work at a moderate price.*

The same morning Véra Pávlovna called upon Julie. "She does not know my present name; say Mademoiselle Rozálsky," said she to the servant.

"You come to see me without a veil, your face exposed; you give your name to the domestic; why, this is madness! You will ruin yourself, dear child!"

"Oh, now I am married, and I can go everywhere and do as I like."

"And if your husband should find it out?"

"In an hour he will be here."

Julie plied her with questions about her marriage. She

was enchanted, she kissed her, weeping all the while. When her enthusiasm had at least quieted down, Véra Pávlovna spoke of the object of her visit.

"You know that we remember old friends only when we need them. I have a great favor to ask of you. I am about to establish a dressmaker's shop. Give me your orders and recommend me to your friends. I sew well, and my assistants are equally good seamstresses; you know of them."

Indeed, Julie did know one of them as an excellent needle-woman.

"Here are some samples of my work. I made this dress myself. See how well it fits!"

Julie examined very carefully the cut of the dress and its seams, and the examination satisfied her.

"You ought to be very successful; you have talent and taste. But for this you need a fine store on the Nevsky."

"In time I shall have one, be sure; meantime I take orders at my house."

These things arranged, they returned to the subject of Vérochka's marriage.

"Storéshnikov led a very dissipated life for a fortnight, but afterward became reconciled to Adèle. I am very glad for Adèle: he is a good fellow; only it is a pity that Adèle has no character."

Started in this direction, Julie launched into gossip about Adèle's adventures and those of others.

Now that Mademoiselle Rozálsky was no longer an unmarried girl, Julie did not deem it necessary to restrain herself. At first she talked reasonably; then, as her excitement increased, she painted orgies glowingly and in colors more and more licentious. Véra Pávlovna became confused, but Julie did not notice it; then, recovering from her first impression, Véra Pávlovna listened with that pitiful interest with which one examines a dear face disfigured by disease. Lopukhóv came, and Julie for a moment transformed herself into a woman of society, serious and full of tact. But she could not play that *rôle* long. After congratulating Lopukhóv on having so beautiful a wife, she again became excited.

"We must celebrate your marriage."

She ordered an impromptu breakfast, to be washed down with champagne. Vérochka had to drink half a glass in honor of her marriage, half a glass in honor of her workshop, and half a glass to the health of Julie herself. Her head began to turn, and she and Julie became terribly noisy; Julie pinched Vérochka, and began to run; Vérochka started after her: they ran through the apartments, leaping over chairs; Lopukhóv sat in his arm-chair, laughing; Julie presumed to boast of her strength, which brought all this tumult to an end:

"I will lift you with one hand."

"You will not lift me."

Beginning to struggle, both of them fell on the sofa, and, not wishing to rise, began to shout and laugh; finally they went to sleep.

Four days later Julie carried Véra Pávlovna a large number of orders of her own and the addresses of some of her friends from whom she might also receive orders. She took Serge with her, saying to him: "We cannot do otherwise; Lopukhóv came to see me, you must return his visit."

Julie acted like a positive woman, and her enthusiasm did not cease, so that she stayed at the Lopukhóvs' a long time.

The noise of Julie's elegant carriage and fine horses made a great impression upon the dwellers in the fifth line between the central and the Small Prospect, where nothing like it had been seen since the days of Peter the Great, if not since a period still more remote. Many watched the surprising phenomenon, and saw it stop near the carriage gate (which was closed) of a one-story wooden house with seven windows; they saw get out a phenomenon more wonderful still, a young woman splendid and brilliant, an officer whose bearing was of the most dignified.

Thanks to this adventure, the Lopukhóv landlady— Petróvna—acquired for four whole days a great importance at the grocery which she was accustomed to frequent. For three whole days this grocery drew a portion of the trade of the neighboring grocery. Petróvna, devoting herself to the interest of public instruction, even neglected her mending a little during this time in order to satisfy those who had a thirst for knowledge.

All this had results. A week later Pável Konstantínych appeared at his son-in-law's. Mária Alexévna obtained information about the life of her daughter and her rascal of a son-in-law, not in a constant and careful way, but from time to time and out of pure curiosity. One of her friends, a gossip of the lowest rank, who lived in Vassilievsky Island, was charged with inquiring about Véra Pávlovna, whenever she happened to pass that way. The gossip brought her information sometimes once a month, sometimes oftener, according to circumstances. The Lopukhóvs live on good terms. They do nothing extraordinary, the only thing remarkable being that they are visited by a great many young people, all of them men and modestly dressed. It cannot be said that they live richly; nevertheless, they have money. Very far from selling anything, they buy. She has made two silk dresses for herself. They have bought a sofa, a table, and a half-dozen second-hand arm-chairs for forty rubles, which were worth perhaps a hundred. They have given their proprietors notice to look for new tenants in a month, for then they intend to move into their furnished apartment,— "though remaining grateful to you for your civility," they added. The proprietors of course said that on their side the feeling was the same.

Mária Alexévna was happy to hear this news. She was a very coarse woman. She tortured her daughter, she would have killed her if she had found it to her advantage. She cursed her as she thought of the ruin of her plan for adding to her riches; all that was true, but did it follow that she had no love for her daughter? Not at all. The affair over and her daughter irrevocably escaped from her hands, what had she to do? Whatever falls into the trench is for the soldier. Vérochka was none the less her daughter; and now, in case of need, Véra Pávlovna might readily be useful to Mária Alexévna. The mother therefore sincerely wished her daughter well. There was nothing peculiar about this affection. Mária Alexévna did not watch her carefully; what she did was simply for form's sake, to satisfy the what-will-people-say consideration, and to show that Véra was really her daughter. Why not become reconciled? Especially since the brigand son-in-law, according to all accounts, is a positive man, with whom one may in time do something. So Mária Alexévna gradually came to the conclusion that it would be better to renew her relations with her daughter. It would have taken six months longer and perhaps even a whole year to reach this result; for there was nothing pressing, and time enough ahead. But the news about the general and his wife suddenly advanced matters at least one-half. The *brigand* had indeed shown himself shrewd enough. He, a poor devil of a student who had left college without a degree, with two cents in his pocket, had formed a friendship with a young general; he had also made his wife a friend of the general's wife; such a man will go far. Or else Véra has formed a friendship with the general's wife, and has made her husband a friend of the general. What is the difference? That would simply show that Véra may go far.

So, as soon as the visit was known, the father was sent to tell his daughter that her mother had pardoned her, and that she was invited to the house.

Véra Pávlovna and her husband went back with Pável Konstantínych and remained a portion of the evening. The interview was cold and formal. Fédya was the principal subject of conversation, because he was the least thorny subject. He was at school, Mária Alexévna having been persuaded to place him at boarding-school; Dmítry Sergéich promised to go to see him, and holidays he was to spend at Véra Pávlovna's. Thus they managed to kill time until the tea-hour; then they hastened to break up, the Lopukhóvs pretending that they were expecting visitors that evening.

For six months Véra Pávlovna had been breathing a vivifying air. Her lungs had already become completely unaccustomed to the atmosphere of strategy, in which every word was uttered with a pecuniary end in view; her ear was no longer used to the discussion of swindling schemes and vile conspiracies. As a result this return to the cellar made a horrible impression on her. This corruption, this triviality, this cynicism struck her like a new thing.

"How did I avoid succumbing to such surroundings? How was I able to breathe in that cellar? And not only did I live there, but I kept my health! Incomprehensible! How could I have been brought up there, and still acquire a love of the good? It is incredible!" thought Véra Pávlovna, on returning to her apartment, with that sense of comfort which one feels on breathing freely after having been stifled.

Shortly after their arrival their accustomed visitors came, —namely, Alexey Pétrovich with Natalya Andrevna, and Kirsánov; they passed the evening as usual. What a new pleasure Véra Pávlovna felt after this interview, in living amid pure ideas and in the society of pure people! The conversation was, as usual, now gay and mingled with souvenirs, now serious and upon all imaginable subjects, including the historical events of that day, such as the civil war in the

Caucasus (the prologue of the great war now going on between the South and the North in the United States, which in its turn is the prologue of events still greater and of which the scene will not be America only). Now everybody talks politics, but at that time those interested in them were few in number; of this small number were Lopukhóv, Kirsánov, and their friends. They even entered into the discussions then prevailing of Liebig's theory of agricultural chemistry, as well as the laws of historical progress, a subject never forgotten in such circles. They concerned themselves also with the importance of distinguishing real desires, which seek and find satisfaction, from whimsical desires, which it is impossible and unnecessary to satisfy. For example, when one has a hot fever, he is always thirsty, but the only truly desirable satisfaction is not in drink but in cure. The unhealthy condition of the system provokes artificial desires while changing normal desires. Besides this fundamental distinction then put forward by anthropological philosophy, they went into other analogous subjects, or, if different, subjects leading back to the same point. The ladies also from time to time took part in these scientific discussions conducted in a simple fashion; they sometimes asked questions; but as a general thing they did not listen, and had even been known to sprinkle Lopukhóv and Alexey Pétrovich with clean water when they seemed too much impressed with the great importance of mineral manure. But Alexey Pétrovich and Lopukhóv discussed their favorite subjects with an invincible tenacity; Kirsánov did not help them much; he generally took the ladies' side, and all three played and sang and laughed until a late hour, when, exhausted, they would finally succeed in separating the indefatigable zealots of serious conversation.

: III :

VÉRA PÁVLOVNA'S SECOND DREAM

Véra Pávlovna, sleeping, saw a field in a dream; her husband —that is, her darling—said: "You wish to know, Alexey Pétrovich, why one sort of soil produces the good, the pure, the delicate wheat, and why another sort does not produce it? You shall account for this difference yourself. See the

root of this fine ear; around the root there is soil, but fresh
soil, pure soil, you might say; smell of it; the odor is damp
and disagreeable, but there is no mouldy or sour smell. You
know that in the language of our philosophy that is real soil.
It is dirty, to be sure; but look at it closely, and you will see
that all the elements of which it is composed are healthy.
This is the soil that they constitute in this combination; but
let the disposition of the atoms be a little changed, and
something different will result; and this something will be
equally healthy, since the fundamental elements are healthy.
What is the reason of that? Look closely at this portion of
the field; you see that there is an outlet for the water, so that
there can be no putridity."

"Yes, motion is reality," said Alexey Pétrovich, "because
motion is life. Now, the principal element of life is labor,
and consequently the principal element of reality is labor,
and the characteristic by which it can be most surely recognized is activity."

"Thus, Alexey Pétrovich, if the sun should warm this soil
and the heat should displace the elements and form them
into more complex chemical combinations,—that is, combinations of a higher degree,—then the ear which would
grow out of this soil would be a healthy ear?"

"Yes, because this is real soil," said Alexey Pétrovich.

"Now, let us pass to this part of the field. Here take likewise a plant, and examine in the same way its root. This
too is dirty. Look well at this soil. It is not difficult to see
that this is putrescent soil."

"That is, abnormal soil," said Alexey Pétrovich.

"I mean, the elements of this soil being unhealthy, it is
natural that, whatever their combination and whatever the
resulting product, this product must be in a state of corruption."

"Evidently, since the elements themselves are unhealthy,"
said Alexey Pétrovich.

"It is not difficult for us to discover the cause of this corruption."

"That is, this abnormal putridity," said Alexey Pétrovich.

"That's it; examine this part of the field again. You see
that the water, having no outlet, stagnates and rots."

"Yes, absence of motion is absence of labor," said Alexey
Pétrovich, "for labor appears in anthropological analysis as
the fundamental form of motion, the form which is the

basis of all the other forms,—distraction, rest, games, amusements; without labor preceding them these forms would not be real. Now, without motion there is no life,—that is, no reality; consequently this soil is abnormal,—that is, rotten. Not until modern times was it known how to make such parts of the earth healthy; now the way has been found in drainage; the superfluous water flows away, and there remains only just what is necessary; this moves, and thus makes the fields healthy. But, as long as this means is not employed, the soil remains abnormal,—that is, rotten; under these conditions it cannot produce good vegetation, while it is very natural that real soil should produce good plants, since it is healthy."

Véra Pávlovna came up to them and said:

"Enough of your analyses, identities, and anthropologisms. Change your conversation a little, gentlemen, I beg of you, in order that I may join in it; or, rather, let us play."

"Let's play," said Alexey Pétrovich: "let us confess."

"Let's confess. That will be fun," said Véra Pávlovna: "but, as you started the idea, it is for you to set the example."

"With pleasure, sister," said Alexey Pétrovich: "but how old are you? Eighteen, are you not?"

"Nearly nineteen."

"But not quite; we will say eighteen, then, and confess, all of us, up to that age, for we must have equality of conditions. I will confess for myself and for my wife. My father was the sexton in the chief town of a government where he followed the trade of bookbinder, and my mother rented rooms to theological students. From morning till night they did nothing but talk and worry about our daily bread. My father was inclined to drink, but only when poverty bore too heavily and painfully upon him or when the income was more than sufficient: in the latter case he would bring my mother all the money and say to her: 'Now, Mother, we have, thank God, all we shall need for two months; and I have kept some change with which to buy a drink in honor of this joyful occasion.' To him it was a real happiness. My mother got angry very often, and sometimes beat me, but this was at times when, as she said, she had strained her back by lifting too many iron pots, or by doing the washing for the five of us and the five students, or by scrubbing the floor soiled by our twenty feet without galoshes, or by taking care of the cow; in short, it was because of excessive nervous fatigue occasioned by wearing and ceaseless labor. And when, with all that, 'the two ends did not meet,' as she expressed it,—that is, when there was no money with which to buy boots for her sons and shoes for her daughters,— then it was that she beat us. She caressed us also when, though children, we offered to help her, or when we did something intelligent, or when she got a rare moment of rest and her back became limber, as she said. To us those were real joys. . . ."

"To the devil with your real sorrows and joys!" said Véra Pávlovna.

"Well, then, in that case, kindly listen to my confession for Natasha."

"I do not wish to listen; she has similar real joys and sorrows, I am sure."

"You are perfectly right."

"But perhaps you would like to hear my confession?" said Serge, mysteriously making his appearance.

"Let us see," said Véra Pávlovna.

"My parents, although they were rich, did nothing but worry and talk about money; rich people are no more exempt from such anxieties . . ."

"You do not know how to confess, Serge," said Alexey Pétrovich, in an amiable tone: "tell us why they worried about money, what the expenses were that tormented them, what were the needs that it embarrassed them to satisfy."

"I well understand why you ask me that," said Serge, "but let us lay that subject aside and view their thoughts from another standpoint. They, too, were anxious about their children."

"Were their children sure of their daily bread?" asked Alexey Pétrovich.

"Certainly, but it was necessary to look out that . . ."

"Do not confess, Serge!" said Alexey Pétrovich: "we know your history; care of the superfluous, preoccupation with the useless. That is the soil out of which you have grown; it is an abnormal soil. Just look at yourself; you are by birth a fairly intelligent and very polite man; perhaps you are no worse or more stupid than we are; but what are you good for?"

"I am good to escort Julie wherever she wishes to go, I am useful to Julie in helping her lead a dissipated life," answered Serge.

"Thereby we see," said Alexey Pétrovich, "that the abnormal unhealthy soil . . ."

"Ah, how you bore me with your realism and your abnormalism! They know that it is incomprehensible, and yet they never stop talking about it!" said Véra Pávlovna.

"Then you do not wish to talk a little with me?" said Mária Alexévna, also appearing mysteriously: "you, gentlemen, withdraw, for this mother wishes to speak to her daughter."

Everybody disappeared, and Vérochka found herself face to face with Mária Alexévna. Mária Alexévna's countenance assumed a scornful expression.

"Véra Pávlovna, you are an educated person; you are so pure, so noble," said Mária Alexévna in a tone of irony; "you are so good; am I, a gross and wicked drunkard, the person to be talking to you? You, Véra Pávlovna, have a bad mother; but tell me, if you please, Madam, with what this mother has been concerned? With daily bread; that is what, in your learned language, is called the real, the veritable human anxiety, is it not? You have heard bad words; you have seen wicked and corrupt conduct; but tell me, if you please, what the object was. Was it a futile, a senseless object? No, Madam. No, whatever the life of your family, it was not a futile, whimsical life. See, Véra Pávlovna, I have picked up your learned style. But you are ashamed and distressed at having so bad a woman for a mother. You would like it if I were good and honest. Well, I am a sorcerer, Véra Pávlovna, I know how to use magic; therefore I can realize your desire. Kindly look; your desire is fufilled; your wicked mother has disappeared; there is a good mother with her daughter; look!"

A room. Near the door a dirty drunken man snores. He is unrecognizable, his face being covered half by his hand and half by bruises. A bed. On the bed lies a woman,—yes, it is she, it is Mária Alexévna, but the good Mária Alexévna! Further, she is pale, decrepit at the age of forty-five, worn out! Near the bed is a young girl of about eighteen; yes, it is you, Vérochka, yourself, but in what rags! What does this mean? You are so yellow and your features so gross, and the room itself is so poor! There is almost no furniture.

"Vérochka, my friend, my angel," says Mária Alexévna: "lie down a little while. Take a rest, my treasure. Why do you

look at me? It is wholly unnecessary. This is the third nigh.
that you have not slept."

"That's nothing, Mamma; I am not tired," says Vérochka.

"And I feel very sick, Vérochka; what will become of you
when left without me? Your father's earnings are small, and
he is a poor support for you. You are pretty; there are many
wicked people in the world. There will be nobody to put
you on your guard. How I fear for you!"

Vérochka weeps.

"My dear child, do not take offence; I do not mean to reproach you, but simply to put you on your guard: why did
you go out Friday, the day before I fell so seriously ill?"

Vérochka weeps.

"He will deceive you, Vérochka. Leave him!"

"No, Mamma."

Two months later. How two months have slipped away in
a single moment! On a chair an officer is seated. On the table
in front of the officer a bottle, and it is she, Vérochka, upon
the officer's knees!

Two months more slip by in a moment.

On a sofa is seated a lady. Before the lady stands Vérochka.

"And do you know how to iron, Vérochka?"

"Yes, I know how."

"What are you, my dear, a serf or free?"

"My father is an office-holder."

"Then you are of gentle birth, my dear? I can't take you.
What kind of a servant would you make? Go, my dear, I
can't take you."

Vérochka is in the street.

"Mamzelle, mamzelle!" says some drunken youth, "where
are you going? I will escort you."

Vérochka runs to throw herself into the Néva.

"Well, my dear child, how do you like having such a
mother?" said the old, the real Mária Alexévna: "am I not
clever in the use of magic? Why are you silent? Have you
no tongue? But I will make you speak just the same. Have
you been in the stores much?"

"Yes," said Vérochka, trembling.

"Have you seen, have you heard?"

"Yes."

"Is their life honorable? Are they educated? Do they read
old books, do they dream of your new order of things, of

the way in which men may be made happy? Do they dream of it? Speak out!"

Vérochka, trembling, said not a word.

"You've lost your power of speech, it seems to me. Is their life honorable? I ask you."

Vérochka maintained her silence and felt a shudder.

"You have then really lost your power of speech? Is their life honorable? Are they virtuous young girls, I ask you again? Would you like to be as they are? You are silent! Don't turn away your face! Listen, then, Vérka, to what I am going to tell you. You are learned; thanks to the money that I have stolen, you are educated. You dream of the good, but, if I had not been wicked, you would never have known what the good is. Do you understand? It *all* comes from me; you are my daughter, *mine*. I am your mother."

Vérochka weeps and shudders.

"What do you wish of me, Mamma? I cannot love you."

"Do I ask you to love me?"

"I should like at least to esteem you, but I cannot do that either."

"Do I need your esteem?"

"What do you want, then? Why have you come to talk to me in so dreadful a way? What do you wish of me?"

"Be grateful, without loving or esteeming me, you ingrate. I am wicked; is there any chance for love? I am dishonest; is there any chance for esteem? But you should understand, Vérka, that, if I were not what I am, you too would not be what you are. You are honest because I have been dishonest; you are good for the reason that I have been wicked. Understand it, Vérochka, and be grateful."

"Withdraw, Mária Alexévna; it is now my turn to speak to my sister."

Mária Alexévna disappeared.

The sweetheart of so many lovers, the sister of so many sisters took Vérochka by the hand.

"I have always wanted to be good with you, Vérochka, for you are good yourself. Now, I am whatever the person is to whom I am talking. At present you are sad; so am I. Look! Though sad, am I still good?"

"Always the best in the world."

"Kiss me, Vérochka; we are both in distress. Your mother told you the exact truth. I do not like your mother, but I need her."

"Can you not do without her?"

"Later I shall be able to, when it shall be useless for men to be wicked. But at present I cannot. The good, you see, cannot get a foothold of themselves, for the wicked are strong and cunning. But the wicked are not all of the same sort. To some of them it is necessary that the world should grow worse and worse, to others it is essential that it should improve, essential in their own interest. It was a good thing for your mother that you should be educated; and why? In order that you might give lessons and thus earn money; in order that you might catch a rich husband. Her intentions were bad, but did you profit by them any the less? With the other class of wicked people this is not the case. For instance, if you had had Ánna Petróvna for a mother, could you have had an education? Would you have known the good? Would you have loved it? No. Either you would not have been allowed to learn, or you would have been made into a puppet. The daughter of such a mother must be a puppet, for the mother herself is nothing else, and lives only to play to puppets with puppets. Now, your mother is bad, but she has been of more value to you, for it was essential to her that you should not be a puppet. You see, then, that the wicked are not all of the same sort. Some prevent the existence of men worthy of the name, and would have them only puppets. But wicked people of the other sort come unconsciously to my aid by giving men the possibility of development and gathering the means that permit this development. That is exactly what I need. Yes, Vérochka, I cannot do without this kind of wicked people to oppose the other wicked people. My wicked people are wicked, but good grows under their wicked hand. Therefore be grateful to your mother. Do not love her, since she is wicked, but do not forget that you owe everything to her, that without her you would not exist."

"Will this always be the case? It will not, will it?"

"Later, when the good shall be strong, it will be otherwise. The time is approaching when the wicked will see that it is against their interest to be wicked, and most of them will become good: they were wicked simply because it was disadvantageous to them to be good, but they know, however, that good is better than evil, and they will prefer the good as soon as they can love it without injury to their own interests."

"And the wicked who were puppets, what will become of them? I pity them too."

"They will play puppets without injuring any one. Their children will not resemble them, for all members of the human family I shall make good, strong, intelligent human beings."

"Oh, how good that will be!"

"But those who prepare the war for this future are among the good from now on. When you help the cook in getting your dinner, do you not feel good, though the air of the kitchen is stifling? Every one feels good at the table, but the one who helped in getting the dinner feels better than the others: the dishes seem much better to her. You like sweets, if I'm not mistaken?"

"Yes," said Vérochka, smiling to see herself thus convicted of a fondness for pastry and of having fussed over them in the kitchen.

"Why grieve? Don't grieve any more."

"How good you are!"

"And gay, Vérochka. I'm always gay, even when I'm sad. Isn't that so?"

"Yes, when I am sad, you appear sad also; but you drive away my sorrow. It is very pleasant to be with you."

"You have not forgotten my song: *Donc vivons?*"

"Oh, no."

"Let us sing it."

"Oh, let's!"

"Vérochka! Why, I seem to have awakened you! But, at any rate, tea is all ready. You really frightened me: I heard you groan; I come in, and find you singing."

"No, my darling, you did not awaken me; I should have awakened without you. What a dream I have just had! I will tell you about it at tea. Leave me. I am going to dress. But how did you dare to enter my room without permission, Dmítry Sergéich? You forget yourself. You were frightened about me, my darling? Come here and let me kiss you. And now leave me quickly, for I must dress."

"You are so late that I had better act as your dressing-maid to-day; shall I?"

"Very good, my darling . . . but somehow it's so embarrassing."

: I V :

Véra Pávlovna's shop was quickly established. At first the organization was so simple that nothing need be said about it. Véra Pávlovna had told her first three seamstresses that she would give them a little higher wages than the stores paid. The three working girls, appreciating the character of Véra Pávlovna, had willingly consented to work for her. They were not at all puzzled at a poor woman's desiring to establish a dressmaker's shop.

These three young girls found four more, choosing them with all the circumspection that Véra Pávlovna had recommended to them: these conditions of choice had nothing in them to excite suspicion, nothing of an extraordinary character. What is there extraordinary in the fact that a young women should want her shop-girls to be of good and open character? She wants no quarrels, that is all; it is only prudence on her part.

Véra Pávlovna also formed a somewhat intimate acquaintance with the girls newly selected before telling them that she accepted them; this was very natural; she still acted like a prudent woman.

They worked a month for the wages agreed upon. Véra Pávlovna was always at the shop, so that the seamstresses had plenty of time to know her more closely and see that she was economical, circumspect, reasonable, and at the same time good; therefore she obtained their confidence very quickly. There was but one thing further to say,—that she was a good employer, who knew how to manage her affairs.

When the month was over, Véra Pávlovna came to the shop with an account book, and asked her seamstresses to stop their work and listen. Then she said to them in simple language things such as the seamstresses had never heard before:

"Now we know each other. For my part, I can say of you that you are good workers and good characters. And I do not believe that you will speak very ill of me. I am going to talk to you without reserve, and if what I say seems strange, you will reflect before deciding upon it; you will not regard my words as futile, for you know me for a serious woman.

"This is what I have to say:

"People of heart say that dressmakers' shops can be established in which the seamstresses shall work with greater profit than in the shops generally known. It has been my wish to make the attempt. Judging from the first month, we must conclude that these people are right. Your wages you have had. I am now going to tell you how much profit remains to me after deducting your wages and the running expenses."

Véra Pávlovna read them the account of the expenses and receipts for the month just over. Under the head of expenses were placed, besides the wages paid, all the other costs,— the rent of the room, lights, and even Véra Pávlovna's carriage-hire in conducting the business of the shop.

"I have so much left," she continued; "what's to be done with this money? I have established a workshop in order that the profits resulting from the work may go to the workers; that is why I come, for this first time, to distribute it among you equally. Then we shall see if that is the best way, or if it would be better to employ this money otherwise."

Having said this, she made the distribution. For some minutes the seamstresses could not recover from their astonishment; then they began to thank her. Véra Pávlovna let them go on, fearing that she would offend them if she refused to listen, which would have seemed in their eyes indifference and disdain.

"Now," she continued, "I have to tell you the most difficult thing that I shall ever have to say to you, and I do not know whether I shall succeed in making it clear. Nevertheless I must try. Why have I not kept this money? And of what use is it to establish a workshop if not to make a profit from it? I and my husband have, as you know, the necessities: although we are not rich, we have everything that we need and enough of it. Now, if I needed anything, I should only have to say so to my husband; or, rather, even that would be needless, for if I wanted anything, he would perceive it himself and give it to me. His business is not of the most lucrative sort, but it is what he likes best. As we love each other a great deal, it is infinitely pleasant to him to do what pleases me; on my side, I love to do what pleases him. Therefore, if I needed money, he would engage in more lucrative business than he is doing now. And he would find it quickly, for he is intelligent and skillful,—but you are somewhat acquainted with him. Now, if he does not do it, that means that the money which we have is enough for me. I have no passion for money; every one has his passion, which is not always the passion for money. Some have a passion for dancing, others for dress, others for cards, and all are ready to ruin themselves to satisfy their ruling passion; many actually do it, and nobody is astonished at it. Now, I have a passion for the things in which I am engaged with you, and, far from ruining myself for my passion, I spend scarcely any money upon it, and I am happy to indulge myself in it without making any profit thereby. Well, there is nothing strange in that, it seems to me. Whoever thinks of making a profit out of his passion? Every one even sacrifices money for it. I do not even do that; I spend nothing on it. Therefore I have an advantage over others in that my passion, though agreeable to me, costs me nothing, while others pay for their pleasure. Why have I this passion? This is why: good and intelligent people have written many books concerning the way in which we should live in order that all may be happy; and the principal means that they recommend is the organization of workshops on a new basis.

"I, wishing to see if we can establish a workshop of this sort, act just as anyone does who desires to build a beautiful house or lay out a fine garden or a hothouse in order to enjoy them; I wish to establish a good dressmaker's shop in order that I may have the pleasure of watching it. Certainly it would be something gained already, if I confined myself to distributing the profits among you monthly, as I do now. But good people say that we can manage in a much better and more profitable way. I will tell you little by little all that we can do besides, if we take the advice of intelligent people. Moreover, you yourselves, by watching things closely, will make your own observations, and when it shall seem to you possible for us to do something good, we will try to do it, but gradually and in proper season. I must only add that without your consent I shall make no innovations. Whatever is new will be according to your wishes. Intelligent people say that nothing succeeds unless it is done voluntarily. I am of their opinion, and shall do nothing without your consent.

"Here is my last order: you see that it is necessary to keep books, and look out that there may be no useless expenditures. During this first month I have done this alone, but I do not care to do so any more. Choose two of you to help me. I shall do nothing without their advice. The money is yours and not mine; therefore it is for you to watch its employment. We are hardly well enough acquainted with each other yet to know which of you is best fitted for such work; we must make a trial and choose only for a limited time; in a week you will know whether to appoint other delegates or let the old ones continue."

These extraordinary words gave rise to long discussions. But Véra Pávlovna had gained the confidence of the working girls. She had talked to them in a very simple way, without going too far or unfolding attractive prospects before them which, after a temporary enthusiasm, give birth to distrust; consequently the young girls were far from taking her for a crank, and that was the principal point. The business went on very satisfactorily.

Here, for the rest, in an abridged form, is the history of the shop during the three years that this shop constituted the principal feature in the history of Véra Pávlovna herself.

The founders were directly interested in the success of the business, and naturally it went on very well. The shop never lost customers. It had to undergo the jealousies of a few other shops and stores, but this proved no serious obstacle. All that Véra Pávlovna had to do was to obtain the right to put a sign over the shop-door. They soon had more orders than the working girls originally employed could execute, and the force went on steadily growing. When the business had been in operation eighteen months, it kept twenty young girls at work; afterwards, more still. One of the first measures of the collective administration was a decision that Véra Pávlovna no more than the others should work without reward. When this was announced to her, she told the working girls that they were perfectly right. They wished to give her a third of the profits. She laid this aside for a certain time until she was able to convince the young girls that this was contrary to the fundamental idea of their institution. For a long time they did not understand; but finally they were convinced. The business was already so large that Véra Pávlovna could not do all the cutting; they gave her another cutter to aid her. Both received the same wages, and Véra

Pávlovna succeeded at last in inducing the society to receive
into its treasury the sum of the profits that it had obliged
her to accept, first deducting that to which she was entitled
as a cutter. They used this money to open a bank.

For a year Véra Pávlovna spent a great portion of the day
at the shop, where she worked as many hours as any of the
seamstresses, perhaps more than any of them. When it became needless for her to work all day at the shop, she caused
her wages to be decreased in proportion to the decrease of
her hours of labor.

How should the profits be divided? Véra Pávlovna wanted
to achieve an equal division. Not until the middle of the
third year did she succeed in this. Prior to that, they passed
through several stages, beginning by dividing in proportion
to the wages. First they saw that, if a working girl was kept
from work for several days by sickness or some other cause
deserving of consideration, it was not right to cut her share
of the profits, which she acquired not exactly by her own
day's work, but rather by the progress of the work as a
whole and the general condition of the shop. Later they decided that the cutters, and such of the other workers as received separate pay for delivering the work at houses or
fulfilling other functions, were sufficiently compensated by
their individual wages, and that it was not just that they
should receive more of the profits than the others. The
simple seamstresses were so delicate about the matter that
they did not ask for this change, even when they saw the
injustice of the old method of distribution established by
themselves. For the rest, it must be added that there was
nothing heroic in this temporary delicacy, inasmuch as the
affairs of all were improving constantly. The most difficult
thing of all was to make the simple working girls understand that one ought to receive just as much of the profits
as another, although some earned more than others, and
that those who labored most skilfully were already sufficiently rewarded by their larger wages. This was the last
change to be made in the division of the profits, and it was
not reached, as has already been said, until towards the middle
of the third year, when the associates had come to understand that the profits were not a reward for the talent of
one or another, but rather a result of the general character
of the workshop, a result of its organization and its object.
Now, this object was the greatest possible equality in the

distribution of the fruits of collective labor among all the working girls, regardless of the personal peculiarities of each. Upon this character of the workshop depended the participation of the laborers in the profits. But as the character of the workshop, its spirit, and its order were produced by the mutual understanding of all, the tacit consent of the most timid or the least capable was not useless in maintaining and developing this understanding.

I pass by many details, because it is not the workshop that I am describing; I speak of it only so far as is necessary to exhibit the activity of Véra Pávlovna. If I mention some of its peculiarities, it is solely with a view of showing how Véra Pávlovna acted in this affair, and how she guided it gradually, with an indefatigable patience and a remarkable steadfastness of purpose. She never commanded, confining herself to advising, explaining, proposing her coöperation, and aiding in the execution of whatever the group had resolved upon.

The profits were divided every month. At first each working girl took her entire share and spent it separately: each had urgent needs, and they were not accustomed to acting in concert. When, through constant participation in the business, they had acquired the habit of combining their efforts in the shop, Véra Pávlovna fixed their attention upon the circumstance that in their trade the amount of patronage is very uneven, depending upon the months of the year, and that it would not be a bad plan to lay aside during the most profitable months a portion of the income in order to make up for the decrease of profits in the other months.

The accounts were kept very exactly, and the young girls knew well that, if any one of them should leave the shop, she would receive without any delay the share belonging to her. Consequently they consented to this proposition. A small reserve capital was formed; it went on growing steadily; they began to seek various uses for it. Everybody understood, in the first place, that loans would be made to those of the participants who should chance to have a great need of money, and no one wanted to lend at interest: poor people believe that financial aid should be extended without interest. The establishment of this bank was followed by the foundation of a purchasing agency: the young girls found that it would be advantageous to buy their tea, coffee, sugar, shoes, and in short many other things, through the agency of the association, which bought merchandise in large quantities and consequently at lower rates. Some time later they went further still: they saw that it would be advantageous to organize in the same way for the purchase of bread and other provisions which they bought every day at the bakeshops and groceries; but they realized at the same time that to do that it would be necessary for the associates to live not far apart. They began to draw together, several living in one house, or taking rooms near the shop. After which the asociation established an agency for its dealings with the bakers and grocers. About eighteen months later almost all the working girls were living in one large house, had a common table, and bought their provisions as they do in large establishments.

Half of these young girls were without family. Some had aged relatives, mothers or aunts; two of them supported their old father; several had little brothers and sisters. Because of these family relations three of them were unable to live in the house with the others: one had a mother difficult to get along with; another had a mother in government employ who objected to living with girls from the country; the third had a drunken father. These profited only by the purchasing agency; it was the same with the married seamstresses. But with these exceptions all those who had relatives to support lived in the common house. They lived two and three in a room; their relatives arranged themselves each in his or her own fashion; two old women had each a separate chamber, but the others roomed together. The little boys had a room of their own; for the little girls there were two.

It was agreed that the boys could not remain there after the age of eight; those who were older were sent to learn a trade as apprentices.

The accounts were kept in the most exact manner in order that no one in the association might injure any one or profit by another's injury.

It would be too long and tedious to enter into fuller details, but there is one point more that must be explained.

Véra Pávlovna, from the very first, took books to the shop. After having given her directions, she began to read aloud, continuing half an hour if not interrupted sooner by the necessity of distributing more work. Then the young girls rested from the attention which they had given to the reading; afterwards they resumed it, and then rested again. It is needless to say that the young girls from the first acquired a passion for reading; some had already acquired it before they came to the shop. Three weeks later, reading during work had become a regular thing. When three or four months had passed, some of the more skillful seamstresses offered to do the reading; it was agreed that they should replace Véra Pávlovna, that each should read half an hour, and that this half-hour should be counted as a part of their labor.

As long as Véra Pávlovna was obliged to do the reading, she sometimes replaced it by stories: when relieved of the reading, she multiplied the stories, which soon became a sort of course of lessons. Then—and this was a great step— Véra Pávlovna succeeded in establishing a regular system of instruction: the young girls became so eager to learn and their work went on so successfully that they decided to interrupt their work to listen to the lessons in the middle of the day's work and before dinner.

"Alexey Pétrovich," said Véra Pávlovna, when calling on the Mertzálovs one day, "I have a request to make of you: Natasha already agrees with me on the idea. My shop is becoming a college of all sorts of learning. Be one of our professors."

"What then shall I teach them? Latin or Greek, perhaps, or even logic and rhetoric?" said Alexey Pétrovich, laughing: "my specialty is not very interesting in your opinion and in the opinion of some one whom I well know."

"No, you are needed precisely as a specialist; you will serve us as a moral buckler and a proof of the good tendency of our teaching."

"You are right. I see clearly that without me this would be immoral. What shall I teach?"

"Russian history, for instance, or an outline of universal history."

"Exactly. That is what I will teach, and it shall be supposed that I am a specialist. Delightful! Two functions,—a professor and a buckler."

Natalya Andrevna, Lopukhóv, three students, and Véra Pávlovna herself were the other professors, as they jokingly called themselves.

They mingled instruction with amusements. They had evening parties, suburban walks, at first seldom, and then, when money was plentiful, more frequently; they also went to the theatre. The third winter they subscribed regularly to gallery seats at the Italian opera.

How much joy and happiness for Véra Pávlovna! But how much effort also, and anxiety, and even sorrow! The most painful impression of this sort, not only to Véra Pávlovna, but to all her little circle, was caused by the misfortune of one of the best of the working girls, Sásha Pribýtkova. She was pretty, and was engaged to an office clerk. One evening, when walking in the street a little later than usual, a man ran after her and took her by the hand. Wishing to release herself, she pulled her arm away quickly, thus causing the man's watch to fall. "Thief, thief!" he cried. The police came and the young girl was arrested. The fiancé, on hearing this news, began a search for the individual, found him, and challenged him to a duel; he refused; then the fiancé struck his adversary; the latter took a stick to strike back, but, before he could do so, received a blow in the breast and fell stone dead. Then the fiancé was imprisoned in his turn, and endless court proceedings began. And then? Then nothing, except that after that it was pitiful to look at Sásha Pribýtkova.

Connected with the shop were many other stories, less dramatic but equally sorrowful. These adventures, inevitable amid the prevailing ideas and surroundings, certainly caused Véra Pávlovna much sorrow and still more embarrassment.

But much greater—oh, much greater!—were the joys. The general progress of the association was gay and prosperous. Therefore, though distressing accidents sometimes happened, happy occurrences were much more frequent. Véra Pávlovna succeeded in finding good situations for the little brothers or sisters of various working girls. In the course of the third year, two of the working girls passed an examination for a governess's situation,—to them a great piece of good fortune! Cases of this sort abounded; but most joyous of all were the marriages. There were many of them and all were happy.

Véra Pávlovna was twice invited to stand godmother and twice refused. This *rôle* was almost always taken by Madame Mertzálov, or by her mother, who was also a very good lady. The first time that she refused, it was thought that she was displeased at something, and refused for that reason; but no: Véra Pávlovna was very happy to be invited, and it was simply out of modesty that she did not accept, not wishing to appear officially as the patron of the bride. She always avoided the appearance of influence; she tried to put others forward and succeeded in it, so that a number of ladies, on coming to the shop to give orders, did not distinguish her from the two other cutters. Her greatest pleasure was to demonstrate that the association had been established and was maintained by the working girls themselves. She wished to persuade herself that the shop might be able to go on without her and that others of the same sort might emerge quite unexpectedly. "And why not? How good that would be! What better thing could happen?"

Such was Véra Pávlovna's fondest dream.

: V :

Thus nearly three years since the establishment of the workshop rolled away, and more than three years since Véra Pávlovna's marriage. By what smoothness and activity had these years been marked! With what tranquillity, joys, and contentment of all sorts had they not been filled!

Véra Pávlovna, waking in the morning, dozes a long time in bed; she loves to doze; while appearing to sleep, she thinks of what there is to do; after which her thought wanders, and she says to herself: "How warm this bed is! How nice it is thus to doze in the morning!" and so she dozes until from the neutral room (now we must say from one of the neutral rooms, for there are two in this fourth year of their marriage)—until from one of the neutral rooms her husband—that is, "her darling"—calls out: "Vérochka, are you awake?"

"Yes, my darling."

This "yes" means that the husband may begin to make the tea: for he makes the tea in the morning, while Véra Pávlovna—no, in her room she is not Véra Pávlovna, but Vérochka—is dressing. She dresses quickly, but she likes to let the water stream over her a long time; then she is a long time in combing her hair, or, rather, not exactly that; she combs her hair quickly, only she likes to play with her tresses, of which she is very fond; sometimes too, it must be added, she pays particular attention to one feature of get-

ting dressed,—her boots: Vérochka dresses with much simplicity, but she has beautiful boots; to have beautiful boots
is her passion.

Now she goes out to drink her tea; she kisses her husband.
"Did you sleep well, my darling?"

While drinking the tea, she talks about various subjects,
trivial or serious. Furthermore Véra Pávlovna—no, Vérochka (during the morning meal she is still Vérochka) —
does not take as much tea as cream: the tea is only a pretext
for taking the cream, and she puts in much more cream than
tea; cream also is her passion. It is very difficult to get good
cream in St. Petersburg, but she knows where to find real
cream, excellent cream. She dreams of owning a cow; if
affairs go on for another year as they have already gone on,
perhaps she may have one. But it is nine o'clock. Her darling
goes off to give his lessons or attend to his other business:
he is also employed in a manufacturer's counting-room.
Véra Pávlovna now becomes Véra Pávlovna until the next
morning. She attends to her household duties; she has but
one servant, a very young girl, who has to be shown everything; and as soon as she has become familiar with affairs,
a new one has to be shown, for servants do not stay long
with Véra Pávlovna. They are always marrying. After six
months or a little more Véra Pávlovna makes a pelerine or
some ruffles as a preparation for standing godmother. On
this occasion she cannot refuse. "But then, Véra Pávlovna,
you have arranged everything; no one but you can be godmother," they would say, with reason.

Yes, she has many household cares. Then she has to go
to give her lessons, numerous enough to occupy her ten
hours a week: to have more would be fatiguing to her, and
furthermore she has no time. Before the lessons she has to
go to the shop and spend some time there; on returning
from the lessons she has to call in again and take a glance
at affairs. Then it is time to dine with her "darling." Often
there are one or two persons to dine with them. Not more
than two; they cannot have more; and even two cause considerable trouble. If Véra Pávlovna comes home tired, then
the dinner is simpler; she goes to her room to rest, and the
dinner begun under her direction is finished without her.
But if on coming home she is not tired, she runs to the
kitchen and goes actively to work; in that case the dinner
is ornamented with some bit of pastry, generally something

to be eaten with cream,—that is, something that may serve
as a pretext for eating cream. During the meal she talks and
asks questions, but generally talks; and why shouldn't she
talk? How many new things she has to communicate concerning the shop alone! After the meal she remains a quarter
of an hour longer with her "darling"; then they retire to their
respective rooms. Now Véra Pávlovna again lies down upon
her bed, where she reads and dozes; very often she sleeps;
perhaps that is the case half of the time. It is her weakness,
a vulgar weakness perhaps; but Véra Pávlovna sleeps after
dinner. And she even loves to sleep; she is neither ashamed
nor repentant of this vulgar weakness. She rises after having slept or simply dozed for an hour and a half or two
hours; she dresses and goes once more to the shop, where
she stays until tea-time. Then, if they have no guests to take
tea with them, she talks again with her "darling," and
they spend about half an hour in the neutral room. After
which, "Till tomorrow, my darling"; they kiss each other
and separate until the following morning.

Then for some time, occasionally until two o'clock in the
morning, she works, reads, finds recreation at the piano
(which is in her room). This grand piano has just been
bought; previously she had hired one. It was a great pleasure
to her when this piano was bought; in the first place it was
a saving. The piano, which was a small second-hand one,
cost one hundred rubles; it only had to be repaired at a
cost of seventy rubles, and then she had a piano of excellent
tone. Sometimes her darling comes in to hear her sing, but
only rarely: he has so much to do! So the evening passes:
working, reading, playing, singing; but especially reading
and singing. This when nobody is there. But very often they
receive visitors, generally young people not as old as Véra
Pávlovna herself, among the number the workshop professors. All hold Lopukhóv in high esteem, consider him one
of the best minds of St. Petersburg, and perhaps they are
not wrong. This is the motive of their intimacy with the
Lopukhóvs: they find Dmítry Sergéich's conversations useful to them. For Véra Pávlovna they have a boundless veneration; she even permits them to kiss her hand without
feeling herself humiliated, and conducts herself toward them
as if she were fifteen years their elder; that is, she so conducts herself when not indulging in gayeties (but, to tell
the truth, the most of the time she does indulge in gayeties);

she runs, she plays with them and they are enchanted, and all dance, and waltz, and run, and chatter, and laugh, and make music, and, above all, sing. So much gayety does not at all prevent these young people from profoundly venerating Véra Pávlovna, and from esteeming her as one rarely esteems an elder sister and as one does not always esteem a good mother. Moreover, the song is not always a gay one; in fact, Véra Pávlovna oftenest sings serious things; sometimes she stops singing and plays serious airs on her piano; her hearers listen in silence. They also receive older visitors, their equals,—for the most part Lopukhóv's old comrades, acquaintances of his old comrades, and two or three young professors, almost all bachelors: the only married people are the Mertzálovs.

The Lopukhóvs visit more rarely, scarcely ever going to see any one but the Mertzálovs and Madame Mertzálov's parents: these good and simple old people have a large number of sons filling positions of considerable importance in all the different ministries; at the houses of these, who live in a certain degree of luxury, Véra Pávlovna meets a society of all colors and shades. This free, active life, not without a touch of sybaritism,—dozing in her soft, warm bed, taking cream, eating pastry with cream,—this life is very pleasant to Véra Pávlovna.

Does the world afford a better life? To her as yet it seems not.

Yes, and for the beginning of youth perhaps she is right.

But the years roll on, and with the lapse of time life grows better, provided it comes to be what it already is for some and what it one day will be for all.

: **VI** :

One day—the end of the summer was already near at hand —the young girls were getting ready to take their customary Sunday walk in the suburbs. On almost every holiday during the summer they went in boats to the islands.* Ordinarily Véra Pávlovna alone went with them, but on this occasion Dmítry Sergéich was going too, which was very extraordinary; it was the second time that year that he had

---

* That is, the islands situated in the suburbs of St. Petersburg and formed by the various arms of the Neva.

done so. This news caused much joy in the shop. Véra Páv-lovna, thought the girls, will be gayer than usual, and the walk will be a very lively one. Consequently some of the girls, who had intended to pass this Sunday otherwise, changed their plans and joined the promenaders. They had to engage five yawls instead of four, and found that even five would not be enough; they had to take a sixth. There were more than fifty persons, over twenty of whom were seamstresses. Only six were absent. There were three women advanced in years; a dozen children; mothers, sisters, and brothers of the seamstresses; three young men who had sweethearts among them, one being a clockmaker's foreman, another a small merchant, and both scarcely yielding in point of manners to the third, who was a schoolteacher in the district; and finally five other young men of various pursuits, of whom two were officers, and eight students from the University and Medical Academy.

They took four great *samovars* and piles of all sorts of provisions, bread, cold veal, etc. For the young people were very active, and in the open air could be relied on to have good appetites: they did not forget half a dozen bottles of wine: for fifty people, fifteen of whom were children, this was certainly none too much.

Really the trip couldn't have been better. Nothing was wanting. They danced quadrilles with sixteen and even twenty couples. In the races twenty-two couples took part; they hung three swings between trees; in between times they drank tea or ate. For half an hour a part of the gay company listened to a discussion between Dmítry Sergéich and two students, the most intimate of his younger friends; they mutually charged each other with erroneous reasoning, mod-erantism, and *bourgeoisisme*. These were general charges, but in each individual some special fault was pointed out. In one of the students it was romanticism, in Dmítry Sergéich schematism, and in the other student, rigorism; it is needless to say that it was very difficult for a simple listener to give attention to such a discussion for more than five minutes.

One of the disputants was not able to keep it up over an hour and a half, after which he fled to join the dancers, but his flight was not altogether inglorious. He had become indignant against some moderate or other. Undoubtedly this moderate was myself, though I was not present, and knowing that the object of his wrath was already well along in years, he cried out: "What are you talking about? Let me quote you some words that I heard uttered lately by a very estimable and very intelligent lady: 'Man is incapable of useful thought after the age of twenty-five years.'"

"But I know the lady to whom you refer," said an officer, who, unfortunately for the romanticist, came up just then. "She is Madame N., and she said that in my presence. She is indeed an excellent lady, only she was convicted on the spot of having boasted half an hour before of being twenty-six years old, and you remember, do you not, how she joined all the others in laughing at herself."

And now all four laughed, and the romanticist, while laughing, took advantage of the opportunity to run away. But the officer took his place in the discussion, which grew still more animated and lasted until tea was ready. The officer answered the rigorist and the schematist more rudely than the romanticist had done, but showed himself a thorough-going follower of Auguste Comte.

After tea the officer declared that, inasmuch as he was still at that age when one can think correctly, he was ready to join the other individuals of the same age; Dmítry Sergéich and even the rigorist followed his example in spite of themselves; it is true that they did not dance, but they joined in the races. When the contests in running and leaping the brook began, the three thinkers showed themselves among the most enthusiastic. The officer proved himself the superior when it came to leaping the brook. Dmítry Sergéich, who was endowed with great strength, became greatly excited on being thrown by the officer; he counted on being the first in this sort of exercise after the rigorist, who very easily lifted into the air and threw to the ground Dmítry and the officer together. That did not clash with the ambition of the officer or of Dmítry Sergéich, for the rigorist was a recognized athlete; but Dmítry Sergéich did not like to pocket the disgrace of being conquered by the officer, and so he returned to the struggle five times, and five times the officer, though not without difficulty, threw him. The sixth time he acknowledged himself conquered. Both could do no more. The three thinkers, stretching themselves upon the grass, resumed their discussion; this time Dmítry Sergéich took the Comtean view and the officer was the schematist, but the rigorist remained a rigorist. At eleven o'clock they started homeward. The old women and children slept in the

boats; fortunately they had taken many warm wraps along;
the others on the contrary talked incessantly, and the games
and laughter in the six yawls did not stop until their arrival.

: V I I :

Two days afterward, at the breakfast table, Véra Pávlovna
told her husband that he had a bad color. He answered that
that night he had not slept very well, and had been feeling
badly since the previous evening; but that it was nothing;
he had taken a little cold on the excursion, especially while
lying on the ground after the racing and wrestling; he admitted that he had been a little imprudent, but convinced
Véra Pávlovna that it was nothing at all.

Then he went about his usual business, and at tea-time
said that his indisposition had left him. But the next morning he was obliged to confess that he must remain a while
in the house. Véra Pávlovna, very anxious, became seriously
frightened, and urged Dmítry Sergéich to send for a doctor.

"But I am a doctor myself, and can care for myself if
need be; at present it isn't necessary."

But Véra Pávlovna insisted, and he wrote a note to Kirsánov, in which he told him that his sickness was insignificant and that he called him only to please his wife.

Consequently Kirsánov was in no hurry about coming.
He remained at the hospital until dinner-time, and, when
he reached the Lopukhóvs, it was already after five o'clock.

"I did well, Alexander, in calling you," said Lopukhóv:
"although there is no danger, and probably will be none,
I have pneumonia. I should certainly have cured myself
without you, but take care of me just the same. It is necessary to ease my conscience. I am not a bachelor like you."

They sounded each other's chests for a long time, and both
came to the conclusion that Lopukhóv's lungs were really
inflamed. There was no danger, and probably would be none,
but this disease is always grave. The patient must keep his
bed a dozen days.

Kirsánov had to talk a long time to Véra Pávlovna to
ease her mind. She finally was persuaded that they were not
deceiving her; that the disease, in all probability, was not
only not dangerous, but even quite light; only it was "in

all probability," and how many things happen against all probability! Kirsánov came twice a day to see his patient: they both saw that the disease was not dangerous. On the morning of the fourth day Kirsánov said to Véra Pávlovna:

"Dmítry is getting on well: for the next three or four days he will be a little worse, after which his recovery will begin. But I wish to speak seriously to you of yourself; why do you not sleep nights? You are doing wrong. He has no need of a nurse, or of me. In acting in this way you are injuring yourself, and quite uselessly. You are too nervous."

To all these arguments Véra Pávlovna answered:

"Never!" "Impossible!" Or else, "I should like to, but I cannot,"—that is, sleep nights and leave Lopukhóv without a nurse.

At last she said: "But all that you are saying to me now he has already told me many times over, as you well know. Certainly I would have yielded to him rather than to you; therefore I cannot."

Against such an argument there was nothing to be said. Kirsánov shook his head and went away.

Coming back to his patient after nine in the evening, he remained by his side in company with Véra Pávlovna about half an hour; then he said:

"Now, Véra Pávlovna, go and rest. We both beg you to. I will spend the night here."

Véra Pávlovna was much confused: she was half convinced that her presence all night by the bedside was not absolutely necessary. But then why does Kirsánov, a busy man, remain? Who knows? No, her "darling" cannot be left alone; no one knows what might happen. He will want to drink, perhaps he will want some tea; but he is so considerate that he won't ask for it. Therefore it is necessary to remain by his side. But that Kirsánov should spend the night there is out of the question; she will not allow it. Therefore she refused to go away, pretending that she was not very tired and that she had rested a great deal during the day.

"I beg you to go; forgive me, but I insist that you leave."

And Kirsánov took her by the hand, and led her almost by force to her room.

"You really confuse me, Alexánder," said the sick man. "What a ridiculous *rôle* you play in remaining all night with a patient who does not need you! and yet I am obliged to you, for I have never been able to induce her to get a nurse, since she fears to leave me alone. She cannot trust me to any one else."

"If I did not see that she doesn't trust you to any one, you may be sure that I would not disturb my comfort. But now I hope that she is going to sleep, for I am a doctor and your friend besides."

In fact, Véra Pávlovna had no sooner reached her bed than she threw herself upon it and went to sleep. Three sleepless nights alone would be nothing, and the hurry and worry alone would be nothing. But the hurry and worry and the three sleepless nights together, without any rest in the daytime, were really dangerous; forty-eight hours more of it, and she would have been sicker than her husband.

Kirsánov spent three nights with his patient; it didn't tire him at all, for he slept very soundly, only taking the precaution to lock the door so that Véra Pávlovna might not know of his negligence. She strongly suspected that he slept, but didn't worry about it. He is a doctor; what, then, is there to be afraid of? He knows when to sleep and when to go without it. She was ashamed at not having been able to calm herself sooner. But in vain she tried to assure him that she would sleep even if he were not there; he didn't believe her, and answered:

"It is your fault, Véra Pávlovna, and you must take the consequences. I have no confidence in you."

Four days afterward she saw clearly that the sick man was almost cured; the most decisive proofs conquered her doubts. That evening they played cards, three-handed. Lopukhóv was no longer completely on his back, but in a half-sitting posture, and had regained the voice of a man in health. It was safe for Kirsánov to leave, and he told them so.

"Alexánder Matvéich, why are you neglecting me so? With Dmítry you are on a good footing. He sees you often enough; but, as for you, you have not been to see us, it seems to me, for more than six months; and it has been so for years. Do you remember that at the beginning we were close friends?"

"Men change, Véra Pávlovna. And I do an enormous amount of work; I can boast of it. I visit nobody, for lack of time and will. I tire myself so from nine till five in the hospital that, when I go home, I can put on nothing but my dressing-gown. Friendship is good, but—do not be offended at what I am going to say—to lie in one's dressing-gown, with a cigar between one's lips, is better still."

In fact, Kirsánov, for more than two years, had not been a visitor at the Lopukhóvs'. The reader has not noticed his name among their ordinary visitors, or even among their rare visitors; for a long time he had been the rarest of all.

: VIII :

The reader with a penetrating eye says: "I see where this is going to end; a new romance is beginning, in Véra Pávlovna's life, in which Kirsánov is to play the principal *rôle*. I see even farther. Kirsánov has long been in love with Véra Pávlovna, and that is why he has ceased to visit the Lopukhóvs." How perceptive you are! As soon as you are told something, you note it instantly and glory in your penetration. Accept my admiration, reader with the penetrating eye!

Thus, in the history of Véra Pávlovna a new personage appears, and I should have to introduce him, had this not already been done. Whenever I spoke of Lopukhóv, I set my wits to work to distinguish him from his intimate friend, and yet I could say almost nothing of him that I should not have to repeat in speaking of Kirsánov. Yes, all that the reader with the penetrating eye will be able to guess of Kirsánov's character will be a repetition of what has been said about Lopukhóv. Lopukhóv was the son of a *petit bourgeois*, tolerably well-to-do for his station,—that is, generally having meat in his cabbage soup. Kirsánov was the son of a law copyist,—that is, of a man who often had no meat in his cabbage soup. Lopukhóv, from his earliest years, had earned his own living; Kirsánov, at the age of twelve, began to aid his father in copying. As soon as he reached the fourth form at school he began to give lessons. Both paved their own way, without aids or influential acquaintances.

What kind of a man was Lopukhóv? At school, French had not been taught him. As for German, he had been taught just enough to enable him to decline *der, die, das* almost faultlessly. After entering the Academy he soon saw that with Russian alone one cannot make much progress in science; he took a French-Russian dictionary and a few French books ready to his hand,—*Télémaque*, Madame de Genlis's novels, a few numbers of our wise *Revue Etrangère*, not very attractive works,—he took these, and, though a great lover of reading, said to himself: "I will not open a single Russian book until I am able to read French easily"; and he succeeded. With German he managed another way; he hired a bed in a room occupied by many German workingmen. The lodging was frightful, the Germans tiresome, the Academy a long way off, but nevertheless he slept there long enough to learn German.

With Kirsánov it had been otherwise. He had learned German with books and a dictionary, as Lopukhóv had learned French, and his French he acquired in still another way,—by means of a single book and no dictionary. The Gospel is a well-known book: he procured a copy of a Geneva translation of the New Testament; he read it eight times, the ninth time he understood it all,—he knew French.

What kind of a man was Lopukhóv? This will show. One day in his much-worn uniform he was going along the Kamenny-Ostrov Prospect to give a lesson for fifty copecks two miles away from the Lyceum. He saw approaching him some one with an imposing air, evidently out for exercise, who marched straight upon him without turning aside. Now, at that time Lopukhóv had made this rule: "I turn aside first for nobody except women." Their shoulders touched. The individual, half turning back, said: "What's the matter with you, pig? Cattle!" and was about to continue in this tone, when Lopukhóv, quickly turning around, seized the individual around the waist and threw him into the gutter with great dexterity; then, standing over his adversary, he said to him: "Don't move or I will drag you into a muddier place." Two peasants passing saw and applauded; a clerk passing saw, did not applaud, and confined himself to a half smile. Carriages passed, but their occupants could not see who was in the gutter. After remaining some time in this attitude, Lopukhóv again took his man, not around the waist, but by the hand, helped him get up, led him into the road, and said to him: "Ah, sir, what a misstep you made! I hope you have not hurt yourself? Allow me to wipe you off." A peasant passing helped to wipe him, as did two passing *petits bourgeois.* After the man was cleaned up, each went his way.

To Kirsánov a similar but somewhat different thing once happened. A certain lady had formed an idea of cataloguing the library which her husband, an admirer of Voltaire, had left her at his death twenty years before. Exactly why a catalogue became necessary after twenty years is not known. It was Kirsánov who happened to apply to the lady for her purpose, and they agreed on eighty rubles as the price; Kirsánov worked for six weeks. Suddenly the lady changed her fancy and decided that the catalogue was useless; so she went into the library, and said:

"You have done enough; I have changed my mind: here is the pay for your work," and she handed him ten rubles.

"I have already done, your — (he gave the lady her title), more than half of the work: of the seventeen cases I have copied ten."

"Do you consider yourself badly paid? Nicolas, come here and talk to his gentleman." Nicolas hurried to the scene.

"How dare you be rude to my mother? Servants! Hey— There!"

"Ah! your servants! I will teach you." The lady gave a shrill scream and fainted, and Nicolas saw clearly that it was impossible for him to make any movement with his arms fastened against his sides by Kirsánov's right hand as if by a band of iron. Kirsánov, after pulling his hair with his left hand, placed it at his throat and said:

"Do you see how easy it is for me to strangle you?"

He gave his throat a grip, and Nicolas saw that it was indeed very easy to strangle him. The grasp was loosened. Nicolas found that he could breathe, but was still at the mercy of his conqueror. To the Goliaths who made their appearance Kirsánov said:

"Stop there, or I will strangle him. Keep your distance, or I will strangle him."

Nicolas, at once comprehending the situation, made signals which meant:

"This fellow means business."

"Now, brother, will you see me to the stairs?" said Kirsánov, again addressing Nicolas though continuing to hold his arm around him. He went out into the hall and descended the stairs, the Goliaths looking at him in astonishment; on the last step, letting go his hold of Nicolas's throat, he hurled him from him, and started for a hat store to buy a cap in place of that which he had left upon the battleground.

Well, then, aren't these two men alike in character? All the prominent traits by which they are marked are traits, not

of individuals, but of a type, so different from those you are
accustomed to see, reader with the penetrating eye, that these
general peculiarities hide from you their personal differences. These people are like a few Europeans scattered
among the Chinese, whom the Chinese cannot distinguish
from each other, seeing but one and the same nature, "bar-
barians with red hair and without manners." In their eyes
the French have "red hair" as well as the English. Now, the
Chinese are right: compared to them all Europeans are as
a single individual; not individuals, but representatives of a
type and nothing more. None of them eat cockroaches or
wood-lice; none of them cut men up into little pieces; all
alike drink brandy and wine made of grapes instead of rice;
and even the common drink, tea, is prepared by the Europeans with sugar, and not without as the Chinese prepare it.
It is the same with people of the type to which Lopukhóv
and Kirsánov belonged: they seem identical to men who do
not belong to this type. Each is bold and resolute, knowing
what to do under all circumstances, and doing it with a
strong arm when necessary. That is one side of their character. On the other side each is of irreproachable honesty, of
honesty such that one cannot even ask concerning either:
"Can this man be relied on fully and absolutely?" It is as
clear as the air that they breathe. As long as those breasts
heave, they will be warm and unshakeable; lay your head
upon them boldly, it will rest there safely. These general
traits are so prominent that they eclipse all individual peculiarities.

Recently this type has appeared in our midst. Previously,
only isolated personalities foreshadowed it. They were exceptions, and as such felt their isolation and weakness; hence
their inertia, their *ennui,* their exaltation, their romanticism,
their whimsicality. They could not possess the principal
traits of this type,—tact, coolness, activity, all well balanced,
the realization of common sense in action. They were really
people of the same nature, but this nature had not yet developed itself into the condition of a type. This type, I repeat, appeared but recently. I can remember when it did not
exist, although I am not very old. I have not succeeded in
becoming one of them, for I was not brought up in their
time; consequently I can without scruple express my esteem
for these new men, for unfortunately I do not glorify myself in saying of them: "These are excellent men." Recently

this type has been multiplying rapidly. It is born of an epoch; it is a sign of the times, and—must I say it?—it will disappear with the fast-flying epoch which produced it. Its life, new as it is, is fated to last but a short time.

We did not see these men six years ago; three years ago we despised them: and now—but it matters little what we think of them now; in a few years, in a very few years, we shall appeal to them: we shall say to them: "Save us!" and whatever they say then will be done by all. A few years more, perhaps even a few months, and we shall curse them; they will be driven from the scene amid hisses and insults. What does it matter? You may drive them away, you may curse them, but they will be useful to you, and that will satisfy them. They will quit the scene, proud and modest, austere and good, as they ever were. Not one will remain upon the scene? Not one! How shall we live without them? None too well. But after them things will go on better than before. Many years will pass, and then men will say: "Since their day things have been better, but still they are bad." And when they shall speak thus, that will mean that it is time for this type to be born again: it will reappear in a greater number of individuals under better forms, because goodness will then be plentier, and all that is now good will then be better. And so history will begin again in a new phase. And that will last until men say: "Now we are good," and then there will be no longer any special type, for all men will be of this type, and it will be difficult for any one to understand that there ever was a time when it was regarded as special and not as the common nature of all mankind.

: IX :

But just as Europeans seem to the Chinese to have the same faces and the same customs when contrasted with those of the Chinese, while in reality there is a much greater difference between Europeans than between Chinese, so it is with these modern men who seem to constitute but a single type. Individual diversity develops itself in more numerous differences, and they are more sharply distinguished from each other than are individuals of any other type. They include all sorts of people,—sybarites and stoics, the stern and the tender, in short, all varieties. But as the most savage European is very gentle, the most cowardly very courageous, the most epicurean very moral compared with the Chinese, so it is with the new men; the most austere believe that man needs more comfort than others dream of for him; the most sensual are more rigid in their morality than the moralists found in the common run of men. But they have ideas of their own in all these things; they view morality and comfort, sensuality and virtue in a way wholly peculiar to themselves.

But they all view these things in the same way and as if they were one and the same thing, so that to them comfort, sensuality, virtue, morality seem identical. But all this is true only from the Chinese standpoint; they themselves, on the contrary, find very great differences in their views corresponding to the diversity of their natures. How can one grasp all these differences?

When Europeans talk over their affairs with each other, but only with each other and not with the Chinese, the diversity of their natures is visible. So is it with our new men; we see in them a great diversity when the relations between themselves and not with others are before us. We have seen two individuals of this type, Véra Pávlovna and Lopukhóv, and we have seen what their relations were. A third individual now appears upon the scene. Let us see what differences will grow out of the possibility now open to one of the three of making a comparison between the two others. Véra Pávlovna now has before her Lopukhóv and Kirsánov. Formerly she had no choice to make; now she may make one.

: X :

Nevertheless two or three words must be said of Kirsánov's outer man.

He too, like Lopukhóv, had regular and handsome features. Some thought the latter more handsome, others the former. Lopukhóv, who was darker, had hair of a deep chestnut color, sparkling brown eyes that seemed almost black, an aquiline nose, thick lips, and a somewhat oval face.

Kirsánov had moderately thick light hair, blue eyes, a

Grecian nose, a small mouth, and an oblong face of rare whiteness.

Kirsánov's position was a fairly good one. He already had a chair. The electors were against him by an enormous majority, and he not only would not have obtained a chair, but would not even have been made a doctor at the final examination at the Academy, had it been at all possible. Two or three young people and one of his old professors, a man already advanced in age, all his friends, had long since reported to the others that there existed in the world a man named Virchow and that this Virchow lived in Berlin, and a man named Claude Bernard and that this Claude Bernard lived in Paris, and I know not how many more names of men of this sort, which my memory does not retain and who also lived in different cities; they had also said that these Virchows, Claude Bernards, and others were scientific luminaries.

All that was improbable in the last degree, for we well know the luminaries of science,—Bœrhoave, Hufeland; Harvey was also a great *savant,* being the discoverer of the circulation of the blood; likewise Jenner, who taught us vaccination; these we know, but, as for these Virchows, and these Claude Bernards, we do not know them. What sort of luminaries are they, then? The devil knows. This same Claude Bernard showed appreciation of Kirsánov's work before he had finished his last year as a student; of course, then, it was impossible to avoid electing him. So they gave Kirsánov a physician's diploma and about eighteen months afterward a chair. The students said that he was a valuable addition to the number of good professors. Of practice he had none, and said that he had abandoned the practice of medicine. But he spent many hours at the hospital; he often dined there and sometimes slept there. What did he do there? He said that he worked there for science and not for the sick: "I do not treat patients, I only observe and experiment." The students sustained this opinion and added that none but imbeciles treat the sick now, for no one yet knows how to treat them. The hospital attendants thought otherwise: "See, Kirsánov takes this patient into his ward; the case must be a serious one," said they to each other; and then they said to the patient: "Don't worry, no disease can stand against this doctor; he is a master, and a father besides."

: XI :

For the first few months after Véra Pávlovna's marriage Kirsánov visited the Lopukhóvs very often, almost every other
day, I might say almost every day and be nearer the truth.
He became soon, if not from the very first, as intimate a
friend of Véra Pávlovna as of Lopukhóv himself. That lasted
about six months. One day their conversation flowed, as
usual, without constraint. Then, Kirsánov, who was the
most voluble, suddenly grew silent.

"What is the matter with you, Alexánder?"

"Why do you stop, Alexánder Matvéich?"

"Oh, it is nothing. Just sad, I guess."

"That's something that rarely happens to you, Alexánder
Matvéich," said Véra Pávlovna.

"It never happens to me without cause," said Kirsánov, in
a tone which seemed strained.

A little later, somewhat sooner than usual, he rose and
went away, taking his leave, as he always did, unceremoniously.

Two days later, Lopukhóv told Véra Pávlovna that he
had been to see Kirsánov and that his reception struck him
as rather peculiar. Kirsánov, it seemed, wanted to be nice to
him—all of which was quite pointless between them. Thereupon Lopukhóv, having looked at him, remarked frankly,
"Alexánder, you seem to be annoyed. Is it with me, perhaps?"

"No."

"With Vérochka?"

"No."

"But what is the matter, then?"

"Nothing; you take notions, I don't know why."

"You do not feel right toward me today; something is the
matter with you."

Kirsánov was profuse with his assurances: nothing was
the matter; in what way had he shown himself put out?
Then, as if ashamed, he again threw off ceremony and became very cordial. Lopukhóv, seizing the opportunity, said
to him:

"Now, Alexánder, tell me, why are you out of sorts?"

"I never dreamed of such a thing,"—and again he became
mawkish and affected.

What an enigma! Lopukhóv recalled nothing that could have offended him; indeed, such a thing was not possible, considering their mutual esteem and profound friendship. Véra Pávlovna, too, asked herself if she had not offended him, but was as unable to find anything, knowing perfectly well that she, no more than her husband, could have offended him.

Two days more passed. Not to come to the Lopukhóvs' for four days in a row was an extraordinary thing for Kirsánov. Véra Pávlovna even wondered if he wasn't sick. Lopukhóv went to see if he was sick. Sick? No, not at all: but still he was out of sorts. To Lopukhóv's urgent inquiries, and after several times saying "No" and several times "It is your imagination," he began to talk all sorts of nonsense about his feelings toward Lopukhóv and Véra Pávlovna: he loved them and esteemed them highly. From all that it was to be inferred that they had wronged him, and the worst of it was that in his remarks there was no allusion to anything of the kind. It was evident that they had offended him. It seemed so strange to Lopukhóv to see this in a man like Kirsánov that he said: "Listen, we are friends: all this really ought to make you blush." Kirsánov answered with an affected sorrow that perhaps he was too sensitive, but that on several occasions he had felt hurt.

"But at what?"

He began to enumerate a great number of things that had happened lately, all of them things of this sort:

"You said that the lighter the color of a man's hair, the weaker he is. Véra Pávlovna said that tea had risen in price. One was an ill-natured jest on the color of my hair. The other was an allusion to the fact that I was your guest."

Lopukhóv stood stupefied: "Pride governs all his thoughts, or, rather, he has become simply a fool, a fool in four letters."

Lopukhóv went home quite saddened. It was painful to see such failings in a man whom he so much loved. To Véra Pávlovna's questions on the subject he replied sadly that it was better not to talk about it, that Kirsánov said disagreeable things, and that probably he was sick.

Three or four days later Kirsánov came back to himself, recognized the imbecility of his words, and called on the Lopukhóvs, behaving himself as he used to. Then he began to tell how stupid he had been. From Véra Pávlovna's words he saw that his conversation had not been reported; he sincerely thanked Lopukhóv for his discretion, and to punish himself told all to Véra Pávlovna; he feelingly excused himself, saying that he was sick and had been in the wrong. Véra Pávlovna bade him drop the subject, declaring that these were stupidities; he caught at the word "stupidities," and began to talk all sorts of twaddle no less senseless than the things he had said to Lopukhóv. He said with much reserve and *finesse* that certainly these things were "stupidities," for he fully realized his inferiority to the Lopukhóvs, but that he deserved nothing else, etc., the whole being said with veiled allusions and accompanied by the most amiable assurances of esteem and devotion.

Véra Pávlovna, at hearing him go on in this way, stood as stupefied as her husband had before her. After Kirsánov's departure they remembered that some days before their friend had shown signs of very singular stupidity. At the time they had neither remarked upon nor understood it; now his remarks became clear to them; they were of the same sort, only less pronounced.

Kirsánov again began to visit the Lopukhóvs frequently; but the continuation of the former simple relations was no longer possible.

Soon the Lopukhóvs grew cold toward him. Finding in this an excuse, he stopped his visits. But he saw Lopukhóv at the house of one of their friends. Some time after, his conduct improving, Lopukhóv's aversion to him began to weaken, and he began to visit him again. Within a year Kirsánov resumed his visits at the Lopukhóvs'; he again became the excellent Kirsánov of former days, unaffected an loyal. But he came rarely: it was plain that he was not at hi ease, remembering the foolish part that he had played. Lopukhóv and Véra Pávlovna had almost forgotten it. But relations once broken off are never quite reëstablished. To all appearances, he and Lopukhóv had become friends again, and Lopukhóv really esteemed him now almost as much as before and visited him often; Véra Pávlovna, too, had restored to him a portion of her good will, but she saw him only rarely.

: XII :

Lopukhóv's sickness, or, better, Véra Pávlovna's extreme attachment to her husband, having forced Kirsánov to maintain intimate daily relations with the Lopukhóvs for more
than a week, he clearly saw that he was entering upon a
perilous path in deciding to pass his nights near Lopukhóv
in order to prevent Véra Pávlovna from being her husband's
sick-nurse. He was very happy and proud at having succeeded so well in doing all that he had considered necessary
to arrest the development of his passion when he had noticed its symptoms three years before. Two or three weeks
afterward he had been unable to avoid returning to the
Lopukhóvs'. But even at those times he had felt more pleasure over his firmness in the struggle than suffering at his
privation, and a month later he did not suffer at all; the
only feeling left being that of satisfaction with his upright
conduct. His soul was so peaceful and pure.

But now the danger was greater than then. In these three
years Véra Pávlovna had certainly greatly developed morally.
Then she was half a child, now it was quite a different thing.
The feeling that she inspired could no longer be the light
attachment that one feels for a little girl whom one loves
and at the same time admires in her innocence. And not only
had she developed morally; with us here in the North, when
a woman is really beautiful, she grows more and more so
every year. Yes, at that age three years of life do a great deal
to develop the good and the beautiful in the soul, in the
eyes, in the features, and in the entire person, if the person
be moral and good.

The danger was great, but for him only; as for Véra Pávlovna, what risk had she to run? She loved her husband, and
Kirsánov was not thoughtless and foolish enough to believe
himself a dangerous rival of Lopukhóv. It was from no false
modesty that he thought so. All who knew them looked on
them as equals. No, Lopukhóv had on his side this enormous
advantage, that he had already deserved love, that he had
already completely won Véra Pávlovna's heart. The choice
was made; she was very contented and happy; could she
dream of anything better? Wasn't she happy? It was even
ridiculous to think of such a thing. To her and to Lopuk-

hóv such an apprehension would have been but an absurd vanity on Kirsánov's part.

Indeed, should Kirsánov permit a lady to have nervous prostration or run the risk of contracting so serious an illness from over-exertion by nursing nights at a sick man's bedside —should he permit all this for such a bit of nonsense as a month or two of heartache? Indeed, to avoid disturbing the tranquillity of his own life for a little while, ought he to allow another individual, no less worthy, to run a serious risk? That would not have been honest. Now, a dishonest action would have been much more disagreeable to him than the slightly painful struggle with himself through which he had to pass, and of the result of which he felt sure as of his firmness.

These were Kirsánov's thoughts, on deciding to take Véra Pávlovna's place at her husband's bedside.

The necessity for watching passed. To save appearances and not make the change in their relations so abrupt as to call attention to it, it was necessary for Kirsánov to visit his friends at first two or three times a week, then from month to month, and then every six months. He could readily explain his absence by his occupations.

: XIII :

What Kirsánov foresaw was realized; his attachment was renewed, and became more intense than before; but to struggle against it gave him no difficulty, no serious torment. Visiting the Lopukhóvs for the second time during the week following the end of his treatment of Dmítry Sergéich, he would stay till nine o'clock in the evening. This was enough, appearances were saved; he would need not come again for a fortnight, and it would be over. But this time he must stay an hour longer. The week was not yet over, and his passion was already half stifled; in a month it would entirely disappear. Therefore he was well contented. He took an active part in the conversation and with so much ease that he was delighted at his success, and this contentment added still further to his self-possession.

But Lopukhóv was arranging to go out for the first time

since his sickness. At this Véra Pávlovna was much pleased, her joy perhaps being greater than that of the convalescent himself.

The conversation turning upon the sickness, they made fun of Véra, and ironically extolled her conjugal self-denial. Barely had she escaped falling sick herself in her exaggerated alarm.

"Laugh, laugh," said she, "but I am sure that in my place you would have done the same."

"What an influence the cares of others have upon a man!" said Lopukhóv; "he is so affected by them that he finally comes to believe that all the precautions of which he is the object are useful. For instance, I might have been out for the last three days, and yet I stay in the house. This very morning I wanted to go out, but I said: 'To be on the safe side I will wait till tomorrow.'"

"Yes, you might have gone out long ago," added Kirsánov.

"That is what I call heroism, for really it is a great bore to me, and I should much like to run away at once."

"Darling, it was for my peace of mind that you played the hero. Really, let's get going, if you want to end the quarantine sooner. I have to go to the shop for half an hour. Let's all three go there; it will be very nice of you to make our shop the object of your first visit. The working-girls will notice it and be much pleased at the attention."

"Good! Let's go together," said Lopukhóv, visibly delighted at the prospect of breathing the fresh air that very afternoon.

"Here is a friend full of tact," said Véra Pávlovna: "it did not even occur to her that you might not wish to come with us, Alexánder Matvéich."

"On the contrary, I am much interested; I've been meaning to see it a long time. Your idea is a very happy one."

In truth, Véra Pávlovna's idea was a happy one. The young girls were much pleased at receiving Lopukhóv's first visit. Kirsánov was much interested in the shop. An hour passed before they knew it. Véra Pávlovna went with Kirsánov through the different rooms, showing him everything. They were going from the dining-room to the work-rooms, when Véra Pávlovna was approached by a young girl who originally was not there. The working girl and Kirsánov looked at each other.

"Nastenka!"

"Sásha!" *

And they kissed each other.

"Sáchenka,† my friend, how happy I am to see you!"

The young girl, laughing and crying, covered him with kisses. When she had recovered from her joy, she said:

"Véra Pávlovna, I cannot talk business today. I cannot leave him. Come to my room, Sáchenka."

Kirsánov was equally overjoyed. But Véra Pávlovna noticed also much sorrow in his first look after that of recognition. And it was not at all astonishing: the young girl was in the last stage of consumption.

Nastenka Kryúkov had entered the shop a year before, being even then very sick. If she had remained in the store where she had worked up to that time, over-work would have killed her long before. But in the shop a way was found of prolonging her life a little. The working girls excused her from sewing altogether, finding her a task less tiresome and less injurious to the health. She performed different functions in the shop, took part in the general administration, and received the orders for work, so that no one could say that she was less useful in the shop than the others.

The Lopukhóvs went away without awaiting the end of Nastenka's interview with Kirsánov.

: XIV :

THE KRYÚKOV STORY

The next morning Nastenka Kryúkov came to see Véra Pávlovna.

"I wish to talk with you about what you saw yesterday, Véra Pávlovna," said she,—and for some minutes she did not know how to continue,—"I shouldn't like you to think unfavorably of him, Véra Pávlovna."

"Think unfavorably of him! as you yourself think unfavorably of me, Nastásya Borísovna."

"Another would not have thought as I do; but you know I am not like others."

* Nastenka and Sásha are the diminutives of Nastasya and Alexánder.

† A more affectionate diminutive than Sásha.

"Nastásya Borísovna, you have no right to treat yourself thus. We have known you for a year, and several members of our little society have known you longer."

"Ah! I see that you know nothing of me."

"On the contrary, I know much about you. Recently you were the waiting-maid of the actress N.; when she married, you left her to avoid her husband's father; you were employed in the store of —, before you came to us; I know all that and many details besides."

"Of course I was sure that Maximov and Cheine, who knew what I used to be, would not run to you with the story. But I thought that you or the others might have heard of it in some other way. Ah! how happy I am that they do not know. But I will tell you everything so that you may know how good he is. I was a very wicked girl, Véra Pávlovna."

"You, Nastásya Borísovna?"

"Yes, Véra Pávlovna. And I was very insolent, shameless and always drunk, that was the origin of my sickness: I drank too much for my weak chest."

Véra Pávlovna had seen three or four similar cases. Young girls whose conduct had been irreproachable ever since she knew them had told her that formerly they led a bad life. The first time she was astonished at such a confession; but after reflecting upon it a little, she said to herself: "And my own life? The mud in which I grew up was also very bad; nevertheless it did not soil me, and thousands of women, brought up in families like mine, remain pure just the same. Why is it, then, at all extraordinary that from this humiliation should come out unstained those whom a favorable opportunity has helped to escape?" The second time she was not astonished to learn that the young penitent had preserved truly human qualities,—disinterestedness, fidelity in friendship, deep feelings, and even some degree of innocence.

"Nastásya Borísovna, I have already had interviews like the one you wish to begin. Such interviews are painful both to the speaker and the listener; my esteem for you will not diminish, but will rather increase, since I know now that you have suffered much; but I understand it all without hearing it. Let's say no more about it. To me explanations are superfluous. I, too, have passed many years amid great sorrows; I try not to think of them, and I do not like to speak of them, for it is very painful to me."

"No, Véra Pávlovna, I have another motive: I wish to tell you how good he is; I should like some one to know how much I owe to him, and whom shall I tell if not you? It will be a relief to me. As to the life that I led, of course there is no occasion to speak of it. It is always the same with poor women of that sort. I only wish to tell you how I met him. It is so agreeable to me to talk about him. I'm going to live with him; so you ought to know why I leave the shop."

"If it will please you to tell this story, Nastásya Borísovna, I am very happy to listen to you. Only let me get my work."

"My work! Alas, I cannot say that. How good these girls were to find me an occupation suited to my health! I wish to thank them one and all. Tell them, Véra Pávlovna, that I begged you to thank them for me. I was walking along the Nevsky Prospect. I had just gone out, and it was still early. I saw a student coming, and directed my steps toward him. He did not say a word, but simply crossed to the other side of the street. I followed him, and grasped him by the arm. 'No,' I said to him, 'I will not leave you, you are so good-looking.'

" 'But I beg you to leave me,' he said.

" 'Oh, no; come with me.'

" 'I have no reason to.'

" 'Well, I will go with you. Where are you going? For nothing in the world will I leave you.' I was impudent, as impudent as any and more so."

"Perhaps that was because you were really timid and were making an effort to be bold."

"Yes, that may be. At least I have noticed it in others,— not at that time, mind you; it was afterwards that I understood the reason. So, when I told him that I absolutely must go with him, he smiled and said:

" 'Come, if you must; only it will be in vain.'

"He wanted to rebuke me, as he afterwards told me; he was impatient at my persistence. So I went, talking all sorts of nonsense to him: but he didn't say a word. We arrived. For a student he lived very comfortably; his lessons brought him about twenty rubles a month, and he lived alone. I stretched myself upon the divan and said:

" 'Some wine!'

" 'No,' said he, 'I shall not give you any wine; only tea, provided you want it.'

" 'With punch,' said I.

" 'No, without punch.'

"I began to act riotously; he remained calm, and looked at me without paying the slightest attention to my conduct: that offended me. In these days we meet such young people, Véra Pávlovna,—young people have grown much better since then,—but then it was very exceptional. Therefore I felt offended and began to insult him.

" 'If you are made of wood,'—and I added an insult,— 'then I am going away.'

" 'But why go now?' said he; 'have some tea first; the landlady will bring the *samovar* presently. Only no insults.'

"And he invariably addressed me in the polite form.

" 'Tell me rather who you are and how you have reached this condition.'

"I began to tell him a story of my own invention. We invent all sorts of stories, and that is why nobody believes us. Sometimes, nevertheless, these stories are not invented: there are noble and educated persons among us. He listened a little while and then said:

" 'No, it isn't a clever story. I should much like to believe it very much, but I cannot.'

"We were already taking tea. Then he said:

" 'Do you know, I see by your complexion that it is bad for you to drink; your chest is in bad condition because of it. Permit me to examine you.'

"Well, Véra Pávlovna, you will not believe me, but I suddenly felt a sense of shame, though a moment earlier I had been behaving very boldly! He noticed it.

" 'Why, no,' said he, 'I only want to sound your chest.'

"He began to listen at my chest.

" 'Yes,' he said, 'you must not drink at all; your chest is not in good condition.'

" 'That is impossible,' I said.

"And indeed it was impossible, Véra Pávlovna.

" 'Then abandon this life.'

" 'As if I'd leave it! It's such fun!'

" 'Not quite,' said he. 'Now leave me; I've got work to do.'

"And I went away, provoked at having lost my evening, to say nothing of the fact that his indifference had offended me. We girls have our pride in these matters. A month later I happened to be passing that way.

" 'Shall I call,' thought I, 'upon my wooden gentleman, and amuse myself a little with him?'

"It wasn't dinner-time yet, the night before I had slept well, and I hadn't been drunk. He was reading a book.

" 'How do you do, my wooden sir?'

" 'How do you do? What have you to say?'

"Again I began my nonsense.

" 'I will show you the door,' said he. 'Stop it! I've told you that I don't like this. You're not drunk and can understand me. Think rather of this: your face is still more sickly than before; you must cut out wine. Fix your clothing, and let us talk seriously.'

"In fact, I had already begun to feel pains in my chest. Again he sounded it, told me that the disease was growing worse, said a great deal. My chest really pained me so badly that, seized with a sudden access of feeling, I began to weep. I didn't want to die, and he filled me with fears of consumption.

" 'But,' I said to him, 'how shall I leave this life? My mistress will not let me go away, for I owe her seventeen rubles. They always keep us in debt so that we have to keep on.'

" 'Seventeen rubles? I cannot give them to you now, for I don't have them; but come the day after to-morrow.'

"That seemed to me very strange, for it was not with this in view that I had spoken as I did. Besides, how could I have expected such an offer? I could not believe my ears, and I began to cry still harder, believing that he was making fun of me.

" 'You shouldn't make fun of a poor girl, when you see that I am crying.'

"For some minutes longer I refused to believe it. Finally he assured me that he was not joking. Would you believe it? He got the money and gave it to me two days afterwards. I could scarcely believe it then.

" 'But how is this?' said I; 'but why do you do this, when you don't want to have anything to do with me?'

"I freed myself from my mistress and hired a little room. But there was nothing that I could do. In freeing us they give us a special kind of certificate; where could I turn with such a document? And I had no money. Consequently I lived as before, though not exactly as before. I received only

my best acquaintances, those who did not abuse me. I left
wine alone. What was the difference, then, you ask? My life
was much easier than it had been. But it was still hard; and
let me tell you something. You will think that it was distressing because I had many friends, five perhaps. No, for I
felt an affection for all of them; hence it wasn't that. Pardon
me if I speak thus to you, but it is because I am sincere with
you: today I am still of the same mind. You know me; am I
not modest? Who has heard anything but good of me? How
much time I spend in playing with the children in the shop,
and they all love me, and the old ladies will not say that I
teach them anything but the best. It is only with you, Véra
Pávlovna, that I am sincere; today I am still of the same
mind: if you feel affection, there is no harm, provided there
is no deceit; if there is deceit, that is another thing. And in
that way I lived. Three months went by, and in that time,
I obtained considerable rest, and although I had to get the
money that I needed in this manner, I no longer considered
that I was leading a wicked life.

"Sáchenka often visited me in those days. I too went sometimes to see him. And now I have got back to my subject,
from which I should not have wandered. Only he didn't
visit me for the same purpose that the others did. He
watched over me, so that I shouldn't slip back into my former addiction—wine. And indeed, during the first days he
restrained me, for I had a terrible yearning for wine. I was
afraid lest he should come in and catch me . . . And truly,
without him, I couldn't have resisted the urge because my
friends—nice fellows—would say, 'I'll send out for some
wine.' But wishing to heed Sáchenka's advice, I answered
them: 'No, don't!'

"In three weeks' time my will was already much stronger:
the desire for drink had gone, and I had already thrown off
the manners peculiar to victims of intoxication. During that
time I saved in order to repay him. and in two months I
did repay him everything. He was so glad to see me repay
him! The next day he brought me muslin for a dress and
other articles bought with the same money. After that he
still kept up his visits, always a doctor caring for a patient.
One day when at my room, about a month after I had paid
my debt, he said to me: 'Now Nastenka, you please me.'

"Drunkenness spoils the face; in consequence of my sobriety my complexion had grown softer and my eyes clearer. Further, having thrown off my old manners, I had become more modest.

"On hearing these words I was so happy that I wanted to throw myself on his neck, but I did not dare. He said to me:

" 'You see, Nastenka, that I am not without feeling.'

"He told me also that I had grown pretty and modest, and he covered me with caresses. He took my hand, placed it in his own, and caressed it with his other hand while looking at it. My hands in those days were white and plump. These caresses made me blush. After such a life, too! I felt a sort of maiden bashfulness; it is strange, but it is true. In spite of my shame,—yes, my shame, although the word seems ridiculous when uttered by me,—I said to him:

" 'What gave you the idea of caressing me, Alexánder Matvéich?'

"He answered:

" 'Because, Nastenka, you are now a virtuous girl.'

"These words made me so happy that I burst into tears.

" 'What is the matter with you, Nastenka?' said he, embracing me. This kiss turned my head, and I fainted. Would you believe, Véra Pávlovna, that such a thing could have happened to me after such a life?

"The next morning I wept, saying to myself: What shall I do now, poor girl? How shall I live? There is nothing left for me but to throw myself into the Néva. I felt that I could no longer live as I had lived. I would rather be dead. I had loved him a long time, but as he had shown no sentiment toward me and as I had no hope of pleasing him, this love had become torpid in me, and I did not even realize it. Now all was clear. When one feels such a love, how can one even look at another man? Therefore I wept and said to myself: What shall I do now, without any means of existence? I had this idea: I will go to him, see him once more, and then drown myself. I wept all that morning. Suddenly he entered, kissed me, and said:

" 'Nastenka, will you live with me?'

"I told him what I thought. And we began to live together.

"Those were happy days, Véra Pávlovna, and I believe that few persons have ever enjoyed such happiness. He never stopped gazing at me! The number of times I'd wake up and see him sitting there with his book . He'd come over to look at me, and then he'd sit there and just lose himself looking at me. And he was so shy, Véra Pávlovna. You see, it was only afterwards that I began to understand—after I began to read books and discovered how they describe love in novels. It was only then that I learnt to understand him. But even though he was so shy, he never stopped gazing at me! What a feeling that is, when a man you love gazes at you like that. You can't imagine what happiness that is. It was a bit like that when he kissed me for the first time. My head swam, I sank into his arms and it was a sweet feeling. But then, you know, your blood boils, you feel agitated and there's something painful in those sweet feelings. Although of course you'd lay down your life for just one moment of such happiness—and people *do* just that too, Véra Pávlovna. Well, of course, that is a tremendous joy, but it's not that I'm talking about. I'm talking about the times you sit there on your own, daydreaming. 'Ah, how I love him!' you think to yourself. And at those times there's no agitation, no pain to spoil the pleasure—it's a much steadier, quieter feeling. And when the man you love loves you too it's the same, only a thousand times stronger. You feel so peaceful, your heart doesn't pound with agitation but beats more evenly, more gently, and it feels so good. Your breast seems to swell and you breathe more easily—yes that's certainly true, you actually breathe more easily!

"And everything is so easy! An hour, two hours can pass in a minute—no, not a minute, nor a second, for time doesn't exist. You fall asleep, and when you wake up it seems such a long time since you fell asleep—then you discover it was no time at all, less than a minute. Yet you don't feel at all weary, you feel refreshed and full of energy, well rested, as though you'd had a long sleep. And you *have* rested! As I said, you breathe more easily, and that's the most important thing. There is such power in a person's gaze, Véra Pávlovna. No amount of caresses or sweet looks can warm you like that. This is the most blissful thing about love.

"And so he kissed me and loved me—oh, such pleasure! It's impossible to imagine it if you haven't experienced it yourself. But you know that, Véra Pávlovna.

"He would kiss my hands and my eyes, then my breasts, my legs—everything. And you know, I didn't feel embarrassed a bit. And I was the same person as I am now. You know, I feel shy when women look at me, Véra Pávlovna, indeed I do. Our girls will tell you how bashful I am—I need a room of my own. Now it's a strange thing, and you won't believe it, but when he looked at me and kissed me I didn't feel the slightest bit shy. I loved it, and I breathed more easily. I'm shy with our girls but I'm not shy of his kisses—why do you think that is, Véra Pávlovna? Maybe it's because I never thought of him as separate from me. I always thought of us as one person. It wasn't as if he was looking at me, but as if I were looking at myself. Yes that's it—that was how it seemed to me and that was why I wasn't embarrassed. But I don't need to tell *you* all this, Véra Pávlovna, you know it already. It's just that when you start thinking about these things you can never stop. No, I'm going now, really, I'll not say another word. But I can say no more to you today, Véra Pávlovna. I only wanted to tell you how good Sáchenka is.''

: X V :

Subsequently Nastenka Kryúkov finished telling her story to Véra Pávlovna. She lived with Kirsánov more than two years. The symptoms of incipient disease seemed to have disappeared. But toward the end of the second year, with the opening of spring, consumption showed itself in a considerably advanced stage. To live with Kirsánov would have been to condemn herself to speedy death; by renouncing this tie she could count on again staving off her disease for a long time. They resolved to separate. To give herself to constant labor would have been equally fatal. Therefore she had to find employment as a housekeeper, maid-servant, nurse, or something of the sort, and that too in a house where the work was not too heavy and where—a no less important consideration—there would be nothing disagreeable, conditions rare enough. Nevertheless such a place was found. Kirsánov had acquaintances among the rising artists; thanks to them, Nastenka Kryúkov became the maid of a Russian actress, an excellent woman. They were a long time in making the separation. "Tomorrow I will go," said Nastenka, and tomorrow came with other tomorrows to find her still there. They wept and could not tear themselves from each other's arms. Finally the actress, who knew all, came herself to find Nastenka, and, cutting everything short, took her away in order that the hour of separation might not be further protracted to the injury of her future servant.

As long as the actress remained upon the stage Nastenka was very well fixed. The actress was very tactful, and the young Kryúkov set a high value upon her place. To find another like it would have been difficult, so she devoted herself to her mistress, who, seeing this, showed her even more kindness. The servant therefore lived very quietly, and there was little or no development of her disease. But the actress married, left the stage, and went to live in her husband's family. There, as Véra Pávlovna already knew, the actress's father-in-law made advances to her servant. The latter was in no danger of seduction, but a family quarrel broke out. The ex-actress began to blame the old man, and he began to get angry. Nastenka, not wishing to be the cause of a family quarrel, gave up her job.

That occurred about two years after her separation from

: **X V I** :

Four months have passed. The care that he had had to bestow upon Nastenka and the memory of the poor girl had Kirsánov. During all that time they had not seen each other. At first he visited her; but the joy of the interview had such a bad effect upon her that he obtained her permission, in consideration of her own good, to discontinue the visits.

She tried to live as a servant in two or three other families, but everywhere she found so many incompatibilities that it was preferable to become a seamstress; it was as well to condemn herself to the rapid development of the disease which was bound to develop in any case as a result of her too exciting life; it was better to submit herself to the same destiny as a result of labor alone, unaccompanied by any disagreeable features. When she entered Véra Pávlovna's shop, Lopukhóv, who was the doctor, did his best to slow down the progress of the consumption. He did much,—that is, much considering the difficulty of the case, his success being really insignificant,—but the end was inevitable. The end, precipitated by Kirsánov's visit to the shop, would have been reached two or three weeks later anyway.

absorbed Kirsánov. It seemed to him now that his love for Véra Pávlovna was thoroughly conquered; he did not avoid her when during her visits to the young Kryúkov she met him and talked with him, nor afterwards when she tried to distract him. Indeed, as long as he felt any fear of his feelings toward Véra Pávlovna, he checked them, but now he felt no more than a friendly gratitude toward her, proportional to the service she had done him.

But—the reader knows already in advance the meaning of this "but," as he always will know in advance what is going to happen in the course of the story—but it is needless to say that the feeling of Kirsánov toward the young Kryúkov, at the time of their second coming together, was not analogous to that of her toward him. He no longer loved her; he was only well disposed toward her, as one is toward a woman whom he has loved. His old love for her had been no more than a youth's desire to love some one, no matter whom. It is needless to say that Nastenka was never a match for him, for they were not equals in intellectual development. As he matured, he could do no more than pity her; he could be kind to her for memory's and compassion's sake, and that was all. His sorrow at having lost her disappeared very quickly, after all. But after this sorrow had really disappeared, he believed that he still felt it. When he finally realized that he felt it no longer, and that it was only a memory, he saw that his relations with Véra Pávlovna were fatal.

Véra Pávlovna tried to divert him from his thoughts, and he allowed her to do so, believing himself incapable of succumbing, or, rather, not even believing that he felt a lover's passion for her. During the two or three months that followed he passed almost every evening at the Lopukhóvs', or else accompanied Véra Pávlovna in her walks; often Lopukhóv was with them, but more often they went alone. That was all, but that was too much, not only for him, but for her also.

: XVII :

VÉRA PÁVLOVNA'S THIRD DREAM

At this time Véra Pávlovna had a dream.

After having taken tea and talked with her "darling," she
went to her room and lay down all dressed for a moment,
not to sleep,—it was too early, being only half-past eight,—
but only to read. There she is, on her bed, reading. But the
book falls from her hands. She reflects and says to herself:
Why does *ennui* sometimes come over me of late? It simply
occurred to me that I wanted to go to the opera this evening.
But Kirsánov is so inattentive! He went too late to get the
tickets. He ought to know, however, that, when Bosio sings,
tickets are not to be had at eleven o'clock for two rubles
each. Can Kirsánov be blamed? If he had had to work until
five o'clock, I am sure he would not have admitted it. But
it is his fault just the same. No, in the future I will rather
ask my "darling" to get the tickets, and I will go with him
to the opera: my "darling" will not leave me without tickets,
and, as for accompanying me, he will be always very happy
to; he is so agreeable, my "darling." Now, thanks to this
Kirsánov, I have missed "La Traviata"; it's horrid!

But when did Bosio get time to learn Russian? And to
pronounce it so well? Where did she unearth those verses
that are so licentious? She probably studied Russian with
the same grammar that I used: those verses are quoted in it
as an example of punctuation, which is very stupid. If only
those verses were not so licentious; but there is no time to
think of the words, for one has to listen to her voice.

> *Consacre à l'amour*
> *Ton heureuse jeúnesse,*
> *Et cherche nuit et jour*
> *L'heure de l'ivresse.*

How queer these words are! But what a voice and what
sentiment! Yes, her voice is much improved; it is admirable
now. How did Bosio succeed in reaching such a point? I did
not know how to make her acquaintance, and here she is,
come to make me a visit. How did she learn of my wish?

"You have been calling me a long time," said Bosio, in
Russian.

"I? How could I have done so, when I am not acquainted
with you? No matter, I am glad, very glad, to see you."

Véra Pávlovna opens her curtains to extend her hand to
Bosio, but the singer begins to laugh; it is not Bosio, but
rather De-Merick playing the Bohemian in "Rigoletto." But
if the gay laugh is De-Merick's, the voice is really Bosio's;

she draws back abruptly and hides behind the curtain. What a pity!

"Do you know why I have come?" said the apparition, laughing as though she were De-Merick instead of Bosio.

"But who are you? You are not De-Merick?"

"No."

"Then you are Bosio?"

Fresh laughter. "You recognize quickly, but we must now attend to the business on which I have come. I wish to read your diary with you."

"I have no diary; I never kept any."

"But look! what is that on the little table?"

Véra Pávlovna looks: on the little table near the bed lies a writing-book inscribed: *Diary of V. L.* Where did this writing-book come from? Véra Pávlovna takes it, opens it, —it is written in her hand: but when?

"Read the last page," says Bosio.

Véra Pávlovna reads: "Again it happens that I remain alone entire evenings. But that is nothing: I am used to it."

"Is that all?" says Bosio.

"All."

"No, you do not read all. You cannot deceive me. And what is this here?"

Véra Pávlovna sees a hand stretch forth. How beautiful this hand is! No, this marvellous hand is not Bosio's. And how did it pierce the curtains without opening them? The hand touches the page; at its contact new lines stand out which were not there before.

"Read."

Véra Pávlovna reads: "No, now I am bored in my solitude. Formerly I was not bored. Why is this so?"

"Turn one page back."

Véra Pávlovna turns the leaf: "Summer of this year. We are going, as usual, out of the city to the islands. This time my darling accompanies us; how contented I am!" (Ah! it is August. What day of the month,—the fifteenth or the twelfth? Yes, yes, about the fifteenth; it was after this excursion that my poor darling fell sick, thinks Véra Pávlovna.)

"Is that all?"

"All."

"No, you do not read all. And what is this here?" (And the marvellous hand again stretches forth, and more new lines appear.)

Véra Pávlovna reads without wishing to: "Why doesn't my darling accompany us oftener?"

"Turn another leaf."

"My darling is so busy, and it is always for me, always for me that he works, my darling." (That is really the answer, thinks Véra Pávlovna with joy.)

"Turn one page more."

"How honest and noble these students are, and how they esteem my darling! And I am gay in their company; with them I feel as if I were with brothers, quite at my ease."

"Is that all?"

"All."

"No, read farther" (and for the third time the hand stretches forth causing new lines to appear).

Véra Pávlovna reads unconsciously: "August 16" (that is, the day after the excursion to the islands; it did occur then on the fifteenth, thinks she). "On the excursion my darling talked the whole time with that Rakhmétov, the rigorist, as they jokingly call him, and with his other comrades. He stayed with me scarcely a quarter of an hour." (That is not true; it was over half an hour; over half an hour, I am sure, thinks she, without counting the time when we sat side by side in the boat.) "August 17. Yesterday we had the students here all the evening;" (yes, it was the night before my darling fell sick). "My darling talked with them all the evening. Why does he devote so much time to them and so little to me? He does not work all the time. For that matter he says himself that without rest labor is impossible, that he rests a great deal, and that he reflects upon some special idea in order to rest himself; but why does he meditate alone, without me?"

"Turn another leaf."

"In July of this year we have had the students twice, as usual; I have played with them a great deal, I was so gay. Tomorrow or the day after tomorrow they will come again, and again I shall be gay."

"Is that all?"

"All."

"No, read farther" (the hand reappears, and new lines respond to its contact). Again Véra Pávlovna reads unconsciously:

"From the beginning of the year to the end of spring. Yes, formerly I was gay with these students, but I was gay and that was all. Now I often say to myself: These are children's games; they will probably seem amusing to me for a long time to come, and even when I shall be old. When I shall be no longer of an age to take part in them, I shall contemplate the games of youth and thus recall my childhood. But even now I look upon these students as younger brothers, and I should not like to transform myself forever into playful Vérochka. I am Véra Pávlovna now; to amuse myself as Vérochka is pleasant from time to time, but not always."

"Turn a few pages farther back."

"I went to Julie's to get her orders. She did not let us go away without breakfast; she ordered champagne, and made me take two glasses. We began to sing, run, shout, and wrestle. I was so gay! My darling looked at us and laughed."

"Is that quite all?" says the apparition, again stretching forth the hand, which always produces the same result,— the appearance of new lines.

Véra Pávlovna reads:

"My darling only looked and laughed. Why did he not play with us? It would have been even merrier. Would he have acted clumsily? Not at all. But it is his character. He confines himself to avoid interference; he approves, rejoices, and that is all."

"Turn a page forward."

"This evening we went, my darling and I, for the first time since our marriage, to see my parents. It was so painful to me to see again this interior which oppressed and stifled me before my marriage. Oh, my darling! From what a hideous life he has delivered me! At night I had a horrible dream: I saw Mamma, who reproached me with being ungrateful; it seemed to me that that was the truth, and this conviction made me groan. My darling, hearing my groans, ran to my side; when he entered my room, I was singing (though still asleep); the presence of the fair one, whom I love so much, had soothed me. My darling wished to dress me. I was terribly embarrassed, but he is so reserved; he only kissed my shoulder."

"Is that really all that is written there? You cannot deceive me. Read." Again under the fatal hand other characters arise, and Véra Pávlovna reads them, still unconsciously:

"And as if that were offensive!"

"Turn a few pages back."

"Today I waited for my friend D. on the boulevard near the Pont Neuf: there lives the lady by whom I wished to be employed as a governess. But she would not give her consent. D. and I returned to the house very much worried. Going to my room before dinner, I had ample time to consider that it would be better to die than to live as I had lived. Suddenly at dinner D. said to me: 'Véra Pávlovna, let us drink to the health of my sweetheart and yours.' I could scarcely keep from weeping tears of joy before everybody for this unexpected deliverance. After dinner I talked a long time with D. as to the way we should live. How I love him: he is helping me leave my cellar."

"Read, read the whole."

"There is no more there."

"Look." (The hand stretches forth.)

"I do not wish to read," says Véra Pávlovna, seized with fright. "Do I really love him because he delivered me from my cellar? *No, I love not him, but my deliverance.*"

"Turn farther back; read the first page."

"Today, the anniversary of my birth, I talked with D. for the first time, and formed an affection for him. I have never heard any one speak such noble and strengthening words. How he sympathizes with everything that is worthy, how he longs to aid all that calls for aid! How sure he is that the happiness of mankind is possible and must come some day; that wickedness and pain are not perpetual, and that a new and peaceful life is approaching with ever hastening steps! How my heart beat with joy when I heard these things from a learned and serious man! They confirmed my own thoughts. How good he was when he spoke of us, poor women! Any woman would love such a man. How wise, noble, and good he is!"

"Exactly; turn again to the last page."

"But I have already read that page."

"No, that was not quite the last. Turn one leaf more."

"Read, read! Do you not see? So much is written there." And the contact of the hand calls forth lines which were not there at first.

Véra Pávlovna trembles:

"I do not wish to read; I cannot."

"I command you. You must."

"I am neither willing nor able."

"Well, I will read what you have written there. So listen:

'He has a noble soul, he is my liberator. But a noble character inspires esteem, confidence, a disposition to act in
concert, friendship; the liberator is rewarded by gratitude,
devotion, and that is all. His nature, perhaps, is more ardent
than mine. His caresses are passionate. But he has another
need; he needs a soft and slow caress; he needs to slumber
peacefully in tender sentiment. Does he know all that? Are
our natures, our needs, analogous? He is ready to die for me,
and I for him. But is that enough? Does he live in the
thought of me? Do I live in the thought of him? Do I love
him as much as I need to love? In the first place, I do not
feel this need of a soft and tender sentiment; no, my feeling
towards him is not . . .' "

"I will hear no more," and Véra Pávlovna indignantly
threw away the diary. "Wicked woman, why are you here?
I did not call you; go away!"

The apparition laughs, but with a gentle and good laugh.

"No, you do not love him; these words are written with
your own hand."

"Damnation!" Véra Pávlovna awoke with this exclamation, and had no sooner regained possession of herself than
she rose and ran.

"My darling, embrace me, protect me! I have had a frightful dream!" She presses herself against her husband. "My
darling, caress me, be affectionate with me, protect me!"

"What is the matter, Vérochka? You are trembling all
over," said Lopukhóv, as he embraced her. "Your cheeks are
moist with tears, and your brow is covered with a cold sweat.
You have walked in bare feet over the floor; let me kiss your
feet to warm them."

"Yes, caress me, save me! I have had a horrible dream; I
dreamed that I did not love you."

"But, dear friend, whom do you love, then, if not me?
That's a very strange dream!"

"Yes, I love you; but caress me, embrace me! I love you,
and I wish to love you."

She embraced him with intensity, she pressed her whole
form against him, and, soothed by his caresses, she gently
fell asleep in his embrace.

: XVIII :

That morning Dmítry Sergéich did not have to call his wife

to take tea; she was there, pressing herself against him; she still slept; he looked at her and thought: "What is the matter with her? What has frightened her? What does this dream mean?"

"Stay here, Vérochka, I am going to bring the tea; do not rise; my darling, I am going to bring the water for you to wash so that you won't have to disturb yourself."

"Yes, I will not rise, I will remain in bed a while longer, I am so comfortable here. How good you are, my darling, and how I love you! There! I have washed; now bring the tea; no, embrace me first."

And Véra Pávlovna held her husband a long time in her arms. "Ah, my darling, how strange I am! How I ran to your side! What will Másha think now? We will hide this from her. Bring me my clothes. Caress me, my darling, caress me; I wish to love you, I need to love! I wish to love you as I have not yet loved you!"

Véra Pávlovna's room remains empty. Véra Pávlovna conceals nothing more from Másha, and is completely established in her husband's room. "How tender you are! How affectionate, my darling! And I imagined that I did not love you! How strange I am!"

Two weeks pass. Véra Pávlovna takes her ease. Now she stays in her room only when her husband is not at home or when he is at work; but no, even when he is at work, she stays in his study, except when Dmítry Sergéich's task demands all his attention. But such tasks are rare, and very often scientific work is purely mechanical; so three-quarters of the time Lopukhóv saw his wife by his side. They lacked but one thing; it was necessary to buy another divan, a little smaller than her husband's. This was done, and Véra Pávlovna took her ease after dinner on her little divan, watching her husband sitting before her.

"My dear friend, why do you kiss my hands? I do not like that."

"Truly? I had quite forgotten that I offend you; and besides, what does it matter, for I shall do it just the same."

"You deliver me for the second time, my darling: you have saved me from wicked people, you have saved me from myself! Caress me, my dear friend, caress me!"

A month passes. Véra Pávlovna still willingly takes her ease. He sits down beside her on the divan; she throws herself into his arms, but becomes pensive; he embraces her; she is still pensive, and her tears are ready to flow.

"Vérochka, dear Vérochka, why are you so pensive?"

Véra Pávlovna weeps and doesn't say a word.

"No, do not embrace me, my dear friend! That is enough. I thank you."

And she gives him a glance so soft and so sincere.

"I thank you; you are so good to me."

"'Good,' Vérochka? What do you mean?"

"Good, yes, my dear friend, you are good!"

. . .

Two days passed. After dinner Véra Pávlovna, pensive, lay stretched upon her bed. Her husband was near her, held her in his arms, and seemed equally pensive.

"No, that is not it; something is lacking."

"How good he is, and how ungrateful I am!" thought Véra Pávlovna.

Such were their thoughts.

She said in a simple tone and without sadness:

"Go to your room, my dear friend; to work or to rest."

"Why are you driving me away, Vérochka? I'm comfortable here."

He was able to say these words, as he wished, in a simple and gay tone.

"No, go away, my dear friend. You do so much for me. Go and rest."

He embraced her, and she forgot her thoughts and breathed again quite freely and as if nothing saddened her.

"I thank you, my dear friend," she said.

: XIX :

Lopukhóv thought about her dream. It was not for him to consider whether she loved him or not; that was her affair, and in this she was no more mistress than he was master. This was a point that must clear itself up, to be thought of only leisurely; now time was pressing, and his business was to analyze the causes of this presentiment.

At first it was a long time before he could discover anything. He had seen clearly for some days that he could not keep her love. It would be a painful loss, but what was to be done? If he could change his character, acquire this inclination for gentle affection which the nature of his wife demanded, that would be another matter, certainly. But he saw that this would be a vain attempt. If this inclination is not given by nature or developed by life independently of the intentions of the man himself, it cannot be created by the effort of his will; now, without the inclination nothing is as it should be. Hence for him the question was solved. So this was the problem of his first reflections. Now, after having meditated on his own situation (as an egoist thinking first of himself and of others only secondarily), he could approach the affair of another,—that is, of his wife. What can be done for her? She does not yet understand what is going on within her, she is not yet as well versed as he in affairs of the heart, and very naturally, being four years younger, which at that early age is a great deal. Couldn't he, as the more experienced, trace this dream back to its cause?

Immediately this supposition came into Lopukhóv's mind. The cause of her thoughts must be sought in the circumstance which gave rise to her dream. She said that she was vexed because she did not go to the opera.

Lopukhóv began to examine his way of living and that of his wife, and the light dawned on his mind. Most of the time when they had nothing to do she had remained in solitude, as he did. Then had come a change: she had had distractions. Now the more sober life had returned. She had not been able to accept it with indifference, for it was no more in her nature to do so than in that of the great majority of mankind. So far there is nothing extraordinary. The solution of the enigma lay in her association with Kirsánov, an association followed by the latter's separation. But why did Kirsánov go away? The cause seems only too natural,—lack of time, pressure of duties. But one cannot deceive, though he use all possible stratagems, an honest, intelligent man, experienced in life.

After a half-hour's meditation all was clear to Lopukhóv in Kirsánov's relations with Véra Pávlovna. It was clear, indeed, but nevertheless Lopukhóv did not cease to ponder over it, and this reverie ended in a decisive and complete discovery, which so impressed him that he could not sleep. But why wear out one's nerves through insomnia? It is three o'clock. If one cannot sleep, he must take morphine. He took two pills; "I will take just one look at Vérochka." But instead of going and looking, he drew his armchair up to the divan upon which his wife lay asleep, and sat down there; then he took her hand and kissed it.

"You are still at work, my darling, and always for me! How good you are, and how I love you!" she murmured in her sleep. No laceration of the heart can endure against morphine in sufficient quantities. On this occasion two pills were enough. Therefore sleep took possession of him. This laceration of the heart was approximately equal in intensity (according to Lopukhóv's materialism) to four cups of strong coffee, to counteract which one pill would not have **been enough while three pills would have been too many. He went to sleep, laughing at the comparison.**

: X X :

A THEORETICAL CONVERSATION

Scarcely had Kirsánov stretched himself out the next day like a veritable sybarite, a cigar between his lips, to read and to rest after his dinner, which had been delayed by his duties at the hospital, when Lopukhóv entered.

"I am as much in the way here as a dog in a bowling alley," said Lopukhóv in a jocose though not at all trifling tone; "I am disturbing you, Alexánder. It is absolutely necessary that I should talk seriously with you. It is pressing; this morning I overslept and should not have found you."

Lopukhóv did not seem to be trifling.

"What does this mean? Can he have noticed anything?" thought Kirsánov.

"Let us have a talk," continued Lopukhóv, sitting down; "look me in the face."

"Yes, he is speaking of *that;* there is no doubt about it," said Kirsánov to himself. Then aloud and in a still more serious tone: "Listen, Dmítry; we are friends. But there are things that even friends must not permit themselves. I beg you to drop this conversation. I don't feel like talking today. And on this subject I am never disposed to talk."

Kirsánov's eyes had a steady look of animosity, as if there were a man before him whom he suspected of an intention to commit some act of meanness.

"Quiet! That cannot be, Alexánder," continued Lopukhóv, in a calm though somewhat hollow voice; "I have seen through your manœuvres."

"I forbid you to speak unless you wish me for an eternal enemy, unless you wish to forfeit my esteem."

"You weren't afraid to lose my esteem before! Remember? Now everything is clear. I didn't pay sufficient attention at that time."

"Dmítry, I beg you to go away, or I shall have to go myself."

"You cannot. Is it with your interests that I am concerned?"

Kirsánov did not say a word.

"My position is advantageous. Yours in conversation with me is not. I seem to be performing an act of heroism. But such notions are silly. I cannot act otherwise; common sense forces me to it. I beg you, Alexánder, to put an end to your manœuvres. They accomplish nothing."

"What? Is it too late already? Pardon me," said Kirsánov quickly, unable to tell whether it was joy or chagrin that moved him when he heard the words: "They accomplish nothing."

"No, you do not understand me correctly. It was not too late. Nothing has happened so far. What will happen we shall see. For the rest, Alexánder, I don't understand what we're talking about. We don't understand each other. Am I right? Enigmas that you do not understand are disagreeable to you. But there is no enigma here. I have said nothing. I have nothing to say to you. Give me a cigar; I have carelessly forgotten mine. I will light it, and we will discuss scientific questions; it was not for that that I came, but to spend the time in chatting about science. What do you think of these strange experiments in the artificial production of albumen?"

Lopukhóv drew another chair up to his own to put his feet on it, seated himself comfortably, lighted his cigar, and continued his remarks:

"In my opinion it is a great discovery, if it be not contradicted. Have you reproduced the experiments?"

"No, but I must do so."

"How fortunate you are in having a good laboratory at your disposition! Reproduce them, reproduce them, I beg of

you, but with great care. It is a complete revolution in the
entire alimentary economy, in the whole life of humanity,—
the manufacture of the principal nutritive substance directly
from inorganic matter. That is an extremely important discovery, equal to Newton's. Don't you think so?"

"Certainly. Only I doubt very much the accuracy of the
experiments. Sooner or later we shall reach that point, indisputably; science clearly tends in that direction. But now
it is scarcely probable that we have already got there."

"That is your opinion? Well, it is mine, too. So our conversation is over. *Au revoir,* Alexánder; but, in taking leave
of you, I beg you to come to see us often, as in the past.
Good-bye."

Kirsánov's eyes, fixed on Lopukhóv, shone with indignation.

"So, Dmítry, you wish to leave with me the opinion that
you have low thoughts?"

"Not at all. But you ought to see us. What is there so
extraordinary in that? Aren't we friends? My invitation is a
very natural one."

"I can't. You began upon a senseless and therefore dangerous matter."

"I do not understand of what affair you speak, and I must
say that I don't like this conversation any more than you did
two minutes ago."

"I demand an explanation of you, Dmítry."

"There is nothing to explain or to understand. You are
getting angry for nothing, and that is all."

"No, I can't let you go away like that." Kirsánov seized
Lopukhóv by the hand as he was on the point of starting.
"Sit down. You must listen to me now."

Lopukhóv sat down.

"What right have you," began Kirsánov in a voice still
more indignant than before,—"what right have you to demand of me what is painful to me? Am I under obligation
to you in anything? And what's the use? It's absurd. Stop
this romantic nonsense. What we both recognize as normal
life will prevail when society's ideas and customs shall be
changed. Society must acquire new ideas, it is true. And it
is picking them up with the development of life. And it is
also true that he who has acquired them should aid others.
But until this radical change has taken place, you have no
right to meddle in the destiny of another. It is a terrible

thing. Do you understand? Or have you gone mad?"

"No, I understand nothing. I don't know what you are talking about. You like to attribute an unheard-of significance to a simple request of your friend who asks you not to forget him. I do not understand what reason you have to get angry."

"No, Dmítry, you cannot throw me off this conversation by joking. You are mad; a base idea has taken possession of you. We utterly reject prejudices, for instance. We do not admit that there is anything dishonoring in a blow *per se* (that idea is a silly, harmful prejudice, and nothing more). But do you have a right at the present moment to strike any one? That would be mean on your part. You would deprive such a man of the peace of his life. How stupid you are not to understand that, if I love this man and you demand that I shall strike him, I hold you for a base man and will kill either you or myself, but will not strike the blow. Besides men, there are women in the world, who are also human beings; besides blows, there are other insults. Do you understand that to submit any human being—let alone a woman—to one of these stupidities, now regarded as insults, is a despicable thing? Yes, you have dishonorable thoughts."

"You're completely right, my friend, regarding proper and dishonorable matters; only I don't know why you speak of them, or why you take me to task in the matter. I have not said a single word to you. I have no designs upon the tranquillity of any one whatsoever. You construct chimeras, that is all. I beg you not to forget me, it being agreeable to me to spend my time with you,—nothing more. Will you comply with your friend's request?"

"That is not the point, Dmítry. I will state this theoretical question in another form: has any one a right to submit a human being to a risk, if this human being is in a tolerably comfortable condition without any need of running a risk? There will come a time, we both know, when all desires will receive complete satisfaction, but we also know that that time has not yet arrived. Now, the reasonable man is content if his life is comfortable, even though such a life should not permit the development of all his faculties, the satisfaction of *all* his desires. I will suppose, as an abstract hypothesis, that this reasonable human being exists and is a woman; that the situation in which she finds it convenient to live is the marriage state; that she is content in this situation: and I ask, given these conditions, who has the right to submit this person to the danger of losing the life which satisfies her simply to see if she might not attain a better, more complete life with which she can easily dispense. The golden age will come, Dmítry, as we well know, but it is yet to come. The iron age is almost gone, but the golden age is not yet here. I pursue my abstract hypothesis: if an intense desire on the part of the person in question—suppose it, for instance, to be the desire of love—were receiving little or no satisfaction, I should have nothing to say against any danger incurred by herself, but I still protest against the risk that another might lead her to run. Now, if the person finds in her life a partial satisfaction of her new desire, she ought not to risk losing everything; and if she does not wish to run this risk, I say that he would be acting in a censurable and senseless manner who should try to make her run it. What objection do you have to offer to this hypothetical deduction? None. Admit, then, that you are not right."

"In your place, Alexánder, I should have spoken as you do. I don't say that you are interested in the matter. I know that it scarcely touches us; we speak only as thinkers, on an interesting subject, in accordance with general scientific ideas which seem to us to be just. From the general scientific standpoint, what you say is absolutely true. A in B's place is B; if, in B's place, A were not B, that would mean that he was not exactly in B's place. Am I right? If so, you have nothing to say against that, just as I have nothing to say in answer to your words. But, following your example, I will construct an abstract hypothesis, likewise having no reference to any one whomsoever. Suppose that, given three persons, one of them has a secret which he desires to hide from the second and especially from the third, and that the second discovers the secret of the first and says to him: Do what I ask of you, or I will reveal your secret to the third. What do you think of such a case?"

Kirsánov turned a little pale, and said:

"Dmítry, you are not acting rightly toward me."

"Do I need to act rightly toward you? Is it you that I am interested in? And, moreover, I do not know what you are talking about. We have spoken of science; we have mutually proposed to each other various learned and abstract problems; I have succeeded in proposing one to you which embarrasses you, and my ambition as a *savant* is satisfied. So I break off this theoretical conversation. I have much to do,—no less than you; so, *au revoir*. Do not neglect your good friends and come to see us as before."

Lopukhóv rose.

Kirsánov looked steadily at his fingers, as if each of them were an abstract hypothesis.

"You are not acting rightly toward me, Dmítry. I cannot satisfy your request. But, in my turn, I impose one condition upon you. I will visit you, but unless I go away from your house alone, you must accompany me everywhere without waiting for me to say a word. Do you understand? Without you I will not take a step either to the opera or anywhere else."

"This condition is insulting to me. Must I regard you as a robber?"

"That is not what I meant. I could not so far outrage you as to believe that you could regard me as a robber. I would put my head in your hands without hesitation. I hope that I may expect equal confidence from you. But it is for me to know what is in my thought. As for you, do as I tell you,— that is all." Lopukhóv was so moved by Kirsánov's words, "It is for me to know what is in my thought," that he said to him: "I thank you, my friend. We have never embraced each other; let us do so now."

If Lopukhóv had been able to examine his course in this conversation as a theorist, he would have remarked with pleasure: "How true the theory is, to be sure! Egoism always governs a man. That is precisely the main point, which I have hidden. 'Suppose that this person is contented with her situation,'—it was there that I should have said: 'Alexánder, your supposition is not correct'; and yet I said nothing, for it would not have been to my advantage to say it. Man likes to observe as a theorist what tricks his egoism plays him in practice. One renounces that which is lost, and egoism so shapes things that one sets himself up as a man performing an heroic act."

If Kirsánov had examined his course in this conversation as a theorist, he would have remarked with pleasure: "How true the theory is! I want to preserve my place, to rest on my laurels, and I preach that one has no right to compromise a woman's tranquillity. Now that, you will understand, means: I will act heroically, I will restrain myself, for the tranquillity of a certain person and my own. Bow, then, before my greatness of soul. It is agreeable to a man to observe as a theorist what tricks his egoism plays him in practice. I abandoned this affair so as not to be a coward. I gave myself up to the joy of triumph as if I had performed an heroic and generous act. I refuse to yield to the first word of invitation that I may not be again embarrassed in my conduct and that I may not be deprived of the sweet joy which my noble way of acting causes me, and egoism so arranges things that I have the air of a man who persists in a course of noble heroism."

But neither Lopukhóv nor Kirsánov had time to take a theoretical standpoint for the purpose of making these agreeable observations. For both of them, practice was very difficult.

: XXI :

The temporary absence of Kirsánov explained itself very naturally. For five months he had sadly neglected his duties and consequently had had to apply himself to his work assiduously for nearly six weeks. Now he had caught up and could therefore dispose more freely of his time. This was so clear that any explanation was almost useless. It was, in fact, so plausible that no doubt on the subject suggested itself to Véra Pávlovna.

Kirsánov sustained his *rôle* in the same irreproachable manner as before. He feared that his tact might fail him on his first visit to the Lopukhóvs after the scientific conversation with his friend; he feared lest he should blush with emotion on taking his first look at Véra Pávlovna, or should make it too plain that he avoided looking at her, or should make some similar mistake; but no, the first meeting passed off very well.

Yet, though Kirsánov conducted himself well, the eyes that looked at him were ready to notice many things that other eyes, no matter whose, would have been unable to see. Lopukhóv himself, in whom Mária Alexévna had discerned a man born for the management of the liquor business, was astonished at the ease of Kirsánov, who did not betray himself for a second, and as a theorist he took great pleasure in his observations, in which he was unconsciously interested on account of their psychological and scientific bearings.

His wife's eyes themselves could see nothing, but a suspicion said: "Watch closely, although you cannot see what I see"; and the aforesaid eyes examined, and, although they saw nothing, it was enough for them to examine in order to notice. For instance, Véra Pávlovna goes with her husband and Kirsánov to an evening party at the Mertzálovs'. Why doesn't Kirsánov waltz at this little party of intimate friends, where Lopukhóv himself is waltzing? It is the general rule here. Why, then, doesn't Kirsánov waltz? Finally he throws himself into it, but why does he hesitate a few minutes before beginning? Is it worth while to expend so much reflection on the question whether or not to begin an affair so serious? Not to waltz was to half betray his secret. To waltz, but not with Véra Pávlovna, was to betray it. But he was a very skillful artist in his *rôle*. He would have preferred not to waltz with Véra Pávlovna, but he saw at once that that would be noticed. Hence his hesitation. All this would not have been noticed if this same suspicion had not begun to ask a multitude of other questions quite as insignificant. Why, for instance, when, on returning from the Mertzálovs', they had agreed to go to the opera the following evening to see "Il Puritani," and when Véra Pávlovna had said to her husband: "You do not like this opera; it will tire you; I will go with Alexánder Matvéich; every opera pleases him; were you or I to write an opera, he would listen to it just the same," why didn't Kirsánov sustain the opinion of Véra Pávlovna? Why didn't he say: "That's so, Dmítry; I won't get a ticket for you"? Why was this? That her darling should go in spite of all was not strange, for he accompanied his wife everywhere. Since the time when she had said to him: "Devote more time to me," he had never forgotten it, and that could mean but one thing,—that he was good and should be loved. But Kirsánov knew nothing of this; why, then, did he not sustain the opinion of Véra Pávlovna? To be sure, these were insignificant things scarcely noticed by Véra Pávlovna and which she seldom remembered beyond the moment, but these imperceptible grains of sand fell and fell continually.

Here, for instance, is a conversation which is not a grain of sand, but a little pebble.

The following evening, while going to the opera in a single cab (for economy's sake), they talked of the Mertzálovs, praised their harmonious life, and remarked upon its rarity: so said they all, Kirsánov for his part adding: "Yes, and a very good thing about Mertzálov is that his wife can freely open her heart to him." That was all that Kirsánov said. Each of the three might have said the same thing, but Kirsánov happened to be the one to say it. But why did he say it? What did it mean? Looked at from a certain point of view, it might be a eulogy of Lopukhóv, a glorification of Véra Pávlovna's happiness with him; it might also have been said with no thought of any one but the Mertzálovs; but supposing him to have been thinking of the Mertzálovs and the Lopukhóvs, it was evident that it was said expressly for Véra Pávlovna. With what object?

So it always is: whoever sets himself to look in a certain direction always finds what he is looking for. Where another would see nothing, he very clearly distinguishes a trace. Where another does not see a shadow, he sees the shadow and even the object which throws it, whose features become more distinct with each new look, with each new thought.

Now, in this case there was, besides, a very palpable fact, in which lay hidden the entire solution of the enigma: it was evident that Kirsánov esteemed the Lopukhóvs; why, then, had he avoided them for more than two years?

It was evident that he was a very decent person, how then could he have shown himself so stupid and commonplace? As long as Véra Pávlovna had no need to think this over, she had not done so, any more than Lopukhóv had at that time. Now, however, her thoughts went in this direction.

: XXII :

Slowly and imperceptibly to herself this discovery ripened within her. Produced by Kirsánov's words or acts, even insignificant impressions which no one else would have felt accumulated within her, without any ability on her part to analyze them. She supposed, suspected, and gradually became interested in the question of why he had avoided her for nearly three years.

She became more and more firmly convinced that such a

man would not have taken himself away out of paltry ambition, for he has no ambition. All these things occurred to
her, and to add to the confusion there came into her consciousness from the silent depths of life this thought: "What
am I to him? What is he to me?"

One day after dinner Véra Pávlovna was sitting in her
room sewing and thinking, very quietly, not at first of this,
but of all sorts of things, in the house, at the shop, about
her lessons, when very quietly, very quietly these thoughts
directed themselves towards the subject which for some unknown reason occupied them more and more. Memories,
questions arose slowly; not very numerous at first, they then
increased, multiplied, and swarmed by thousands through
her head; they grew thicker and thicker, and gradually
merged themselves in a single question taking more and
more definite shape. "What is the matter with me? Of what
am I thinking? What is it that I feel?" And Véra Pávlovna's
fingers forgot to stitch, and her sewing fell from her hands,
and she grew a little pale, then blushed, turned pale again,
and then her cheeks inflamed and passed in a twinkling of
an eye from a fiery redness to a snowy whiteness. With almost haggard eyes she ran into her husband's room, threw
herself upon his knees, embraced him convulsively, and laid
her head upon his shoulder that he might support it and
hide her face.

"My dear friend, I love you," said she in a stifled voice,
bursting into tears.

"Well, my dear friend? Is there any reason in that for so
much grief?"

"I don't want to offend you. It's you I wish to love."

"You will try, you will see. If you can. In the meantime,
be calm; time will tell what you can and what you cannot
do. You have a great affection for me; then how could you
offend me?"

He caressed her hair, kissed her head, pressed her hand.
She sobbed a long time, but gradually grew calm. As for
him, he had been prepared for a long time to hear this confession, and consequently he received it imperturbably;
moreover, she did not see his face.

"I will see him no more; I will tell him that he must stop
visiting us," said Véra Pávlovna.

"Think it over yourself, my dear friend; you shall do what

seems best to you. And when you are calm, we will talk it over together."

"Whatever happens, we cannot fail to be friends. Give me your hand; clasp mine; see how warmly you press it."

Each of these words was said after a long interval,—intervals which he spent in lavishing upon her the caresses of a brother for a grieved sister.

"Remember, my friend, what you said to me on the day of our betrothal: 'You are setting me free.' "

Silence and new caresses.

"How did we define love the first time that we spoke of it? To rejoice in whatever is good for the loved one; to take pleasure in doing everything necessary to make the loved one happier,—was that not what we said?"

Silence and new caresses.

"Whatever is best for you pleases me. You will see what is best for you. Why get upset? If no misfortune has come to you, what misfortune can come to me?"

These words, often repeated after interruptions and each time with slight variations, took up considerable time, which was alike painful to Lopukhóv and to Véra Pávlovna. But on becoming calmer Véra Pávlovna began at last to breathe more easily. She embraced her husband with warmth, and with warmth kept on repeating to him: "It is you I wish to love, you alone; I wish to love only you."

He did not tell her that she was no longer mistress of herself in that matter: it was necessary to let the time slip by in order that her strength might be reëstablished by the quieting influence of some thought or other, no matter what. But Lopukhóv seized a favorable moment to write and place in Másha's hands a note for Kirsánov, which read as follows: "Alexánder, do not come in now, and do not visit us for some time. There is nothing the matter; only rest is necessary." Rest necessary, and nothing in particular the matter,—a fine conjunction of words! Kirsánov came, read the note, and told Másha that he had come on purpose to get the note, but had not time to come in now, as he had some distance yet to go, and would drop in on his way back.

The evening passed quietly, at least quietly to all appearance. Half the time Véra Pávlovna remained alone in her chamber after having sent her husband away, and half the time he sat near her, quieting her continually by a few kind words, and not so much by words either, but by his gentle and soothing voice; not gay, of course, but not sad either,— simply a little melancholy like his face. Véra Pávlovna, hearing this voice and looking at this face, began gradually to think that the matter was of no significance, and that she had mistaken for a strong passion a dream which would vanish in a couple of days.

Her feeling told her that this was not the case.

Yes, it is the case, thought she with greater firmness, and the thought prevailed. How could it have been otherwise within the hearing of this gentle voice which said that the matter was of no significance?

Véra Pávlovna went to sleep to the soft whisperings of this voice, did not see the apparition, slept quietly, and woke late and thoroughly rested.

: XXIII :

"The best relief from sad thoughts is to be found in labor," thought Véra Pávlovna (and she was quite right); "I will stay in the shop from morning till night until I am cured. That will cure me."

And so she did. The first day she really found a great deal to divert her thoughts; the second resulted in fatigue without much diversion; on the third she found no diversion at all. Thus passed a week.

The struggle was a painful one. Véra Pávlovna grew pale. But outwardly she was quite calm. She even tried to seem gay, and in this she almost always succeeded; but, though no one noticed anything and though the paleness was attributed to a slight indisposition, Lopukhóv was not at all deceived. He did not even need to look at her; he knew the whole situation.

"Vérochka," he said a week later, "in our life we are realizing the old and popular belief that the shoemaker always goes barefooted and that the tailor's clothes never fit him. We are teaching others to live according to our economic principles, and we scarcely dream of governing our own life in accordance with these same principles. One large household is much more advantageous than several small ones. I should like very much to apply this rule to our home.

If we were to bring someone else into our household, then we would all save almost half of our expenses. I could give up the lessons that I'm simply fed up with. My salary at the factory would suffice. With less work I could rest, resume my studies, and make a career for myself. It is only necessary to select persons who are congenial. What do you think about it?"

All this time Véra Pávlovna had been looking at her husband with as much distrust and indignation as Kirsánov had shown on the day of the theoretical conversation. When he had finished, she was red with anger.

"I demand that you stop this talk. It's irrelevant."

"Why, Vérochka? I am talking merely of financial advantages. Poor people like ourselves must not overlook them. My work is hard and some of it is disagreeable."

"I am not to be talked to thus." Véra Pávlovna rose. "I will permit no one to approach me with equivocations. Explain what you mean, if you dare."

"I mean, Vérochka, that, having taken our interests into consideration, we could profit."

"Again! Keep quiet! Who gave you the right to set yourself up as my guardian? I shall begin to hate you!" She ran hurriedly to her room and shut herself up.

It was their first and last quarrel.

Véra Pávlovna remained shut up in her room until late in the evening. Then she went to her husband's room.

"My dear, I spoke too severely to you. But do not be offended. You see, I am struggling. Instead of helping me, you put within my reach that which I am pushing away with the hope,—yes, with the hope of triumph."

"Forgive me, my friend, for having approached the question so crudely. Are we reconciled? Let's have a talk."

"Oh, yes, we are reconciled, dear. Only don't work against me. I have already enough to do to struggle against myself."

"And it's in vain, Vérochka. You have taken time to examine your feeling, and you see that it is more serious than you were willing to believe at first. What is the use of tormenting yourself?"

"No, dear, it is you whom I wish to love, and I do not wish, I do not wish in any way, to offend you."

"My friend, you wish me well. Do you think, then, that I find it pleasant or useful that you should continue to torment yourself?"

"But, darling, you love me so much!"

"Much, Vérochka, but what is love? Doesn't it consist in this,—to rejoice in the joy and suffer in the suffering of the person loved? In tormenting yourself you will torment me also."

"That is true, darling, but you will also suffer if I yield to this sentiment, which . . . Ah! I don't understand why this feeling was born in me! Damnation!"

"It matters very little how or why it was born. We can do nothing about that any more. There is only one choice now. Either you suffer, and I suffer on account of it, or you stop suffering and I likewise."

"But, my dear friend, I shall not suffer. This will pass. You'll see that it will pass away."

"I thank you for your efforts. I appreciate them because they show that you have the will to do what you deem necessary. But remember this, Vérochka: they seem necessary only to you, not to me. As an onlooker, I see your situation more clearly than you do. I know that this will be useless. You may struggle while you have strength; but do not think of me. Don't be afraid of offending me. You know my way of looking at these things. You know that my views are firm and really judicious. You know all that. Do you expect to deceive me? Will you stop respecting me? I might ask further: will your good feelings towards me, in changing their character, grow weaker? Won't they, on the contrary, be strengthened by this fact,—that you have not found an enemy in me? Do not pity me: my fate will be in no way deserving of pity because, thanks to me, you have not been deprived of happiness. But enough. It is painful to talk too long about these things, and still more so for you to listen to them. Go to your room, reflect, or, rather, sleep. Do not think of me, but think of yourself. Only by thinking of yourself can you prevent me from feeling useless sorrows."

: XXIV :

Two weeks later, while Lopukhóv was busy with his factory accounts, Véra Pávlovna spent the morning in a state of extreme agitation. She threw herself upon her bed, hid her face in her hands, and a quarter of an hour afterwards rose abruptly, walked up and down her room, fell into an armchair, began again to walk with an unsteady and jerky movement, threw herself again upon her bed, and then resumed her walk. Several times she approached her writing table, remained there a few moments, and went away rapidly. At last she sat down, wrote a few words, and sealed them; but half an hour afterwards she took the letter, tore it up, and burned the pieces. And her agitation began again. She wrote another letter, which she tore up and burned in turn. Finally she wrote for the third time, and as soon as she had sealed it and without taking time to address it, ran into her husband's room and threw the letter on the table. Thereupon she returned to her room, and fell into an armchair, where she remained motionless for half an hour, or perhaps an hour. A ring! It's he! She runs into his room to get the letter, tear it up, and burn it,—but where is it? It isn't there. She looks for it hastily. Where is it, then? But there was Másha opening the door. From the threshold Lopukhóv saw how Véra Pávlovna, distraught and pale, passed swiftly from his study to her own room. He did not follow her. Instead, he went to his study directly. Slowly and calmly he inspected the writing table and around it. In fact, for some days now he had been expecting something of this sort—either a talk or a letter. Ah, here it was, an unaddressed letter with her seal. It is evident that she was looking for it to destroy it. She could not have come in that condition to bring it. His papers are all in disorder, but could the poor woman have found it in her present state of agitation and mental disturbance? She had thrown it as one would throw a piece of coal which burned his fingers, and the letter had fallen on the casement behind the table. It is almost useless to read it: the contents are known. Let us read it nevertheless.

> "My dear friend, I was never so strongly attached to you as at this moment. If I could only die for you! Oh! how happy I should be to die if it would make you happy! But I cannot live without him. I offend you, I kill you, my dear friend, and I do not wish to. I act in spite of myself. Forgive me! Forgive me!"

For more than a quarter of an hour Lopukhóv remained before his table, his eyes lowered and fixed. Although the blow was expected, it was none the less terrible. Although everything necessary after such a confession had been con-

sidered and decided in advance, at first he was very much
agitated. At last he collected himself, and went to the
kitchen to speak to Másha.

"Másha, wait a little, please, before setting the table. I
don't feel well and am going to take some medicine before
dinner. As for you, don't wait for us. Eat your dinner leisurely. When I'm ready to sit down to dinner, I will tell
you."

From the kitchen he went to his wife's room. She was
lying down with her face in the pillows; on his entrance she
trembled.

"You have found it, you have read it! I must be mad!
What I have written is not true; this letter is the result of a
moment of fever and delirium."

"Certainly, my friend. There is no need of paying any attention to this letter, since you were too excited. Things of
this importance cannot be decided in such a fashion. We
have plenty of time to think the matter over, and to talk
about it calmly several times, considering its importance to
us. Meanwhile I wish to talk to you of my affairs. I've managed to make quite a few changes—all that were essential—
and am very well satisfied. Are you listening to me?"

She did not know herself whether she was listening or
not.

"Listen, then, for these are very important matters to me,"
continued the husband. It is true that she knew three-
fourths of these things. She even knew them all, but what
difference did it make? It was so good to listen. Lopukhóv
complained again of the lessons which for a long time had
been disagreeable to him. He told why, and named the families to which he felt the greatest aversion. He added that
his work of keeping the factory books was not unpleasant.
It was important and permitted him to exert an influence
over the workmen in the factory, with whom he might succeed in doing something. He had given elementary instruction to a few ardent friends, and shown them the necessity
of teaching reading and writing. He had managed to get
for these teachers payment from the owners of the factory,
once they saw that educated workmen injured the ma-
chinery less, worked better, and got drunk less frequently.
He told how he had rescued workmen from lives of drunkenness, with which object he frequented their taverns,—
and I know not what besides. But the most important thing

was that his employers esteemed him as an active and skillful man, who had gradually taken the affairs of the house
into his own hands, so that the conclusion of the story, and
the part that Lopukhóv had most at heart, was this: he had
been given the position of assistant superintendent of the
factory. The superintendent, a member of the firm, was to
have only the title and the usual salary, while he was to be
the real superintendent. It was only on this condition that the
member of the firm had accepted the position of superintendent.

"I can't . . . it's not for me."

"You just accept the post so that an honest man may occupy it. You needn't bother with the management of affairs. I'll take care of everything."

"In that case I can accept."

But it was not the power conferred that concerned Lopukhóv. The essential thing with him was that he would receive a salary of thirty-five hundred rubles, almost a thousand rubles more than before, thus enabling him to give
up all his other jobs, much to his delight. This story lasted
more than half an hour, and towards the end Véra Pávlovna
was already able to say that she really felt very well and,
after arranging her hair, would go to dinner.

After dinner Másha was given eighty copecks to get a
cab with which to carry in all directions a note from Lopukhóv, saying: "I am free, gentlemen, and shall be very glad
to see you." The horrible Rakhmétov appeared shortly, followed soon by a number of young people, and a learned
discussion began between these confident and obstinate de-
baters. They accused each other of all imaginable violations
of logic; a few traitors to this elevated discussion aided Véra
Pávlovna to pass a tolerable evening. She had already
guessed the purpose of Másha's errands. "How good he is!"
she thought to herself. Indeed, this time Véra Pávlovna was
definitely delighted with her young friends, even though she
did not participate in their levity. She sat quietly, gazed
upon them with joy and was ready to kiss Rakhmétov.

They did not break up till three o'clock in the morning.
Véra Pávlovna, tired, was no sooner in bed than her husband entered.

"In speaking to you of the factory, I forgot, my dear Vérochka, to say one thing which, however, isn't of great importance. Passing over the details,—I'm very sleepy and

you must be,—I will tell you in two words. In accepting the place of assistant superintendent, I have reserved the privilege of taking a month, or even two if I like, before entering upon my duties. I want to make good use of this time. It is five years since I've visited my parents at Ryazan; so I want to get over to see them. Till tomorrow, Vérochka. Don't get up. You'll have time tomorrow. Sleep well."

: XXV :

When Véra Pávlovna emerged from her room the next day her husband and Másha were packing two valises with his things. Másha was very busy. Lopukhóv had given her so many things to pack that she could not manage them.

"Help us, Vérochka."

All three drank their tea together while the packing was going on. Scarcely had Véra Pávlovna begun to come to herself when her husband said:

"Half past ten! It's time to go to the station."

"I'm going with you, dear."

"Dear Vérochka, I shall have two valises; there will be no room for you. Go with Másha in another cab."

"That is not what I said. To Ryazan."

"Well, in that case Másha shall take the valises, and we will go together."

In the street the conversation could not be very intimate, the noise of the pavements was so deafening!

Many things Lopukhóv did not hear; to many others he replied in such a way as not to be heard himself, or else did not reply at all.

"I am going with you to Ryazan," repeated Véra Pávlovna.

"And your things? How can you go without your things? Get ready, if you wish to. Do as you think best. I will ask only this of you: wait for my letter. It shall reach you tomorrow; I will send it by some one coming this way."

How she kissed him at the station! What names she called him when he was boarding the train! But he did not stop talking of the factory affairs, of what a good state they were in, and how glad his parents would be to see him. Nothing in the world is so precious as health. She must take care of herself. At the very moment of parting he said to her through the railing:

"You wrote me yesterday that you were never so attached to me as now. That's true, dear Vérochka. I am no less attached to you. Good feelings toward those whom we love implies a great desire for their happiness, as both of us know. Now, there is no happiness without liberty. You would not wish to stand in my way; no more do I wish to stand in yours. If you should stand in your own way for my sake, you would offend me. Therefore do nothing of the kind. And aim for your greatest good. Then we will see. You'll let me know by letter when I am to return. Goodbye, my friend! The bell rang the second time. It's time to go. Good-bye!"

: XXVI :

This happened towards the end of April. In the middle of June Lopukhóv returned to St. Petersburg for three weeks; then he went to Moscow,—on factory business, as he said. He started on the ninth of July, and on the morning of the eleventh occurred the baffling episode at the hotel near the Moscow railway station, and two hours later the scene which was enacted in a country-house on the Kamenny Island. Now the perceptive reader can no longer miss his stroke and will guess who it was that blew his brains out. "I saw long ago that it was Lopukhóv," says the reader with the penetrating eye, enchanted by his talent for divination. What has become of Lopukhóv, and how does it happen that his cap is pierced by a ball? "I do not know, but it was surely he who played this rascally bad trick," repeats the reader with the penetrating eye. So be it, obstinate reader; judge in your own way. It is impossible to make you understand anything.

: XXVII :

AN UNUSUAL MAN

About three hours after Kirsánov's departure Véra Pávlovna came back to herself, and one of her first thoughts was this: the shop cannot be abandoned. Much as Véra Pávlovna might like to demonstrate that the shop would go on of itself, she really knew very well that this was only a seductive idea, and that, to tell the truth, the shop required some such management as her own to keep it from falling to pieces. For the rest, the business was now well under way, and the management caused her but little trouble. Madame Mertzálov had two children; but she could give half an hour to it two or three times a day. She certainly would not refuse, especially as she had already accepted opportunities to do many things in the shop. Véra Pávlovna began to unpack her things for a sale, and at the same time sent Másha first to Madame Mertzálov to ask her to come, and then to a huckster named Rachel, one of the shrewdest of Jewesses, but an old and good acquaintance of Véra Pávlovna, toward whom Rachel practised the same absolute honesty that characterizes almost all the small Jewish merchants in their dealings with honest people. Rachel and Másha were to enter the apartments in the city, get all the clothes that had been left at the fur-dealer's, where Véra Pávlovna's cloaks had been deposited for the summer, and then, with all this baggage, come to the country-house, so that Rachel, after estimating the value of the goods, might buy them all at once.

As Másha stepped through the carriage entrance, she met Rakhmétov, who had been rambling about in the vicinity for half an hour.

"Are you going away, Másha? For a long time?"

"I do not expect to get back before night. I have so much to do."

"Is Véra Pávlovna alone?"

"Yes."

"Then I will go in and see her. Perhaps I will stay in your place, in case I can be useful."

"Oh, yes, do so; I am afraid for her. I have forgotten to notify any of the neighbors; there are, however, a cook and a child's nurse, two of my friends, to serve her at dinner, for she has not yet dined."

"That is nothing; no more have I; I have not dined; we can serve ourselves alone. But you,—have you dined?"

"Yes, Véra Pávlovna would not let me go away otherwise."

"Well again! I should have supposed that it would have been forgotten."

With the exception of Másha and those like her, every-

one was somewhat afraid of Rakhmétov. Lopukhóv, Kirsánov, and all those who were afraid of nothing sometimes
felt, in his presence, a sort of fear. Véra Pavlovna did not
regard him as a friend. She found him too much of a bore,
and he never mingled in her circle. But he was Másha's
favorite, although he was less amiable and talkative with
her than were Lopukhóv's other visitors.

"I have come without an invitation, Véra Pávlovna," he
began: "but I have seen Aléxander Matvéich, and I know
all. Hence I thought that I might be useful to you in some
way; so I'm going to stay with you the whole evening."

Offers of service were not to be disdained at such a moment.

Any one else in Rakhmétov's place would have been invited, and would have proposed himself, to unpack the
things; but he did not do it and was not asked to. Véra
Pávlovna pressed his hand and said to him with sincere
feeling that she was very grateful to him for his attentions
to her.

"I will stay in the study," he answered: "if you need anything, you will call me; and, if any one comes, I will open
the door. Don't disturb yourself."

Having said this, he went very quietly into the study,
took from his pocket a large piece of ham and a slice of
black bread, weighing in all about four pounds, sat down
in an armchair, ate the whole, and in trying to chew it well
drank half a decanter of water. Then he went up to the
bookshelves and began to look for something to read.

"Familiar . . . Imitation . . . Imitation . . . Imitation
. . ." This word *Imitation* referred to the works of Macaulay, Guizot, Thiers, Ranke, and Gervinus.

"Ah! here's something . . ." said he, reading on the
backs of several large volumes "Newton's Complete
Works"; he turned over the leaves, found what he was
looking for, and with a gentle smile exclaimed:

"Here it is! Here it is! 'Observations on the Prophecies
of Daniel and the Apocalypse of St. John.'

"Yes, I know little of such things as these. Newton wrote
these commentaries in his extreme old age when he was half
mad. They constitute a classic source for those studying the
question of the mingling of intellect with insanity. This is
a universally historical question; this mixture is found in all
events without exception; in almost all books, in almost all

heads. But here it must be in perfect form. In the first place, it concerns the greatest genius known. Then, the insanity mingled with this intellect is a recognized, indisputable insanity. Therefore this is a capital book of its kind. The most delicate indications of the general phenomenon must appear here in a more striking manner than in the case of any other individual, no matter who he may be, and no one can doubt that these are really the indications observable in phenomena concerning the mingling of insanity with intellect. In short, it's a book worth studying!"

So he began to read the book and with pleasure,—this book which no one had read for a century, except, perhaps, those who corrected the proofs. To any one else reading this book would have been like eating sand or sawdust, but for Rakhmétov it was a delicacy.

People like Rakhmétov are scarce. I have met but eight (of whom two were women). They resembled each other in nothing, save one point. There were among them the amiable and the stern, the melancholy and the gay, the fiery and the phlegmatic, the impressionable and the imperturbably calm. They resemble each other in only one point, I have said; but that is enough to make a special type of them and distinguish them from all other men. I laughed at those whom I knew, when I was with them; they got angry or not, but they could not help doing as much themselves. And indeed there were many ridiculous things about them, and it was in that respect that they resembled each other. I like to laugh at such people.

The one whom I met in the circle of Lopukhóv and Kirsánov, and whom I am about to describe, serves to prove that the opinions of Lopukhóv and Alexey Pétrovich on the qualities of the soil, in Véra Pávlovna's second dream, allow one exception,—namely, that, whatever the quality of the soil, one may always find little patches of ground capable of producing healthy ears.

Rakhmétov belonged to a family known since the thirteenth century,—that is, to one of the oldest families not only in Russia, but in all Europe. Among the chiefs of the Tartar regiments massacred at Tver with their army, for having tried to convert the people to Mohammedanism, according to the reports, but in reality simply for having exercised tyranny,—among these chiefs was one named Rakhmét, who had had a child by a Russian whom he had abducted, a niece of the principal court official at Tver,—that is, the high court marshal and field marshal. The child was spared on account of the mother and rebaptized as Latyfe-Mikhaïl. It is from Latyfe-Mikhaïl Rakhmétovich that the Rakhmétovs descend. At Tver they were boyars, at Moscow they were only grand officers of the crown, and at St. Petersburg in the last century they were generals-in-chief,—not all of them, of course; the family having become very numerous, certainly not all its members could be generals-in-chief. The father of the great-grandfather of our Rakhmétov was a friend of Ivan Ivanych Shuvalov, who got him out of the disgrace into which he had fallen in consequence of his friendship for Munich. His great-grandfather was the colleague of Rumiantsov, had attained the rank of general-in-chief, and was killed at the battle of Novi. His grandfather accompanied Alexánder to Tilsitt, and would have gone farther than any of the others, but his friendship with Spéransky put an early end to his career. At last his father served the government without success or disgrace. At the age of forty he resigned, and went to live as a retired lieutenant-general on one of his estates scattered along the banks of the Medvéditza and near its source. The estates, however, were not very large, containing in all about twenty-five hundred souls. But he had many children, —eight, we believe. Of these eight children Rakhmétov was the next to the last, there being one sister younger than himself; consequently his inheritance was rather small: he received about four hundred souls and seven thousand acres of land. What he did with these souls and fifty-five hundred acres of the land no one knew. Likewise no one knew that he kept fifteen hundred acres, that he was a squire, and that he derived an income of three thousand rubles from the leases of that part of the land which he kept; no one knew that while he lived among us. We did not learn it till later, but we supposed of course that he belonged to the family of Rakhmétovs containing so many rich landowners, whose aggregate wealth was estimated at seventy-five thousand souls. We knew also that our friend Rakhmétov spent four hundred a year; for a student that was much in those days, but for a landowner Rakhmétov it was very little. But it was difficult to get information, and we simply said to ourselves that our Rakhmétov belonged to some branch of the family that had fallen into poverty,—that perhaps he was a son of the counsellor of some financial board who had left his children a small capital. But of course all these things interested us but little.

Now he was twenty-two years old; he had been a student since the age of sixteen, but he had spent almost three years away from the University. At the end of his second year he went to his estate, arranged his affairs, and, after having overcome the resistance of his tutor, won the curses of his brothers, and behaved himself in such a way that the husbands of his sisters had forbidden them to pronounce his name, he began to travel through Russia by land and water in ordinary and extraordinary ways,—on foot, for instance, and in decked boats, and in boats of not much speed. He had many adventures for which he himself was responsible. He set up at his own expense two men at the University of Kazan and five at Moscow University. However, he didn't bring anyone along with him to St. Petersburg, where he planned to live himself. Consequently no one knew that he had an income of thirty thousand rubles rather than four hundred. This information didn't come out till later. Then we only saw that he had disappeared for a long time, that two years before he had entered the philological faculty, that still earlier he had been in that of the natural sciences, and that was all.

But though none of his St. Petersburg acquaintances knew anything of his relatives or his fortune, all, on the other hand, knew him by two nicknames. One of these, "the rigorist," the reader knows already; this name he accepted with his slight smile of half-content. But when they called him Nikítushka,* or Lómov, or by his full nickname, Nikítushka Lómov, a broad smile lit up his face, which was justifiable, since it was not by birth but by the firmness of his will that he had acquired the right to bear this illustrious name among millions of men. But this name is glorious only in a strip of land one hundred versts† wide crossing eight governments; to readers living in other parts of Russia this name requires explanation. Nikítushka Lómov, a boat-hauler who went up the Volga fifteen or twenty years ago, was a giant of Herculean strength; who, because of this strength, received four times the regular wages. When his boat would dock in a Volga town and its men went to

* A diminutive of Nikita.
† A verst is equivalent to a little more than half a mile.

the market or bazaar (as they call it on the Volga), people would say: "There's Nikítushka Lómov! There's Nikítushka Lómov!" and everybody ran into the street leading from the wharf to the bazaar. The people followed their hero-athlete in crowds.

When Rakhmétov, at the age of sixteen, came to St. Petersburg, he was an ordinary youth of somewhat above the average height and strength, but very far from being remarkable for his muscular force: of ten of his equals in age taken at random two surely could have thrown him. But in the middle of his seventeenth year he formed the idea of acquiring physical strength and acted accordingly. At first he practised gymnastics; it was a good plan, but gymnastics only perfects the original material; it was necessary, therefore, to equip himself with the material, and during twice as long a period as he had spent in gymnastics he became for several hours every day a laborer in search of work requiring strength; he carried water, delivered firewood, chopped it up, cut stone, dug in the earth, sawed wood, and forged iron; he tried many different kinds of work, changing very often, for with each new task, with each change, new muscles were developed. He adopted the diet of pugilists: he ate food known exclusively as strengthening, especially almost raw beef-steak, and from that time on he always lived so. A year later he took his trip, and found in it still more favorable opportunities for developing his physical strength. He had been an agricultural laborer, a carpenter, a boatman, and a worker at all sorts of healthy trades; once he even went along the Volga from Dubovka to Rybinsk as a boat-hauler. To say that he wanted to be a boat-hauler would have seemed in the last degree absurd both to the master of the boat and to the boat-haulers, and they would not have accepted him; but he took the riverbank simply as a traveller. Having put himself on friendly terms with the boat-haulers, he began to aid them in pulling the rope, and a week later became a veritable boat-hauler. They soon saw how he pulled, and they measured strength with him; he vanquished four of the strongest boat-haulers; he was then twenty years old, and his fellow-workmen christened him Nikítushka Lómov, in memory of the hero who was by then dead. The following summer he travelled by steamboat; one of the men with whom he had worked at boat-hauling happened to be in the crowd on deck, and it was in this way that some students, his fellow-travellers, learned that he had been called Nikítushka Lómov. In fact, by devoting his time to it, he had acquired and learned how to use extraordinary strength. "I must do it," he had said; "it will make me liked and esteemed by common people. And it is useful; some day it may prove good for something." And thus it was that he acquired this extraordinary strength. At the age of sixteen he came to St. Petersburg as an ordinary school-graduate, who had worthily completed his early studies. He passed his first months of study after the manner of beginners. Soon he saw that among his comrades there were some especially intelligent who did not think as the others did, and having learned the names of five or six of them (they were few in number), he interested himself in them and cultivated the acquaintance of one of them, who was no other than Kirsánov, and then his transformation into the rigorist, into Nikítushka Lómov, into an uncommon man, began. He listened to Kirsánov with passionate eagerness. The first evening that they spent together he wept; he interrupted Kirsánov with exclamations of hatred against that which must die and enthusiastic panegyrics of that which must endure.

"What books shall I begin with?" he asked.

Kirsánov informed him on this point. The next morning at eight o'clock he walked up and down the Nevsky between the Admiralty Plaza and the Police Bridge awaiting the opening of a French and German book-store where he could buy what he wanted. He read three days and nights continuously, from Thursday at eleven in the morning till Sunday at nine in the evening,—eighty-two hours in all. To keep him awake the first two nights his will alone sufficed; to keep awake the third night he drank eight cups of very strong coffee; the fourth night his strength failed him, the coffee had no effect, he fell on the floor, and slept there about fifteen hours. A week later he came to Kirsánov to ask him for the titles of some new books and explanations concerning the books he had just read; he became fast friends with him, and through him with Lopukhóv.

Six months later, although but seventeen years old, while they were already twenty-one, he was treated by them as an equal, and became thenceforth an uncommon man.

What circumstances had helped him to become an uncommon man?

His father was very intelligent, very well-informed, and ultra-conservative,—in this like Mária Alexévna, only more respectable. So far as his father went, then, the son's life was certainly a painful one. If this were all, however, it would be nothing. But his mother, a rather delicate woman, suffered from the trying character of her husband; besides, he was a witness of the life of the peasantry. And even this would be nothing. But, when about fifteen years old, he fell in love with one of his father's mistresses. The resulting to-do was, of course, quite something. He was sorry for the woman, who had suffered a great deal on his account. Thoughts began passing through his head—and here Kirsánov served the same function for him, that Lopukhóv had for Véra Pávlovna. His past life may have counted for something, it is true, in the formation of his character; but he could not have become what he was going to be if he had not been specially endowed by nature. Some time before he left the University to go first to his estate and then on his journey through Russia he had already adopted special rules for the government of his physical, moral, and intellectual life; and on his return these rules had been transformed into a complete system, to which he always held unchangeably. He had said to himself: "I will not drink a single drop of wine. I will not touch a woman." Why this resolution? So extreme a course was not at all necessary. "It must be," said he; "we demand that men may have a complete enjoyment of their lives, and we must show by our example that we demand it, not to satisfy our personal passions, but for mankind in general; that what we say we say from principle and not from passion, from conviction and not from personal desire."

For the same reason he forced himself to lead a very austere life. To become and to remain Nikítushka Lómov he had been obliged to eat meat, much meat, and he ate it in large quantities. But he looked long at a copeck spent for any food other than meat; consequently he ordered his landlady to get the best of meat, the best pieces for him, while all the other food that he ate at home was of the cheapest. He gave up white bread, and ate only black bread at his table. For whole weeks he did not taste sugar, for months together he did not touch fruit or veal or poultry, nor did he buy anything of the kind: "I have no right to spend money on a whim which I need not gratify." Yet he

had been brought up on a luxurious diet and had a keen
taste, as could be seen from his remarks about food when
dining out: he ate with relish many dishes which he denied
himself at his own table, while there were others which he
ate nowhere, and this for a well-founded reason: "Whatever the people eat, though only at intervals, I may eat
also, when occasion offers. I must not eat that which is entirely out of the reach of common people. This is necessary
so that I may feel, though but in a very slight degree, how
much harder is the life of common people than my own."
So, when fruits were served, he always ate apples, but never
apricots: at St. Petersburg he ate oranges, but refused them
in the provinces. Because at St. Petersburg common people
eat them, which is not the case in the provinces. He ate
sweets because a good cake is no worse than pie, and pie
made of puff-paste is known to common people; but he did
not eat sardines. He was always poorly clad, though fond
of elegance, and in all other things lived a Spartan's life;
for instance, he allowed himself no mattress and slept on
felt without so much as doubling it up.

But he had one thing to trouble his conscience; he did
not leave off smoking. "Without my cigar I cannot think;
if that is a fact, it is not my fault; but perhaps it is due to
the weakness of my will." He could not smoke bad cigars,
having been brought up amid aristocratic surroundings, and
he spent money for cigars at the rate of three hundred and
seventy-five rubles a thousand. "Abominable weakness," as
he expressed it. But it was only this weakness that made
it possible for him to repel his assailants. An adversary, cor-
nered, would say to him: "Perfection is impossible; even
you smoke." Then Rakhmétov redoubled his attacks, but
aimed most of his reproaches at himself, his opponent receiving less, still without being quite forgotten. He succeeded in doing a great deal, since in the employment of
his time he imposed equally strict rules upon himself. He
did not lose a quarter of an hour, and had no need of rest.

"My occupations are varied; change of occupation is a
rest."

The circle of friends which had its center in Kirsánov
and Lopukhóv he visited just often enough to enable him to
keep on an intimate footing with its members.

This was necessary. Daily experience proves the usefulness
of intimate relations with some circle or other of men;

one must always have on hand sources for all sorts of information. Aside from the meetings of this circle, he never visited any one except on business, and nowhere did he stay five minutes longer than his business required. Likewise, at home, he neither received any one nor allowed any one to stay except on these conditions. He said plainly to his visitor: "Our conversation is finished. Now let me turn to something else, for my time is precious."

During the first months of his new birth he spent almost all his time in reading; but that lasted only a little more than half a year. When he saw that he had acquired a systematic method of thinking in the line of the principles which he had found to be true, he then said to himself: "Henceforth reading is a secondary thing. So far as that is concerned I am ready for life," and he began the habit of devoting to books only such time as he had left after attending to his other business,—that is, very little time. In spite of this the range of his knowledge extended with an astonishing rapidity and at the age of twenty-two he was already a learned man. In this matter, too, he imposed rules upon himself.

"No luxury, no caprices; nothing but the necessary. Now, what is necessary? Upon each subject there are only a very few first-class works; in all the others there are nothing but repetitions, rarefactions, modifications of that which is more fully and more clearly expressed in these few. There is no need of reading any but these; all other reading is but a useless expenditure of time. Take, for example, Russian *belles lettres*. I say to myself: 'First I will read all of Gogol's works.' In the thousands of other novels I have only to read five lines on five different pages to see that I shall find nothing in them but Gogol spoiled. Then what is the use of reading them?"

It was the same in economic science; there the line of demarkation was even more sharply drawn.

"If I have read Adam Smith, Malthus, Ricardo, and Mill, I know the alpha and omega of this school. I read only that which is original, and I read it only so far as is necessary in order to know this originality."

Consequently there was no way of inducing him to read Macaulay; after spending a quarter of an hour in reading several pages, he said to himself: "I know the quality of these rags." He read, and with pleasure, Thackeray's "Vanity

Fair," and began to read "Pendennis," but closed the book at the twentieth page.

"It is all in 'Vanity Fair'; he has nothing more to say; hence to read him further is useless."

Gymnastics, labor for the development of his strength, and reading were Rakhmétov's personal occupations, but after his return to St. Petersburg they took but a quarter of his time; the rest of the time he occupied in the affairs of some one else or in matters not relating especially to his own person, always holding to the rule by which he governed his reading,—not to spend time on secondary matters and with second-rate men, but to attend only to important matters and important men. For instance, outside of his circle, he made the acquaintance of no one save those that had an influence over others. A man who was not an authority for several others could by no means enter into conversation with him. He said, "Excuse me, I have no time," and went his way. Likewise, if he wished to make the acquaintance of any one, there was no way of getting rid of him. He came directly to you and said what he had to say with this introduction: "I wish to make your acquaintance; it is necessary. If you have no time now, fix some other time." To your minor affairs he lent no attention even though you were his most intimate friend and had begged him to take an interest in your concerns: "I have no time," he would say, turning away. But he concerned himself about important matters when in his opinion it was necessary, even though no one asked him to do so: "It is my duty," he would say. In all that he said and did he didn't stand on ceremony.

This, for instance, is the way in which I made his acquaintance. I was already past my youth and living very comfortably; so from time to time five or six young people of my province used to meet at my house. This made me a precious man for him: these young people were well-disposed toward me, and they found in me a similar disposition toward them.

It was on such an occasion that he heard my name spoken. When I saw him for the first time at Kirsánov's, I had never heard of him: it was shortly after his return from his travels. He came in after I did; I was the only member of the company whom he did not know. Scarcely had he entered when he took Kirsánov aside and, pointing to me with his eyes, said a few words to him. Kirsánov, too, said a few words in reply, and left him. A moment later Rakhmétov sat down directly opposite me at a distance no greater than the width of a little table near the divan, and he began to look me in the face with all his might. I was irritated: he looked at me without the slightest ceremony, as if I were a portrait, and I frowned. That did not disturb him in the least. After having looked at me two or three minutes, he said to me: "M. N., I wish to make your acquaintance. I know of you, but you do not know me. Go to Kirsánov and those present in whom you have the most confidence, and ask them about me." This said, he rose and went into another room.

"Who is this character?" I asked.

"It's Rakhmétov. He wants you to ascertain whether he deserves confidence unconditionally and whether he deserves consideration. He is worth more than all of us put together," said Kirsánov, and the others bore him out.

Five minutes later he came back into the room where we all were. He did not try to talk with me, and talked but very little with the others; the conversation was not a learned one nor one of much importance. "Ah, ten o'clock already!" said he a little while later; "at ten o'clock I have business elsewhere. M. N. [he addressed himself to me], I must say a few words to you. When I took Kirsánov aside to ask him who you were, I pointed you out with my eyes; even if I had not done so, you would have noticed that I was inquiring about you. Why should we not make the gestures that are natural in asking a question of this sort? When will you be at home to receive me?"

At that time I did not like to make new acquaintances, and, besides, I didn't like this brazenness.

"I only sleep in the house; I am not at home through the day."

"But you do sleep at home? What time do you go to bed?"

"Very late."

"For instance?"

"Toward two or three o'clock."

"Very well, set the hour."

"If you absolutely wish it, day after tomorrow, at half past three in the morning."

"Surely I ought to look upon your words as rude and

insulting; however, it is possible that you have good reasons. In any case, I will be at your house day after tomorrow at half past three in the morning."

"If you are so bent upon it, come a little later instead; I shall be at home all the morning until noon."

"Good! I will call at ten o'clock. Will you be alone?"

"Yes."

"Good!"

He came, and with the same directness went straight to the matter which prompted his making my acquaintance. We talked about half an hour. The subject of our conversation is of little consequence; it is enough to remember that he said, "It is necessary," and I answered, "No"; that he added, "You ought to," and I replied, "Not at all." At the end of the half-hour he said: "It is clear that it would be useless to continue. Are you convinced that I am a man worthy of absolute confidence?"

"Yes; all have told me so, and now I see it for myself."

"And in spite of all you persist in your opinion?"

"I persist."

"Do you know what follows from that? That you are either a liar or a man of little value!"

What do you say to that? What should one do to another who uses such language toward him? Provoke him to a duel? But he spoke so calmly, without any trace of personality, like a historian who judges things coldly, not with an intent to offend any one, but to serve the truth, that it would have been ridiculous to take offence, and I could only laugh.

"But these amount to the same thing," said I.

"In the present case they do not amount to the same thing."

"Then perhaps I am both at once."

"In the present case to be both at once is impossible. But one or the other,—certainly. Either you do not think and act as you speak, and in that case you are a liar; or you do think and act as you speak, and in that case you are a man of little value. One of the two,—certainly. The first, I suppose."

"Think as you please," said I, continuing to laugh.

"Good day. In any case remember that I keep my confidence in you, and am ready to resume our conversation whenever you see fit."

However queer this was, Rakhmétov was perfectly right,

both in having begun as he did, since he had inquired about me before approaching the matter, and in having ended the conversation in this way. In fact, I did not say what I thought, and he had the right to call me a liar; and "in the present case," as he expressed it, I could not take offence at or even exception to his words, the case being such that he could really keep his confidence in and even his esteem for me. Yes, however odd his manner, every man he dealt with was convinced that Rakhmétov acted in precisely the most reasonable and most simple way, and his terrible insults, his terrible reproaches were so given that no sensible man could be offended at them; and, with all his phenomenal rudeness, he was at bottom very gentle. Consequently his prefaces were in this tone. He began every difficult explanation in this way:

"You know that I am going to speak without any personal feeling. If you find the words I am about to say to you disagreeable, I will ask you to forgive them. I simply think that one should not take offence at what is said conscientiously and with no intention of offending. For the rest, whenever it may seem to you useless to listen to my words, I will stop; it is my rule to offer my opinion wherever I ought to, and never to impose it."

And, in fact, he did not impose it: he could not be prevented from giving his opinion when he deemed it useful; but he did it in two or three words, and added: "Now you know what the end of our conversation would be; do you think it would be useful to discuss further?" If you said "No," he bowed and went his way.

That is how he talked and acted. He always had a great deal of business not relating to himself personally. He had no personal matters; this everybody knew. But what the matters were to which he gave his attention, the members of his circle did not know. They simply saw that he had a multitude of concerns. He was rarely at home, and was always on the go, either on foot or in a cab, but generally on foot. At the same time he received many people, and for this purpose had made it a rule to be always at home from two o'clock till three. During this time he talked business and dined. But very often, for several days together, he did not go home, and then one of his friends, devoted to him body and soul and silent as a tomb, received his visitors for him. About two years after his entrance into Kirsánov's study, where we now see him reading Newton's commentaries on the Apocalypse, he left St. Petersburg, after telling Kirsánov and two or three of his most intimate friends that he had nothing more to do in the city, that he had done all that he could, that nothing more could be done for two or three years, and that consequently he was free for that length of time and wished to use it for the benefit of his future activity. We have learned since that he went to his old estate, sold the land remaining to him, received about thirty-five thousand rubles, went to Ryazan and Moscow, and distributed about five thousand rubles among his seven fellows so that they might finish their studies. And here ended his authentic history. What became of him after his departure from Moscow is not known. Several months went by, and no news came from him. Those who knew most about him no longer kept silence regarding several matters which, at his request, they had concealed during his stay among us. It was then that the members of our circle learned that he financed students and the various other details about him which I have just given. We heard also a multitude of stories which, instead of making him better known to us, only rendered his character more enigmatic,—stories astonishing from their singularity, stories which sometimes flatly contradicted the opinion we had formed of him, as a man wholly without feeling, having, if I may so express myself, no heart beating with personal emotions. To relate all these stories would be out of place. I will give but two here,—one of each class,—one queer and the other upsetting the theory of his pretended hardness of heart. I choose them from those told me by Kirsánov.

A year before he disappeared for the second and probably the last time from St. Petersburg Rakhmétov said to Kirsánov: "Give me a large quantity of salves for healing wounds inflicted by sharp tools." Kirsánov filled an enormous jar for him, thinking that Rakhmétov intended to take it to a carpenters' shop or that of some other workmen liable to cuts. The next morning Rakhmétov's landlady ran to Kirsánov in great fright:

"Doctor, I do not know what has got into my tenant: he is late, he has not left his room, the door is locked; I looked through the crack of the door and saw him covered with blood; when I began to cry out, he said to me through the door: 'It is nothing, Agraféna Antonovna.' How can it be nothing! Save him, doctor! Oh, how afraid I am he may die! He is so utterly without pity for himself."

Kirsánov ran in all haste; Rakhmétov opened his door, a broad and dismal smile on his lips. Kirsánov saw a sight at which Agraféna Antonovna might well have been startled; others would have been. The back and sides of Rakhmétov's shirt (he was in his shirt) were covered with blood; there was blood under the bed; the felt on which he slept was covered with blood; in the felt were hundreds of little nails, sticking up about an inch; Rakhmétov had lain all night on this bed of his invention.

"What does this mean, Rakhmétov?" cried Kirsánov, thoroughly frightened.

"A trial. It was necessary to make it. Improbable, certainly, but at all events it was necessary to make it. I know now what I can do."

Besides what Kirsánov saw, the landlady evidently could have told many curious things about Rakhmétov, but in her innocence and simplicity the old woman doted on him, and it is needless to say that nothing could be learned from her. On this occasion she ran to Kirsánov only because Rakhmétov himself allowed her to do so for her own peace of mind. She wept very bitterly because she thought that he wanted to commit suicide.

Two months after this affair, at the end of the month of May, Rakhmétov disappeared for a week or more, but no one remarked upon it, as it very often happened that he disappeared for several days. Later Kirsánov told us the following story of the way in which Rakhmétov spent his time while absent. It was the erotic episode of his life. His love grew out of an event worthy of Nikítushka Lómov. Rakhmétov was going from Pargolovo* to the city, in a thoughtful mood and with eyes lowered, as usual; when passing by the Forestry Institute, he was startled from his dreams by the harrowing cry of a woman. Raising his eyes, he saw that a horse, attached to a jaunting-car in which a lady sat, had taken the bit in his teeth and was running as fast as he could; the lady had dropped the reins, which were dragging along the ground; the horse was not more than two steps from Rakhmétov; he threw himself into the middle of the road, but the horse passed rapidly by him

* A village in the suburbs of St. Petersburg.

before he could seize the bridle; he could only grasp the rear axle of the jaunting-car, which he stopped, though he fell himself. The passers-by ran to the spot, helped the lady out of the jaunting-car, and picked up Rakhmétov. His chest was slightly bruised, but his most serious injury was the loss of a good-sized piece of flesh which the wheel had torn from his leg. When the lady had recovered herself, she ordered him to be taken to her country-house, about half a verst distant. He consented, for he felt very weak, but he insisted that Kirsánov be sent for, as he would have no other doctor. Kirsánov decided that the bruises on his chest were not of serious consequence, but he found Rakhmétov himself very weak from loss of blood. He remained in bed ten days. Naturally, the lady whom he had saved cared for him herself. In view of his weakness he could only talk with her,—the time would have been lost at any rate,—so he spoke and for once without reserve. The lady was a young widow nineteen years old, moderately rich, independent, intelligent, and fine-looking. Rakhmétov's ardent words (not of love, be it understood) charmed her.

"I see him in my dreams surrounded with a halo," said she to Kirsánov. He also conceived a passion for her. From his exterior she thought him poor; consequently she was the first to propose marriage when on the eleventh day he rose and said that he could go home.

"With you I have been more outspoken than with others; you can see that men like me have not the right to bind their destiny to that of any one whomsoever."

"Yes, you are right," said she, "you cannot marry. But until you have to leave me, love me."

"No, I cannot accept that offer either; I am no longer free, and must not love."

What has become of this lady since? This adventure must have changed her life. In all probability she herself became an unusual person. I wanted to find out, but couldn't. Kirsánov never told me her name and he didn't know what had happened to her. Rakhmétov asked him not to see her or inquire about her. "If I suppose that you know anything about her, I won't be able to resist asking you—and this must never happen."

When the story came out, everyone recalled that at the time, for a month or two—possibly longer, Rakhmétov was

gloomier than usual and did not get excited regardless of
the teasing about his abominable weakness, that is, cigars.
Neither did he smile broadly and sweetly when they flattered him by using his nickname Nikítushka Lómov. I recall even more. Three or four times that summer he re-
sponded to my teasing (for I teased him when we were
alone, and that is why he was fond of me):

"Yes, pity me; you are right, pity me. I, too, like the
others, am not an abstract idea, but a man who wishes to
live. However, it will pass away."

And in fact it did pass away. Once only, several months
later, I so excited him by my raillery that he happened to
say the same words over again.

The reader with the penetrating eye sees, perhaps, that I
know more about Rakhmétov than I say. It may be so. But
what I really do not know is this,—where Rakhmétov is
now, what has become of him, and whether I shall ever see
him again. About these matters I know no more than his
other friends. Three or four months after his disappearance
from Moscow we supposed, though we had heard nothing
from him, that he was travelling in Europe. This conjecture
seems to have been correct. At least it is confirmed by this
evidence. A year after Rakhmétov's disappearance one of
Kirsánov's acquaintances met in a railway carriage between
Vienna and Munich a young Russian, who said that he had
travelled through all the Slavonic countries, meeting all
classes of society and staying in each country only as long
as it was necessary in order to form a true conception of its
ideas, its customs, its manner of life, its local institutions, its
material condition, and the various branches of its population; that with this view he lived in cities and villages, going on foot from one village to another; that he had studied
in the same way the Roumanians and the Hungarians;
that he had travelled, now on foot and now by rail, through
Northern Germany; that then he had visited in detail
Southern Germany and the German provinces of Austria;
that now he was going to Bavaria, and thence to Switzer-
land by way of Würtemberg and Baden; that afterwards
he would go through France and England in the same
way, which he counted on doing in a year; if there were
enough of the year left, he would see also Spain and Italy;
if not, he would not go there. Why? Because in a year it
was absolutely necessary that he should be in the United

States, a country which he must study more than any other. There he would remain a long time, perhaps more than a year, and perhaps forever should he find occupation there. It was, however, more likely that in three years he would return to Russia, as it seemed to him that at that time it would be necessary to be there. All this is much like Rakhmétov, including the "it is necessary's" impressed upon the memory of the narrator. The age, the voice, the features of the traveller were also confirmatory indications, but the narrator had not paid much attention to his fellow-traveller, who, moreover, had left him two hours later, descending from the train at a little village. Consequently the narrator gave only a vague description of his external appearance, so that the authenticity is not complete. It is also said that a young Russian, an ex-squire, once presented himself to one of the greatest European thinkers of our century, the father of the new German philosophy, and said to him: "I have thirty thousand thalers; I need but five thousand; the remainder I beg you to accept." The philosopher was living in great poverty.

"What for?"

"For the publication of your works."

The philosopher did not accept; but the Russian nevertheless deposited the money in his name at a banker's, and wrote him a note which read as follows: "Do with this money as you will; throw it in the water if you like; but you cannot send it back to me, for you will not find me." The money is said to be still at the banker's. If this report be true, it was Rakhmétov and none other who called on the philosopher. Such, then, is the gentleman whom we now see seated in Kirsánov's study. He is truly an unusual man, an individual of a very rare sort. And I have not spoken to you of him at this length, reader with the penetrating eye, to teach you the proper method of behavior (unknown to you) toward people of his sort. You cannot see a single man of his type; your eyes are not made to see such phenomena; to you these men are invisible; none but honest and fearless eyes can see them. But it was good that you should know, were it only by hearsay, that such men exist.

Yes, people like Rakhmétov are very droll, very amusing. I tell them that they are very droll; I tell them so because I pity them; I say to the noble hearts who are charmed by them: "Do not imitate them. The way along which they lead you is poor in personal joys." But, instead of listening to me, they say: "The way is not poor at all; on the contrary, it is very rich; though it should be poor in some particular spot, it can never long continue so, and we shall have strength enough to scale the difficult points in order to enter into the immense prairies fertile in all sorts of joys." You see, then, reader with the penetrating eye, that it is not for you, but for another portion of the public, that I have said that men like Rakhmétov are droll. I will tell you, however, that they are not wicked; otherwise, perhaps you would not understand; no, they are not·wicked. They are few in number, but through them the life of all mankind expands; without them it would have been stifled. They are few in number, but they put others in a position to breathe, who without them would have been suffocated. Great is the mass of good and honest men, but Rakhmétovs are rare. They are the best among the best, they are the movers of the movers, they are the salt of the salt of the earth.

: XXVIII :

"Ah, then!" thinks the perceptive reader, "so Rakhmétov is to be the principal personage and master of all, Véra Pávlovna is to fall in love with him, and we are to see the story of Lopukhóv begun over again with Kirsánov as the hero."

Nothing of the sort. Rakhmétov will pass the evening in conversation with Véra Pávlovna, and I will not keep from you a single word of what they say. You shall soon see that, if I had not chosen to communicate this conversation to you, I could very easily have kept from doing so, and the course of events in my story would not have been changed in the least. I also tell you in advance that, when Rakhmétov, after talking with Véra Pávlovna, shall go away, he will go away for ever from my story, that he will be neither a principal nor a secondary character, and that he will not figure further in my novel. Why have I introduced him and described him in such detail? There is an enigma for you, perceptive reader. Can you guess it? It should not be difficult, if you had the slightest idea of art, about which you are so fond of chattering; but it is Greek to you. Stop, I will whisper in your ear half of the solution of the enigma. I have shown Rakhmétov in order to satisfy the most essential condition of art, and simply for that. Well, now, find out if you can what this artistic condition is. Look, guess! The feminine reader and the simple-minded masculine reader, who do not chatter about art, know, but to you it is an enigma. Take your time. I draw a long, broad stroke between the lines (see how careful I am with you). Pause over this stroke, and reflect upon it; still, perhaps you will not guess.

Madame Mertzálov came. After having regretted and consoled, she said that she would take charge of the shop with pleasure, but that she feared she might not succeed, and again she began to regret and console while helping to sort out the effects. After having asked the neighbors' servants to go to the bake-shop, Rakhmétov prepared the *samovar,* brought it in, and they began to take tea; Rakhmétov spent half an hour with the ladies, drank five cups of tea, half emptied at the same time an enormous pot of cream, and ate a frightful quantity of rolls, and two plain loaves which served as a foundation.

"I am entitled to this extra indulgence, for I am sacrificing an entire half of my day."

While enjoying his meal and listening to the ladies as they exhausted themselves in grief, he expressed three times his opinion: "It is senseless,"—not that the ladies should exhaust themselves in grief, but that any one should kill himself for any reason whatever except to get rid of an intolerably painful and incurable disease or to avoid a painful and inevitable death,—such, for instance, as torture on the wheel; each time he expressed this opinion concisely, as was his habit. He poured out the sixth cup of tea, at the same time emptying the pot of cream completely, and took all the rolls that were left, and, the ladies having long ago finished their meal, he made a bow and went off with these things to finish his material enjoyment in the study, where he passed some time as a sybarite, stretched out on the sofa, which was used by everybody, but which to him was Capuan luxury.

"I am entitled to this feast, for I am sacrificing twelve or fourteen hours of my time," said he. After having finished his physical enjoyment, he began once more his mental

enjoyment,—the reading of the commentaries on the Apocalypse. About ten o'clock the police official came to communicate the particulars of the affair to the wife of the
suicide. Rakhmétov told him that the wife knew all about
it already, and that there was nothing to be said to her.
The official was very glad to be relieved from participation
in a harrowing scene. Then came Másha and Rachel and
began to sort out the clothing and goods. Rachel advised
the sale of everything except the nice cloak, for, if that
were sold, it would be necessary in three months to have
a new one made. To this Véra Pávlovna consented, and the
price was fixed at four hundred and fifty rubles,—all that
the things were worth, according to Madame Mertzálov.
So at ten o'clock the business deal was closed. Rachel paid
two hundred rubles; she had no more about her, but would
send the balance in two or three days by Madame Mertzálov; she took the things and went away. Madame Mertzálov
remained an hour longer, but it was time to nurse her child,
and she went away, saying that she would come the next
day to accompany Véra Pávlovna to the station.

When Madame Mertzálov had gone, Rakhmétov closed
Newton's commentaries on the Apocalypse, put them carefully back in their place, and sent Másha to ask Véra Pávlovna if he could go into her room. He obtained permission.
He entered, as usual, slowly and coolly.

"Véra Pávlovna, I am now able to console you to a certain extent. It is permissible to do so now; it was not
necessary to do so sooner. First warning you that the general
result of my visit will be of a consoling nature,—you know,
I never say vain words, and you must calm yourself in advance,—I am going to explain the affair to you at length.
I told you that I had seen Alexánder Matvéich and that I
knew everything. That was strictly true. But I did not tell
you that I knew all from him, and I could not have told
you so, since in reality I knew all, not from him, but from
Dmítry Sergéich, who came to see me about two o'clock; I
was notified in advance of his coming, and consequently
was at home; so he came to see me about two o'clock, after
writing the note which has caused you so much grief. And
he it was who asked me . . ."

"You knew what he intended to do and did not stop
him?"

"I asked you to be calm, as the result of my visit was to

be consoling. No, I did not stop him, for his mind was thoroughly made up, as you shall see for yourself. As I began to say, he it was who asked me to spend this evening with you, and, knowing that you would be in sorrow, he entrusted me with a commission for you. He chose me as his agent because he knew me to be a man who carries out the instructions that are given him, and cannot be turned aside by any sentiment or any prayer. He foresaw that you would beg me to violate his will, and he hoped that I would carry it out without being moved by your prayers. So I shall, and I beg you to ask no concession of me. This commission is as follows: In going away to 'quit the scene' . . ."

"My God, what has he done! Why didn't you stop him?"

"Examine this expression, 'quit the scene,' and do not blame me prematurely. He used this expression in the note that you received, did he not? Well, we will adopt the same expression, for it is very happily chosen and expresses the idea exactly."

Véra Pávlovna became more and more perplexed; she said to herself: "What does it mean? What must I think?"

Rakhmétov, with all the apparent absurdity of his circumstantial method of explanation, managed the affair in a masterly way. He was a great psychologist, and knew how to proceed gradually.

"So, in going away, with a view to quitting the scene, to use his accurate expression, he left with me a note for you."

Véra Pávlovna rose abruptly.

"Where is it? Give it to me! And you could stay here all day without delivering it to me?"

"I could because it was necessary. You will soon understand my reasons. They are well-founded. But first I must explain to you the expression that I employed just now: 'the result will be consoling.' By the consoling nature of the result I did not mean the receipt of this note, and that for two reasons, the first of which is this: in the fact of the receipt of this note there would not have been sufficient relief, you see, to deserve the name of consolation; to give consolation something more is necessary. So the consolation must be found in the contents of the note."

Véra Pávlovna rose again.

"Calm yourself; I do not say that you are mistaken. Hav-

ing warned you concerning the contents of the note, let me
tell you the second reason why I could not mean by the
'consoling nature of the result' the fact of the receipt of the
note, but its contents rather. These contents, on the character
of which we have settled, are so important that I cannot
give them to you, but can only show them to you."

"What! You will not give them to me?"

"No. That is precisely why he chose me, for anybody else
in my place would have given them to you. The note cannot
remain in your hands because, considering the extreme
importance of its contents, it must not remain in the hands
of any one. Now, if I should give it to you, you would wish
to keep it. So, not to be obliged to take it away from you
again by force, I shall not give it to you, but shall only
show it to you. But I shall not show it to you until you
have sat down, placed your hands upon your knees, and
given me your word not to raise them."

Véra Pávlovna submissively placed her hands upon her
knees, and cried, in painfully impatient voice: "I swear it!"

Rakhmétov placed on the table a sheet of letter-paper,
on which were written ten or twelve lines.

Scarcely had Véra Pávlovna cast a glance at it when, forgetting her oath, she rose impetuously to seize the note,
which was already far off in Rakhmétov's lifted hand.

"I foresaw that, and for that reason, as you would have
noticed had you been in a condition to notice anything,
my hand did not leave the note. Therefore I will continue
to hold this sheet by the corner as long as it remains on the
table. This will make all your attempts useless."

Véra Pávlovna sat down again and replaced her hands.
Rakhmétov again placed the note under her eyes. She read
it over twenty times with emotion. Rakmétov stood with
much patience beside her chair, holding the corner of the
sheet with his hand. A quarter of an hour passed thus.
Finally Véra Pávlovna raised her hand slowly, evidently
without bad intentions, and hid her eyes.

"How good he is! how good he is!" said she.

"I am not quite of your opinion, and you shall know
why. This will be no part of his commission, but only the
expression of my opinion, which I gave to him, too, at our
last interview. My commission consisted only in this,—to
show you this note and then burn it. Have you looked at it

enough?"

"Again, again!"

She folded her hands anew, he replaced the note, and
with the same patience stood in the position already described a good quarter of an hour longer. Again she hid
her face in her hands and repeated: "Oh! how good he is,
how good he is!"

"You have studied this note as closely as you could. If
you were in a calmer frame of mind, not only would you
know it by heart, but the very form of each letter would
be stamped for ever in your memory, so long and attentively have you looked at it. But in your present state of
agitation the laws of memory do not exist, and memory
may prove false to you. In view of this possibility I have
made a copy of the note; this copy you can always see
at my house whenever you like. Sometime I may even find
it possible to give it to you. Now I think it is time to
burn the original, and then my commission will be completed."

"Show it to me once more."

He again placed the note on the table. This time Véra
Pávlovna repeatedly raised her eyes from the paper: it was
plain that she had learned the note by heart and was verify-
ing her remembrance of it. A few minutes afterwards she
gave a deep sigh, and stopped lifting her eyes from the
note.

"Now, that is enough, it seems to me. It is time. It is
midnight already, and I have yet to give you my thoughts
about this matter, for I think you should know my opinion.
Do you consent?"

"Yes."

On the instant the note was ablaze in the flame of the
candle.

"Ah!" cried Véra Pávlovna, "that is not what I said.
Why . . ."

"Yes, you only said that you consented to listen to me.
But sooner or later I should have had to burn it."

Saying these words, Rakhmétov sat down.

"Besides, the copy of the note remains. Now, Véra Pávlovna, I am going to give you my opinion of the affair. I
will begin with you. You are going away. Why?"

"It would be very painful for me to stay here. The sight
of places which would recall the past would make me

very unhappy."

"Yes, that is a very disagreeable feeling. But do you believe that life would be much less painful to you anywhere else? Very little less, in any case. And yet what do you do? To secure yourself a slight relief, you risk the destiny of fifty individuals dependent upon you. Is that right?"

What has become of the tiresome solemnity of Rakhmétov's tone? He speaks in a spirited, natural, simple, brief, and animated way.

"That is true, but I have asked Madame Mertzálov . . ."

"You do not know whether she will be in a position to replace you in the shop; her capacity is not yet proven. Now, this is a matter which calls for a person of more than ordinary capacity. The chances are ten against one that no one would be found to replace you and that your departure would ruin the shop. Is that well? You expose fifty persons to almost certain, almost inevitable ruin. And for what reason? To secure a little comfort for yourself. Is that well? What an eager tenderness for one's own trivial relief, and what an insensibility to the fate of others! How does this view of your course please you?"

"Why didn't you restrain me?"

"You would not have listened to me. And, besides, I knew that you would come back soon; consequently the matter was not important. You see that you are in the wrong."

"Completely," said Véra Pávlovna, partly in jest and partly in earnest,—almost wholly in earnest, in fact.

"No, that is but one side of your crime. 'Completely' involves much more. But for your repentance you shall receive a reward: I am going to aid you to repair another crime, which it is not yet too late to correct. Are you calm now, Véra Pávlovna?"

"Yes, almost calm."

"Good! Do you need Másha for anything?"

"Certainly not."

"And yet you are already calm; you ought, then, to have remembered that it was time to tell her to go to bed,—it is already past midnight,—especially as she has to rise early. Who should have thought of this, you or I? I will tell her that she may sleep. And at the same time, for this fresh repentance—for you do repent—here is a new reward; I will see what there is for supper. You have not eaten today, and you must have an appetite."

"It is true, and a keen one; I felt it as soon as you reminded me of it," said Véra Pávlovna, laughing this time.

Rakhmétov brought the remains of the dinner. Másha had shown him the cheese and a pot of mushrooms, which made them a good enough supper; he brought two knives and forks, and, in short, did everything himself.

"See, Rakhmétov, how eagerly I eat; that means that I was hungry; and yet I did not feel it. It was not Másha alone that I forgot. I am not, you see, so malicious a criminal."

"Nor am I so very attentive to others. I reminded you of your appetite because I too wanted to eat."

"Ah, Rakhmétov, you are my good angel, and not for my appetite alone. But why did you stay here all day without showing me the note? Why did you keep me so long in torture?"

"The reason is a very serious one. It was necessary that others should witness your sorrow, so that the news of your extreme grief might spread and thus confirm the authenticity of the event which caused it. You would not have wanted to feign sorrow. In fact, it is impossible to completely replace nature by anything; nature in all cases acts in a much more convincing way. Now there are three sources from which the event may be authenticated,— Másha, Madame Mertzálov, and Rachel. Madame Mertzálov is an especially important source, as she knows all your acquaintances. I was very glad that you conceived the idea of sending for her."

"But how shrewd you are, Rakhmétov!"

"Yes, it was not a bad idea to wait until night, but the credit of it belongs to Dmítry Sergéich himself."

"How good he is!" and Véra Pávlovna heaved a profound sigh, not of sorrow, but of gratitude.

"Well, Véra Pávlovna, we will analyze him further. Indeed, of late, his thoughts have been very wise and his conduct perfect. Yet we shall convict him of some pretty serious sins."

"Rakhmétov, do not speak of him in that way, or I shall get angry."

"You rebel! That calls for another punishment. The list of your crimes is only just begun."

"Execute, execute, Rakhmétov."

"For this submission a reward. Submission is always rewarded. If you have any wine, it would not be a bad idea for you to drink some. Where is it? In the sideboard or in the closet?"

"In the sideboard." There he found a bottle of sherry.

Rakhmétov made Véra Pávlovna drink two small glasses of it, and lit a cigar himself.

"It is a pity that I cannot drink three or four small glasses with you. I want it so much."

"Is it possible, Rakhmétov?"

"It is tempting, Véra Pávlovna, it is very tempting," said he, laughing; "man is weak."

"You, too, weak! Why, Rakhmétov, you astonish me! You are not at all what I thought you were. Why are you always so sober? Tonight you are a gay and charming man."

"Véra Pávlovna, I am now fulfilling a gay duty. Why shouldn't I be gay? But this is an exceptional case. Generally the things that I see are not gay at all. How can I help being sober? But, Véra Pávlovna, since you happen to see me as I should very much like to be always, and since we have come to talk so freely to each other, know this,—but let it be a secret,—that it is not to my liking to be sober. It is easier for me to do my duty when it is not noticed that I too should like to enjoy life. In that case no one tries to entertain me, and I am not forced to waste my time in refusing invitations. But that it may be easier for you to think of me only as a sober man, I continue my inquest concerning your crimes."

"But what more do you want, then? You have already convicted me of two,—insensibility toward Másha and insensibility regarding the shop. I am repentant."

"The insensibility toward Másha is only an offence, not a crime: Másha would not die from rubbing her heavy eyes an hour longer; on the contrary, she would have done it with a pleasant feeling, knowing that she was doing her duty. But in regard to the shop, I've a bone to pick with you."

"As if you haven't picked on me enough!"

"Not quite. I want to pick you to the very bone. How *could you* leave the shop to rack and ruin?"

"But I have repented, and, besides, I didn't abandon it. Madame Mertzálov had consented to take my place."

"We've already spoken of that, and your intention of

furnishing her as a substitute is not a sufficient excuse. But by this excuse you have succeeded only in convicting yourself of a new crime.

Rakhmétov gradually resumed his serious, though not solemn, tone.

"You say that she is going to take your place. Is that decided upon?"

"Yes," said Véra Pávlovna, seriously, foreseeing that something bad was to follow.

"Look at it. The affair is decided, but by whom? By you and by her, without taking any further counsel. Whether these fifty persons would consent to such a change, whether they wished it, and whether they have some better way, doesn't matter? That is despotism, Véra Pávlovna. So you are already guilty of two great crimes,—lack of pity and despotism. But the third is even worse. You risked an institution, which more or less aptly corresponded to wholesome ideas on social order, which to a degree served as an important affirmation of their practicability. (As you know, practical proofs of this are so scarce that every bit is precious.) You submitted this institution to the risk of changing from a proof of its practicability into evidence of the impracticability and absurdity of your convictions, into a refutation of your ideas which were so beneficial to mankind. You supplied the champions of darkness and evil with an argument against your sacred principles. I shall not even speak of the fact that you were destroying the well-being of fifty persons! You were harming the cause of mankind and betraying the cause of progress. That, Véra Pávlovna, is what is called, in ecclesiastical language, the sin against the Holy Ghost, the only unpardonable sin. Isn't that true, madam criminal? Fortunately everything has happened as it has, and you have sinned only in intention. Ah! you blush in earnest, Véra Pávlovna. Good. Now I will console you. If you had not suffered so much, you would not have committed such crimes even in your imagination. Therefore the real criminal is he who has occasioned you so much torment. And you repeat continually: 'How good he is! how good he is!' "

"What! Do you think that, if I have suffered, it is through his fault?"

"Whose fault is it, then? He has managed this affair well, I admit, but why all this hubbub? Nothing of the kind should have happened."

"Yes, I should not have had this feeling. But I did not invite it; on the contrary, I tried to suppress it."

" 'I should not have had'—that is good! You do not see wherein you are guilty, and you reproach yourself when there is no occasion to. This feeling had to arise in one way or another, given your character and that of Dmítry Sergéich, and it would have developed itself under any circumstances. The essential point in the matter is not that you are in love with another, which is only a result; it is the dissatisfaction with your former relations. What form was this dissatisfaction obliged to take? If both, or even one of you, had been deficient in intellectual development and refinement, or if you had been bad people, your dissatisfaction would have taken the ordinary form,—hostility between husband and wife; you would have nagged each other, if you had both been bad; or one of you would have tormented the other, and the other would have been pitilessly tormented. It would have been in any case one of those domestic hells that we find in most families. That evidently would not have prevented the appearance of love for another, but in addition there would have been hell, mutual torment, I know not what. With you, dissatisfaction could not take this form, because both of you are honest; so it took only its lightest, mildest, most inoffensive form,— love of another. Of this love there is no occasion to speak: it is not, I repeat, the essential point. The essential point is the dissatisfaction with your former situation, and the cause of your dissatisfaction is the difference in your characters. Both of you are good, but when your character, Véra Pávlovna, matured, when it lost its childish ambiguity and acquired definite traits, it became evident that you and Dmítry Sergéich were not well suited to each other. What is there prejudicial to either of you in this case? I, for instance, am not a bad man. Could you live a long time with me? You would die of *ennui*. In how many days, do you think?"

"In a very few days," said Véra Pávlovna, laughing.

"He is not as sober as I am, but nevertheless there is altogether too much difference between you. Who should have noticed it first? Who is the older? Whose character was formed the earlier? Who has had the greater experience in life? He should have foreseen it all and prepared you, so that you might not be frightened and eaten up with sorrow. He did not realize this until the feeling, that he should have anticipated, was not only developed, but had produced its results. Why did he foresee nothing, notice nothing? Was it stupidity? He doesn't lack common sense. No, it was inattention, negligence, rather; he neglected his relations with you, Véra Pávlovna. That was the real trouble. And still you repeat: 'He is good; he loved me.'"

Rakhmétov was gradually becoming animated, and spoke with warmth. But Véra Pávlovna stopped him.

"I must not listen to you, Rakhmétov," said she in a bitter and discontented tone; "You heap reproaches upon the man to whom I am infinitely indebted. I beg you to be silent, Rakhmétov. I beg you to go away. I am much obliged to you for having sacrificed an evening on my account. But I beg you to go away."

"Good," said he, laughing. "No, Véra Pávlovna, you cannot get rid of me so easily. I foresaw this contingency, and took my precautions. The note which I burned was written of his own accord. And here is one which he wrote because I asked him to. This I can leave with you, because it is not an important document. Here it is."

Rakhmétov handed the note to Véra Pávlovna.

> *My dear Vérochka:*
>   Listen to all that Rakhmétov has to say to you. I do not know what he intends to say to you, I have not charged him to say anything to you, and he has not made the slightest allusion to what he intends to say. I know, however, that he never says anything unnecessary. Yours,   D. L.
>   July 11, 2 o'clock in the morning.

God knows how many times Véra Pávlovna kissed this note.

"Why didn't you give it to me sooner? Perhaps you have something else from him."

"No, I have nothing more, because nothing more was necessary. Why didn't I give it to you? There was no reason for giving it to you until it became necessary."

"But to give me the pleasure of receiving a few lines from him after our separation."

"Yes. Perhaps only for this reason,—well, that's not so

important."

"Ah, Rakhmétov, you want to drive me mad!"

"So this note is the cause of a new quarrel between us?" said he, smiling again. "If that is the case, I will take it away from you and burn it. You know well what they say of such people as we are,—that to them nothing is sacred. Hence we are capable of all sorts of violence and meanness. May I continue?"

They both became calm,—she, thanks to the note; he, because he remained silent while she kissed the note.

"Yes, I must listen to you."

"He did not notice what he should have noticed," began Rakhmétov calmly: "that has produced bad results. Though we cannot call it a crime in him, neither can we excuse it. Suppose that he didn't know that a rupture was inevitable; still, given your character and his own, he should nevertheless have prepared you at all events against anything like it, just as one would against any accident which is not to be desired and which there is no reason to expect, but which is to be provided for. One cannot answer for the future and the changes that it may bring. With this axiom—that we are exposed to all sorts of accidents—he was familiar, we may be sure. Why did he leave you in ignorance to such an extent that, when the present circumstances arose, you were not at all prepared for them? His lack of foresight came from negligence, injurious to you, but in itself an indifferent thing, neither good nor bad; but, in failing to prepare you against any contingency, he acted from an absolutely bad motive. To be sure, he had no data to act upon, but it is precisely in those matters, where one acts without data, that nature best manifests itself. It would have been contrary to his interests to prepare you, for thereby your resistance to the feeling not in harmony with his interests would have been weakened. Your feeling proved so strong that your resistance could not overcome it; but it was not at all unlikely that this feeling would manifest itself with less force. If it had been inspired by a man less exceptionally worthy, it would have been weaker. Feelings against which it is useless to struggle are an exception. There are many more chances that this feeling will manifest itself in such a way that it may be stifled, if the power of resistance is not wholly destroyed. It was precisely in view of these, the most probable chances, that he did not wish to lessen your power of resistance. Those were his motives for leaving you unprepared and subjecting you to so much suffering. What do you say to this?"

"It's not true, Rakhmétov. He didn't hide his ways of thinking from me. His convictions were as well known to me as to you."

"To hide them would have been difficult. To oppose in your presence convictions corresponding to his own and to pretend for such a purpose to think otherwise than he did would have been simply dishonesty. You would never have loved such a man. Have I pronounced him bad? He is very good; I could say nothing else; I will praise him as highly as you like. I only say this: at the time of your rupture his conduct was very good, but before that his conduct towards you was bad. Why did you distress yourself? He said that it was because you did not wish to grieve him. Why was this thought, that you could thereby greatly grieve him, able to find a place in your mind? It should not have found a place there. What grief? It is stupid. Jealousy?"

"You do not admit jealousy, Rakhmétov?"

"A man with a developed mind should not have it. It is a distorted feeling, a false feeling, an abominable feeling; it is a phenomenon of our existing order of things, based upon the same idea that prevents me from permitting any one to wear my linen or smoke my pipe: it is a result of the fashion of considering one's companion as an object that one has appropriated."

"But, Rakhmétov, not to admit jealousy leads to horrible consequences."

"To those who are jealous they are horrible, but to those who are not there is not only nothing horrible about them, but nothing even of importance."

"You preach utter immorality, Rakhmétov!"

"Does it seem so to you after living with him for four years? That is precisely where he has done wrong. How many times a day do you dine? Only once. Would any one find fault with you if you dined twice? Probably not. Why do you not do so? Do you fear that you may grieve some one? Probably because you do not feel the necessity of it. Yet dinner is a very agreeable thing. But the mind and (more important still) the stomach say that one dinner is agreeable and that a second would be disagreeable. But if the fancy seized you or you had an unhealthy desire to dine twice, would the fear of grieving some one deter you? No, if any one felt grieved or prohibited you, you would hide and eat your food in a nasty way, you would soil your hands in taking it hastily, you would soil your clothes by hiding bits in your pockets, and that would be all. The question here is not one of morality or immorality, but only this: is smuggling a good thing? Who is restrained by the idea that jealousy is a feeling worthy of esteem and respect? Who says to himself: 'Ah! if I do this, I shall cause him grief'? Who is tormented by these useless struggles? Few people, the best, just those whose nature would not lead them into immorality. The mass are not restrained by these stupidities; they only resort to further strategy. They fill their lives with deceit and become really bad. That is all. Don't you know this?"

"Why, certainly."

"Where, then, do you find the moral benefit of jealousy?"

"Why, we have always talked in this vein ourselves."

"Not exactly in this vein, probably, or perhaps you talked so without believing your own words, not believing them because on this as on other questions you heard continually the opposite views. If that was not the case, why did you torment yourself? Why all this confusion about such trivial matters? What an embarrassment to all three of you, and especially to you, Véra Pávlovna! Whereas you might all three live as in the past, as you lived a year ago, or take apartments together, or arrange your life in any other way, according to your choice, but without any upset, and all three take tea or go to the opera together as in the past. Why these anxieties? Why these catastrophes? All because, owing to his wrong policy of keeping you in ignorance on this matter, he has caused you much useless sorrow."

"No, Rakhmétov, you say horrible things."

" 'Horrible things' again! Groundless anxieties and need-less catastrophes are the things that seem horrible to me."

"Then, in your eyes, our whole story is only a stupid melodrama?"

"Yes, an utterly useless melodrama coupled with utterly useless drama. And instead of a simple and peaceful con-versation there has been a harrowing melodrama and the guilty party is Dmítry Sergéich. His honest conduct at the last hardly suffices to cancel his original fault. Take another glass of sherry and go to bed. I have accomplished the

object of my visit. It is already three o'clock, and, if not
disturbed, you will sleep a long time. Now, I told Másha
not to call you till half past ten, so that tomorrow you will
hardly have time to take breakfast, but will have to hurry
to the depot. If you don't have time to pack all your
things, you will come back soon, or else they will be sent
to you. Do you wish Alexánder Matvéich to go directly
after you, or do you prefer to come back yourself? But it
would be painful for you to be in Másha's presence, for
she must not notice that you are entirely calm. She will not
notice this during half an hour of hurried preparations.
With Madame Mertzálov it is another thing. I will go to
her tomorrow morning, and tell her not to come because
you went to bed late and must not be waked; that she must
go directly to the depot instead."

"How attentive you are to me!" said Véra Pávlovna.

"This attention, at least, you need not attribute to him;
it comes from me. Except that I rebuke him for the past
(to his face I said much more) on account of his responsi-
bility for this useless anxiety, I find that, as soon as you
actually began to suffer, he acted very commendably."

: XXIX :

AN INTERVIEW WITH THE PERCEPTIVE
READER, AND HIS EXPULSION

Tell me, then, perceptive reader, why I have shown you
Rakhmétov, who has just gone away to appear no more in
my story. I have already told you that he would take no
part in the action.

"It is not true," interrupts the perceptive reader. "Rakhmétov is a personage, for he brought the note which . . ."

Why, how weak you are, my good sir, in the aesthetic discussions of which you are so fond! In that case Másha too
is, in your eyes, a personage? She also, at the beginning of
the story, brought a letter, which horrified Véra Pávlovna.
And perhaps Rachel is a personage?

"Ah! now I know," says the penetrating reader. "Rakhmétov appeared to pronounce judgment on Véra Pávlovna
and Lopukhóv. He was needed for the conversation with
Véra Pávlovna."

Your weakness is really deplorable, my worthy friend. You construe the matter in just the wrong way. Was it necessary to bring a man in simply that he might pronounce his opinion of the other personages? Your great artists do it, perhaps. As for me, though a feeble writer, I understand the conditions of art a little better than that. No, my good sir, Rakhmétov was not at all necessary for that. How many times has Véra Pávlovna herself, how many times have Lopukhóv and Kirsánov themselves, expressed their own opinion concerning their own actions and relations! They are intelligent enough to judge what is good and what is bad. Do you believe that Véra Pávlovna herself, recalling at her leisure a few days later the tumult just experienced, would not have blamed herself for having forgotten the shop in the same way that Rakhmétov blamed her? Do you believe that Lopukhóv himself did not think of his relations with Véra Pávlovna quite as Rakhmétov spoke of them to Véra Pávlovna? Honest people think of themselves all the evil that can be said of them, and that is the reason, my good sir, why they are honest people. Didn't you know that? Did you think that Rakhmétov, in his conversation with Véra Pávlovna, acted independently of Lopukhóv? Well, he was only Lopukhóv's agent. He understood it so himself, and Véra Pávlovna saw it a day or two later; and she would have seen it as soon as Rakhmétov opened his mouth, if she had not been so excited. Certainly Lopukhóv told the truth in his second note. He had said nothing to Rakhmétov and the latter had said nothing to him about the conversation which was to take place; but Lopukhóv knew Rakhmétov and knew what the latter thought of things and what he would say under certain circumstances. Honest people understand each other without explaining themselves. Lopukhóv could have written in advance, almost word for word, all that Rakhmétov would say to Véra Pávlovna, and that is exactly why he asked Rakhmétov to be his agent. Lopukhóv knew perfectly well that all he thought about himself, Rakhmétov, Mertzálov and his wife, the officer who had wrestled with him on the islands thought also, and that Véra Pávlovna was sure to think so within a short time even though no one should say it to her. She would see it as soon as the first flush of gratitude passed. Therefore, figured Lopukhóv, I really lose nothing by sending Rakhmétov to her, although he will rebuke me, for she would reach the same opinion herself; on the contrary, I gain in her esteem: she will see that I foresaw the substance of the conversation, and that *I arranged it.*

That was the plan which Lopukhóv devised, and Rakhmétov was only his agent. You see, my good penetrating reader, what sly dogs honest people are and how their egoism works. Their egoism is different from yours, because they do not find their pleasure in the same direction that you do. They find their greatest pleasure, you see, in having people whom they esteem think well of them, and that is why they trouble themselves to devise all sorts of plans with no less zeal than you show in other matters. But your objects are different, and the plans that you devise are different. You concoct evil plans, injurious to others, while they concoct honest plans, useful to others.

Now, my good sir, a question: why, then, do I give you Rakhmétov's conversation with Véra Pávlovna? Do you understand now that when I give you, not the thoughts of Lopukhóv and Véra Pávlovna, but Rakhmétov's conversation with the latter, I thereby signify the necessity of giving you, not alone the thoughts which constitute the essence of the conversation, but the actual conversation itself?

When two men talk, one sees more or less the character of these men; do you see whither this tends? Was Véra Pávlovna's character sufficiently well known to you before this conversation? It was; you have learned nothing about her: you already knew that she flares up, that she jests, that she likes good things to eat and a glass of sherry to drink; therefore the conversation was necessary to show the character, not of Véra Pávlovna, but of whom then? There were but two in the conversation, she and Rakhmétov. To show the character, not of Véra Pávlovna, but—well, guess!

"Rakhmétov," shouts the penetrating reader.

Bravo! You have hit it; I like you for that. Well, you see, it is just the contrary of what you first thought. Rakhmétov is not shown for the sake of the conversation, but the conversation is given to make you better acquainted with Rakhmétov and solely for that purpose. Through this conversation you have learned that Rakhmétov had a desire for sherry, although he never drank wine; that Rakhmétov was not absolutely solemn and morose; that on the contrary, when engaged in agreeable business, he forgot his sorrowful thoughts, his bitter sadness, and gaily jested and made merry: only, as he explained it, "that is rarely the case with me, and I am sorry that it is so rarely the case. I do not like to be solemn, but circumstances are such that a man with my ardent love of good cannot help being solemn. If it were not for that, I should jest, I should laugh, perhaps I should sing and dance all day long." Do you understand now, why, though many pages were used in directly describing Rakhmétov, I have devoted additional pages to the accomplishment of the same purpose indirectly? Tell me, now, why I have shown and described this figure in such detail. Remember what I have already told you,—"solely to satisfy the most essential condition of art." What is this condition, and how is it satisfied by the fact that I have put Rakhmétov's figure before you? The first demand of art consists in this,—to so represent objects that the reader may conceive them as they really are. For instance, if I wish to represent a house, I must see to it that the reader will conceive it as a house, and not as a hovel or a palace. If I wish to represent an ordinary man, I must see to it that the reader will not conceive him as a dwarf or as a giant.

It has been my purpose to represent ordinarily upright people of the new generation, people whom I meet by hundreds. I have taken three of them: Véra Pávlovna, Lopukhóv, and Kirsánov. I consider them ordinary people, they consider themselves such, and are considered such by all their acquaintances (who resemble them). Have I told extraordinary things? I have represented them with affection and esteem, it is true, but that is because every upright man is worthy of such affection and esteem.

But when have I bowed before them? Where have you seen in me the slightest tendency to adoration, or hint that they are ideal characters? As I conceive them, so they act,—like simple, upright people of the new generation. What do they do that is remarkably elevated? They do not do cowardly or nasty things. They have honest but ordinary convictions, they try to act accordingly, and that is all. Where is their heroism? Yes, it has been my purpose to show human beings acting just as all ordinary men of this type act, and I hope I have succeeded. Those of my readers who are intimately acquainted with living men of this type have seen from the beginning and up to the present moment that my principal characters are not at all ideal and not above the general level of people of their type, and that these men do not act in real life in any other way than that in which I picture them as acting. Suppose that other upright people had been confronted with a slightly different situation. It is not a matter of absolute necessity or fatality that all husbands and all wives should separate; not all upright wives feel a strong passionate love for their husband's friend; not all upright men have to struggle against their passion for a married woman during three whole years; nor is one always forced to blow his brains out on a bridge or to disappear from a hotel to go no one knows where. But no upright man in the place of the people pictured by me would have considered it heroic to do as they have done. He would do likewise under similar circumstances. And the friends of such a man, resembling him (for these people form friendships only with those who act and think as they do), consider him an estimable man, but never dream for a moment of dropping on their knees before him; they say to themselves: We, too, are like him.

I hope, I say, that I have succeeded in making every upright man of the new generation recognize the type of his friends in my three characters. But those who from the beginning of the story have been able to think of Véra Pávlovna, Kirsánov, and Lopukhóv as "our friends, people like ourselves simply,"—these are still but a minority of the public. The majority are still much below this type. A man who has never seen anything but dirty huts might take an engraving of a very ordinary house for the picture of a palace. How shall the house be made to seem to such a man a house and not a palace? Only by showing in the same picture even a little wing of a palace. He will then see from this wing that the palace must be quite a different thing from the building represented in the picture, and that the latter is really but a simple house. If I had not shown the figure of Rakhmétov, the majority of readers would have had a false idea of the principal characters of my story. I will wager that up to the concluding paragraphs of this chapter Véra Pávlovna, Kirsánov, and Lopukhóv have seemed to the majority of the public to be heroes, individuals of a superior nature, if not ideal persons, if not even persons impossible in real life by reason of their very noble conduct. No, my poor friends, you have been wrong in this thought: they are not too high. It is you who are too low. You see now that they simply stand on the surface of the earth; and, if they have seemed to you to be soaring in the clouds, it is because you are in the infernal depths. The height where they stand all men should and can reach.

Elevated natures are not like these. I have shown you a faint outline of the profile of one of them; the features are different, as you clearly see. Now, it is possible for you to become equals of the men whom I represent, provided you will work for your intellectual and moral development. Whoever is beneath them is very low.

Come up from your caves, my friends, ascend! It is not so difficult. Come to the surface of this earth where one is so well situated and the road is easy and attractive! Try it: development! development! Observe, think, read those who tell you of the pure enjoyment of life, of the possible goodness and happiness of man.

Read them, their books delight the heart; observe life,—it is interesting; think—it is a pleasant occupation. And that is all. Sacrifices are unnecessary, privations are unnecessary, unnecessary. Desire to be happy: this desire, this desire alone, is indispensable. With this end in view you will work with pleasure for your development, for there lies happiness.

Chapter Fourth

THE LIFE OF
VÉRA PÁVLOVNA WITH
HER SECOND HUSBAND

: I :

Madame and highly esteemed Véra Pávlovna:

My intimacy with Dmítry Sergéich Lopukhóv, who has just perished, and my profound esteem for you lead me to hope that you will kindly admit me among the number of your acquaintances, although I am entirely unknown to you. However that may be, I make bold to believe you will not accuse me of importunity. I but execute effectively the will of this poor Dmítry Sergéich; and you may consider the information which I have to communicate to you on his account as perfectly authentic, for the good reason that I am going to give you his own thoughts in his own words, as if he were speaking himself.

These are his words upon the matter which it is the object of my letter to clear up:

"The ideas which have resulted in pushing me to the act that has so much alarmed my intimate friends [I give you the very words of Dmítry Sergéich, as I have already told you] ripened in me gradually, and changed several times before taking their definitive form. It was quite unexpectedly that I was struck by the event which threw me into these thoughts, and only when she [Dmítry Sergéich refers to you] told me the dream that had horrified her. This dream made a great impression on me, and as a man who analyzed the feelings which caused it I understood from that moment that new horizons were about to dawn upon her life, and that sooner or later the nature of our relations would completely change. I wished to believe, and I did really believe, that this change would not be of long duration, that our old relations would be reëstablished. She even tried to escape this change by holding herself to me as closely as possible. That had its influence upon me, and for some days I believed it possible to realize her hope. But I soon saw, nevertheless, that this hope was vain. The whole trouble lay in my character.

"In speaking thus I do not mean to blame my character. I understand it in this manner.

"A man who employs his time well, divides it into three parts,—work, pleasure, rest or distraction. Pleasure demands rest as much as work does. In work and in pleasure the human element predominates over individual peculiarities. We are driven to labor by the preponderant motive of external rational needs; to pleasure by the preponderant motive of other needs of human nature,—needs quite as general. By rest and distraction the individual seeks to reëstablish his forces after the excitement which has exhausted them. In this the individual decides freely for himself in accordance with his personal tastes and proclivities. In work and in pleasure men are drawn to each other by a powerful general force above their personal peculiarities,—in work by a clearly understood self-interest, and in pleasure by the identical needs of the organism. In rest it is not the same. Here there is no general force acting to dominate individual peculiarities: leisure is of all things the most personal, the thing in which nature demands most liberty. Here man most individualizes himself, each seeking the satisfaction most agreeable to him.

"In this respect men are divided into two principal categories. For those of one category leisure or distraction is most agreeable in the society of others. Solitude is essential for everyone. For these, however, it is important that it be an exception, since life with others is the rule for them. This class is much more numerous than the other, which needs the opposite. Those of the latter class are more at ease in solitude than in society. This divergence has been remarked by general opinion, which has signified it by the expressions 'sociable men' and 'unsociable men.' I belong to the category of the unsociables, she to that of the sociables. That is the whole secret of our history. It is clear that neither of us is to blame for this, any more than either of us is to blame for not having strength enough to remove this cause. Man can do nothing against his own nature.

"It is rather difficult to understand the peculiarities of other natures, for each man regards others in line with the nature of his own individuality. Whatever I do not need, others don't either. The naturalness of this mode of thinking is my real excuse for my not having noticed sooner the difference between her character and mine. This is important. When we began to live together, she placed me on too high a pedestal: so at that time we did not stand on an equality. She had too much esteem for me; my way of living seemed to her exemplary; she considered my individual peculiarity as a characteristic befitting all men, and for a time she was under its influence. There was still another, stronger reason.

"The inviolability of the inner life is very lightly esteemed among immature people. Every member of the family—especially the oldest members—unceremoniously pokes his nose into your private life. Not that our secrets are thereby violated: secrets are things more or less precious, which one does not forget to conceal and guard. Moreover, not every one has them, and many haven't anything to hide from their relatives. But every one wishes to keep a little corner of his inner life into which no one may penetrate, just as every one wishes to have a room of his own. Immature persons pay small respect either to the one or the other: even if you have a room of your own, everybody walks into it, not exactly to watch you or intrude upon you, but because they do not dream that they may disturb you. They imagine that you can object to unexpected visits from none but those whom you dislike. They do not understand that, even with the best intentions, one may be intrusive. The threshold, which no one has a right to cross against the will of the interested party, is respected only in one case, that of the head of the family, who may put out by the shoulders whoever intrudes upon him. All the rest must submit to any and every intrusion and on the most idle pretexts, or even without any pretext at all.

"It is natural that these intrusions, without purpose or intention, should provoke a reaction; and as soon as the individual finds himself in a position to live alone, he takes pleasure for some time in solitude, though naturally inclined to society.

"To come back to the person in question. Before marrying she was in an exceptionally acute situation; she was intruded upon, her thoughts were scrutinized, not simply to kill time, or even through indelicacy, but systematically, shamelessly, grossly, and with bad intentions. Consequently the reaction was very strong in her.

"For this reason my fault must not be judged too severely. For some months, perhaps a year, I was not mistaken: she did, indeed, need solitude, and took pleasure in it. And during that time I formed my idea of her character. Her intense temporary need of solitude was identical with my constant need; why is it astonishing, then, that I should have taken a temporary phenomenon for a constant trait of her character? Every one is led to judge others by himself!

"This is a fault and a pretty serious one. I do not accuse myself, but I am moved, nevertheless, to justify myself; that is, I foresee that others will not be as indulgent for me as I am for myself. That is why, in order to soften the blame and help to an understanding, I must give some details about my character pertinent to the subject which we are considering.

"I have no idea of rest except in solitude. To be in society means to me to busy one's self with something, or to work, or to delight one's self.

"I feel completely at my ease only when I am alone. What shall we call this feeling? What is its origin? In some it comes from dissimulation; in others, from timidity; in a third class, from a tendency to melancholy; in a fourth, from a lack of sympathy for others. It seems to me that I have none of these things. I am straightforward and sincere; I am always ready to be gay, and am never sad. Company pleases me: only it is all combined for me either with work or with pleasure. But these occupations must be relieved by rest,—that is, by solitude. As far as I can understand myself, I am moved by a desire of independence, of liberty.

"So the force of the reaction against her old family life led her to accept for a time a way of life contrary to her steady inclinations; her esteem for me maintained these temporary dispositions in her longer than they would otherwise have lasted. In this period I formed a false idea of her character: I mistook her inclinations of the moment for steady inclinations; and I rested assured. That is the whole story. On my side there is a fault, but it isn't wide. On hers there is no fault at all. How much suffering all this has cost her. And with what a catastrophe it ended for me!

"When the fright occasioned by her horrible dream had opened my eyes to the state of her feelings, it was already too late to repair my fault. But if we had seen sooner what she lacked, it is possible that, by making a persistent effort over ourselves, we could have achieved a sort of contentment with each other. But I do not believe that, had we succeeded, anything good would have resulted from it. Suppose we had reconstructed our characters sufficiently to render them harmonious; conversions, nevertheless, are good only when brought into action against some evil proclivities; now, the proclivities that we should have had to change are in no way blameworthy. In what respect is sociability worse or better than the desire for solitude, and *vice versa?* Now, conversion, after all, is violence, dispersion; in dispersion many things are lost, and the effect of violence is to stupefy.

"The result that we might have attained would not have been a compensation. We should have become insignificant and should have withered more or less the freshness of our life. And why? To keep certain places in certain rooms? If we had had children, that would have been another matter; then we should have had to consider carefully the possibly bad influence that our separation would have had upon their fortunes. In that case it would have been necessary to make every possible effort to avoid this *dénoûement,* and the result—the joy of having done all that was necessary to make those dear to us happier—would have rewarded adequately all our efforts. But in the actual state of things what rational object could our efforts have had?

"Consequently, the present situation being given, all is arranged for the best. We have not had to violate our natures. We have had much sorrow, but, had we acted otherwise, we should have had much more, and the result would not have been as satisfactory."

Such are the words of Dmítry Sergéich. From his persistence in dwelling on this aspect of the matter, you can easily see that he felt embarrassed. And he added quickly, "I feel that I'll continue to remain somewhat at fault in the opinion of those who analyze this affair without any sympathy for me. But I am sure of her sympathy. She will judge me even better than I judge myself. Now, for my part, I believe that I have done perfectly right. Such is my opinion of my conduct up to the time of the dream."

Now I am going to communicate to you his feelings concerning the subsequent events:

"I have said [Dmítry Sergéich's words] that from the first words that she uttered about her dream I understood that a change in our relations was inevitable. I expected that this change would be a pretty radical one, for it was impossible that it should be otherwise, considering the energy of her nature and the intensity of her discontent at that time; and her discontent was all the greater from having been long suppressed. Nevertheless, I looked only for an external change and one quite to my advantage. I said to myself: 'For a time she will be under the influence of a passionate love for some one; then, a year or two having gone by, she will come back. I am an estimable man; the chances of finding another man like me are very rare (I say what I think, and have not hypocrisy enough to underrate my merits); her feeling will lose a portion of its intensity by satisfaction; and she will see that, although one side of her nature is less satisfied in living with me, on the whole she is happier and freer with me than with any one else. Then things will again shape themselves as in the past. Having learned by experience, I shall bestow more attentions upon her, she will have a greater and keener attachment for me, and we shall live more harmoniously than in the past.'

"But (this is a thing which it is a very delicate matter for me to explain, and yet it must be done),—but what effect did the prospect of this reëstablishment of our relations have upon me? Did it make me happy? Of course! But was that all? No, I looked forward to it as a burden, a very agreeable burden, to be sure, but still a burden. I loved her much, and would have violated my nature to put myself in greater harmony with her; that would have given me pleasure, but my life would have been under restraint. That

was the way in which I looked at things after the first
impression had passed away, and I have seen that I was not
mistaken. She put me to the proof of that, when she wished
me to force myself to keep her love. The month of com-
plaisance which I devoted to her was the most painful
month of my life. There was no suffering in it,—that expression would be out of place and even absurd, for I felt
only joy in trying to please her,—but it wearied me. That
is the secret of the failure of her attempt to preserve her
love for me.

"At first blush that may seem strange. Why wasn't I
bored with devoting so many evenings to students, for
whom I certainly would not have seriously disturbed myself, and why did I feel so much fatigue from devoting only
a few evenings to a woman whom I loved more than myself and for whom I was ready to die, and not only to die,
but to suffer all sorts of torments? It is strange, I admit,
but only to one who has not fathomed the nature of my
relations with the young people, to whom I devoted so much
time. In the first place, I had no personal relations with
these young people. When I was with them, I did not seem
to have men before me, but abstract types exchanging ideas;
my conversations with them were hardly to be distinguished
from my solitary dreams; but one side of the man was
occupied, that which demands the least rest,—thought. All
the rest slept. And furthermore the conversation had a practical, a useful object,—coöperation for the development of
the intellectual life and the perfecting of my young friends.
This was so easy a task that it rather reëstablished my
strength, exhausted by other work,—a task which did not
tire me, but, on the contrary, refreshed me; nevertheless, it
was a task, and it was not rest that I was after, but a useful
object. In short, I let my whole being go to sleep, thought
excepted, and that acted without being troubled by any
personal prepossession regarding the men with whom I was
talking; consequently, I felt as much at my ease as if I had
been alone. These conversations did not take me out of
my solitude, so to speak. There was nothing in them similar
to the relations in which the entire man participates.

"I know what a delicate matter it is to utter the word
'*ennui*'; but sincerity will not permit me to withhold it.
Yes, with all my love for her, I felt a sense of relief when
later I became convinced that our relations were forever

broken. I became convinced of it about the time when she perceived that to comply with her desires was a burden to me. Then my future seemed to assume a more agreeable shape. Seeing that it was impossible to maintain our old relations, I began to consider by what method we could soonest—I must again use a delicate expression—effect a separation. That is why those who judge only by appearances have been able to believe in my generosity. Nevertheless I do not wish to be hypocritical and deny the good that is in me; therefore I must add that one of my motives was the desire to see her happy. But this was only a secondary motive, a strong one enough, to be sure, but far inferior in intensity to the first and principal motive,—the desire to escape *ennui*. That was the principal motive. It was under this influence that I began to analyze attentively her manner of life, and I easily discovered that the person in question was dominated in her feelings and acts by the presence and absence of Alexánder Matvéich. That made me consider him also. Then I understood the cause of her strange actions, to which at first I had paid no attention. That made me see things in a still more agreeable light. When I saw in her not only the desire for a passionate love, but also the love itself, an unconscious love for a man entirely worthy of her and able to completely replace me at her side; when I saw that this man too had a great passion for her,—I was thoroughly delighted. It is true, however, that the first impression was a painful one: no grave change takes place without some sorrow. I saw now that I could no longer conscientiously consider myself indispensable to her, as I had been accustomed to think. This new change, therefore, had a painful side. But not for long. Now I was sure of her happiness and felt no anxiety about her. That was a source of great joy. But it would be an error to believe that that was my chief pleasure; no, personal feeling was dominant even here. I saw that I was to be free. I do not mean that single life seemed to me freer than family life. No, if husband and wife make each other mutually happy without effort and without thought, the more intimate their relations the happier they are. But our relations were not of that nature. Consequently to me separation meant freedom.

"It is obvious from all this that I acted in my own interest, when I decided not to stand in the way of their happiness. There was a noble side to my conduct, but the motive power was the desire of my own nature for a more comfortable situation. And that is why I had the strength to act well, to do without hesitation and without pain what I believed to be my duty. This is always easy when it coincides with the dictates of one's own nature.

"I started for Ryazan. Some time afterwards she called me back, saying that my presence would not trouble her. I took the contrary view,—for two reasons. It was painful to her to see the man to whom (in her opinion) she owed so much. She was mistaken. She was under no obligation to me, because I had always acted much more in my own interest than in hers. But she saw it differently, and moreover she felt a very profound attachment for me, which was a source of pain. This attachment had also its agreeable side, but this could not have become dominant unless it had been less intense, for, when intense, it is very painful. The second motive (another delicate explanation, but I must say what I think) arose from the fact that her rather abnormal situation in the matter of social conditions was disagreeable to her. Thus I came to see that the proximity of my existence to hers was painful to her. I will not deny that to this new discovery there was a side incomparably more painful to me than all the feelings that I had experienced in the preceding stages of the affair. I retained very good dispositions toward her: I wished to remain her friend. I hoped that such would be the case. And when I saw that it could not be, I was much grieved. And my chagrin was compensated by no personal interest. I may say, then, that my final resolution was taken only through attachment to her, through a desire to see her happy. Consequently, my conduct toward her even in our happiest days never gave me so much inner satisfaction as this resolution. Then at last I acted under the influence of what I may call nobility, or, to speak more accurately, noble design, in which the general law of human nature acts wholly by itself without the aid of individual peculiarities; and I learned to know the lofty pleasure of seeing one's self act nobly,—that is, in the way in which all men without exception, ought to act.

"I do not need to explain this side of my conduct, which would have been senseless to the last degree in dealing with other men; it is, however, only too well justified by the character of the person to whom I yielded. When I was at Ryazan, not a word passed between her and Alexánder Matvéich. Later, at the time when I took my final resolution, not a word passed between him and me or between her and me. But to know their thoughts I did not need to hear them."

I have transmitted literally the words of Dmítry Sergéich, as I have already said.

I am an entire stranger to you, but the correspondence upon which I enter with you, in carrying out the will of poor Dmítry Sergéich, is of so intimate a nature that you will be curious perhaps to know who this unknown correspondent is, who is so familiar with Dmítry's inner life. I am a medical student who has renounced his profession; I can tell you nothing more about myself. Of late years I have lived in St. Petersburg. A few days ago I conceived the idea of travelling and seeking a new career in foreign lands. I left St. Petersburg the day after you learned of Dmítry's loss. By the merest chance I did not have my passport, but I succeeded in getting that of another, which one of our common acquaintances had the kindness to furnish me. He gave it to me on condition that I would do some errands for him on the way. If you happen to see M. Rakhmétov, be kind enough to tell him that all his commissions have been attended to. Now I am going to wander about for a while,—probably in Germany observing the customs of the people. I have a few hundred rubles, and I wish to live at my ease and without doing anything. When I grow weary of idleness, I shall look for work. Of what sort? It is of no consequence. Where? It matters not. I am as free as a bird, and I can be as careless as a bird. Such a situation enchants me.

Probably you will wish to reply, but I do not know where I shall be a week hence,—perhaps in Italy, perhaps in England, perhaps at Prague. Now I can live according to my caprice, and where it will take me I know not. Consequently, upon your letters place only this address: *"Berlin, Friedrichstrasse 20, Agentur von H. Schmeidler";* within this envelope place another containing your letter, and upon the inner envelope, instead of any address, write the figures 12345; to the Schmeidler agency that will mean that the letter is to be sent to me. Accept, Madame, the assurance of the high esteem of a man unknown to you, but profoundly devoted to you, who signs himself

A QUONDAM MEDICAL STUDENT.

My much esteemed Monsieur Alexánder Matvéich:
In conformity with the wishes of poor Dmítry Sergéich, I must tell you that he considered the obligation to yield his place to you the best conclusion possible. The circumstances which have induced this change have gradually come about within the last three years, in which you had almost abandoned his society, and without, consequently, any share in them on your part. This change results solely from the acts of two individuals whom you have tried in vain to bring together, and the conclusion was inevitable. It is needless to say that Dmítry Sergéich could in no way attribute it to you. Of course this explanation is superfluous, and it is only for form's sake that he has charged me with making it. He was not fitted for the situation which he occupied, and in his opinion it is better for all that he has yielded his place to you.
I shake your hand.

A QUONDAM MEDICAL STUDENT.

"And, for my part, I know . . ."
What's that? The voice is familiar to me. I look behind me; it is he, it is really he, the penetrating reader, lately expelled for knowing neither A nor B on a question of art, here he is again, and with his usual penetration again he knows something.
"Ah! I know who wrote that . . ."
I seize precipitately the first object that comes to my hand,—it is a napkin, inasmuch as, after copying the letter of the quondam student, I sat down to breakfast,—I seize the napkin and I close his mouth. "Well! know then! but why cry out like a madman?"

: II :

St. Petersburg, August 25, 1856

Monsieur:

You cannot imagine how happy I was to receive your letter. I thank you with all my heart. Your intimacy with Dmítry Sergéich, who has just perished, entitles me to consider you a friend, and permit me to call you so.

In each of the words which you have communicated to me I have recognized the character of Dmítry Sergéich. He was always searching for the most hidden causes of his acts, and it pleased him to apply thereto the theory of egoism. For that matter it is a habit common to all our circle. My Alexánder also is fond of analyzing himself in this fashion. If you could hear how he explains his conduct towards me and Dmítry Sergéich for the last three years! To hear him, he did everything from selfish design, for his own pleasure. I, too, long since acquired this habit. Only it occupies us— Alexánder and me—a little less than Dmítry Sergéich; we have the same inclination, only his was stronger. Yes, to hear us, we are all three the greatest egoists that the world has yet seen. And perhaps it is the truth.

But, besides this trait, common to all three of us, the words of Dmítry Sergéich contain something peculiar to himself: the object of his explanations is evident,—to calm me. Not that his words are not wholly sincere,—he never said what he did not think,—but he makes too prominent that side of the truth calculated to give me peace. I am very grateful to you, my friend, but I too am an egoist, and I will say that his anxiety on my account was useless. We justify ourselves much more easily than others justify us. I too do not consider myself at all guilty towards him; I will say more: I do not even feel under any obligation to have an attachment for him. I appreciate highly his noble conduct, but I know that he acted nobly, not for me, but for himself; and I, in not deceiving him, acted, not for him, but for myself,—not because, in deceiving him, I should have been injust to him, but because to do so was repugnant to me. I say, as he does, that I do not accuse myself. But like him also I am moved to justify myself; to use his expression (a very correct one), which means that I foresee others will not be as indulgent as myself regarding some phases of my conduct. I have no desire to justify myself regarding that part of the matter upon which he touches; but, on the other hand, I have a desire to justify myself regarding the part upon which he does not need to justify himself. No one will call me guilty on account of what took place before my dream. But, then, is it not my fault that the affair took so melodramatic an aspect and led to a theatrical conclusion? Ought I not to have taken a much simpler view of a change of relations already inevitable, when my dream for the first time opened the eyes of Dmítry Sergéich and myself to my situation? In the evening of the day when Dmítry Sergéich died, I had a long conversation with that ferocious Rakhmétov. What a good and tender man that Rakhmétov is! He said I know not how many horrible things about Dmítry Sergéich. But, if one should repeat them in a friendly tone, they would be almost just.

I believed that Dmítry Sergéich knew perfectly well what Rakhmétov was going to say to me, and that he had counted on it. In my state of mind I needed to hear him, and his remarks did much to quiet me. Whoever planned that conversation, I thank you very very much, my friend. But the ferocious Rakhmétov himself had to confess that in the last half of the affair the conduct of Dmítry Sergéich was perfect. Rakhmétov blamed him only for the first half, concerning which it pleased Dmítry Sergéich to justify himself.

But I am going to justify myself concerning the second half, although no one has told me that I was guilty. But every one of us—I speak of ourselves and our friends, of our whole circle—has a severer censor than Rakhmétov himself,—his or her own mind. Yes, I understand, my friend, that it would have been much easier for all if I had taken a simpler view of the affair and had not given it so tragic a significance. And, if we leave it to the opinion of Dmítry Sergéich, I shall have to say further that he would then have had no need to resort to a sensational climax very painful to him: he had to act as he did only because he was pushed by my impetuous way of looking at things.

I suppose that he must have thought so too, although he did not charge you to tell me so. I set the higher value on his good feelings towards me from the fact that, in spite of all that happened, they did not weaken. But listen, my friend; this opinion is not just. It was not from any fault of mine, it was not my unnecessary exaggeration of feeling that forced Dmítry Sergéich into an experience which he himself calls very painful. It is true that, if I had not attached excessive importance to the change of relations, the journey to Ryazan might have been dispensed with, but he says that that was not painful to him; in this respect, then, my excitement caused no great harm. It was only the necessity of dying that was painful to him. He explains by two reasons why he was forced to adopt that resolution.

In the first place, I suffered from my extreme attachment for him; in the second, I suffered because I could not give my relations with Alexánder the character demanded by public opinion. In fact, I was not altogether tranquil; my situation was hard, but he did not guess the real cause. He believed that his presence was painful to me on account of the depth of my gratitude; this was not quite the case. We are very much disposed to look for consoling thoughts, and when Dmítry Sergéich saw the inevitability of dying, that inevitability had long ceased to exist. My gratitude had decreased to that moderate degree which constitutes an agreeable feeling. Now, deep gratitude was the sole cause of my painful exaggeration of feeling. The other cause mentioned by Dmítry Sergéich—the desire to give my relations with Alexánder the character demanded by society—did not depend at all upon my way of viewing the affair. It was the result of society's ideas. That cause I could not have controlled; but Dmítry Sergéich was absolutely mistaken if he supposed that his presence was painful to me for that reason. If a husband lives with his wife, that is enough to prevent scandal, whatever the relations of his wife with another. That is a great step already. We see many examples where, thanks to the noble character of the husband, affairs are thus arranged, and in that case society lets the woman alone. Now, I consider that the best and easiest way of arranging affairs of this sort. Dmítry Sergéich at first proposed this plan to me. I then refused on account of my exaggeration of feeling. I do not know what would have happened if I had accepted; but, if I had been able to content myself with being left alone and the avoidance of scandal regarding my relations with Alexánder, it is evident that the plan proposed by Dmítry Sergéich would have been sufficient, and that, if I had adopted it, there would have been no need of his decision to die. In that case evidently I should have had

no reason to want to make formal my relations with Alexánder. But it seems to me that such an arrangement, satisfactory in most cases similar to ours, would not have worked
in ours. Our situation had one peculiar feature,—the three
individuals whom it concerned were of equal force. If
Dmítry Sergéich had felt an intellectual and moral superiority in Alexánder; if, in yielding his place to him, he had
yielded to moral superiority; if his withdrawal, instead of
being voluntary, had been only the withdrawal of the weak
before the strong,—why, then certainly nothing would have
weighed upon me. Likewise, if I had been superior in mind
and character to Dmítry Sergéich; if he himself, before the
birth of my passion, had been one of the two heroes of a
certain anecdote which once made us laugh so heartily,—
all would have been arranged, he would have submitted.
The anecdote was of two gentlemen who, after having con-
versed some time and being pleased with each other, desired
to make each other's acquaintance:

"I am Lieutenant So-and-So," said one, with an air of
dignity.

"And I am the husband of Madame Tedesco," said the
other.

If Dmítry Sergéich had been the husband of Madame
Tedesco, why, then he would have had no need to resort to
extremities, he would have submitted to his fate, he would
have seen nothing offensive to him in his submission, and
everything would have been delightful. But his relations
with me and with Alexánder were not at all of such a character. In no respect was he either our inferior or our superior; this was evident to all. My liberty could depend only
on his good will and not at all on his weakness. You cannot
deny it, my friend.

What, then, was my situation? I saw myself dependent on
his good will. That was why my situation was painful to me,
that was why he found it useful to adopt his noble resolution. Yes, my friend, the cause of my feeling, which forced
him to this step, was much more deeply hidden than he explains in your letter. The overwhelming degree of gratitude
no longer existed. To satisfy the requirements of society
would have been easy in the way proposed by Dmítry Sergéich himself, and, after all, these requirements did not affect
me, living in my little circle, entirely beyond the reach of
gossip. But I remained dependent upon Dmítry Sergéich.

That was the painful part of it. What had my view of the change of our relations to do with this? Dmítry Sergéich remained the master. Now, you know and approve my feeling. I do not wish to be dependent upon the good will of any one, though he be the most devoted of men, the man whom I most esteemed, in whom I believed as in another self, and in whom I had full confidence. I do not wish it, and I know that you approve this. But why so many words? Why this analysis of our inmost feelings, which no one would have gone into? Like Dmítry Sergéich, I have a mania for undressing my feelings in order that I may say: It is not my fault, but the result of a circumstance beyond my control? I make this remark because Dmítry Sergéich liked remarks of this character. I wish to insinuate myself into your mind, my friend. But enough of this! You have had so much sympathy for me that you have thought nothing of the few hours required to write your long and precious letter. From it I see (whether from Dmítry Sergéich's style or yours),— yes, I see that you will be curious to know what became of me after Dmítry Sergéich left me to go to Moscow and then to come back and die. On his return from Ryazan he saw that I was embarrassed. This was manifest in me only in his presence; as long as he was at Ryazan, I did not think so much about him. But, when he started for Moscow, I saw that he was meditating something grave. He settled up his affairs at St. Petersburg. He had been waiting for a week only to get everything arranged for his departure, and why should I not have foreseen this? During the last days I sometimes saw sadness on his face, on that face which knew so well how to hide secrets. I foresaw that something decisive was to be expected. And when he boarded the train, I was so sad! The next day and the day after my sorrow increased. Suddenly Másha brought me a letter. What a painful moment! What a painful day! You know it. How much better I know now the strength of my attachment for Dmítry Sergéich! I had no idea myself that it was so deep. You know the strength of our mutual attachment. You certainly know that I had then decided to see Alexánder no more; all day I felt that my life was broken forever, and you know of my childish enthusiasm when I saw the note of my good, my very good, friend, the note that changed completely all my thoughts (notice the prudence of my expressions; you must be contented with them, my friend). You know all this, because Rakhmétov, after escorting me to the train, went to accompany you to the station. Dmítry Sergéich and he were right in saying that I ought nevertheless to leave St. Petersburg in order to produce the effect desired by Dmítry Sergéich so much that he inflicted upon me horrible torments for an entire day. How grateful I am to him for having had so little pity on me! He and Rakhmétov were also right in advising Alexánder not to see me or escort me to the station. But, as I no longer needed to go as far as Moscow, it being necessary only to leave St. Petersburg, I stopped at Novgorod. A few days later Alexánder came there with the documents establishing the death of Dmítry Sergéich. We were married a week later, and have lived almost a month at Chudovo,* near the railroad, in order that it may be easy for Alexánder to go three or four times a week to his hospital. Yesterday we returned to St. Petersburg, and that is why I am so late in answering your letter. It had remained in Másha's box, who had almost forgotten it. And you had probably framed all sorts of ideas in consequence of receiving no reply.

Embracing you, my friend,

Yours,

VÉRA KIRSÁNOV.

I shake your hand, my dear; only I beg you not to send compliments, at least to me; else I will let my heart flow out before you in a torrent of adoration, which would certainly be disagreeable to you in the highest degree. But do you know that for us to write so briefly to each other shows considerable stupidity in me as well as in you? It seems that we are somewhat embarrassed in each other's presence. Supposing that this were pardonable in me, why should you feel any embarrassment? Next time I hope to talk freely with you, and I shall forthwith write you a heap of St. Petersburg news.

Yours,

ALEXÁNDER KIRSÁNOV.

* A large village situated about sixty-five miles from St. Petersburg.

: I I I :

These letters, while perfectly sincere, were indeed a little exclusive, as Véra Pávlovna herself remarked. The two correspondents evidently tried to make the painful shocks which they had felt seem less intense to each other. They are very shrewd people. I have very often heard them—them and those like them—say things which made me laugh heartily in the midst of their pathetic assertions that such and such a thing was nothing and could easily be endured.

I laughed at such assertions when made privately to me, a stranger. And when I heard them said before a man who could not help listening, I corroborated them, and said that such and such a thing was indeed nothing. An honest man is very queer; I have always laughed at them when I have met them.

They are sometimes even absurd. Take, for example, these letters. I am a little accustomed to such things, being on terms of friendship with them. But what an impression they must make on a total stranger, or on the penetrating reader, for instance!

The penetrating reader pronounces sentence, shaking his head:

"Immoral!"

"Bravo! Do me the favor of saying one word more."

"The author also is an immoral man to approve such things," says the penetrating reader, adding to the sentence.

"No, my dear, you are mistaken. There are many things in this that I do not approve, and, to tell the truth, I do not even approve any of it. It is all much too ingenious, much too far-fetched; life is much simpler."

"Then you are still more immoral?" asks the penetrating reader, opening his eyes wide, astonished at the inconceivable immorality into which humanity has fallen in my person.

"Much more immoral," I say, and no one knows whether I am telling the truth or laughing at the penetrating reader.

The correspondence lasted three or four months longer,—actively on the part of the Kirsánovs, negligently and inadequately on the part of their correspondent. The latter soon ceased to answer their letters; they saw that his sole intention was to communicate to Véra Pávlovna and her husband the thoughts of Lopukhóv, and that, after having fulfilled this duty, he deemed further correspondence useless. Having obtained no reply to two or three letters, the Kirsánovs understood this and stopped writing.

: I V :

Véra Pávlovna is resting on her soft couch, waiting for her husband to come back from the hospital to dinner. Today she does not fuss over dessert or dinner; she prefers to rest, for she has worked hard all the morning. It has been so for a long time, and it will be so for a very long time to come. She is starting another workshop for seamstresses at the other end of the city. Véra Pávlovna Lopukhóv lived on Vassilievsky Island. Véra Pávlovna Kirsánov lives on Sergeievsky Street, her husband requiring rooms in the neighborhood of the Vilborg district.

Madame Mertzálov proved equal to the management of the shop on Vassilievsky Island, which was quite natural, she and the shop being old acquaintances. On her return to St. Petersburg Véra Pávlovna saw that she did not need to visit the shop often to see that things went well, and, though she continued to visit it almost daily, it was solely because she was drawn by affectionate attachment. It must be added, however, that her visits were not quite useless, for Madame Mertzálov often needed her advice; but that took very little time, besides being needed less and less frequently. Madame Mertzálov will soon have as much experience as herself, and will be able to conduct things herself. After her return to St. Petersburg Véra Pávlovna visited Vassilievsky Island more as a dear friend than as an indispensable person. What, then, was to be done? Establish a new workshop for seamstresses, in her own neighborhood, at the other end of the city.

So, in fact, a new shop was established in one of the smaller streets between Basseiny Street and Sergeievsky Street. There is much less work here than in the first shop. The first five of the working-girls are from the old shop, where their places have been filled by others; the rest of the force is made up of acquaintances of the seamstresses in the old shop. So, everything is half done, to start with. The purpose and organization of the shop was well known to the staff. The young girls came filled with a desire to establish promptly in the new shop the organization which had been effected so slowly in the old. Oh! now the organization went ahead ten times faster than then, and with three times less embarrassment. But none the less there was a great deal of work to be done, and Véra Pávlovna was tired, as she had been yesterday, and day before yesterday, and as she had been for about two months. Two months only, although six months had elapsed since her second marriage. After all, it was necessary to have a honeymoon; and she had a long one. Now she got back to work.

Yes, she had worked a great deal; now she was resting and thinking of many things, especially of the present; it is so beautiful and so full! So full of life that but little time is left for memories; memories will come later. Oh! much later! Not in ten years, nor even in twenty, but later still. Nevertheless, they do come even now, though rarely. At this moment, for example, she is recalling what has most impressed her. Here is what her memory brings back to her.

: V :

"My darling, I am going with you."

"But you have not your things."

"I will go tomorrow, since you will not take me with you today."

"Reflect, meditate. And wait for my letter. It will reach you tomorrow."

There she is on her way back from the station to the house; what does she feel and what does she think as she retires with Másha? She hardly knows, herself, so shaken has she been by the rapid shaping of events. It is but twenty-two hours since he found in his room the letter which she had written, and already he is gone! How quickly, how suddenly! At two o'clock in the morning she foresaw nothing of this. He waited till, conquered and exhausted by fatigue, she was overcome by sleep; then he entered her room and said a few not over-sensible words as a scarcely comprehensible preface to this bit of information:

"I have not seen my old parents in a long time; I am going to see them; they will be very glad."

Only that, and then he went out. She ran after him, although he had made her promise not to do so.

"Where is he, then? Másha, where is he, where is he?"

Másha, who was still engaged in clearing the tea-table just left by visitors, answered:

"Dmítry Sergéich went out; he said, as he passed by, 'I am going for a walk.'"

She had to go back to bed. How could she sleep? She did not know that his departure was to take place in a few hours. He had said that they still had time to talk over all these things together. And when she awoke, it was time to go to the station.

All this passes before her eyes like a flash, as if it had not happened to her, but had been the experience of some one else, which had been told to her hastily. Only on reaching the house does she regain possession of herself, and begin to think: What is she now? what is to become of her?

Yes, she will go to Ryazan. She will go. To do otherwise is impossible. But the letter? What will it say? Why wait for it before deciding? She knows the contents in advance. No, it is necessary to wait until the letter comes. But what is the use of waiting? She will go. Yes, she will go. She repeats it to herself for one, two, three, four hours. But Másha, getting hungry, is already calling her to dinner for the third time, and this time she orders rather than calls; well, it is at least a distraction.

"Poor Másha, she must be very hungry on account of me. Why did you wait for me, Másha? You would have done better to dine without waiting for me."

"That cannot be, Véra Pávlovna."

And again the young woman reflects for two hours:

"I will go. Tomorrow. Only I will wait for the letter, for he begged me to. But, whatever its contents,—I know what it will contain,—I will go."

That is what she thinks; but is that really all? No, her thought still runs upon five little words: *He does not wish it,* and these little words dominate her thought more and more. The setting sun finds her still absorbed. And just at the moment when the importunate Másha comes to demand that she shall take tea, six words add themselves to the five: *Nor do I wish it either.* Másha has entered; and has driven away these six new bad little words. But not for long. At first they do not dare to make their appearance, and give place to their own refutation: *But I must go.* Then they yield, only to come back escorted by this refutation. In a twinkling they return to Véra Pávlovna's thought: *He does not wish it—Nor do I wish it either.* For half an hour they dance a saraband in her brain; then against these words so often uttered, *I will go,* rush these three, *Shall I go?* But here comes Másha again.

"I gave a ruble to the bearer, Véra Pávlovna, for it was written on the envelope that, if he brought the letter before nine o'clock, he should be given a ruble; if after that, only half as much. Now, he brought it before nine o'clock. To go faster he took a cab; 'I did as I promised,' he said to me."

A letter from him! She knows what it contains: "Do not come." But she will go just the same; she does not wish to listen to this letter. The letter contains something else,— something which cannot be disregarded:

> "I am going to Ryazan, but not directly. I have many business matters to attend to on the way. Besides Moscow, where press of business will oblige me to spend a week, I must stop at two cities this side of Moscow and three places the other side, before reaching Ryazan. How much time I shall have to spend thus I cannot tell. For instance, I have to collect some money from our commercial representatives, and you know, my dear friend [these words, *dear friend,* were repeated in the letter that I might see that he was still well-disposed towards me; how I kissed these words!],—you know, my dear friend, that, when one has to collect money, he often has to wait several days where he expected to stay but a few hours. So I absolutely cannot fix the day of my arrival at Ryazan, but it surely will not be immediately."

Véra Pávlovna still remembers word for word the contents of this letter. What, then, is to be done? He deprives her of all dependence upon him by which she may remain attached to him. And the words, *I must go to him,* change into these: *Nevertheless I must not see him,* and in the latter sentence the word *him* refers to another person. She repeats these words for an hour or two: *I must not see him.*

Of this thought is born another: *Is it possible that I wish to see him? No.* When she goes to sleep, this last thought gives way to another: *Will it be possible for me to see him?* No answer, but a new transformation: *Is it possible that I may not see him?* And she sleeps till morning in this last thought: *Is it possible that I may not see him?*

And when she awakes very late in the morning, all the thoughts of the evening before and of the night give way to these two, which clash against each other: *I will see him! I will not see him!* That lasts all the morning. *I will see him!* No! no! no! But what is she doing? She has taken her hat, she looks in the glass instinctively to see if her hair is in order, and in the glass she sees her hat; everything vanishes then before these three words: "No going back! No going back! No going back!"

"Másha, do not wait for me to come to dinner. I shall not dine at home."

"Alexánder Matvéich has not yet returned from the hospital," says Stepán to her, calmly. Indeed, there is no reason for Stepán to be astonished at the presence of Véra Pávlovna, who had come very often lately.

"I suspected as much, but it makes no difference. I'll wait. Don't tell him that I am here."

She takes up a literary review,—yes, she can read, she sees that she can read; yes, now that there is no going back, now that her resolution is taken, she feels very calm.

A new life is about to begin. How astonished and happy he will be! A new life is about to begin. How happy we are! A ring; she blushes slightly and smiles; the door opens.

"Véra Pávlovna!"

He staggers; yes, he staggers; he has to support himself against the door, but she runs to him, and kissing him, says:

"Darling, oh my dearest! How noble *he* is! How I love you! I could not live without you!"

What took place then, how they crossed the room, she does not remember; she only remembers running to him and kissing him; for that matter, he remembers no more than she. They only remember that they passed by armchairs and by the table, but how did they leave the door? . . . Yes, for a few seconds their heads were turned, their sight disturbed by this kiss . . .

"Vérochka, my angel!"

"My friend, I could not live without you. How long you

have loved me without telling me so! How noble you are, and how noble he is, too!"

"Tell me, then, Vérochka, how did this happen?"

"I told him that I could not live without you; the next day—that is, yesterday—he went away. I wanted to follow him. All day yesterday I thought that I would go to him; yet here I have been waiting a long time."

"But how thin you have grown in the last two weeks, Vérochka! How delicate your hands are!"

He kisses her hands.

"Yes, my friend, it was a painful struggle! Now I can appreciate how you have suffered to avoid disturbing my peace. How did you succeed in maintaining such self-possession that I noticed nothing? How you must have suffered!"

"Yes, Vérochka, it was not easy."

And he still covers her hands with kisses. Suddenly she begins to laugh:

"Ah! how inattentive I am to you! You are tired, Sásha, you are hungry!"

She escapes and runs away.

"Where are you going, Vérochka?"

But she does not answer. She is in the kitchen already talking to Stepán in gay and urgent tones.

"Get dinner for two! Quick, quick! Where are the plates, and knives and forks? I will set the table. Bring in something to eat; Alexánder is so tired from his hospital duties that his dinner must be served in a hurry."

She returns with the plates, on which rattle knives, forks, and spoons.

"You know, my darling, that the first thought of lovers at the first interview is to dine as quickly as possible," says she, laughing.

He laughs also, and helps her set the table; but delays her still more, for he is constantly kissing her hands.

"Ah! my darling, how delicate your hands are!" And he kisses them again.

"Come to the table, Sásha, and be quiet!"

Stepán brings the soup. During dinner she tells him how this all happened.

"Ah! my darling, how we eat for lovers! It is true, though, that yesterday I ate nothing."

Stepán enters with the last course.

"Stepán, I have eaten your dinner."

"Yes, Véra Pávlovna, I shall have to buy something at the shop."

"Do so, and now you must know that in the future you will always have to prepare for two, not counting yourself. Sásha, where is your cigar-case? Give it to me."

She cuts a cigar herself, lights it, and says to him:

"Smoke, my darling; meantime I will prepare the coffee; or perhaps you prefer tea? Do you know, my darling, our dinner ought to be better; you are too easy with Stepán."

Five minutes later she returns; Stepán follows her with the tea-service, and, as she comes in, she sees that Alexánder's cigar has gone out.

"Ha! ha! my darling, how dreamy you have become in my absence!"

He laughs too.

"Smoke, then," and again she lights his cigar.

In recalling all this now, Véra Pávlovna laughs over again: "How prosaic our romance is! The first interview and the soup; our heads turned at the first kiss, then a good appetite,—what a strange love-scene! It is very queer. And how his eyes shone! But indeed they shine still in the same way. How many of his tears have fallen on my hands, which were then so delicate, but which certainly are not so now. But really my hands are beautiful; he speaks the truth." She looks at her hands and says: "Yes, he is right. But what has that to do with our first interview and its accompaniments? I sit down at the table to pour the tea."

The tea is not yet finished when a terrible ring is heard; two students burst into the room and in their hurry do not even see her.

"Alexánder Matvéich, an interesting patient!" they say, all out of breath; "an extremely rare and very curious subject [here they give the Latin name of the disease] has just been brought in, Alexánder Matvéich, and aid is needed immediately. Every half-hour is precious. We even took a cab."

"Quick, quick, darling, hurry!" says she. Only now do the students notice her and bow, and in a twinkling they drag away their professor, who was not long in getting ready, having kept on his military overcoat. Again she hurries him.

"From there you will come to my place?" says she, as she takes leave of him.

"Yes."

In the evening he makes her wait a long time. It is ten o'clock, and he does not come; eleven,—it is useless to expect him. What does it mean? Certainly she is not at all anxious; nothing can have happened to him; but why is he obliged to stay with the interesting patient? Is this poor interesting patient still alive? Has Sásha succeeded in saving him? Yes, Sásha was detained a long time, and remained at the hospital till four in the morning.

"The case was very difficult and interesting, Vérochka."

"Saved?"

"Yes."

"But why did you rise so early?"

"I've not been in bed."

"You have not been in bed! To avoid delaying your arrival you did not sleep last night! Impious man! Go to your room and sleep till dinner-time; be sure that I find you still asleep."

In two minutes he was driven away.

Such were their first two interviews. But the second dinner went off better; they told each other of their affairs in a reasonable manner. The night before, on the contrary, they did not know what they were saying. They laughed, and then were gloomy. It seemed to each of them that the other had suffered the more.

Ten days later they hired a little country-house on Kamenny Island.

: V I :

It is not very often that Véra Pávlovna recalls the past of her new love: the present is so full of life that but little time is left for memories. Nevertheless these memories come back more and more often, and gradually she feels the growth within her of a certain discontent, faint, slight, vague, at first,—a discontent with whom, with what? Ah! there it is; at last she sees that it is with herself that she is discontented, but why? She was too proud for that. Is it only with the past that she is discontented? That was the case at first, but she notices that this discontent refers also to the present. And of how strange a character this feeling is! As if it were not she, Véra Pávlovna Kirsánov, who felt this discontent, but as if it were the discontent of thousands and millions of human beings reflected in her. For what reason are these thousands and millions of human beings discontented with themselves? If she had lived and thought as she used to when she was alone, it is probable that this feeling would not have shown itself so soon; but now she was constantly with her husband, they always thought together, she thinks of him in the midst of these other thoughts. That aids her much in determining the character of her feeling. He has been unable to find the solution of the enigma. This feeling, obscure to her, is still more so to him. It is even difficult for him to understand how one can feel discontent without this discontent referring to something personal. This is a singularity a hundred times more obscure to him than to her. Nevertheless she feels much aided by the fact that she thinks always of her husband, that she is always with him, observes him, and thinks with him. She has noticed that, when the feeling of discontent comes, it is always followed by a comparison (it is even contained in this comparison) between herself and her husband, and her thought is illuminated by the right word: "A difference, an offensive difference." Now all is clear to her.

: VII :

"How agreeable N. N. is, Sásha! [The name spoken by Véra Pávlovna was that of the officer through whom she had desired to make the acquaintance of Tamberlik in her horrible dream.] He has brought me a new poem, which is not to be printed for a long time yet," said Véra Pávlovna, at dinner. "When we have dined, we will read this poem, if you like. I have waited for you, though I am terribly anxious to read it."

"What, then, is this poem?"

"You shall judge. We shall see if he has succeeded. N. N. says that he himself—I mean the author—is almost satisfied with it."

They sat down in Véra Pávlovna's room, and she began to read:

> *Oh! comme la corbeille est pleine!*
> *J'ai de la perse et du brocart.*

Ayez pitié, ô mon amour,
De l'épaule du garçon.

"Now I see," said Kirsánov, after hearing several dozen lines: "it is a new style peculiar to the author. But it is easy to see who wrote it. Nékrassov, is it not? I thank you very much for having waited for me."

"I believe it is!" said Véra Pávlovna. And they read twice the little poem, which, thanks to their intimacy with a friend of the author, they thus had the privilege of seeing three years before its publication.

"But do you know the lines which most impress me?" said Véra Pávlovna, after they had several times read and re-read several passages of the poem; "these lines do not belong in the principal passages, but they impress me exceedingly. When Kátya* was awaiting the return of her lover, she grieved much:

Inconsolable, elle se serait consumée de douleur

Si elle avait eu le temps de se chagriner;
Mais le temps des travaux pénibles pressait,
Il aurait fallu achever une dizaine d'affaires.
Bien qu'il lui arrivât souvent
De tomber de fatigue, la pauvre enfant,
Sous sa faux vaillante tombait l'herbe,
Le blé criait sous sa faucille;
C'est de toutes ses forces
Qu'elle battait le blé tous les matins,
Et jusqu'à la nuit noire elle étendait le lin
Sur les prairies pleines de rosée.

These lines are only the preface of the episode where this worthy Kátya dreams of Vanya;† but, I repeat, they are the ones which most impress me."

"Yes, this entire picture is one of the finest in the poem, but these lines do not occupy a prominent place in the poem. You find them so beautiful because they correspond so closely to the thoughts that fill your own mind. What, then, are these thoughts?"

"These, Sásha. We have often said that it is probable that

* Kátya is the diminutive of Katérina.
† Vanya is the diminutive of Ivan.

woman's organization is superior to man's, and that it is probable, therefore, that intellectually man will be thrown back by woman to a second place when the reign of brute force is over. We have reached this supposition by watching real life and especially by noting the fact that the number of women born intelligent is greater than that of men. Moreover, you rest this opinion on various anatomical and physiological details."

"What insulting things for men you bring forth. And these are more your pronouncements than mine, Vérochka. It is insulting for me! Fortunately, the time that you foresee is still far off. Otherwise I should quickly change my opinion to avoid being relegated to a second place. For that matter, it is only a probability; science has not yet observed facts enough to solve this grave question properly."

"But, dear, have we not also asked ourselves why the facts of history have been hitherto so contradictory of the deduction which may be drawn, with almost entire certainty, from observations of private life and the constitution of the organism? Hitherto woman has played but a minor part in intellectual life, because the reign of violence deprived her of the means of development and stifled her aspirations. That is a sufficient explanation in itself; but here is another. So far as physical force is concerned, woman's organism is the weaker, but it has at the same time the greater power of resistance, has it not?"

"This is surer than the difference in native intellectual powers. Yes, woman's organism is more effective in its resistance to the destructive forces,—climate, inclement weather, insufficient food. Medicine and physiology have paid but little attention to this question as yet, but statistics has already given an eloquent reply: the average life of women is longer than that of men. We may infer from this that the feminine organism is the more vigorous."

"The fact that woman's manner of life is generally even less healthy than man's makes this all the truer."

"There is another convincing consideration given us by physiology. Woman's growth may be said to end at the age of twenty, and man's at the age of twenty-five; these figures are approximately correct in our climate and of our race. Let us suppose, roughly speaking, that out of a given number there are as many women who live to the age of seventy as men who attain the age of sixty-five, and if we take into consideration the difference in the periods of development, the preponderance of vigor in the feminine organism becomes even more evident than the statisticians suppose, since they have never taken into account the difference in the ages of maturity. Seventy years is twenty times three and five-tenths; sixty-five years is twenty-five times two and six-tenths. Therefore woman's life is three and one-half times as long as the period of her development, while man's is but little more than two and one-half times as long as the period of his development, which is a little slower. Now, the respective strength of the two organisms should be measured by this standard."

"The difference is greater than my readings had led me to believe."

"You have read only the statistical summaries bearing on the average length of life. But if to these statistical facts we add physiological facts, the difference will appear very much greater yet."

"That is so, Sásha; I thought—and the thought now strikes me still more forcibly—that, if the feminine organism is better fitted to resist destructive forces, it is probable that woman could endure moral shocks with the greater ease and firmness. But in reality the opposite seems to be the truth."

"Yes, it is probable. But it is only a supposition. It is true, nevertheless, that your conclusion is derived from indisputable facts. The vigor of the organism is very intimately connected with the vigor of the nerves. Woman's nerves are probably more elastic and of more solid texture, and, if that is the case, they ought to endure painful shocks and sensations with the greater ease and firmness. In actual life we have far too many examples of the contrary. Woman is very often tormented by things that man endures easily. Not much effort has been made as yet to analyze the causes which, given our historical situation, show us phenomena the opposite of what we are justified in expecting from the very constitution of the organism. But one of these causes is plain; it governs all historical phenomena and all the phases of our present condition. It is the force of bias, a bad habit, a false expectation, a false fear. If a person says to himself, 'I can do nothing,' he finds himself unable to do anything. Now, women have always been told that they are weak, and so they feel weak and to all intents and purposes are weak. You know instances where men really in good health have been seen to waste away and die from the single thought that they were going to weaken and die. But there are also instances of this in the conduct of great masses of people, entire humanity. One of the most remarkable is furnished by military history. In the Middle Ages, infantry imagined that it could not hold its own against cavalry, and actually it could not. Entire armies of foot soldiers were scattered like flocks of sheep by a few hundred horsemen; and that lasted until the English foot-soldiers, small proprietors, proud and independent, appeared on the Continent. These did not share this fear, and were not accustomed to surrender without a struggle. They conquered every time they met the innumerable and formidable French cavalry. Do you remember those famous defeats of French horsemen by small armies of English foot-soldiers at Crécy, Poitiers, and Agincourt? The same fact was repeated when the Swiss foot-soldiers once got the idea that they had no reason to think themselves weaker than the feudal cavalry. The Austrian horsemen, and afterwards those of Burgundy, still more numerous, were beaten by them in every fight. The other horsemen wanted to meet them also, and were always routed. Everybody saw then that infantry was a more solid body than cavalry: but entire centuries had gone by in which infantry was very weak in comparison with cavalry, simply because it thought itself so."

"True, Sásha. We are weak because we consider ourselves so. But it seems to me that there is still another cause. I have us two in mind. Does it not seem to you that I changed a great deal during the two weeks when you did not see me?"

"Yes, you grew very thin and pale."

"It is precisely that which is revolting to my pride when I remember that no one noticed you grow thin or pale, though you suffered and struggled as much as I. How did you do it?"

"This is the reason, then, why these lines about Kátya, who escapes sorrow through labor, have made such an impression on you! I endured struggle and suffering with reasonable ease, because I had not much time to think about them. During the time that I devoted to them I suffered horribly, but my urgent daily duties forced me to forget them the greater part of the time. I had to prepare my lessons and attend to my patients. In spite of myself I rested during that time from my bitter thoughts. On the rare days when I had leisure, I felt my strength leaving me. It seems to me that, if I had abandoned myself for a week to my thoughts, I should have gone mad."

"That's it, exactly. Of late I have seen that the origin of the difference between us was there. One must have work that cannot be neglected or postponed, and then one is incomparably securer against sorrow."

"But you had a great deal of work too."

"My household duties, to be sure, but I was not obliged to attend to them, and often, when my sadness was too strong, I neglected them to abandon myself to my thoughts; one always abandons that which is least important. As soon as one's feelings get firm possession of them, these drive all petty cares out of the mind. I have lessons; these are more important. My main support then came from Dmítry's work as it now comes from yours. The lessons allow me to flatter myself that I am independent, and are by no means useless. But then I could get along without them.

"Then I tried, in order to drive away tormenting thoughts, to busy myself in the shop more than usual. But I did it only by an effort of will. I understood well enough that my presence in the shop was necessary only for an hour or an hour and a half, and that, if I stayed longer, I was tying myself down to a fatigue that, though certainly useful, was not at all indispensable. And then, can such altruistic occupation sustain persons as ordinary as I am? The Rakhmétovs are another sort of people: they are so much concerned about the common welfare that to work for public ends is a necessity to them, so much so that to them altruistic life takes the place of private life. But we do not scale these high summits, we are not Rakhmétovs, and our private life is the only thing, properly speaking, that is indispensable to us. The shop was not my matter, after all; I was concerned in it only for others and for my ideas; but I am one of those who take little interest in the affairs of others, though they are suffering themselves. What we need in such cases is a personal, urgent occupation, upon which our life depends; such an occupation, considering my feelings and condition, would weigh more with me than all the impulses of passion; it alone could serve to support me in a struggle against an omnipotent passion; it alone gives strength and rest. I want such an occupation."

"You are right, my friend," said Kirsánov, warmly, kissing his wife, whose eyes sparkled with animation. "To think that it hadn't occurred to me before, when it would have been so simple; I didn't even notice it! Yes, Vérochka, no one can think for another. If you wish to be comfortable, think for yourself of yourself; no one can take your place. To love as I love, and not to have understood all this before you explained it to me! But," he continued, laughing, and still kissing his wife, "why do you think this occupation necessary now? Are you becoming amorously inclined towards any one?"

Véra Pávlovna began to laugh heartily, and for some minutes mad laughter prevented them from speaking.

"Yes, we can laugh at that now," she said, at last: "both of us can now be sure that nothing of the kind will ever happen to either of us. But seriously, do you know what I am thinking about now? Though my love for Dmítry was not the love of a completely developed woman, neither did he love me in the way in which we understand love. His feeling for me was a mixture of strong friendship with the fire of amorous passion. He had a great friendship for me, but his amorous transports needed but a woman for their satisfaction, not me personally. No, that was not love. Did he care much about my thoughts? No, no more than I did about his. There was no real love between us."

"You are unjust to him, Vérochka."

"No, Sásha, it is really so. Between us it is useless to praise him. We both know very well in what high esteem we hold him; it is vain for him to say that it would have been easy to separate me from him; it is not so; you said in the same way that it was easy for you to struggle against your passion. Yet, however sincere his words and ·yours, they must not be understood or construed literally.

"Oh! my friend, I understand how much you suffered. And this is how I understand it."

"Vérochka, you stifle me. Confess that, besides the force of sentiment, you also wanted to show me your muscular force. How strong you are, indeed! But how could you be otherwise with such a chest?"

"My dear Sásha!

. . .

"But you did not let me talk business, Sásha," began **Véra** Pávlovna, when, two hours later, they sat down to tea.

"I did not let you talk? Was it my fault?"

"Certainly."

"Who began the indulgence?"

"Are you not ashamed to say that?"

"What?"

"That I began the *indulgence.* Fie! the idea of thus compromising a modest woman on the plea of coldness!"

"Indeed! Do you not preach equality? Why not equality of initiative as well?"

"Ha, ha, ha! a fine argument! But would you dare to accuse me of being illogical? Do I not try to maintain equality in initiative also? I take now the initiative of continuing our serious conversation, which we have too thoroughly forgotten."

"Take it, if you will, but I refuse to follow you, and I take the initiative of continuing to forget it. Give me your hand."

"But we must finish our talk, Sásha."

"We shall have time enough tomorrow. Now, you see, I am absorbed in an analysis of this hand."

: VIII :

"Sásha, let's finish our conversation of yesterday. We must do so, because I am getting ready to go with you, and you must know why," said Véra Pávlovna the next morning.

"You are coming with me?"

"Certainly. You asked me, Sásha, why I wanted a job upon which my life should depend, which I should look upon as seriously as you on yours, which should be as interesting as yours, and which should require as much attention as yours requires. I want this job, dearest, because I am very proud. When I think that during my days of trial my feelings became so visible in my person that others could analyze them, I am thoroughly ashamed. I do not speak of my sufferings. You had to struggle and suffer no less than I, and you triumphed where I was conquered. I want to be as strong as you, your equal in everything. And I have found the way; I have thought a great deal since we left each other yesterday, and I have found it all alone; you were unwilling to aid

me with your advice; so much the worse for you. It is too
late now. Yes, Sásha, you may be very anxious about me, my
dear friend, but how happy we shall be if I am successful!"

Véra Pávlovna had just thought of an occupation which,
under Kirsánov's guidance and her hand in his, she could
engage in successfully.

Lopukhóv, to be sure, had not hindered her at all; on the
contrary, she was sure of having his support in all serious
matters. But it was only under serious circumstances that
he was as devoted and firm as Kirsánov. This he had shown
when, to marry her and deliver her from her oppressive
situation, he had sacrificed all his scientific dreams and exposed himself to the sufferings of hunger. Yes, when the
matter was serious, his hand was always held out to her. But
only then. Véra Pávlovna, for instance, organized her shop
herself. If, in any way whatever, his aid had been needed,
Lopukhóv gave it with pleasure. But he had his own life as
she had hers. Now it is not the same. Kirsánov does not
wait for his wife to ask him to participate in all that she
does. He is as interested in everything that is dear to her as
she is in everything that relates to him.

From this new life Véra Pávlovna derives new strength,
and what formerly seemed to her as if it would never leave
the realms of the ideal now appears entirely within reach.

As for her thoughts, this is the order in which they came
to her:

: IX :

"Almost all the paths of civil life are formally closed to
us, and those which are not closed by formal obstacles are
closed by practical difficulties. Only the family is left us.
What occupation can we engage in, outside of the family?
That of a governess is almost the only one; perhaps we have
one other resource,—that of giving lessons (such lessons as
are left after the men have chosen). But we all rush into
this single path and stifle there. We are too numerous to
find independence in it. There are so many to choose from
that no one needs us. Who could care to be a governess?
When any one wants one, he is besieged by ten, a hundred,
or even more applicants, each trying to get the place to the
detriment of the others.

"No, until women launch out into a greater number of careers, they will not enjoy independence. It is difficult, to be sure, to open a new road. But I occupy an especially favorable position for doing it. I should be ashamed not to profit by it. We are not prepared for serious duties. For my part, I do not know how far a guide is indispensable to me in order to confront them. But I do know that every time I need him I shall find him, and that he will always take great pleasure in helping me.

"Public prejudice has closed to us such paths of independent activity as the law has not forbidden us to enter. But I can enter whichever of these paths I choose, provided I am willing to brave the usual gossip. Which shall I choose? My husband is a doctor; he devotes all his leisure time to me. With such a man it would be easy for me to attempt to follow the medical profession.

"Indeed, it is very important that there should be women-physicians. They would be very useful to persons of their own sex. It is much easier for a woman to talk to another woman than to a man. How much distress, suffering, and death would thus be averted! The experiment must be tried."

: X :

Véra Pávlovna finished the conversation with her husband by putting on her hat to follow him to the hospital, where she wished to try her nerves and see if she could stand the sight of blood and whether she would be capable of pursuing the study of anatomy. In view of Kirsánov's position in the hospital, there certainly would be no obstacles in the way of this attempt.

I have already compromised Véra Pávlovna several times from the poetical standpoint; I have not concealed the fact, for instance, that she dined every day, and generally with a good appetite, and that further she took tea twice a day. But I have now reached a point where, in spite of the depravity of my tastes, I am seized with scruples, and timidly I ask myself: Would it not be better to conceal this circumstance? What will be thought of a woman capable of studying medicine?

What coarse nerves, what a hard heart, she must have! She is not a woman, she is a butcher. Nevertheless, remembering that I do not set up my characters as ideal types, I calm myself: let them judge as they will of the coarseness of Véra Pávlovna's nature; how can that concern me? She is coarse? Well! so be it.

Consequently I calmly state that she found a vast difference between idle contemplation of matters and active work on them for the good of one's own self and of others. Indeed whoever is at work has no time to be frightened and feel repugnance or disgust. So Véra Pávlovna studies medicine, and I number among my acquaintances one of those who introduced this novelty among us. She felt transformed by the study, and she said to herself: In a few years I shall get a foothold.

That is a great thought. There is no complete happiness without complete independence. Poor women that you are, how few of you enjoy this happiness!

: XI :

One year, two years pass; yet another year will pass from the time of her marriage to Kirsánov, and Véra Pávlovna's occupation will be the same as now; many years will pass, and her days will still be the same, unless something special happens. Who knows what the future will bring? Up to the time when I write these lines, nothing special has happened, and Véra Pávlovna's occupations have not changed. Now that the frank confession of Véra Pávlovna's bad taste in daring to study medicine and succeed in it has been made, it is easy for me to speak of anything; nothing else can harm her as much in the estimation of the public.

Many things in Véra Pávlovna's life have remained the same as before in this new and peaceful life.

The rooms are divided into the neutral and the non-neutral; all the rules regarding entrance into the non-neutral rooms are still the same. However, there are a few notable changes.

For instance, permission to enter the non-neutral rooms is now set once and for all for a certain time of day, since two of the three main events of the day have been transferred to these rooms: they are now in the habit of drinking their morning tea in her room, and evening tea in his. Evening tea takes place without formalities; the servant, the same Stepan, merely brings the samovar and tea-things into Alexander's room, then leaves. Morning tea, however, has its own special routine. Stepan puts the samovar and the things on the table in the neutral room adjacent to Véra Pávlovna's, then goes off to Alexander Matveich's study to tell him it is ready—if, that is, he is there. If not, well then Stepan has no need to announce anything and just hopes that they'll remember it is time for tea. So they have agreed on this rule for their morning ritual: in the morning, when Véra Pávlovna is waiting for her husband to come in with the tea, he does not have to knock. Anyone would think she simply could not manage without Sasha, until she gets up.

On awaking in the morning she dozes and tosses about as of old, now sleeping, now meditating. She now has two new subjects of reflection which in the third year of her marriage were followed by a third, the little Mítya,* so named in honor of her friend Dmítry. The two others are, first, the sweet thought of the independence that she is to acquire, and, second, the thought of Sásha; the latter cannot even be called a special thought, being mingled with all her thoughts, for her dear husband participates in her whole life. But when thoughts of him are foremost in her mind—as they very often are—what should one call it? Thinking or dreaming? Dozing or waking? Her eyes are half-closed, her cheeks are slightly flushed like the flush of sleep—yes, she is dreaming.

Now as you see, Véra Pávlovna spends a long time dozing before she gets up to take her bath, which is a carefully organised operation requiring considerable pre- paration. It means bringing a tap into her room from the boiler in the kitchen, and it must be said that it takes a great deal of wood to heat the water for this luxury. But what of it, she can indulge herself now. Then, after taking her bath, Véra Pávlovna often goes straight back to bed, luxuriating there until Sásha comes back. More often than not, however, she lies there dreaming and dozing, and does not get up for her bath until Sásha actually walks through the door.

But how she enjoys her bath every morning! First she

* Mítya is the diminutive of Dmítry.

runs the hot water, then turns off the hot tap and turns on the cold, and the water gradually cools—and how good that is! Sometimes she lies in it for half an hour or longer, sometimes she stays in there for a whole hour.

And all this she does without servants—and dresses herself on her own too. It is so much better this way. And she doesn't just dream away the time when she is on her own. And if she did miss her bath, then she would just have to do without it. Why? Why, so that Sásha won't have to be her chambermaid! Sásha is so terribly funny! When that woman singer was staying with them she had touched his arm and whispered something in his ear: "That sort of thing is utterly offensive!" he had noted in his mental diary. Be all that as it may, though, her darling does unfailingly preside over the morning tea.

This is an excellent arrangement, Sásha is absolutely right: it is really very pleasant to drink tea—or rather thick cream heated up with a dash of strong tea—in bed. Sásha gets up and fetches the tea-things (which always takes him some time), then comes back and pours it out while she dozes and drinks and lounges about—not in the bed but on the sofa, which is as soft and wide as a feather-bed—until ten or eleven o'clock, the time when Sásha is to go to the hospital or the clinic or the academic lecture-room. But her mornings were not on that account devoted to idleness. As soon as Sásha, after drinking his last cup, had lit his cigar, one of the two said to the other: "Let's go to work," or else: "Enough! enough! now for work!" What work? you ask. The private lesson. Sásha is her private tutor in medicine; she is aided by him still further in mathematics, and in Latin, which is perhaps even more tiresome than mathematics, but for that matter the Academy of Medicine requires but very little. I should be very careful about asserting that Véra Pávlovna will ever know enough Latin to translate even two lines of Cornelius Nepos, but she already knew enough to decipher the Latin phrases which she met in medical books, and that was what she needed. This is the finishing touch; I see that I am compromising Véra Pávlovna enormously . . . .

A DIVERSION ON BLUE STOCKINGS

"Blue stockings! Don't talk to me about blue stockings! I cannot endure blue stockings! They are stupid and dull, these blue stockings!" cries the perceptive reader, in the heat of the moment although not without conviction.

See how attached the perceptive reader and I are to one another. He cursed me once, I threw him out twice, and still we go on exchanging heated insults. It's a secret attraction of hearts and there's nothing to be done about it!

"Oh perceptive reader, you are right", I say to him; "The blue stocking is truly stupid and unendurably dull, as you have discovered. But you have not discovered *who* this blue stocking is. Look in the mirror and you will find out. These smug blue stockings express a lot of foolish, affected opinions about literature and science, and there's not a jot of sense in any of it. They speak not because they're interested, but because they want to flaunt their intelligence with which nature has so meagrely endowed them, their lofty aspirations (of which they have as many as the chair they sit on), and their education (of which they have as much as a scarecrow). Whose crude image or sleek figure do you see in the mirror? Why, your own, my friend. Yes, you may grow your beard long or you may carefully shave it, but there's not a shadow of doubt that you are the truest blue stocking of them all, and that is why I have thrown you out on two occasions: because I cannot endure blue stockings, who are ten times more numerous amongst us men than amongst women.

"Any person who pursues their goal, in a businesslike fashion, whether they are dressed in men's or women's attire makes no difference: that person is simply a hard-working human being—and there's an end to it!"

: XII :

This little discussion about blue stockings has been useful to the perceptive reader, for it was about him. But it has also taken me away from my story about how Véra Pávlovna spends her time now. What do we mean by "now"? Well, any time, say some time between now and the time she moved to Bergievsky Street. Anyway, let us continue our narrative, pausing only to mention the complete change in Véra Pávlovna's evenings, a process that started ever since she first renewed her acquaintance with Kirsanov on Vasilevsky Island.

The Kirsánovs were now the centre of a large number of young families living just as congenially and happily as they and sharing their ideas and tastes. These associations took half of their leisure time. But there is one thing of which unfortunately it is necessary to speak at too great length to many individuals in order to be understood. Whoever has not felt it himself must at least have read that there is great difference between a simple evening party and one where the object of your love is present. That is well known. But what very few have felt is that the charm which love gives to everything in man's life, this intense gleam of life, should light not only the period of desire, of aspiration, the period called courting, or seeking in marriage. No, this period should be only the ravishing dawn of a day more ravishing yet. Light and heat increase during the greater part of the day; so during the course of life love and its delights should increase. Among people of the old society such is not the case; the poetry of love does not survive satisfaction. The contrary is the rule among the people of the new generation whose life I am describing. The longer they live together, the more they are warmed by the poetry of love, until the time when the care of their growing children absorbs them. Then this care, sweeter than personal enjoyment, becomes uppermost; but until then love grows incessantly. That which the men of former times enjoyed only for a few short months the new men keep for many years.

And why so? It is a secret which I will unveil to you, if you wish. It is a fine secret, one worth having. It is not difficult, but one must have a pure heart, an upright soul, and that new and just conception of the human being which prompts respect for the freedom of one's life companion. Look upon your wife as you looked upon your sweetheart; remember that she at any moment has the right to say to you: "I am dissatisfied with you; leave me." Do this, and ten years after your marriage she will inspire in you the same enthusiasm that she did when she was your sweetheart, and she will have as much charm for you as then and even more. Recognize her liberty as openly, as explicitly, and with as little reserve, as you recognize the liberty of your friends to be your friends or not, and ten years, twenty years, after marriage you will be as dear to her as when you were her sweetheart. This is the way in which the people of our new generation live. Their condition in this respect is very enviable. Among them husbands and wives are loyal, sincere, and love each other always more and more.

After ten years of marriage they do not exchange false kisses or false words. "A lie was never on his lips; there was no deception in his heart," was said of some one in a certain book. In reading these things we say: The author, when he wrote this book, said to himself that this was a man whom all must admire as one to be celebrated. This author did not foresee that new men would arise, who would not admit among their acquaintances people who had not attained the height of his unparalleled hero, and the readers of the aforesaid book will have difficulty in understanding what I have just said, especially if I add that my heroes do not consider their numerous friends as exceptions, but simply as estimable, though very ordinary, individuals of the new generation.

What a pity that at the present hour there are still more than ten antediluvians for every new man! It is very natural, however. An antediluvian world can have only an antediluvian population.

: XIII :

"See, we have been living together for three years already [formerly it was one year, then two, next it will be four, and so on], and we are still like lovers who see each other rarely and secretly. Where did the idea come from, Sásha, that love grows weaker when there is nothing to disturb possession? People who believe that have not known true love. They have known only self-love or erotic fancies. True love really begins with life in common."

"Am I not the inspiration of this remark?"

"You? You will in a few years forget medicine, unlearn to read, and lose all your intellectual faculties, and you will end by seeing nothing but me."

Such conversations are neither long nor frequent, and, indeed, what is there for long and frequent conversation here!

"Yes, it grows stronger every year."

"You know those stories about people who take opium, and find their passion for it increases with every year? Once you experience that passion it can never weaken, and can only grow stronger."

"Passion can never be sated! Utter satisfaction never lasts longer than a few hours."

"A surfeit of passion does not come from the heart; it is a product of barren fantasy, of spoilt dreamers withdrawn from life, not of living active people."

"As though my appetite would weaken and my taste grow dull if I ate well every day and did not fast! In fact it is just the opposite: my taste develops precisely because I have good food on the table. And I lose my appetite only when I lose my desire to live, for without it I cannot live." (Vulgar materialism, the perceptive reader and I may note.)

"Can it really be in our nature for this appetite to weaken with time, rather than strengthen, when a friendship can develop and grow more loving over a week, a month, a year or twenty years? People need only to get on well together if they are to remain friends."

They are continually having discussions like this, although they are always brief and infrequent.

And yet these conversations are more and more frequent and lengthy.

"Sásha, how your love bolsters me up! It inspires in me the power of independence even against you. Does my love give you nothing?"

"To me? No less than to you. This continuous, strong, healthy excitement necessarily develops the nervous system [gross materialism, let us note with the penetrating reader]; consequently my intellectual and moral forces grow in proportion to your love."

"Yes, Sásha, I understand when they say that your eyes are becoming clearer and your expression more intense and powerful."

"There is no reason to praise me for that, even in your behalf, Vérochka. We are one and the same being. Of course, my thought, having become much more active, must be reflected in my eyes. When I come to draw inferences from my observations, I now do in an hour what formerly required several hours. I can hold in my mind many more facts than before, and my deductions are larger and more complete. If I had had any germ of genius in me, Vérochka, with this sentiment I should have become a great genius. If I had been given a bit of creative power, along with the sentiment which dominates me, I could have acquired the strength to revolutionize science. But I was born to be only a drudge, an ordinary and obscure laborer able to handle special questions only. That is what I was without you. Now, you know, I am something else: much more is expected of me; it is believed that I will revolutionize an entire branch of science, the whole theory of the functions of the nervous system. And I feel that I shall meet this expectation. At the age of twenty-four man has a broader and bolder intellectual view than at the age of twenty-nine, or thirty, or thirty-two, and so on. I am as strong as I was at twenty-four. And I feel that I am still growing, which would not be so were it not for you. I did not grow during the two or three years preceding our union. You have restored to me the freshness of early youth and the strength to go much farther than I could have gone without your love."

"And energy for work, Verochka, surely that means something? We carry the energy aroused by our passions into our work too, for this is the basis of our entire life. You know how a cup of coffee or a glass of wine affects our mental work—that superficial energy which lasts an hour and is followed by a feeling of weakness corresponding to the initial brief exhilaration? Well, I feel as though my nerves were permanently in that state—I feel so strong and alive!"(Vulgar materialism, we may once again observe.)

These conversations became longer, more frequent:

"If one hasn't experienced love's power to arouse all one's strength, one hasn't known real love."

"Love means rising up, and helping the other to do the same."

"Love gives power to those who cannot achieve anything, and to those who can, she gives the strength to make use of it."

"A man loves a woman only if he is prepared to help his beloved to rise up and be independent."

"A person loves only if love brightens their thoughts and strengthens their hands."

Conversations like these are very frequent also.

"My dear, I am reading Boccaccio now [what immorality! let us note to the penetrating reader. Only we men may read that; but for my part I am going to make this remark: a woman will hear the penetrating reader give utterance to more conventional filth in five minutes than she will find in all Boccaccio, and she will not hear from the penetrating reader a single one of those luminous, fresh, and pure words in which Boccaccio abounds]: you are right in saying that he has very great talent. Some of his tales deserve to be placed beside the best dramas of Shakespeare for depth and delicacy of psychological analysis."

"How do you like those humorous stories of his where he is somewhat impudent?"

"Some of them are funny, but generally they are tiresome, like every farce, from being too coarse."

"But he must be pardoned; he lived five hundred years before our time. What now seems to us too filthy was not considered improper then."

"It is the same with many of our manners and customs; they will seem coarse and unclean in much less than five hundred years. But I pay no attention to the license of Boccaccio. I speak of those novels of his in which he describes an elevated and passionate love so well. It is there that his great talent appears. I come back to what I was going to say: he paints very well and very vividly. But, judging from his writings, we may say that they did not know in those days that delicacy of love which we know now; love was not felt so deeply, although it is said to have been the epoch when they enjoyed it most completely. No, the people of that day did not enjoy love so well. Their sentiments were too superficial and their intoxication too mild and transient."

"The power of sensation corresponds to the depth of the organism from which it arises. If it is stirred only by external things it will be a mere transient feeling, embracing only a small part of one's life. Just as a person who drinks wine simply because someone passes him a glass is unlikely to appreciate the taste or get any pleasure out of it. Pleasure is so much more powerful when its roots are in the imagination, when the imagination seeks out the object and cause of its pleasure. Then the blood courses more powerfully around the body, which grows perceptibly warmer, thus increasing the sensual experience. But even this experience of pleasure is weak in comparison to those relations which are deeply rooted in the moral life. For then the entire nervous system is suffused with passions of a deep and long-lasting power. Then the chest is filled with warmth—and this is not just the beating of the heart, aroused by fantasy; no, one's whole chest expands with the most remarkable freshness and lightness, as if the very atmosphere we breathe had changed and the air itself was clearer, richer in oxygen. We occasionally experience

something like this on a warm sunny day, when we sit outside in the sun. But the difference is that when this freshness and warmth is in our very nerves we sense them directly, our sensual powers unmediated by the elements."
And:
"I'm so glad I gave up wearing those uncomfortable clothes before it was too late. It's quite true, one shouldn't wear tight things that constrict the circulation. Why should one rejoice that they make the skin softer? Such rubbish, and it ruins one's feet! A stocking can perfectly well stay up on its own. And one's figure improves when it's no longer squeezed and constricted.

"It doesn't improve immediately, though. You know, I only wore a corset for three years, and had stopped wearing one before we started living together. But even without corsets, our dresses are far too tight at the waist. I wonder if this deformity will pass with time, just as bound feet did? Yes, it must! Why, it's happening even now— soon all this will be a thing of the past! Those Greek women were so much cleverer than us—we should have learnt a lesson from them long ago, and worn those wide tunics that flow from the shoulders. What a horrible style our dresses are—it completely ruins our figures! Well, at least my figure is its natural shape now, I'm pleased about that!"

"How lovely you are, Verochka!"
"How happy I am, Sasha!"

> His sweet words are like a murmuring stream,
> So sweet his smile, his kiss.
> Extinguish your kisses, dear friend
> For even without them you are on fire!
> Your blood seethes, your chest heaves,
> Your cheeks burn, your eyes blaze,
> Gleaming like stars in the night.

: XIV :

VÉRA PÁVLOVNA'S FOURTH DREAM

And Véra Pávlovna had a dream, and this is what she dreamt:

There comes to her from the distance a familiar, oh so familiar voice, singing:

> Wie herrlich leuchtet
> Mir die Natur!
> Wie glänzt die Sonne,
> Wie lacht die Flur!*

And that is exactly how it is in Véra Pávlovna's dream...

Cornfields flooded with shafts of sunlight, golden meadows strewn with flowers, flowers on every bush in the copses surrounding the meadows, and rising up in the distance beyond the copses, a green and whispering forest, bright with flowers and fluttering with birds. The fragrance of the flowers and the twittering of the birds waft over fields, meadows, copses and forests. And beyond the forest, yet more shining, flowering cornfields, meadows and copses stretching away to the distant mountains, covered in trees and gleaming in the sun. Above their summits, bright transparent clouds cast shadows of purple, silver and gold on the light blue horizon. The sun is risen and nature is rejoicing, pouring forth endless light and warmth, fragrance and song, and flooding our hearts with love and bliss. And from our hearts pour sweet songs of love, joy and goodness: "Oh earth! Oh Bliss! Oh Love! Love, golden and beautiful as the morning clouds on the mountain peaks!"

> O Erd'! O Sonne!
> O Glück! O Lust!
> O Lieb', O Liebe,
> So goldenschön.
> Wie Morgenwolken
> Auf jenen Höh'n! **

---

*How gloriously nature glows!
How the sun shines,
How the fields laugh!
(From Goethe's *Mailied*)

** Oh earth, oh sun,
Oh light, oh laughter!
Oh golden love, gleaming
Like a cloud in the heavens...
(From Goethe's *Mailied*)

"Now do you know who I am? Can you see how beautiful I am? No, you do not know me yet, none of you yet knows me in all my beauty. Take a look at the past, the present and the future – look now, and listen:

> Wohl perlet im Glase der purpurne Wein,
> Wohl glänzen die Augen der Gäste . . . *

At the foot of the mountains, on the outskirts of the forest, a palace rises up amid thick alleys of flowering shrubs.

"Come, let us go there."
They go on wings.

A sumptuous feast is in progress. The wine is foaming in the glasses, and the feasters' eyes are bright. Beneath the sounds of shouting and laughter, secrets are whispered, hands are squeezed, and furtive kisses exchanged.

"Give us a song!" they shout. "Our celebration isn't complete without a song!"

The poet rises, his brow bright with inspiration. To him Nature confides her secrets and history reveals its purpose, and thousands of years, like a series of pictures, fly past as he sings.

– i –

The poet's words ring out, and this is the picture they conjure up.

A nomadic encampment, sheep, horses and camels grazing beside tents. Further in the distance lie groves of figs and olives, and far away on the horizon to the north-west are two lofty mountain ranges, their peaks covered in snow, their slopes covered in cedars. But more shapely than the cedars are the shepherds, and more shapely than the palm-trees are their wives. They lead carefree, idle lives; pleasure and love is their only concern, and all their days are spent in caresses and songs of love.

"No, that is not me," says our bright beauty. "I didn't exist then. That woman was a slave. A place without equality is no place for me. That tsaritsa was Astarte. Look,

---

* How merrily they pass the goblet,
How bright the eyes of the feasters.
(The opening lines of Schiller's *Four Ages*)

here she is."

A splendid woman appears, with thick gold bracelets on her wrists and ankles, and round her neck a heavy necklace of pearls and corals set in gold. Her hair is oiled with myrrh. Her expression is one of voluptuous servility, her eyes are sensual, mindless.

"You must submit to your lord," she says to the woman lying in the dust, at her feet. "Fill his idle hours with delight while he rests from the fray. You must love him because he has bought you, and if you do not, he will kill you."

"See, that is not me," says our beauty.

– ii –

Again the poet's inspired words ring out, and a new picture appears.

A city. Mountains stretch away to north and east. In the south and east, and further to the west, lies the sea. This city is a marvellous place. The houses are neither large nor luxurious, but what a quantity of magnificent temples! Especially on the hill, up which leads a flight of stairs adorned with gates of extraordinary splendour. The entire hillside is covered with temples and buildings, each one of which would enhance and ennoble the most splendid of our capital cities now. Inside the temples, and indeed in every corner of the town, there are thousands of statues— each one of which would make the museum which contained it the finest in the world. And the people, too, are so beautiful, crowds of them walking about the squares and streets. Each one of these young men, each one of these girls and young women, might well serve as the model for a statue. Bright, lively, cheerful people, leading busy and elegant lives. Their houses, so unpretentious from the outside, are filled inside with such a wealth of elegance, such a highly developed sense of pleasure—each dish, each piece of furniture would evoke our admiration. For these people, so skilled in the arts of beauty, live for love and in the service of beauty.

Here comes an exile, returning to the city after attempting to overthrow the government. He is returning to take power—everyone knows this. Yet not one hand is raised against him. And why? Why, because riding in the chariot beside him is a woman of quite exceptional beauty, even in this city of beautiful women, and she is showing him to the people, begging them to accept him and telling them that she supports him. Bowing to her beauty, the people grant her lover Pisistratus the right to rule over them.

Here is the court, and here are the judges, stern old men. The people may be carried away, but *they* are not so easily swayed. For the Areopagus is known for its impartiality; gods and goddesses have submitted their affairs to its judgement. And now this woman, considered by all to be guilty of horrendous crimes, is to appear before them; she must die, this destroyer of Athens, each of the judges has already secretly decided this. Yet, no sooner does the guilty Aspasia appear before them than they all fall to the ground before her, saying; "We cannot condemn you, you are too beautiful!" For is this not the kingdom of beauty? Is this not the kingdom of love?

"No, I did not exist then," says our bright beauty. "They worshipped woman, but they did not consider her as an equal. They worshipped her only as a source of pleasure, and granted her no human dignity! A place which does not respect woman as a human being is no place for me. That tsaritsa was Aphrodite. Here she is."

This tsaritsa is completely unadorned—she is so beautiful that her worshippers do not wish her to wear clothes that would conceal her heavenly form from their rapturous gaze.

What does she say to the woman, almost as beautiful as herself, who is scattering incense on her altar?

"You must be the source of man's pleasure. He is your master. Live not for yourself but for him!"

In her eyes is the langour of physical pleasure. She bears herself proudly, and her expression is proud, but she is proud only of her physical beauty. What sort of life was a woman condemned to live during her reign? She had no freedom. A man would lock up his wife in the *gyneceum* so that nobody but he might enjoy her beauty, for it belonged to him alone. There were certain women who called themselves free, but they sold the enjoyment of their beauty—and thus they sold their liberty. No, they were not free either. This tsaritsa was half-slave. Where there is no freedom there is no happiness, and that is no place for me.

– iii –

Again the poet's words ring out and another scene unfolds:

A castle, and before it an arena surrounded by an amphi-theatre, filled with a dazzling crowd of spectators. There are two knights in the arena. In the balcony of the castle above sits a maiden, holding a scarf in her hand. The knights are fighting to the death, and he who wins will take the scarf from her and kiss her hand.

Toggenburg is victorious. "Knight, I love you like a sister," says the maiden. "Ask no other love of me. My heart beats no faster when you appear, and beats no faster when you leave."

"My fate is decided," he says, and sets sail for Palestine. The glory of his deeds spreads far and wide through the whole of Christendom. But he cannot live without seeing the tsaritsa of his soul, and cannot find oblivion in battle. He returns.

"Do not knock, Knight. She is in a convent."

So he builds himself a hut from whose windows, unbeknownst to her, he secretly watches her when she opens the shutters of her cell every morning. His entire life is spent waiting for her to appear at the window, beautiful as the sun. He has no other life but this, waiting every morning for the tsaritsa of his soul to appear. And since he has no other life, his life soon runs out, and as his life is ebbing away he sits at the window of his hut with just one thought: will he ever see her again?

"No, no! That has nothing to do with me!" says our bright beauty. "He loved her only so long as he did not touch her. If she had become his wife she would have been his slave. She would have had to tremble before him, he would have locked her up and ceased to love her; he would have gone to war, hunted, feasted with his companions, ravished his slaves, and his wife would have been abandoned, locked up and despised. No, I was not there, where a man would cease to love a woman the moment he touched her. That tsaritsa was Chastity. Look, here she is."

Modest, meek, gentle, beautiful—more beautiful than Astarte, more beautiful than Aphrodite—but pensive and sorrowful. People kneel before her and bring her crowns of roses, and she says: "My soul is mortally sad. A sword has pierced my heart. You too must grieve. You too are unhappy. Earth is a vale of tears."

"No, no, I was not there!" says our bright beauty.

"No, those tsaritsas were not me. They still reign, but their kingdoms are gradually disappearing. With the birth of each one of them the realm of her predecessor begins to collapse. I was born just as the reign of Chastity was beginning to collapse. Since I was born their realms have begun to collapse yet faster, and now they are beginning to vanish altogether. Their successors cannot replace them yet, for they still exist. But I shall soon replace all of them, and then I shall rule the entire world. They had to reign before me, for without them I could never have existed.

"People were like wild animals once. They ceased being so only when man began to value woman's beauty. But woman had not man's physical strength and man was a rough, crude creature. Everything was decided by physical strength in those days. Man learnt to appreciate woman's beauty—then merely took her. She became his property, his chattel. This was the reign of Astarte.

"As man grew more highly developed he valued her beauty more highly—he worshipped her beauty. But her consciousness was still barely developed. He valued her only for her beauty, while she thought only what he had taught her to think. He told her that she was not a person, and that only he was a person. She saw herself merely as a beautiful jewel that belonged to him, and did not consider herself to be human. This was the reign of Aphrodite.

"But slowly she did grow conscious of herself as a human being. What grief these glimmerings of her human dignity must have caused her! For she was still not regarded as such, and man had no other use for her but as his slave. And she said to him: "I do not want to be your companion on these terms." Then man's passion for her made him implore her to stay; he submitted to her wishes, forgot that he did not regard her as a human being, and loved her as an innocent maiden, inaccessible and untouchable. But as soon as she yielded to his entreaties, as soon as he touched her—woe betide her! For then she was in his hands, and those hands were stronger, coarser than hers, and he turned her into a slave and despised her. Woe betide her! This was the sad reign of the virgin.

"But the centuries passed. And my sister—do you know her?—did her work. She existed before I did, before all the others, and her work has been indefatigable. Her labours were hard, her success was slow, but still she worked, and her success grew. And so it was that man became more reasonable, woman became conscious of her equality, and the time came for me to be born.

"This was not so long ago, not so long ago at all. Do you know who first discovered that I had been born, and told others? It was Rousseau, in *La Nouvelle Eloise*. It was in that work that people first learnt about me. And since then my power has grown—it does not rule over many yet, but it is growing nevertheless, and the time is not far off when I shall rule the earth. Only then will people appreciate my beauty. At present, those who recognise me cannot yet obey me, for they are surrounded by people who are hostile to me, and would persecute them and poison their lives if they did my bidding. Above all things, I want happiness and an end to suffering, so I say to them: "Look, do nothing for which you would be tormented. Do my bidding only so far as it will cause you no harm."

"But can I ever know you fully?" asks Véra Pávlovna.

"Yes, you can, for you are in a very fortunate position and have nothing to fear. You can do anything you want. And if you wish to know my will, no harm will come to you; you must not and will not desire anything which might cause people to torment you. You are perfectly content with what you have; you must not and will not desire anything or anybody you do not have. To you I can reveal myself fully."

"Tell me your name then. You have told me the names of princesses of the past, but you still have not told me your name."

"You want to know my name? Look at me then, and listen."

– v –

"Look at me, listen to me. Do you recognise my voice? Do you recognise my face? Have you ever beheld my face before?'

No, she had never seen her face, yet why did it seem to her as though she had? She had seen it for a year now, ever since she had spoken to her Dmítry and he had looked at her and kissed her. For a year she had seen this beautiful woman who revealed herself to her as openly as she revealed herself to her husband; for a year this woman had been appearing constantly before her eyes in all her radiance.

"No I have never seen you fully nor set eyes on your face, for although you revealed yourself to me before, you were surrounded with such radiance that I could barely see you. I saw only that you were more beautiful than anyone else. Your voice I heard too, but I could hear only that it was more beautiful than any other."

"Look then, for your sake I shall dim for a moment the brightness of my aura, and my voice will sound for you without the enchanting power I give to it. For one moment I shall cease to be a tsaritsa. Did you see, did you hear, have you discovered who I am? Enough! I am a tsaritsa again, and a tsaritsa I shall always be." She was again surrounded by an ineffable aura, and again her voice was inexpressibly enchanting. But for that one moment, when she ceased to be a tsaritsa so that we might know her – could it really be true? Did Véra Pávlovna really see her own face, hear her own voice?

"Yes," says the tsaritsa. "You wanted to know who I am, and now you know. You wanted to know my name, but I have no name other than hers to whom I appear. My name is her name. You have seen who I am. There is nothing nobler than a man; there is nothing nobler than a woman. I am the person in whose image I appear, the person who loves and is loved."

Yes, it is herself that Véra Pávlovna has seen—a goddess. The countenance of the goddess is her own living countenance, whose features are so far from perfection— every day she sees more than one face more beautiful than hers. Yes, this is her own face, glowing with love, a face more beautiful than all the ideals bequeathed to us by all the sculptors of antiquity, all the great painters from the great age of art. Yes, it is she, glowing with the radiance of love, and even though there might be hundreds of faces much lovelier than hers in St Petersburg—which is so poor in beauty—yet she is more beautiful than the Aphrodite in the Louvre, more beautiful than all the beauties of the past.

"You see your reflection in the mirror, just as you are, without me. In me you see yourself as you are seen by him who loves you. For him, you and I are one. For him there is no one lovelier than you. For him, all ideals pale beside you. Isn't that so?"

It is indeed so!

– vi –

"Now that you know who I am, you shall discover what I am . . .

"In me is all the sensual pleasure you saw in Astarte. She is the mother of all us tsaritsas who followed her. In me is the ecstasy at the sight of beauty which was in Aphrodite. And in me is the veneration of purity which was in Chastity.

"But in me all these things are fuller, loftier and stronger than in them. I embody the virtues of Chastity, the qualities of Astarte and Aphrodite, and unite these with other powers, each one of which becomes greater from the union. But in me there is something new, something far, far more powerful than anything in the previous tsaritsas. And what distinguishes me from them is Equality—the equality of all who love, an equality in their relations. And it is this that gives me a power and beauty far, far greater than theirs.

"When a man recognises a woman as his equal he ceases to regard her as his property. Then she loves him, as he loves her, because she *wants* to. And if she does not, he has no rights over her nor her over him. So in me there is Liberty.

"Liberty, Equality—everything in me takes on a new, more exalted charm, unknown before me. Compared to this, all else before me is reduced to nothing.

"Before I appeared, people had never experienced the full pleasure of their senses, for unless both lovers are freely attracted to one another, neither of them can know true ecstasy. Before I appeared, people had never experienced the full pleasure of contemplating beauty, for if beauty is not revealed through free attraction there is no rapture in its contemplation. Pleasure and ecstasy without free attraction are dull experiences indeed, compared to these experiences in me.

"My chastity is purer than that of Chastity, who spoke only of purity of body. I am free because I am free of deceit. I never utter a word I do not mean, nor give kisses which are not from the heart.

"All this gives me a new charm, more powerful than any other and loftier than anything in the previous tsaritsas. Masters are embarrassed before their servants, servants are embarrassed before their masters; we feel free only with our equals. It is so dull being with our inferiors—we are completely happy only with those who are our equals. That is why man had not experienced the full joy of love before I appeared, but merely a momentary excitement, not worthy of the name of happiness. And as for woman— what a poor wretch she was before I appeared! She was nothing but an abject slave living in fear and knowing little of love; for where there is fear there can be no love . . .

"So if you want to describe me in a word, that word is Equality. For without equality the pleasures of the body and the contemplation of beauty are dull, dismal and joyless. Without equality there is no purity of heart, only the false purity of body. Equality is the origin of freedom, and without freedom I cannot exist.

"I have told you everything so that you may now tell others what I am. But my kingdom is still small. I cannot yet reveal my will to everyone, and must protect my people from the slander of those who do not yet know me. I will reveal it fully only when my kingdom rules the world; only when all men and women are beautiful in body and pure in heart will I reveal my beauty to the world. But you, your fate is particularly fortunate. I shall not harm or disturb you if I tell you what will be when everyone, not just the few, is worthy of recognising me as their tsaritsa. To you alone I shall confide the secrets of my future. Swear to keep silent, and listen."

– vii –

. . . .
. . . .

– viii –

"Oh my love, now I know your will, now I know what will be. But *how* will it be then? How will people live?"

"I alone cannot tell you this—for this I must call upon my elder sister, she who appeared to you long ago. She is my sovereign and my servant. I am what she has made me, yet she works for me. Sister, come to my aid."

The sister of sisters appeared, the bride of her bride-grooms.

"Greetings, sister," she says to the tsaritsa. "And you are here too?" she says to Véra Pávlovna. "So you want to see how people will live when this tsaritsa, who is my ward, rules the earth? Look!"

A vast building, of an immensity seen only in the greatest capital cities of the world—but no, there are none so vast! It stands in the midst of cornfields, meadows, groves and gardens. The cornfields—it is like our corn, yet not such as we have now, for it grows so rich and abundant. Whoever saw such ears? Whoever saw such grain? Can it really be corn? You could grow such corn only in a greenhouse now. The fields are like our fields, but such flowers as these would be found only in flower-gardens. And those orchards, of lemons and oranges, figs and apricots—how can they grow in the open air? Oh, but they are surrounded by columns, open to the summer air. Yes, they are greenhouses. Those groves are the same as ours: oaks, limes, elms and maples, yes, the groves are such as we have now. Great care has been lavished on them and there is not a single sick tree to be seen, but they are the same, only the trees have remained the same. But this building, what is it? What sort of architecture is this? There is nothing like it now. No, there is just a hint of it in the palace which now stands on Sydenham Hill,* and which is built of glass and wrought iron, nothing but glass and wrought iron. But this is not all, this is only the outer cover, the building's outer walls. Inside is a real house, a house of vast proportions.

The outer building, of crystal and wrought iron, is merely a case, forming broad galleries which surround it on every storey. The architecture of the inner building is so simple. What narrow spaces there are between the windows—and how immense and wide these windows are; why they stretch from floor to ceiling! Its stone walls, like rows of pilasters, make a frame for these windows, which open out on to the galleries. But what are the walls and ceilings made of? What about the doors and the window-frames? What is this? Silver? Platinum? Almost all the furniture is of the same material too. Wooden furniture is an eccentricity here, merely there for the sake of variety. But what *is* the other furniture made of? And the walls and ceiling? "Try and move this chair," says the elder tsaritsa. This metal furniture is lighter than ours, lighter than walnut. What *is* it? Ah, *now* I know! Sasha once showed me

* The Crystal Palace, built for the Great Exhibition of 1851 and burnt down in 1936.

a disc of this metal; it was as light as glass, they make necklaces and bracelets of it now. Yes, Sasha said that sooner or later aluminium would replace wood, maybe stone too. How rich it looks! Aluminium, aluminium everywhere, and every space between the windows is adorned with great mirrors. And look at those carpets on the floors! In that hall there the floor is uncovered, and you can see that it too is made of aluminium. "See, it is unpolished so that it won't be too slippery. The children play here, and so do the older people. And the floor in that hall is uncarpeted, for dancing." There are young trees and plants everywhere. The whole house is a huge winter garden.

But who lives in this house, more splendid than any palace? "Many, many people live here. Come, let's take a look at them." They go out on to the balcony which projects from the gallery on the upper storey of the house. How is it that Véra Pávlovna did not notice before? Groups of people are scattered about the cornfields, men and women, young and old, children. The majority of them are young; there are a few old men, even fewer old women, and more children than old people, but there are not many of them here either. For more than half the children are indoors, doing the housework. They do almost everything in the house, and like doing it very much. There are a few old women with them, but there are not many old people; here they grow old very late, for life is healthy and peaceful, and preserves youth.

The groups in the fields are all singing. What is the work they are doing? Ah, they are harvesting the corn. How quickly they are working! But they have good reason to sing and to work so fast! For almost everything is done for them by machines—reaping, binding the sheaves and carting them away—and the people do virtually nothing but walk, drive around and attend to the machines. And how comfortable they have made themselves. It is a sweltering day, but this does not bother them, of course. Over the part of the field where they are working they have hung an immense canopy, which makes a nice cool shade! When the work moves on, this too is moved. They have good reason to sing and work so cheerfully! I would like to be a harvester too! Songs, and yet more songs—unfamiliar and new, all of them. Yet they have remembered one of ours, which I too know:

> You and I will live like kings,
> These people are our friends.
> Whatsoever your heart desires
> They and I will give you.

But now the work is finished and they are all walking towards the building. "Let us go into the hall again, and see them have dinner," says the elder sister. They enter the mightiest of the halls, half of which is covered in tables, which are already laid. How many tables there are! Will a lot of people be eating here? Why, a thousand or more! Not everyone is here, for some prefer to eat on their own. The meal has been prepared by the old men, women and children who did not go to the fields. "Cooking, cleaning, housework—this work is too light for the others," says the elder sister, "So it's done by those who can no longer do anything else, or have not yet learnt how."

The dishes are splendid, all aluminium and crystal. Vases and flowers have been set along the middle of the broad tables and the food is already on the table. The workers have come in and are sitting down to eat, along with those who made the dinner.

"But who will serve them?" asks Véra Pávlovna.

"When? During dinner? But what for? There are only five or six courses, and the main dishes are put in special places to keep them hot. You see those dents in the table there? Those are pans filled with hot water,' says the elder sister. "You live well, you like good food on the table—how often do *you* enjoy such a meal as this?"

"A few times a year, perhaps."

"Yet for these people, this is just an everyday meal! Anyone who wants to can have something a bit better, and then a separate account is kept for them. But if one demands no more than what all the others have, then no such account is kept. Everything is arranged in this way: anything which the whole collective can afford costs nothing, but for every special luxury there is a separate price."

"Are these really our people? Is this really our land? I heard them singing, and it was in Russian."

"Yes. You see that river not far from here? That is the Oka. These are our people—for when I am with you, I am Russian!"

"And was it you who brought all this about?"

"It was all done for me, because I wished it. It was I who inspired them to achieve it and encouraged them to complete it, but it is she, my elder sister, who is doing all the work. For she is a worker–I merely enjoy the fruits of her labours."

"And will everyone live like this?"

"Yes, everyone," says the elder sister. "Everlasting spring and summer, everlasting joy. But you have only seen them at work, at the end of my half of the day and the beginning of her half. We shall come back in two months' time, and see them in the evening!"

– ix –

The flowers have withered now, the leaves are falling and the picture is more desolate.

"See how dreary it is," says the younger sister. "How miserable it must be to live there now. *I* wouldn't want to live there!"

"The halls are empty, there's not a soul in the fields or gardens," says the elder sister. "I did this because my sister the tsaritsa wished it."

"So the palace is really empty?"

"Yes, it's cold and damp now—why stay? Of the two thousand people who live here, only some ten or twelve eccentrics have remained, thinking it would make a nice change to stay on in this remote and solitary place and watch the northern autumn. In a little while it will be winter, and then there will be constant changes. Small groups of winter sports enthusiasts will arrive and spend several days here, enjoying winter."

"But where are the others?"

"Wherever it is hot and sunny," says the elder sister. "In the summer, when there is a lot of work here and the weather is good, all sorts of guests arrive from the south. When we were in the house, the company consisted entirely of people like you. But there are a great many other houses built to contain these guests, and in these, people of many races settle in with their hosts—you live with whoever you want to, you can choose the company you keep. And then, having taken in a multitude of these guests over the summer to help with the work, you can go south, or wherever you want, for the remaining seven or eight months of the year. There is one special place, however, where most of your people crowd to. And that is New Russia."

"Is that near Odessa and Kherson?"

"That was in your time—look, *there* is New Russia!"

Mountains clad in orchards; steep valleys and broad ravines beneath the crags. "These mountains used to be bare," says the elder sister. "Now they are covered in a thick layer of earth, with gardens and groves of tall trees. Below them in the moist hollows are coffee plantations, and above are date palms, fig-trees, vineyards and sugar plantations. In the fields they grow some wheat, but mainly rice."

"But what country is this?"

"Let us go a little higher for a moment, and you will see its borders."

Far away to the north-east are two rivers, which unite and flow together straight to the east, where Véra Pávlovna is standing. To the south-east there is a wide bay, and to the south the land stretches into the distance, growing wider between this bay and the long thin strip of sea which forms its western border. Between this narrow bay on the west and the sea, far, far away to the north-west, there is a narrow isthmus.

"But we are in the middle of the desert!" says the astonished Véra Pávlovna.

"Yes indeed, we are in the centre of what was once desert," says the elder sister. "Now, as you see, this huge expanse of land from the north, from that great river in the north-east, has been turned into fruitful land, as it was in the past. That region in the south, by the sea, is once again as it used to be in the days when it was described as 'flowing with milk and honey'. We are not far, as you see, from the southern border of this cultivated desert. The mountainous part of this peninsula is still sandy, infertile steppe, as this entire region used to be in your day. But every year you Russians are moving the boundaries of the desert a little further south. Others are working in other countries. There is room for everyone, and enough work to go round, there is space and prosperity. Yes, this whole region is green and flourishing, from the great river in the north-east to the entire expanse in the south as far as the peninsular. Dotted about this region, as in the north, are huge buildings, four or five miles apart, like countless giant chess pieces on a giant chess board. Let us go down and visit one of them," says the elder sister.

Another huge crystal house, only the columns of this one are white. "They are made of aluminium," says the elder sister, "because it is very hot here and white burns less in the sun. It's a bit more expensive than cast-iron, but better suited to the climate here!"

And look what they have devised: encircling the entire palace are rows of tall thin pillars, and on these is stretched a white canopy which covers the entire palace and half a mile beyond. "It is always cool and moist in here," says the elder sister. "See, in each pillar there is a little fountain. The water rises up above the canopy and scatters its drops as it falls, making it nice and cool inside. You see, they can change the temperature to suit them."

"And what about those who like the intense heat and the bright southern sun?"

"You see those pavilions and tents over there? Here everyone can live as best suits them. Everyone should live as they please, that is the purpose of all my work."

"And are there still cities, then, for those who like living in them?"

"Yes, but there are few such people left now. There are far fewer towns than before, almost all of them on the best harbours; they provide centres of communication, and for the transport of goods from other centres. But these cities are far more magnificent than cities in the past. Some people take their holidays there, just for a change; the inhabitants are constantly on the move, and usually go there only for a short time, to work."

"But who would want to live in them permanently?"

"Well, people do, as you live in your Petersburgs and Londons. Whose business is it but theirs? Who is to stop them? Everyone here lives as they want to. But the vast majority of people, ninety-nine out of a hundred, live as we've shown you, since they find this more pleasant and comfortable. But come, let us go into the palace. It is already late in the evening, and it's time now to watch them."

"No, first of all I want to know how all this was brought about."

"What do you mean?"

"I mean, how was barren desert turned into fertile land, where almost all of us now spend two thirds of the year?"

"How was it brought about? But what is so surprising

about it? It wasn't done in a year, of course, nor in ten years, and I brought it about gradually. First they brought clay from the banks of the great river in the north-east and from the shores of the great sea in the south-west—they have powerful machines to do this. The clay bound the sand, they built canals, they irrigated the land, gradually green shoots began to appear, the air became more moist and the work progressed, one step at a time, a few miles a year, sometimes just one mile a year, but moving steadily south all the time, as they are now. What is so surprising about that? They have simply grown wiser, turned to their advantage the colossal power and resources of the earth, which they had until then merely wasted or used destructively. So I haven't worked and taught in vain! In the early days it was hard for people to understand what was good for them, for then they were primitive, mindless, coarse and cruel. But I taught them wisdom. And when they finally came to their senses, it wasn't hard for them to achieve it. I don't demand anything difficult from people, you know that. You are doing something for me yourself— is it so difficult?"

"No."

"Of course it isn't. Think of your sewing workshop. Did you have a lot of money and resources to run it? More than others?"

"Resources? Why, we had nothing!"

"There you are then! Yet your seamstresses are ten times more comfortable, twenty times happier and have a hundred times fewer worries than other workshops with the same resources. You yourself have proved that people can live freely, even in your own time. You have only to be reasonable, organise your life properly and use your resources profitably."

"Yes, yes, I know that."

"Come then, let us go once more and see how people will live when they too understand what you understood long ago."

– x –

They go into the building, and into yet another vast and magnificent hall. A party is in full swing. It is three hours after sunset—this is the hour of pleasure. How brightly the hall is lit—but where does this light come from? There are no candelabras here, no chandeliers—ah, that is it! In the dome of the hall there is a great sheet of opaque glass through which pours light. That is exactly how it should be—a pale, soft bright light, just like that of the sun, but yes, it is electric! There are about a thousand people in the hall, although it could easily hold three times that number. "And of course when there are guests there must be many more," says the bright beauty. "So what is happening now? Is this just an ordinary weekday evening?"

"Of course."

"But the women are dressed so splendidly—nowadays this would be a court ball. But you can see from the cut of their dresses that this is another time. A few women are wearing the sort of dresses we wear now, but they are clearly dressed like this only to be different, for fun. Yes, they are just playing, making fun of their own clothes. Everyone is wearing something different, there is an extraordinary variety of styles. Many of them are wearing southern and eastern costumes, for these are so much more graceful than our own. But the predominant fashion is a light, loose dress, such as Greek women used to wear in the most refined Athenian period. The men too wear long wide tunics, without waists, something like a cloak or mantle. This is evidently what they wear every day at home. And what a tasteful, beautiful fashion it is! How gracefully it outlines the human form and enhances the grace of its movements! And what an orchestra that is— over a hundred men and women! And what a choir!"

"Yes, you have not ten voices in the whole of Europe such as you would find in all hundred singers in this hall alone. And it is the same in all the other halls too. But the way of life here is so different from the old days – it is a healthy and cultured life, so that the chest expands and the voice is better," says the bright tsaritsa. The people in the orchestra and choir are constantly changing places; people leave, others replace them, some go off to dance, dancers take their places.

This is a normal weekday evening for them, for they dance and enjoy themselves like this every evening. Did you ever see such joyful energy? But how could they not have this energy, this joy which is beyond our experience? They have worked hard all day, and anyone who has not put in a good day's work has not prepared their nervous system to enjoy the evening's entertainments to the full.

Even now the celebrations of simple people—if by chance they do succeed in enjoying themselves—are always so much more cheerful and lively than the celebrations of the mighty. Yet there are scant possibilities for our simple people to enjoy themselves, whereas here they are so much richer. Our simple people's celebrations are always marred by memories of deprivation, suffering, misery and discomfort, and by premonitions of these things in the future—they are mere brief moments when poverty and grief are forgotten. Yet, can poverty and grief ever be forgotten? Does not the sand build up to make a desert? Does not a miasma of mud infect the smallest lump of good earth lying between the desert and the swamp?

Here there are no such memories, no fears of poverty and suffering. Here there are memories only of contentment, happiness, prosperity and labour freely given, and the anticipation of these things in the future. What a contrast! And then again, our working people have strong constitutions to be sure, which means they can endure a lot of carousing, yet they are coarse and insensitive. Here they also have strong constitutions, but these people are cultured and sensitive. They, however, have something which we do not, for it comes only with hard physical labour and sound health, and that is a powerful and healthy thirst for pleasure. This is joined to all the delicacy of feelings we know now. They have both our morality and culture, and the strength and energy of working people. One can easily understand why their joys, passions and festivities are so much fuller and livelier than ours. What happy people!

No, we do not know what real pleasure is, for we do not yet have the sort of life or people which would make it possible. But these people know how to enjoy themselves— they have known all the rapture of true joy! Joyful and beautiful, these men and women lead free lives of toil and pleasure. How they bloom with energy and health, how graceful and elegant they are, how lively and expressive their features are. What a blessed, happy people!

Half of them are now enjoying themselves at the party in the hall, but where is the other half?

"Where are the others?" says the bright tsaritsa. "Why they are everywhere. Some are actors, some musicians, some spectators—everyone does whatever they want. There are people scattered about the lecture halls, museums and libraries, people strolling about the gardens or sitting in their rooms, resting on their own or playing with their children. But as for most of them—well, that is my secret. You saw in the hall how people's cheeks burnt and their eyes shone? You saw people going off and people arriving? They left because I enticed them away. The room of every man and woman here is my sanctuary, and in them my secrets are inviolable. Over the doors hang sumptuous carpets which muffle all sounds, and behind those doors is complete privacy. It is I who return them from the realm of my secrets and send them back to the festivities. For I am sovereign here; here everything is done for my sake. Here they toil to refresh their energies and feelings for me; here their festivities are a preparation for me. And after me they rest. Here I am the purpose of life—here I am life."

– xi –

"In my sister is the supreme happiness of all life," says the elder sister. "But as you see, here there is every pleasure that anyone could possibly want. Here every person lives in the way best suited to them, for here each person has free will and complete liberty."

"What we have sown you will take time to develop, as you know. Many generations will elapse before all that you have glimpsed comes to pass. No, not many generations; my work is advancing more rapidly now, more rapidly with each year. You will not enter my sister's kingdom, but at least you have seen it; you know the future and it is bright and beautiful. Love it, strive for it, work for it, bring it nearer, do your utmost to bring it into the present.

"The closer you bring the future, the brighter, richer and happier your life will be. Strive for it, work for it, bring it nearer and do everything you can to bring it into the present."

: X V :

A year had passed; the new shop, thoroughly organized, was doing well. The two shops coöperated: when one was overworked, it sent orders to the other. They kept a running account with each other. Their means were already so large that they were able to open a store on the Nevsky Prospect but they had to coöperate more closely, which embarrassed

Véra Pávlovna and Madame Mertzálov quite a bit. Although the two associations were friendly, met frequently, and ofteh took walks together in the suburbs, the idea of complete coöperation between the two enterprises was new, and a great deal had to be done. Nevertheless the advantage of having their own store on the Nevsky Prospect was evident, and, after experimenting for some months, Véra Pávlovna and Madame Mertzálov finally succeeded. A new sign appeared on the Nevsky Prospect in French: *Au bon travail. Magasin de Nouveautés.* With the opening of the new store, business began to improve rapidly and was done to better and better advantage. Madame Mertzálov and Véra Pávlovna cherished the dream of seeing the number of shops rise from two to five, ten, twenty.

Three months after the opening of the store Kirsánov received a visit from one of his colleagues with whom he was somewhat acquainted. The latter talked to him a great deal of various medical applications, and especially of the astonishing efficacy of his method, which consisted in placing on the breast and abdomen two small bags, narrow and long, filled with pounded ice and each wrapped in four napkins. In conclusion, he said that one of his friends wished to make Kirsánov's acquaintance.

Kirsánov complied with this desire. The acquaintance was an amiable chap, and the conversation turned on many things,—among others the store. Kirsánov explained that it had been opened for an exclusively commercial purpose. They talked a long time about the sign; was it well to have the sign bear the word *travail?* Kirsánov said that *Au bon travail* meant in Russian a house that filled its orders well: then they discussed the question whether it would not be better to substitute for this motto the name of the manager. Kirsánov objected that his wife's *Russian* name would drive away many customers.* At last he said that his wife's name was Véra, which, translated into French, was *foi,* and that it would be sufficient to put on the sign, instead of *Au bon travail, A la bonne foi.* This would have a most innocent meaning,—simply a house that was conscientious,—and besides the name of the manager would appear. After some discussion they decided that this was feasible. Kirsánov led the conversation on such subjects with especial zeal, and,

* The most famous and well-known dressmaking and millinery establishments in St. Petersburg used to be kept by Frenchwomen.

as a general thing, carried his point, so that he returned home well satisfied.

Madame Mertzálov and Véra Pávlovna, however, had to abate their fine hopes, and think only of preserving what had been already achieved.

The founders of the establishment considered themselves fortunate in the *status quo*. Kirsánov's new acquaintance continued his visits and proved very interesting. Two years went by, and nothing of especial note happened.

: XVI :

LETTER OF KATERÍNA VASSÍLIEVNÁ PÓLOZOV

St. Petersburg, August 17, 1860.

My dear Polina,

I want to tell you about something completely novel that I learned about recently, something in which I am now deeply involved. I am sure that you will also be interested in it. The main point is that you yourself will probably find it possible to take up something of the same sort. It's wonderful, my dear.

It is about a sewing-women's shop,—two shops, to be more accurate, both based on the same principle, both founded by one woman, whose acquaintance I made only a fortnight ago and whose friend I have already become. I am now helping her on condition that she will help me to organize a similar shop. This lady's name is Véra Pávlovna Kirsánov, still young, kind, gay, quite to my fancy; she resembles you, Polina, more than your Kátya, who is so quiet. She is an energetic and fearless person. Hearing of her shop by chance, —they told me of but one,—I came directly to her without recommendation or pretext, and simply told her that I was much interested in her shop. We became friends at our first interview, and the more easily because in her husband, Kirsánov, I found again that Doctor Kirsánov who rendered me so great a service, you remember, five years ago.

After talking with me for half an hour and seeing that I was really in sympathy with these things, Véra Pávlovna took me to her shop, the one which she personally superintends (the other shop is now in charge of one of her friends, also a very excellent person). Now I want to give you an account of the impression made upon me by this first visit. This impression was so vivid and new that I hastened to write it in my journal, long since abandoned, but now resumed in consequence of a peculiar circumstance which I perhaps will tell you about some time. I am very glad that I thus fixed my thoughts; otherwise I should now forget to mention many things which struck me at the time. Today, after two weeks, what astonished me so much seems ordinary. And, curiously enough, the more ordinary I find it all, the more I become attached to it.

Having said thus much, dear Polina, I now copy my diary, adding to it some later observations.

We then went to the shop. On entering, I saw a large room, well furnished and containing a grand piano, as if the room belonged to the residence of a family spending four or five thousand rubles a year. It was the reception room; the sewing-women also spent their evenings there. Then we visited the twenty other rooms occupied by the working-women. They are all very well furnished, although the furniture is not alike in all of them, having been bought as occasion required.

After seeing the rooms where the working-women slept, we went into the rooms where they worked. There I found young girls very well dressed in inexpensive silk or muslin. It was evident from their gentle and tender faces that they lived comfortably. You cannot imagine how I was struck by all this. I made the acquaintance of several of these young girls on the spot. Not all had reached the same degree of intellectual development: some already used the language of educated people, had some acquaintance with literature, like our young ladies, and knew a little about history and foreign countries; two of them had even read a great deal. Others, who had been in the shop but a short time, were less developed, but still one could talk with any of them as with a young girl who has received a certain amount of education. Generally speaking, the degree of their development is proportional to the time that they have been in the shop.

We stayed there to dinner. The dinner consists of three dishes; that day they had rice soup, baked fish with sauce, and veal; after dinner tea and coffee were served. The dinner was so good that I ate with great relish; I should not consider it a privation to eat so always, and yet you know that my father has always had a very good cook.

When we returned to Véra Pávlovna's, she and her husband explained to me that there was nothing astonishing in this. All that I saw, they said, was due to two causes.

On the one hand a greater profit for the sewing-women, and on the other a greater economy in their expenses.

Do you understand why they earn more? They work on their own account, they are their own employers, and consequently they get the part which would otherwise remain in their employer's pocket. But that is not all; in working for their own benefit and at their own cost, they save in provisions and time: their work goes on faster and with less expense.

It is evident that there is a great saving also in the cost of their maintenance. They buy everything at wholesale and for cash, and consequently get everything cheaper than if they bought on credit and at retail.

Besides this, many expenses are much diminished, and some become utterly useless.

According to the calculation made for me by Kirsánov, the sewing-women, instead of the hundred rubles a year which they ordinarily earn, receive two hundred, but, by living in coöperation and buying everything at wholesale and in quantities not exceeding the wants of the association (for instance, the twenty-five working-women have only five umbrellas), they use these two hundred rubles twice as advantageously.

Such is the marvel that I have seen, dear Polina, the explanation of which is so simple. Now I am so accustomed to this marvel that it seems strange to me that I was ever astonished at it. Why did I not expect to find everything as I did find it?

Write me whether you can interest yourself in a shop of this sort. I am doing so, Polina, and find it very pleasant.

Yours,

K. PÓLOZOV.

Chapter Fifth

NEW CHARACTERS

AND THE CONCLUSION

: I :

Mademoiselle Pólozov said in her letter to her friend that she was under obligations to Véra Pávlovna's husband. To understand this it is necessary to know who her father was.

Pólozov had been a captain or lieutenant, but had resigned his office. Following the custom of the good old days, he had led a dissipated life and devoured a large inheritance. After having spent all he had, he reformed and sent in his resignation, in order to make a new fortune. Gathering up the *débris* of his old fortune, he had left about ten thousand rubles in the paper money of that time.* With this sum he started as a small dealer in wheat: he began by taking all sorts of little contracts, availing himself of every opportunity when his means permitted, and in ten years he amassed a considerable capital. With the reputation of so positive and shrewd a man, and with his rank and name well known in the vicinity, he could select a bride from the daughters of the merchants in the two provinces in which he did business. He reasonably chose one with a dowry of half a million (likewise in paper). He was then fifty years old; that was twenty years before the time when his daughter and Véra Pávlovna became friends, as we have seen. With this new fortune added to his own, he was able to do business on a

---

* A silver ruble was worth at that time three and one-half times as much as a paper ruble.

large scale, and ten years later he found himself a millionaire in the money then in circulation. His wife, accustomed to country life, had kept him away from the capital; but she died, and then he went to St. Petersburg to live. His business took a still better turn, and in another ten years he was reputed to be worth three or four millions. Young girls and widows set their caps for him, but he did not wish to marry again, partly through fidelity to his wife's memory, and still more because he did not wish to impose a step-mother upon his daughter Kátya, of whom he was very fond.

Pólozov's operations grew larger and larger; he might already have been the possessor, not of three or four millions, but of a good ten, had he taken the liquor privilege. However he felt a certain repugnance to that business, which he did not consider as respectable as contracts and supplies. His millionaire colleagues made great fun of this casuistry, and they were not wrong; but he, though wrong, held to his opinion: "I am a merchant," said he, "and I do not wish to get rich by extortion." Nevertheless, about a year before his daughter made Véra Pávlovna's acquaintance, he was furnished with only too glaring a proof that his business at bottom was scarcely distinguishable from the liquor monopoly, although in his opinion it differed much. He had an enormous contract for a supply of cloth, or provisions, or shoe leather, or something or other,—I don't know exactly what; age, his steady success, and the growing esteem in which he was held rendering him every year more and more haughty and obstinate, he quarreled with a man who was necessary to him, flew into a passion, insulted him, and his luck turned.

Afterwards he was told to submit. He refused.

He was utterly ruined. His merchandise lay upon his hands; further, some evidences of neglect or sharp practice were found; and his three or four millions vanished. Pólozov, at the age of seventy, became a beggar,—that is, a beggar in comparison with what he had been; but, comparisons aside, he was comfortably well off. He still had an interest in a stearine factory, and, not in the least humiliated, he became manager of this factory at a very fair salary. Besides this, some tens of thousands of rubles had been saved by I know not what chance. With this money, had he been ten or fifteen years younger, he could have begun again to make his fortune, but at his age this was not to be thought of.

And Pólozov's only plan, after due reflection, was to sell the factory, which did not pay. This was a good idea, and he succeeded in making the other stockholders see that a prompt sale was the only way to save the money invested in the enterprise. He thought also of finding a husband for his daughter. But his first care was to sell the factory, invest all his capital in five per cent bonds,—which were then beginning to be fashionable,—and live quietly out the remainder of his days, dwelling sometimes on his past grandeur, the loss of which he had borne bravely, losing with it neither his gayety nor his firmness.

: II :

Pólozov loved Kátya and did not let ultra-aristocratic governesses hold his daughter too severely in check. "These are stupidities," said he of all efforts to correct her attitudes, manners, and other similar things. When Kátya was fifteen, he agreed with her that she could dispense with the English governess as well as with the French one. Then Kátya, having fully secured her leisure, was at perfect liberty in the house. To her liberty then meant liberty to read and dream. She had but few friends, being intimate with only two or three; but her suitors were innumerable: she was the only daughter of Pólozov, possessor—immense!—of four millions! But Kátya read and dreamed, and the suitors despaired. She was already seventeen, and she read and dreamed and did not fall in love. But suddenly she began to grow thin and pale, and at last fell seriously ill.

: III :

Kirsánov was not in active practice, but he did not consider that he had a right to refuse to attend consultations of physicians. And at about that time—a year after he had become a professor and a year before his marriage with Véra Pávlovna—the bigwigs of St. Petersburg practice began to invite him to their consultations often,—even more often than he liked. These invitations had their motives. The first was that the existence of a certain Claude Bernard of Paris had been established; one of the aforesaid bigwigs, having—no one knows why—gone to Paris for a scientific purpose, had seen with his own eyes a real flesh-and-blood Claude Bernard; he had recommended himself to him by his rank, his profession, his decorations, and the high standing of his patients. After listening to him about half an hour, Claude Bernard had said to him: "It was quite useless for you to come to Paris to study medical progress; you did not need to leave St. Petersburg for that." The bigwig took that for an endorsement of his own labors, and, returning to St. Petersburg, pronounced the name of Claude Bernard at least ten times a day, adding at least five times, "my learned friend," or, "my illustrious companion in science." After that, then, how could they avoid inviting Kirsánov to the consultations? It could not be otherwise. The other reason was still more important: all the bigwigs saw that Kirsánov would not try to take away their practice, for he did not accept patients, even when begged to take them. It was well known that a great many of the bigwig practitioners followed this line of conduct: when the patient (in the bigwig's opinion) was approaching an inevitable death and ill-intentioned destiny had so arranged things that it was impossible to defeat it, either by sending the patient to the springs or by any other sort of exportation to foreign parts, it then became necessary to place him in the hands of another doctor, and in such cases the bigwig was even almost ready to pay money to have the patient taken off his hands. Kirsánov rarely accepted offers of this sort, and to get rid of them generally recommended his friends in active practice, keeping for himself only such cases as were interesting from a scientific standpoint. Why should they not invite to consultations, then, a colleague known to Claude Bernard and not engaged in a race after patronage?

The millionaire Pólozov had one of these bigwigs for a doctor, and, when Katerína Vassílievna fell seriously ill, the medical consultations were always made up of bigwigs. Finally she became so weak that the bigwigs resolved to call Kirsánov. In fact, the problem was a very difficult one for them; the patient had no disease, and yet she was growing perceptibly weaker. But some disease must be found, and the doctor having her in charge invented *atrophia nervorum,* "suspension of nervous nutrition." Whether there is such a disease I do not know, but, if it exists, even I can see that it is incurable.

So a new council was held, which Kirsánov attended. They examined the patient and pressed her with questions; she answered willingly and very calmly; but Kirsánov, after her first words, stood one side, doing nothing but watch the bigwigs examine and question; and when, after having worn themselves out and harassed her, they appealed to Kirsánov: "What do you think, Alexánder Matvéich?" he answered: "I have not examined the patient sufficiently. I will remain here. It is an interesting case. If there is need of another consultation, I will tell Karl Fyódorych"—that is, the patient's doctor, whom these words made radiant with happiness at thus escaping his *atrophia nervorum*. When they had gone, Kirsánov sat down by the patient's bed. A mocking smile lighted up her face.

"It is a pity that we are not acquainted," he began; "a doctor needs confidence; perhaps I shall succeed in gaining yours. They do not understand your sickness; it requires a certain sagacity. To sound your chest and dose you with drugs would be quite useless. It is necessary to know but one thing,—your situation,—and then find some way to get you out of it. You will aid me."

The patient did not say a word.

"You do not wish to speak to me?"

The patient did not say a word.

"Probably you even want me to go away. I ask you only for ten minutes. If at the end of that time you consider my presence useless, as you do now, I will go away. You know that sorrow is the only thing that troubles you. You know that, if this mental state continues, in two or three weeks, perhaps even sooner, you will be past saving. Perhaps you have not even two weeks to live. Consumption has not yet set in, but it is near at hand, and in a person of your age and condition it would develop with extraordinary rapidity and might carry you off in a few days."

The patient did not say a word.

"You do not answer. You remain indifferent. That means that nothing that I have said is new to you. By your very silence you answer: 'Yes.' Do you know what any other doctor would do in my place? He would speak to your father. Perhaps, were I to have a talk with him, it would save you, but, if it would displease you to have me do so, I will not. And why? Because I make it a rule to undertake nothing in any one's behalf against his or her will; liberty is above everything, above life itself. Therefore, if you do not wish me to learn the cause of your very dangerous condition, I will not try to find it out. If you say that you wish to die, I will only ask you to give me your reasons for this desire; even if they should seem to me without foundation, I should still have no right to prevent you; if, on the contrary, they should seem to me well founded, it would be my duty to aid you in your purpose, and I am ready to do so. I am ready to give you poison. Under these circumstances I beg you to tell me the cause of your sickness."

The patient did not say a word.

"You do not deign to answer me? I have no right to question you further, but I may ask your permission to tell you something of myself, which may establish greater confidence between us. Yes? I thank you. You suffer. Well, I suffer too. I love a woman passionately, who does not even know that I love her and who must never find it out. Do you pity me?"

The patient did not say a word, but a sad smile appeared upon her face.

"You are silent, but yet you could not hide from me the fact that my last words impressed you more than any that preceded them. That is enough for me; I see that you suffer from the same cause as myself. You wish to die. That I clearly understand. But to die of consumption is too long, too painful a process. I can aid you to die, if you will not be aided to live; I say that I am ready to give you poison, poison that will kill instantly and painlessly. On this condition, will you furnish me with the means of finding out whether your situation is really as desperate as you believe it to be?"

"You will not deceive me?" said the patient.

"Look me steadily in the eyes, and you will see that I will not deceive you."

The patient hesitated a few moments: "No, I do not know you well enough."

"Anybody else in my place would have already told you that the feeling from which you suffer is a good one. I will not say so yet. Does your father know of it? I beg you not to forget that I shall say nothing to him without your permission."

"He knows nothing about it."

"Does he love you?"

"Yes."

"What shall I say to you now? What do you think yourself? You say that he loves you; I have heard that he is a man of good sense. Why, then, do you think that it would be useless to inform him of your feeling, and that he would refuse his consent? If the obstacle consisted only in the poverty of the man whom you love, that would not have prevented you from trying to induce your father to give his consent; at least, that is my opinion. So you believe that your father doesn't think much of him; your silence towards your father cannot be explained otherwise. Am I not right?"

The patient did not say a word.

"I see that I am not mistaken. Do you know what I think now? Your father is an experienced man, who knows men well; you, on the contrary, are inexperienced. If any man should seem bad to him and good to you, in all probability you would be wrong, not he. You see that I am forced to think so. Do you want to know why I say so disagreeable a thing to you? I will tell you. Perhaps you will resent it, but nevertheless you will say to yourself: 'He says what he thinks; he does not dissimulate and does not wish to deceive me.' I shall gain your confidence. Don't I talk to you like an honest man?"

The patient answered, hesitatingly:

"You are a very strange man, doctor."

"Not at all; I am simply not like a hypocrite. I have spoken my thought frankly. But still it is only a supposition. I may be mistaken. Give me the means of finding out. Tell me the name of the man whom you love. Then—always with your permission—I will go and talk with your father."

"What will you say to him?"

"Does he know him well?"

"Yes."

"Then I will ask him to consent to your marriage on condition that the wedding shall take place, not tomorrow, but two or three months hence, in order that you may have time to reflect coolly and consider whether your father is not right."

"He will not consent."

"In all probability he will. If not, I will aid you, as I have already promised."

Kirsánov talked a long time in this tone. And at last the patient told him the name of the man she loved, and gave him permission to speak to her father. Pólozov was greatly astonished to learn that the cause of his daughter's exhaustion was a desperate passion. He was still more astonished when he heard the name of the man whom she loved, and said firmly: "Let her die rather. Her death would be the lesser misfortune for her as well as for me."

The case was the more difficult from the fact that Kirsánov, after hearing Pólozov's reasons, saw that the old man was right and not his daughter.

: I V :

Suitors by hundreds paid court to the heiress of an immense fortune; but the society which thronged at Pólozov's dinners and parties was of that very doubtful sort and tone which ordinarily fills the parlors of the suddenly rich like Pólozov, who have neither relatives nor connections in the real aristocracy. Consequently these people ordinarily become the hosts of sharpers and fops as destitute of external polish as of internal virtues. That is why Katerína Vassílievna was very much impressed when among her admirers appeared a real gallant of the best tone: his behavior was much more elegant, and his conversation much wiser and more interesting, than those of any of the others.

The father was quick to notice that she showed a preference for him, and, being a positive, resolute, and firm man, he instantly had a talk with his daughter: "Dear Kátya, Solovtsóv is paying you assiduous attention; look out for him; he is a very bad man, utterly heartless; you would be so unhappy with him that I would rather see you dead than married to him; it would not be so painful either for me or for you."

Katerína Vassílievna loved her father and was accustomed to heed his advice, for he never laid any restraint upon her, and she knew that he spoke solely from love of her; and, further, it was her nature to try rather to please those who loved her than to satisfy her own caprices; she was of those who love to say to their relatives: "You wish it; I will do it." She answered her father: "I like Solovtsóv, but, if you think it better that I should avoid his society, I will follow your advice." Certainly she would not have acted in this way, and, in conformity with her nature,—not to lie, —she would not have spoken in this way, if she had loved him; but at that time she had but a very slight attachment for Solovtsóv. He simply seemed to her a little more interesting than the others. She became cold towards him, and perhaps everything would have passed off quietly, had not her father in his ardor gone a little too far, just enough for the cunning Solovtsóv. He saw that he must play the *rôle* of a victim, but where should he find a pretext? One day Pólozov happened to indulge in a bitter jest at his expense. Solovtsóv, with an air of wounded dignity, took his leave and ceased his visits. A week later Katerína Vassílievna received from him a passionate, but extremely humble, letter. He had not hoped that she would love him; the happiness of sometimes seeing her, though even without speaking to her, had been enough for him. And yet he sacrificed this happiness to the peace of his divinity. After all, he was happy in loving her even hopelessly, and so on; but no prayers or desires. He did not even ask for a reply. Other letters of the same style arrived from time to time, and finally had an effect upon the young girl.

Not very quickly, however. After Solovtsóv's withdrawal Katerína Vassílievna was at first neither sad nor pensive, and before his withdrawal she had already become cold towards him; and, besides, she had accepted her father's counsel with the utmost calmness. Consequently, when, two months later, she grew sad, how could her father imagine that Solovtsóv, whom he had already forgotten, had anything to do with it?

"You seem sad, Kátya."

"I? No, there is nothing the matter with me."

A week or two later the old man said to her:

"Are you well, Kátya?"

"No, there is nothing the matter with me."

A fortnight later still:

"You must consult the doctor, Kátya."

The doctor began to treat Kátya, and the old man felt entirely easy again, for the doctor saw no danger, but only weakness and a little exhaustion. He pointed out, and correctly enough, that Katerína Vassílievna had led a very strenuous life that winter,—every evening a party, which lasted till two, three, and often five o'clock in the morning. "This exhaustion will pass away." But, far from passing away, the exhaustion went on increasing.

Why, then, didn't Katerína Vassílievna speak to her father? Because she was sure that it would have been in vain. He had signified his ideas in so firm a tone, and he never spoke lightly! Never would he consent to the marriage of his daughter to a man whom he considered wicked.

Katerína Vassílievna continued to dream, reading Solovtsóv's humble and despairing letters, and six months of such reading brought her within a step of consumption. And she did not drop a single word that could lead her father to think that he was responsible for her sickness. She was as tender with him as ever.

"Are you unhappy about something?"

"No, Papa."

"Are you not in sorrow about something?"

"No, Papa."

"It is easy to see that you are not; you are simply despondent, but that comes from weakness, from sickness. The doctor too said that it came from sickness."

But whence came the sickness? As long as the doctor considered the sickness trivial, he contented himself with attributing it to dancing and tight lacing; when he saw that it was growing dangerous, he discovered "the suspension of nervous nutrition," the *atrophia nervorum.*

: V :

But, though the bigwig practitioners had agreed in the opinion that Mademoiselle Pólozov had *atrophia nervorum,* which had been developed by the fatiguing life that she led in spite of her natural inclinations towards reverie and melancholy, it did not take Kirsánov long to see that the patient's weakness was due to some moral cause. It was evident that the young girl had exercised her independence in concealing her illness so long even from her father, and in so acting through the whole of it that he could not divine its cause; the calmness of her replies at the medical consultation confirmed this opinion. She endured her lot with firmness and without any trace of exasperation. Kirsánov saw that a person of such a character deserved attention and aid. Consumption was about to set in, and soon all the care imaginable would be futile. For two hours he had been striving to gain the patient's confidence; at last he had succeeded; now he had got down to the heart of the matter, and had obtained permission to speak to her father.

The old man was very much astonished when he learned from Kirsánov that it was love for Solovtsóv that was at the bottom of his daughter's sickness. How could that be? Kátya had formerly accepted so coolly his advice to avoid Solovtsóv's society, and had been so indifferent when his visits ceased! How could she have begun to die of love on his account? Does any one ever die of love? Such exaltation did not seem at all probable to so calculating and practical a man. But he was made very anxious by what Kirsánov said, and kept saying in reply: "It is a child's fancy and will pass away." Kirsánov explained again and again, and at last made him understand that it was precisely because she was a child that Kátya would not forget, but would die. Pólozov was convinced, but, instead of yielding, he struck the table with his fist and said with inflexible resolution: "Well, let her die! let her die! better that than be unhappy. For her as well as for me it will be less painful!" Katerína Vassílievna was right, therefore, in believing that it was useless to speak to her father.

"But why are you so obstinate on this point? I am willing to admit that the lover is bad, but is he as bad as death?"

"Yes! He has no heart. She is sweet and delicate; he is a base libertine."

And Pólozov painted Solovtsóv so black that Kirsánov could say nothing in reply. In fact, how could he help agreeing with Pólozov? Solovtsóv was no other than the Jean whom we formerly saw at supper with Storéshnikov, Serge, and Julie. Hence it was evident that an honest young girl had better die than marry such a man. He would stifle and prey upon an honest woman. She had much better die.

Kirsánov thought for a few minutes in silence, and then said:

"No, your arguments are not valid. There is no danger for the very reason that the individual is so bad. She will find it out, if you leave her to examine him coolly."

And Kirsánov persisted in explaining his plan to Pólozov in more detail. Had he not himself said to his daughter that, if she should find out that the object of her love was unworthy, she would renounce him herself? Now he might be quite sure of such renunciation, the man loved being very unworthy.

"It will not do for me to tell you that marriage is not a thing of extreme importance if we view it without prejudice, though really, when a wife is unhappy, there is no reason why she should not separate from her husband. But you think that out of the question, and your daughter has been brought up with the same ideas; to you as well as to her marriage is an irrevocable contract, and, before she could get any other ideas into her head, life with such a man would kill her in much more painful fashion than consumption. Therefore we must consider the question from another standpoint. Why not rely on your daughter's good sense? She is not insane; far from it. Always rely on the good sense of any one whom you leave free. The fault in this matter is yours. You have put chains on your daughter's will; unchain her, and you will see her come to your view, if you are right. Passion is blind when it meets obstacles; remove the obstacles, and your daughter will become prudent. Give her the liberty to love or not to love, and she will see whether this man is worthy of love. Let him be her sweetheart, and in a short time she will dismiss him."

Such a way of viewing things was far too novel for Pólozov. He answered with some asperity that he did not believe in such twaddle, that he knew life too well, and that he saw too many instances of human folly to have any faith in humanity's good sense. Especially ridiculous would it be to trust to the good sense of a little girl of seventeen. In vain did Kirsánov reply that follies are committed only in two cases,—either in a moment of impulse, or else when the individual is deprived of liberty and irritated by resistance. These ideas were Greek to Pólozov. "She is insane; it would be senseless to trust such a child with her own fate; rather let her die." He could not be swerved from his decision. Therefore extreme measures must be taken. There was danger in so doing, it is true, but there was only danger, while any other course meant certain loss. There was but one chance of loss against an infinity of chances of salvation. Kirsánov saw in his patient a young girl of calm and silent firmness, and was sure of her. But had he a right to submit her to this danger? Yes, certainly.

"Very well," said Kirsánov, "you will not cure her by the means within your power; I am going to treat her with my own. Tomorrow I will call another consultation."

Returning to his patient, he told her that her father was obstinate, more obstinate than he expected, and that it was necessary consequently to proceed energetically in opposition to him.

"No, nothing can be done," said the patient in a very sad tone.

"And if I decide to submit you to the risk of death? I have already spoken of this to you, but only to gain your confidence and show you that I would consent to anything in order to be useful to you: now I speak positively. Suppose I were to give you poison?"

"I have long known that my death is inevitable; I have but a few days more to live."

"And suppose it were tomorrow morning?"

"So much the better."

She spoke quite calmly.

When there is but one resource left,—to fall back on the resolve to die,—success is almost sure. He explained his plan to her, although it really needed no further elucidation.

: VI :

Certainly Kirsánov would never have made it a rule in such cases to resort to such a risk. It would have been much simpler to carry the young girl away and let her marry any one she might choose; but in this case the question was made very complex by the young girl's ideas and the character of the man whom she loved. With her ideas of the indissolubility of marriage she would continue to live with this base man, even though her life with him should prove a hell. To unite her to him was worse than to kill her. Consequently there was but one way left,—to cause her death or give her the opportunity of coming back to her right mind.

The next day the medical council reassembled. It consisted of half a dozen very grave and celebrated personages; else how could it have had any effect on Pólozov? It was necessary that he should regard its decree as final. Kirsánov spoke; they listened gravely to what he said, and endorsed his opinion no less gravely. It could not be otherwise, for, as you remember, there was in the world a certain Claude Bernard, who lived in Paris and had a high opinion of Kirsánov. Besides, Kirsánov said things that they did not understand at all; how, then, could they refuse their approval? Kirsánov said that he had watched the patient very carefully, and that he entirely agreed with Karl Fyódorych that the disease was incurable. Now, the agony being very painful, and each additional hour of the patient's life being but another hour of suffering, he believed it to be the duty of the council to decree, for the sake of humanity, that the patient's sufferings should be at once terminated by a dose of morphine, from the effects of which she would never awaken.

The council looked at the patient, sounded her chest once more to decide whether it ought to accept or reject this proposition, and, after a long examination, much blinking of the eyes, and stifled murmurs against Kirsánov's unintelligible science, it came back to the room adjoining the sick chamber and pronounced this decree: The patient's sufferings must be terminated by a fatal dose of morphine. After this proclamation, Kirsánov rang for the servant and asked her to call Pólozov into the council-chamber. Pólozov entered. The gravest of the sages, in a sad and solemn form and a majestic and sorrowful voice, announced to him the decree of the council.

Pólozov was thunderstruck. Between expecting an eventual death and hearing the words: "In half an hour your daughter will be no more," there is a difference. Kirsánov looked at Pólozov with fixed attention; he was sure of the effect; nevertheless it was a matter calculated to excite the nerves; for two minutes the stupefied old man kept silent.

"It must not be! She is dying of my obstinacy! I consent to anything! Will she get well?"

"Certainly," said Kirsánov.

The celebrities would have been seriously offended if they had had time to dart glances at each other signifying that all understood that this youngster had played with them as if they were puppets; but Kirsánov did not leave them time enough for the development of these observations. He told the servant to take away the drooping Pólozov, and then congratulated them on the perspicacity with which they had divined his intention, understanding that the disease was due to moral suffering, and that it was necessary to frighten the opinionated old man, who otherwise would really have caused his daughter's death. The celebrities separated, each

content at hearing his own perspicacity and erudition thus
attested before all the others.

After having given them this certificate, Kirsánov went
to tell the patient that the plan had succeeded. At his first
words she seized his hand and tried to kiss it; he withdrew
it with great difficulty.

"But I shall not let your father visit you immediately to
make the same announcement to you: I have first to give
him a lesson concerning the way in which he must conduct
himself."

He told her what advice he was going to give her father,
saying that he would not leave him until he should be completely prepared.

Disturbed by all that had happened, the old man was
very much cast down; he no longer viewed Kirsánov with
the same eyes, but as Mária Alexévna had formerly viewed
Lopukhóv when, in a dream, she saw him in possession of
the lucrative monopoly of the liquor business. But yesterday
Pólozov naturally thought in this vein: "I am older and
more experienced than you, and, besides, no one in the
world can surpass me in brains; as for you, a beardless boy
and a *sans-culotte,* I have the less reason to listen to you
from the fact that I have amassed by my own wits two
millions [there were really but two millions, and not four];
first amass as much yourself, and then we will talk." Now
his thought took this turn: "What a bear! What a will he
has shown in this affair! He understands how to make men
bend."

Pólozov was seized with fright on hearing, in answer to
his first question: "Would you really have given her a fatal
dose?" this reply, given quite coldly by Kirsánov: "Why,
certainly."

"What a bandit!" said Pólozov to himself. "He talks like
a cook wringing a hen's neck."

"And you would have had the courage?" he continued,
aloud.

"Of course; do you take me for a wet rag?"

"You are a horrible man," Pólozov said and repeated it.

"That only means that you have never seen horrible men,"
answered Kirsánov, with an indulgent smile, at the same
time saying to himself: "You ought to see Rakhmétov."

"But how did you persuade all these physicians?"

"Is it, then, so difficult to persuade such people?" answered Kirsánov, with a slight grimace.

After having put a stop to Pólozov's interminable questions, Kirsánov began his instructions.

"Do not forget that human beings reflect coolly only when not thwarted, that they get heated only when irritated, and that they set no value on their fantasies if no attempt is made to deprive them of them and they are left free to inquire whether they are good or bad. If Solovtsóv is as bad as you say,—and I fully believe you,—your daughter will see it for herself, but only when you stop thwarting her. A single word from you against him would set the matter back two weeks, several words forever. You must hold yourself quite aloof."

The instructions were spiced with arguments of this sort: "It is not easy to make yourself do what you do not wish to do. Still, I have succeeded in such attempts, and so I know how to treat these matters; believe me, what I say must be done. I know what I say; you have only to listen."

With people like Pólozov one can act effectively only with a high hand. Pólozov was subdued, and promised to do as he was told. But while convinced that Kirsánov was right and must be obeyed, he could not understand him at all.

"You are on my side and at the same time on my daughter's side; you order me to submit to my daughter and you wish her to change her mind. How are these two things to be reconciled?"

"It is simple enough; I only wish you not to prevent her from becoming reasonable."

Pólozov wrote a note to Solovtsóv, begging him to be good enough to call upon him concerning an important matter; that evening Solovtsóv appeared, came to an amicable but very dignified understanding with the old man, and was accepted as the daughter's intended, on the condition that the marriage should not take place inside of three months.

: **VII** :

Kirsánov could not abandon this affair: it was necessary to come to Katerína Vassílievna's aid to get her out of her blindness as quickly as possible, and more necessary still to watch her father and see that he adhered to the policy of non-intervention. Nevertheless, for the first few days after the crisis, he refrained from visiting the Pólozovs: it was certain that Katerína Vassílievna's state of exaltation still continued; if he should find (as he expected) her sweetheart unworthy, the very fact of betraying his dislike of him—to say nothing of directly mentioning it—would be injurious and heighten the exaltation. Ten days later Kirsánov came, and came in the morning expressly that he might not seem to be seeking an opportunity of meeting the sweetheart, for he wished Katerína Vassílievna to consent with a good grace. Katerína Vassílievna was already well advanced on the road to recovery; she was still very pale and thin, but felt quite well, although a great deal of medicine had been given her by her illustrious physician, into whose hands Kirsánov had resigned her, saying to the young girl: "Let him attend you; all his drugs cannot harm you now." Katerína Vassílievna welcomed Kirsánov enthusiastically, but she looked at him in amazement when he told her why he had come.

"You have saved my life, and yet need my permission to visit us?"

"But my visit in his presence might seem to you an attempt at interference in your relations without your consent. You know my rule,—to do nothing without the consent of the person in behalf of whom I wish to act."

Coming in the evening two or three days afterwards, Kirsánov found the sweetheart as Pólozov had painted him, and Pólozov himself—behaving satisfactorily: the well-trained old man was placing no obstacles in his daughter's path. Kirsánov spent the evening there, not showing in any way whatever his opinion of the sweetheart, and in taking leave of Katerína Vassílievna he made no allusion to him, one way or another.

This was just enough to excite her curiosity and doubt. The next day she said to herself repeatedly: "Kirsánov did not say a word to me about him. If he had left a good impression on him, Kirsánov would have told me so. Can it be that he does not please him? In what respect can he be displeasing to Kirsánov?" When the sweetheart returned the following day, she examined his manners closely, and weighed his words. She asked herself why she did this: it was to prove to herself that Kirsánov should not, or could not, have found out anything about him. This was really her motive. But the necessity of proving to one's self that a person whom one loves has no faults puts one in the way to find some very soon.

A few days later Kirsánov came again, and still said nothing of the sweetheart. This time she could not restrain herself, and towards the end of the evening she said to Kirsánov:

"Your opinion? Why don't you say something?"

"I do not know whether it would be agreeable to you to hear my opinion; I do not know whether you would think it impartial."

"Don't you like him?"

Kirsánov made no answer.

"He displeases you?"

"I haven't said so."

"It is easy to see that he does. Why, then, does he displease you?"

"I will wait for others to see the why."

The next night Katerína Vassílievna examined Solovtsóv more attentively yet.

"Everything about him is all right; Kirsánov is unjust; but why can't I see what it is in him that displeases Kirsánov?"

Her pride was excited in a direction most dangerous to the sweetheart.

When Kirsánov returned a few days afterwards, he saw that he was already in a position to act more positively. Hitherto he had avoided conversations with Solovtsóv in order not to alarm Katerína Vassílievna by premature intervention. Now he made one of the group surrounding the young girl and her sweetheart, and began to direct the conversation upon subjects calculated to unveil Solovtsóv's character by dragging him into the dialogue. The conversation turned upon wealth, and it seemed to Katerína Vassílievna that Solovtsóv was far too much occupied with thoughts about wealth; the conversation turned upon women, and it seemed to her that Solovtsóv spoke of them much too lightly; the conversation turned upon family life, and she tried in vain to drive away the impression that life with such a husband would be perhaps not very inspiring, but rather painful, to a woman.

The crisis had arrived. For a long time Katerína Vassílievna could not go to sleep; she wept in vexation with herself at having injured Solovtsóv by such thoughts. "No, he is not a heartless man; he does not despise women; he loves me, and not my money." If these replies had been in answer to another's words, she would have clung to them obstinately. But she was replying to herself. Now, it is impossible to struggle long against a truth that you have discovered yourself; it is your own. There is no ground for suspicion of trickery. The next evening Katerína Vassílievna herself put Solovtsóv to the test, as Kirsánov had done the evening before. She said to herself that she wished only to convince herself that she had injured him needlessly, but at the same time she felt that she had less confidence in him than before. And again she could not go to sleep, and this time it was with him that she was vexed. Why had he spoken in such a way that, instead of quieting her doubts, he had strengthened them? She was vexed with herself too, and in this vexation could be seen clearly enough this motive: "How could I have been so blind?"

It is easy to understand that two days later she was completely absorbed by this thought: "It will soon be too late to repair my error, if I am mistaken."

When Kirsánov returned for the first time after his conversation with Solovtsóv, he saw that he might speak to Katerína.

"Earlier you wanted to know my opinion about him," said he. "That is not as important as yours. What do you think of him yourself?"

Now it was she who kept silent.

"I do not dare to press you for an answer," said he. He spoke of other things, and soon went away.

But half an hour afterwards she called on him herself.

"Give me your advice; you see that I am hesitating."

"Why, then, do you need the advice of another, when you know yourself what should be done in case of hesitation?"

"Wait till the hesitation is over?"

"You have said it."

"I could postpone the marriage."

"Why not do so, then, if you think it would be better?"

"But how would he take it?"

"When you see in what way he will take it, you can reflect further as to the better course to follow."

·"But it would be painful for me to tell him."

"If that be the case, ask your father to do it for you; he will tell him."

"I do not wish to hide behind another. I will tell him myself."

"If you feel in a condition to tell him yourself, that is certainly much the better way."

It is evident that with other persons—with Véra Pávlovna, for instance—it would not have taken so long to bring the affair to a conclusion. But each temperament has its own particular requirements: if an ardent nature is irritated by delay, a gentle nature on the contrary rebels against abruptness.

The success of Katerína Vassílievna's explanation with her sweetheart surpassed Kirsánov's hopes, believing that Solovtsóv would have wit enough to drag the matter along by his submission and soft beseechings. No; with all his reserve and tact Solovtsóv could not restrain himself at seeing an enormous fortune escape him, and he himself permitted the escape of the few chances that were left him. He launched out in bitter complaints against Pólozov, whom he called an intriguer, telling Katerína Vassílievna that she allowed her father to have too much power over her, that she feared him, and that in this matter she was acting in accordance with his orders. Now, Pólozov as yet knew nothing about this resolution of his daughter; she felt that she was entirely free. The reproaches heaped upon her father wounded her by their injustice, and outraged her in showing her that Solovtsóv considered her a person lacking in will and character.

"You seem to think me a plaything in the hands of others."

"Yes," he said, thoroughly irritated.

"I was ready to die without thinking of my father, and you do not understand it. From this moment all is over between us," said she, quickly leaving the room.

: VIII :

For a long time Katerína Vassílievna was sad, but her sadness, which grew out of these events, soon turned to something else.

There are characters who feel but little interest in a special fact in itself and are only pushed by it in the direction of general ideas, which then act upon them with much greater intensity. If such people possess minds of remarkable vigor, they become reformers of general ideas, and in ancient times they became great philosophers. Kant, Fichte, Hegel, did not elaborate any single special question; such tasks they found wearisome. This refers only to men, be it understood; women, according to generally received opinion, never have strong minds. Nature, you see, has denied them that. Nature is queer, and that is why there are so few great minds among women.

People of uncommonly small minds, with such a tendency of character, are generally phlegmatic and insusceptible; those having minds of ordinary calibre are prone to melancholy and reverie. Which does not mean that they let their imaginations run riot: many of them are deficient in imagination and very positive, only they love to plunge into quiet reverie.

Katerína Vassílievna's love of Solovtsóv had been inspired by his letters; she was dying of a love created by her imagination. It is evident from this that she had very romantic tendencies, although the noisy life of the commonplace society which filled the Pólozovs' house did not dispose her to exalted idealism. It was one of her traits, therefore. The stir and noise had long been a burden on her; she loved to read and dream. Now not only the stir, but the wealth itself, was a burden on her. It does not necessarily follow that she was an extraordinary person. This feeling is common to all rich women of gentle and modest natures. Only in her it had developed sooner than usual, the young girl having received a harsh lesson at an early age.

"In whom can I believe? In what can I believe?" she asked herself, after her rupture with Solovtsóv; and she was forced to conclude that she could believe in nobody and in nothing. Her father's fortune attracted avarice, strategy, and deception from all quarters of the city. She was surrounded by greedy, lying, flattering people; every word spoken to her was dictated by her father's millions.

Her inner thoughts became more and more serious. General questions—concerning wealth, which wearied her so much, and poverty, which tormented so many others—began to interest her. Her father allowed her a large amount of pocket money; she—in that respect like all charitable women—helped the poor. At the same time she read and reflected; she began to see that help of the kind which she lavished was much less efficacious than might have been expected. She was unworthily deceived by the base or pretended poor; and, besides, even those who were worthy of aid and knew how to profit by the money given them could not get out of their poverty with the alms which they received. That made her reflect. Why so much wealth in the hands of some to spoil them; why so much poverty for others? And why did she see so many poor people who were as unreasonable and wicked as the rich?

She was dreamy, but her dreams were mild, like her character, and had as little brilliance as herself. Her favorite poet was George Sand; but she represented herself neither as a Lélia, or an Indiana, or a Cavalcanti, or even a Consuelo; in her dreams she was a Jeanne, and oftener still a Geneviève. Geneviève was her favorite heroine. She saw her walking in the fields and gathering flowers to serve as models for her work; she saw her meeting André,—what sweet rendezvous! Then they find out that they love each other; those were dreams, she knew. But she loved also to dream of the enviable lot of Miss Nightingale, that sweet and modest young girl, of whom no one knows anything, of whom there is nothing to know, except that she is the beloved of all England. Was she young? Poor or rich? Was she happy in her private life or not? No one speaks of that, no one thinks of it, but all bless the consoling angel of the English hospitals of the Crimea and Scutari. Returning to her country after the war was over, she had continued to care for the sick. This was the dream that Katerína Vassílievna would have liked to realize for herself. Her fancy did not carry her beyond these reveries about Geneviève and Miss Nightingale. Can it be said that she is given to fantasy? Can she be called a dreamer?

Had Geneviève been surrounded by the noisy and commonplace society of the lowest rank of sharpers and

fops, had Miss Nightingale been plunged into a life of idle
luxury, might they not have been sad and sorrowful? Therefore Katerína Vassílievna was perhaps more rejoiced than
afflicted when her father was ruined. It disturbed her to see
him grow old and weak, he who was once so strong. It
weighed upon her also to have less means with which to do
good. The sudden disdain of the crowd which had formerly
fawned upon her and her father offended her somewhat;
but this too had its consoling side,—being abandoned by
the trivial, wearisome, and vile crowd, being no more dis-
gusted by its baseness and treachery, being no more embarrassed by it. Yes, now she was calm. She recovered hope.

"Now, if any one loves me, it will be for myself, and
not for my father's millions."

: IX :

Pólozov wanted to arrange the sale of the stearine factory of
which he was a stockholder and director. After six months
of assiduous search, he finally found a purchaser. The purchaser's card read: *Charles Beaumont,* agent of the London
house of Hodgson, Loter & Co. The factory could not pros-
per; everything about it was in bad condition,—its finances
and its administration; but in more experienced hands it
probably would yield large returns; an investment of five
or six hundred thousand rubles might give an annual profit
of a hundred thousand. The agent was conscientious: he
carefully inspected the factory, and examined its books with
the utmost minuteness before advising his house to purchase. Then began the discussions as to the condition of the
business and how much it was worth. These dragged along
almost interminably. During all this time Pólozov, in accordance with an old custom, was very attentive to the agent
and always invited him to dinner. The agent kept himself
at a respectful distance from the old man, and for a long
time declined his invitations, but one day, feeling tired and
hungry after an unusually long discussion with the directors,
he consented to go to dinner with Pólozov, who lived on
the same floor.

: X :

Charles Beaumont, like every Charles, John, James, or William, was not fond of personal intimacies and effusions; but, when asked, he told his story in a few, clear words. His family, he said, was of Canadian origin; in fact, in Canada a good half of the population consists of descendants of French colonists, and his family belonged to these descendants; hence his French name. In his features he certainly resembled a Frenchman more than an Englishman or a Yankee. But, he continued, his grandfather left the suburbs of Quebec and went to New York to live; such things happen. Therefore his father went to New York when still a child and grew up there. When he became an adult (exactly at that time), a rich and progressive proprietor, living in the southern part of the Crimea, conceived the idea of replacing his vineyards with cotton plantations. So he despatched an agent to find an overseer for him in North America. The agent found James Beaumont, of Canadian origin and a resident of New York,—that is, an individual who had no more seen a cotton plantation than you or I, reader, have seen Mount Ararat from our St. Petersburg or Kursk. Progressive people are always having such experiences. It is true that the experiment was in no wise spoiled by the American overseer's complete ignorance of this branch of production, since growing cotton in the Crimea would have been the same as to grow grapes at St. Petersburg. Nevertheless, this impossibility did come to pass upon the overseer's discharge. He became a distiller of brandy in the government of Tambov, where he passed almost all the rest of his life. There his son Charles was born, and there, shortly afterwards, he buried his wife. When nearly sixty-five years old, having laid aside a little money for his old age, he began to think of returning to America, and finally did return. Charles was then about twenty years old. After his father's death Charles desired to return to Russia, where he was born and where, in the fields of the government of Tambov, he had spent his childhood and youth; he felt himself a Russian. He had lived in New York where he was a clerk in a commercial house but he soon left this position for one in the London house of Hodgson, Loter & Co.: ascertaining that this house did business with St. Petersburg, he took the first opportunity to express a desire of obtaining a place in Russia, explaining that he knew Russia as if it were his own country. To have such an employee in Russia would evidently be of great advantage to the house, so it sent him from the London establishment on trial, and here he is in St. Petersburg, having been here six months, on a salary of five hundred pounds. It was not at all astonishing, then, that Beaumont spoke Russian like a Russian and pronounced English with a certain foreign accent.

: XI :

Beaumont found himself a third at dinner with the old gentleman and his daughter, a very pretty, somewhat melancholy, blonde.

"Could I ever have thought," said Pólozov at dinner, "that my stock in this factory would some day be a matter of importance to me? It is very painful at my age to fall from so high a point. Fortunately Kátya has accepted calmly the loss of her fortune sacrificed by me. Even during my life this fortune belonged more to her than to me. Her mother had capital; as for me, I brought but little; it is true that I earned a great deal and that my labor did more than all the rest! What shrewdness I have had to show!" And the old man talked a long time in this boasting tone.

In accordance with the American habit of seeing nothing extraordinary in rapid fortune or sudden ruin, and in accordance also with his individual character, Beaumont was not inclined either to be delighted at the greatness of mind which had succeeded in acquiring three or four millions, or to be afflicted at a ruin which still permitted the employment of a good cook. But, as it was necessary to say a word of sympathy in answer to this long discourse, he remarked:

"Yes, it is a great relief when one's family bears up so well under reverses."

"But you seem to doubt it, Karl Yákovlich. You think that, because Kátya is melancholy, she regrets the loss of wealth? No, Karl Yákovlich, you wrong her. We have experienced another misfortune: we have lost confidence in everybody," said Pólozov, in the half-serious, half-jocose tone used by experienced old men in speaking of the good but *naïve* thoughts of children.

Katerína Vassílievna blushed. It was distasteful to her to have her father turn the conversation upon the subject of her feelings. Besides paternal love there was another circumstance that went far to excuse her father's fault. When one has nothing to say and is in a room where there is a cat or a dog, he speaks of it, and, if there is no cat or dog, he speaks of children; not until these two subjects are exhausted does he talk about the rain and fine weather.

"No, papa, you are wrong in attributing my melancholy to so lofty a motive. It is not my nature to be gay, and, besides, I am bored."

"One may be gay or not, according to circumstances," said Beaumont; "but to be bored is, in my opinion, unpardonable. Boredom is the fashion among our brothers, the English, but we Americans know nothing about it. We have no time for it: we are too busy. I consider . . . It seems to me," he resumed, correcting his Americanism, "that the same should be true of the Russian people also: in my opinion you have too much to do. But I notice in the Russians just the opposite characteristic: they are strongly disposed to spleen. Even the English are not to be compared with them in this respect. English society, regarded by all Europe, including Russia, as the most tiresome in the world, is more talkative, lively, and gay than Russian society, just as it yields the palm to French society in this particular. Your travellers talk of English spleen; I do not know where their eyes are when they are in their own country."

"And the Russians have reason to feel bored," said Katerína Vassílievna; "what can they busy themselves about? They have nothing to do. They must sit with folded arms. Name me an occupation, and my *ennui* probably will vanish."

"You wish to find an occupation? Oh! that is not so difficult; you see around you such ignorance,—pardon me for speaking in this way of your country, *of your native country*," he hastened to add in correction of his Anglicism; "but I was born here myself and grew up here, and I consider it as my own, and so I do not stand on ceremony,—you see here a Turkish ignorance, a Japanese indifference: I hate your native country, since I love it as my own country, may I say, in imitation of your poet. Why, there are *many things to be done*."

"Yes, but what can one man do, to say nothing of one woman?"

"Why, you are doing already, Kátya," said Pólozov; "I will reveal her secret for you, Karl Yákovlich. To drive away *ennui* she teaches little girls. Every day she receives her scholars, and she devotes three hours to them and sometimes even more."

Beaumont looked at the young girl with esteem: "That is American. By America I mean only the free States of the North; the Southern States are worse than Mexico and almost as abominable as Brazil [Beaumont was a furious abolitionist]. It is like us to teach children; but then, why are you bored?"

"Do you consider that a serious occupation, Mr. Beaumont? It is but a distraction; at least, so it seems to me. Perhaps I am mistaken, and you will call me a materialist?"

"Do you expect such a reproach from a man belonging to a nation which everybody reproaches with having no other thought, no other ideal, than the dollar?"

"You jest, but I am seriously afraid of stating my opinions on this subject before you. My views might seem to you like those preached by the obscurantists concerning the uselessness of education and enlightenment."

"Bravo!" said Beaumont to himself: "is it possible that she can have arrived at this idea? This is getting interesting."

Then he continued aloud: "I am an obscurantist myself; I am for the unlettered Negroes against their 'civilized' proprietors in the Southern States. But pardon me; my American hatred has diverted me. It would be very agreeable to me to hear your opinion."

"It is very prosaic, Mr. Beaumont, but I have been led to it by my experience of life. It seems to me that the matter with which I occupy myself is but one side of the whole, and, moreover, not the side upon which the attention of those who wish to serve the people should be first fixed. This is what I think: give people bread, and they will learn to read themselves. It is necessary to begin with the bread; otherwise it will be time wasted."

"Then why don't you commence at the necessary point?" said Beaumont, already a little animated. "It is possible; I know examples, with us in America," he added.

"I have already told you why. What can I undertake alone? I do not know how to go to work; and, even if I knew, could I do it? A young girl is so hampered in every direction. I am free in my own room. But what can I do there? Put a book on the table and teach people to read it. Where can I go? What can I do alone?"

"Are you trying to make me out a despot, Kátya?" said the father: "but it is not my fault, you having given me so severe a lesson."

"I blush at the thought, papa; I was then a child. No, you are good, you do not thwart me. It is society that thwarts me. Is it true, M. Beaumont, that in America a young girl is much less hampered?"

"Yes, we may be proud of it, although we are far from where we ought to be; but what a comparison with Europeans! All that you hear about the liberty of woman in our country is really the truth."

"Papa, let us go to America, after M. Beaumont has bought the factory," said Katerína Vassílievna, jokingly: "there I will do something. Ah! how happy I should be!"

"One may find an occupation in St. Petersburg also," said Beaumont.

"How?"

Beaumont hesitated two or three seconds. "But why, then, did I come here? And who could better inform me?" said he to himself.

"Have you not heard of it? There is an attempt in progress to apply the principles lately deduced by economic science: are you familiar with them?"

"Yes, I have read a little about them; that must be very interesting and very useful. And could I take part in it? Where shall I find it?"

"The shop was founded by Madame Kirsánov."

"Is she the doctor's wife?"

"You know him? And has he said nothing to you about this matter?"

"A long time ago. Then he was not married. I was sick; he came several times, and saved me. Ah! what a man! Does she resemble him?"

But how was she to make Madame Kirsánov's acquaintance? Should Beaumont give Katerína Vassílievna a letter of introduction to Madame Kirsánov? What was the use? The Kirsánovs had never even heard his name; but no introduction was necessary: Madame Kirsánov surely would be very glad to find so much sympathy. As for her address, it would have to be ascertained at the hospital or the Academy of Medicine.

: XII :

Such was the way in which Mademoiselle Pólozov came to know Véra Pávlovna; she called upon the latter the following morning; and Beaumont was so interested in the matter that he came in the evening to inquire about her visit.

Katerína Vassílievna was very animated. There was no trace of her sorrow left; ecstasy had replaced melancholy. She described to Beaumont, with enthusiasm, what she had seen and heard. She had already told the story to her father, but it was impossible for her to weary of it. Her heart was full for she had found an attractive occupation. Beaumont listened attentively; but does one listen like that? And she said to him, almost angrily: "Mr. Beaumont, I am becoming disappointed in you. How can you be so little impressed? One would suppose that you felt almost no interest."

"Don't forget, Katerína Vassílievna, that I have seen all this in America. I am interested in a few of the details, but as a whole I know it only too well. It is only in the persons who have taken this initiative here that I can be much interested. For instance, what can you tell me of Madame Kirsánov?"

"Ah, my God! of course, I liked her very much. She explained everything to me with so much love."

"You have already said so."

"What more do you want? What else could I tell you? Could you expect me, indeed, to be thinking of her, when I had such a sight before my eyes?"

"I understand that one entirely forgets persons when interested in things; but nevertheless what else can you tell me of Madame Kirsánov?"

Katerína Vassílievna called up her recollections of Véra Pávlovna, but found in them only the first impression that Véra Pávlovna had made upon her. She described very vividly her external appearance, her manner of speech, all that one sees at a glance when first meeting a stranger, but beyond this there was almost nothing in her memory relating to Véra Pávlovna. The shop, the shop, the shop,— and Véra Pávlovna's explanations. These explanations she understood thoroughly, but Véra Pávlovna herself she understood but very little.

"For this once, then, you have disappointed my hopes to learn something from you about Madame Kirsánov. Nevertheless I do not release you; in a few days I will ask you again about her."

"But why not make her acquaintance, if she interests you so much?"

"I should like to do so; perhaps I shall some day. But first I must learn more about her."

Beaumont was silent for a few moments.

"I am considering whether I should ask you a favor. Yes, I better. This is it: if my name happens to be mentioned in your conversations with them, do not say that I have questioned you about her, or that it is my intention to sometime make her acquaintance."

"But this is getting mysterious, Mr. Beaumont," said Katerína Vassílievna, in a serious tone. "Through me as an intermediary you wish to obtain information about them, while you remain concealed yourself?"

"Yes, Katerína Vassílievna; how shall I explain it to you? I am afraid of making their acquaintance."

"All this is very strange, Mr. Beaumont."

"True. I will say more: I fear that it may be disagreeable to them. They have never heard my name. But I have had something to do with one of their relatives, and even with them. In short, I must first be sure that it would be agreeable to them to make my acquaintance."

"All this is strange, Mr. Beaumont."

"I am an honest man, Katerína Vassílievna, and I assure you that I shall never permit myself to compromise you. I see you now only for the second time, but already I have the highest regard for you."

"I see for myself, Mr. Beaumont, that you are an honest man; but . . ."

"If you think me an honest man, you will permit me to come to see you in order that, as soon as you shall feel entirely sure about me, I may ask you for details about the Kirsánovs. Or rather, you shall break the silence yourself, whenever it may seem to you that you can satisfy the request which I have just made of you and which I shall not renew. Are you willing?"

"Certainly, Mr. Beaumont," said Katerína Vassílievna, slightly shrugging her shoulders. "But confess, then . . ."

This time she did not wish to finish.

"That I must now inspire you with some mistrust? True. But I will wait till that has disappeared."

: XIII :

Beaumont visited the Pólozovs very often. "Why not?" thought the old man: "he is a good match. Certainly he is not such a husband as Kátya might once have had. But then she was neither concerned nor ambitious. Now I could not ask for a better one."

In fact, Beaumont was a good match. He said that he thought of living in Russia for the rest of his days, as he regarded it as his native country. Here was a positive man; at thirty years, though born poor, he had a good position in life. If he had been a Russian, Pólozov would have liked it had he been a nobleman, but in the case of foreigners this is not an important consideration, especially when they are Frenchmen and still less when they are Americans. In America one may be today in the employ of a shoemaker or a farmer, tomorrow a general, the day after president, and then again a clerk or a lawyer. They are a people apart, judging individuals only by their wealth and their capacities. "And they are quite right," reflected Pólozov; "I am such a man myself. I began in commerce and married a merchant's daughter. Money is the most important thing; brains also, to be sure, for without brains one cannot get money. He has taken a good road. He will buy the factory and be its manager; then he will become a partner in the house. And their houses are not like ours. He, too, will control millions."

It was very probable that Pólozov's dreams concerning his future son-in-law were no more to be realized than the similar dreams of Mária Alexévna. But, however that may be, Beaumont was a good match for Katerína Vassílievna.

Was not Pólozov mistaken, nevertheless, in his prevision of a son-in-law in Beaumont? If the old man had had any doubts at first, these doubts would have disappeared when

Beaumont, two weeks after he had begun to visit them, said that it was very probable that the purchase of the factory would be delayed a few days. At any rate he wished to defer the drawing-up of the contract, as he was waiting for Mr. Loter, who would soon arrive at St. Petersburg. "At first, when I was not personally acquainted with you," added Beaumont, "I wanted to conclude the matter myself. Now that we are so well acquainted, this would not be proper. And so that later there may be no misunderstandings, I have written to my employers that, during the negotiations, I have made the acquaintance of the manager and principal stockholder, who has nearly his entire fortune invested in the factory, and have asked, in consequence, that the house should send some one to conclude the negotiations in my place; that is the reason, you see, why Mr. Loter is coming."

Prudence and wisdom,—these showed clearly an intention to marry Kátya: a simple acquaintance would not have prompted such precaution.

: XIV :

The next two or three visits of Beaumont were marked at first by a rather cold welcome on the part of Katerína Vassílievna. She began indeed to feel a little distrust of this comparative stranger, who had expressed a puzzling interest in a family to whom, if he were to be believed, he was not known, and yet feared to make their acquaintance in the absence of knowledge that his acquaintance would be agreeable. But even during these first visits, though Katerína Vassílievna viewed him with distrust, she nevertheless was quickly drawn into lively conversation with him. In her past life, before making the acquaintance of Kirsánov, she had never met such men. He sympathized so much with all that interested her, and understood her so well! Even with her dearest friends (for that matter, properly speaking, she had but a single friend, Polina, who had long been living at Moscow, after her marriage to a manufacturer of that city), even with Polina she did not converse so much at her ease as with him.

And he at·first came, not, of course, to see her, but to inquire about the Kirsánovs. Nevertheless from the very first, from the moment when they began to talk of *ennui* and the means of escaping it, it was plain that he was interested in her and was in sympathy with her. At their second interview he was very much drawn to her by her enthusiasm at having found a useful occupation. Now at each new interview his good feeling toward her became more evident. Straightway a friendship of the simplest and most fervent sort was formed between them, so that a week later Katerína Vassílievna had already told him all that she knew about the Kirsánovs: she was sure that this man was incapable of entertaining an evil design.

It is none the less true that, when she broached the subject of the Kirsánovs, he stopped her.

"Why so soon? You hardly know me."

"No, I know you enough, Mr. Beaumont. I see that your unwillingness to explain to me what seemed strange in your desire was probably due to the fact that you had no right to do so; there are secrets."

To which he answered:

"And, you see, I am no longer so impatient to know what I wanted to find out about them."

: X V :

Katerína Vassílievna's animation continued without weakening, but it changed into a perpetual playfulness full of luminous humor. It was precisely this animation which most drew Beaumont to her; that was very evident. After having listened two or three times to the stories that she told him regarding the Kirsánovs, he said to her the fourth time: "Now I know all that I had to find out. I thank you."

"But what do you know, then? I have only told you so far that they love each other and are very happy."

"That is all that I had to find out; besides, I knew it."

And the subject of conversation changed.

The first thought of Katerína Vassílievna, on hearing Beaumont's first question about Madame Kirsánov, had been that he was in love with her. But now it was clear that such was not the case.

As well as Katerína Vassílievna now knew him, she even believed that Beaumont was not capable of falling in love. "Love he may. But if he loves anybody now, it's me," thought Katerína Vassílievna.

: XVI :

But did they really love each other? Did she, for instance, love him? On one occasion she showed some feeling for Beaumont; but how it ended! Not at all as the beginning would have led one to expect.

Beaumont came to the Pólozovs' every day for longer or shorter calls, but every day. It was precisely on this fact that Pólozov based his conviction that Beaumont intended to ask for Katerína Vassílievna's hand; there were no other indications. One day the evening went by, and Beaumont did not come.

"Do you know what has happened to him, Papa?"

"I know nothing about it; probably he did not have time."

Another evening passed, and still Beaumont did not come. The next morning Katerína Vassílievna was getting ready to go out.

"Where are you going, Kátya?"

"To attend to some affairs of mine."

She went to see Beaumont. He was sitting down, in an overcoat with large sleeves, and reading; he raised his eyes from his book when he saw the door open.

"Ah! it is you, Katerína Vassílievna? I am very glad, and I thank you very much."

This was said in the same tone in which he would have greeted her father, except that it was a little more affable.

"What is the matter with you, Mr. Beaumont? Why have you stayed away so long? You have made me anxious about you, and, besides, you have made time hang heavy on my hands."

"Nothing of importance, Katerína Vassílievna; I am well, as you see. Won't you have some tea? See, I am drinking some."

"Very well, but why haven't we seen you for so long?"

"Peter, bring a cup. You see, I am well; there is nothing the matter, then. Stop! I have been to the factory with Mr. Loter, and, in explaining it to him, I was careless and placed my arm on some gearing, which scratched it. And neither yesterday nor the day before could I put on my undercoat."

"Show me your arm; else I shall be anxious and believe that you are mutilated."

"Oh! no [Peter entered with a cup for Katerína Vassílievna], I really have my two hands. But then, if you insist [he pulled his sleeve up to his elbow]. Peter, empty this ashtray and give me my cigar-case; it is on the table in the study. You see that it is nothing; it needed nothing but some court-plaster."

"Nothing? It is swollen and very red."

"Yesterday it was much worse, tomorrow it will be all well. [After emptying the ashtray and bringing the cigar-case, Peter withdrew.] I didn't want to appear before you as a wounded hero."

"But why didn't you write a word?"

"Oh! at first I thought that I should be able to wear my undercoat the next day,—that is, day before yesterday,— day before yesterday I thought that I should be able to wear it yesterday, and yesterday today. I didn't think it worth bothering you about."

"And you have troubled me much more. Your conduct was not good, Mr. Beaumont. When will this matter of the sale be finished?"

"One of these days, probably, but, you know, this delay is not my fault, or Mr. Loter's, but that of the corporation itself."

"What are you reading?"

"Thackeray's new novel. To have such talent and repeat the same thing everlastingly! It is because his stock of ideas is small."

"I have already read it; in fact."

They lamented the fall of Thackeray, and talked for half an hour about other similar matters.

"But it is time to go to Véra Pávlovna's; and, by the way, when will you make their acquaintance? They are excellent people."

"Some day or other I will ask you to take me there. I thank you very much for your visit."

"*Au revoir,* Mr. Beaumont; will you come today?"

"I doubt it . . . no. Tomorrow, surely."

: XVII :

Do young girls who are in love make such visits as these? In the first place, no well-bred young girl would ever permit herself to do anything of the kind; but, if she should permit herself, evidently something very different would result from it. If Katerína Vassílievna's act is contrary to morality, the content of this immoral act, so to speak, is still more contrary to all accepted ideas. Is it not clear that Katerína Vassílievna and Beaumont were not human beings, but fish, or, if they were human beings, that they at least had fish blood in their veins? And when she saw him at her home, she treated him in a manner quite in line with this interview.

"I am tired of talking, Mr. Beaumont," said she, when he stayed too long; "stay with Papa; I am going to my room."

And she went out. Sometimes he answered:

"Stay fifteen minutes longer, Katerína Vassílievna."

"Very well," she then replied.

But generally he answered:

"*Au revoir,* then, Katerína Vassílievna."

What sort of people are these, I should like to know; and I should like to know also if they are not simply honest people, whom no one prevents from seeing each other in their own fashion, whom no one will prevent from marrying whenever the idea occurs to them, and who, consequently, have no reason to bear up against obstacles. Yet I am embarrassed by the coolness of their association, not so much on their account as on my own. Am I condemned, in my capacity of novelist, to compromise all my heroes and heroines in the eyes of well-bred people? Some eat and drink, others do not get excited without reason: what an uninteresting set!

: **XVIII** :

And yet, in the opinion of the aged Pólozov, the affair meant marriage. Considering the nature of the relations between the supposed lovers, how could he imagine such a thing? Hadn't he heard their conversations? Not always, it is true; sometimes they stayed with him, but more often went to other rooms. It is true that this did not change at all the character of their conversation. These conversations were such that a *connoisseur* in matters of the human heart (a *human heart* which men really do not have) would have lost all hope of ever seeing Katerína Vassílievna and Beaumont married. Not that they did not talk of sentiments to each other; they talked of those as they did of everything else, but only a little and in what a tone! Here is an example. A week after the visit for which Beaumont had "very much thanked" Katerína Vassílievna, and two months after the beginning of their acquaintance, the sale of the factory was concluded; Mr. Loter was getting ready to start the next day; the stockholders, including Pólozov, were to receive the very next day half of the sum in cash and half in notes payable in three months. Pólozov, perfectly satisfied, was seated at a table in the drawing-room, turning over his business papers, and half listening to his daughter's conversation with Beaumont as they passed through the drawing-room.

"If a woman, a young girl, is hampered by prejudices," said Beaumont, without further Anglicisms or Americanisms, "man too—I speak of honest men—suffers great annoyance thereby. How can one marry a young girl who has had no experience in the daily relations which will result from her consent to the proposition? She cannot judge whether daily life with a man of such a character as her sweetheart will please her or not."

"But, Mr. Beaumont, if her relations with this man have been daily, that surely gives her a certain guarantee of mutual happiness."

"A certain,—yes; nevertheless it would be much surer if the test were more thorough. The young girl, from the nature of the relations permitted her, does not know enough about marriage; consequently for her it is an enormous risk. It is the same with an honest man who marries. Only he can judge in a general way; he is well acquainted with women of various characters, and knows what character suits him best. She has no such experience."

"But she has had a chance to observe life and characters in her family and among her acquaintances; she has had excellent opportunities for reflection."

"All that is very fine, but it is not sufficient. There is no substitute for personal experience."

"You would have only widows marry," said Katerína Vassílievna, laughing.

"Your expression is a very happy one. Only widows. Young girls should be forbidden to marry."

"You are right," said Katerína Vassílievna, seriously.

At first it seemed very queer to Pólozov to hear such conversations or parts of conversations. But now he was somewhat accustomed to it, and said to himself: "I too am a man devoid of prejudices. I went into commerce and married a merchant's daughter."

The next day this part of the conversation,—the general conversation was usually devoted to other subjects,—this part of the conversation of the night before continued as follows:

"You have told me the story of your love for Solovtsóv. But what was this? It was, I say, a childish sentiment, about which there was no security. It is a good subject for jest, when you look back to it, and also for grief, if you will, for it had a very sad side. You were saved only by a very unusual circumstance, because the matter fell into the hands of a man like Alexánder."

"Who?"

"Matvéich Kirsánov," he finished, as if he had not paused after the first name; Alexánder; "but for Kirsánov you would have died of consumption. You had an opportunity to deduce from his experience well-founded ideas as to the harmful character of the situation which you had occupied in society. And you deduced them. All that is very reasonable, but by no means did it give you the experience necessary to enable you to appreciate the character which it would be good for you to find in a husband. You do not want a rascal, but an honest man,—that is all that you have learned. Good. But should every honest woman be content, whatever the character of the man she may have chosen, provided he is honest? In such matters a better knowledge of characters and relationships is needed,—a wholly different experience. We decided yesterday that only widows should marry, to use your expression. What sort of a widow are you, then?"

"That's true," said Katerína Vassílievna, somewhat sadly, "but at any rate I haven't deceived any one."

"And you would not have succeeded in doing so, for one cannot feign experience when one doesn't have it."

"You are always talking of the insufficiency of the means afforded us, young girls, for making a well-grounded choice. As a general thing, for a choice to be well-grounded, no experience of this sort is necessary. If a young girl is not too young, she may know her own character very well. I, for instance, know mine, and it is evident that I shall not change. I am twenty-two years old. I know what I need in order to be happy: a tranquil life, with no one to disturb my peace, and that is all."

"Evidently you are right.

"Is it so difficult to tell whether these indispensable traits exist or not in the character of any given man? One can find it out from a few conversations."

"You are right. But you have said yourself that this is the exception and not the rule."

"Certainly it is not the rule. Mr. Beaumont, given our conditions of life, our ideas, and our customs, one cannot wish for a young girl to have this knowledge of every-day relations, this knowledge of which we say that, if it is lacking, the young girl runs a great risk of making a bad choice. Under her present conditions there is no way out of her situation. The young girl might, indeed, easily stoop and learn dissimulation. She would have to deceive her parents and the world, or hide herself from them, which is the next thing to deceit; and this would decidedly lower her character. It is very probable also that she would view life far too lightly. And if that did not happen, if she did not become bad, her heart would be broken. And yet she would gain almost no experience of actual life, because these relations, either so dangerous to her character or so painful to her heart, are never more than relations of appearance, not at all the relations of every-day life. You see that that would not be at all advisable, considering our present way of living."

"Certainly, Katerína Vassílievna; but that is just why our present way of living is bad."

"Surely; we're agreed on that point. What does it mean, in fact? The man says: 'I doubt whether you would make me a good wife.' And the young girl answers: 'No, I beg of you, make me a proposal.' Unheard-of insolence! Or perhaps that is not the way? Perhaps the man says: 'I have not so much as to consider whether I should be happy with you; but be prudent, even in choosing me. You have chosen me, but, I pray you, reflect, reflect again. It is much too serious a matter even in relation to me who love you much. Do not give yourself up without a very rigid and systematic examination.' And perhaps the young girl answers: 'My friend, I see that you think, not of yourself, but of me. You are right in saying that we are pitiful beings; that men deceive us and lead us into error with bandaged eyes. But don't be afraid on my account: *I* am sure that *you* are not deceiving me. My happiness is sure. As calm as you are on your account, so am I on mine.'"

"I am astonished only at this," continued Beaumont the next day (they were again walking through the rooms, in one of which was Pólozov): "I am astonished only at this,—that under such conditions there are still some happy unions."

"You speak as if you were displeased that there, are any," said Katerína Vassílievna, laughing. She laughed often now, with a gay and gentle laugh.

"And indeed they may lead you to sad thoughts: if, with such inadequate means of judging the needs and characteristics of men, young girls still know enough to make a tolerably happy choice, what lucidity and sagacity that argues in the feminine mind! With what clear, strong, and just mental vision woman is endowed by nature! And yet it remains useless to society, which rejects it, crushes it, stifles it. If this were not the case, if her mind were not compressed, if such a great quantity of moral power were not destroyed, humanity would progress ten times more rapidly."

"You are a panegyrist of women, Mr. Beaumont. Couldn't all this be explained more simply by *chance?*"

"Chance! explain what you will by chance; when cases are numerous, they are the result of a general cause."

"You reason on the question of women like Mrs. Beecher Stowe, Mr. Beaumont. She demonstrates that the Negro race is endowed with greater intellect than the white race."

"You jest, but I am not jesting at all."

"You are not annoyed with me, I hope? If women and young girls cannot do what you consider is indispensable to them, it is not at all my fault. But I am going to give you my serious opinion, if you wish it, not, however, upon the woman question,—I do not care to be judge in my own cause,—but simply upon yourself, Mr. Beaumont. You, by nature, are a man of great self-control, and you get angry when you talk upon this question. What does this mean? You probably have had some personal experience . . . Probably you have been the victim of what you consider an inexperienced young girl's erroneous choice."

"Perhaps myself, or perhaps some relative of mine. Nevertheless, think about this, Katerína Vassílievna. I will tell you, after I have received your reply. In three days I will **ask** you to give me a reply."

"To a question which is not formulated? Do I know **you** so little that I need to reflect for three days?"

Katerína Vassílievna stopped, placed her hand upon Beaumont's neck, bent the young man's head towards her, **and** kissed him on the forehead.

According to all precedents, and even according to **the** demands of common politeness, Beaumont ought to have embraced her and kissed her lips; but he did not. He only pressed the hand which had been thrown around him. "**Very** well, Katerína Vassílievna, but think about it, nevertheless." And they began to walk again.

"But who told you, Karl, that I have not been thinking about it for much more than three days?" she answered, still holding his hand.

"Of course I saw it clearly. So I will tell you all forthwith; it is a secret; let us go into the other room and sit **down,** that we may not be overheard."

They said these last words as they passed by the old man: he, seeing them walking arm in arm, which had never happened before, said to himself: "He has asked her hand, **and** she has given him her word. Good!"

"Tell your secret, Karl; here Papa will not hear us."

"It seems ridiculous, Katerína Vassílievna, to appear **to** have fears on your account; certainly there is nothing **to** fear. But you will understand why I put you on your guard in this matter when I tell you of the experience through which I have passed. Certainly we might both have lived together. But I pitied her. How much she suffered, and **of** how many years of the life that she needed was she deprived! It is very sad. It matters little where the thing occurred,—say New York, Boston, Philadelphia, or where you will. She was an excellent person and looked upon her husband as an excellent man. They were extremely devoted **to** each other. And yet she must have suffered much. He **was** ready to give his head for his wife's slightest happiness. And yet she could not be happy with him. Fortunately **it** ended as it did. But it was painful to her."

"Can I have heard this story from any one?"

"May be."

"From herself, perhaps?"

"May be."

"I have not yet given you an answer?"

"No."

"You know it."

"I know it," said Beaumont, and the ordinary scene that occurs between lovers began with ardent embraces.

: XIX :

The next day at three o'clock Katerína Vassílievna called at Véra Pávlovna's.

"I am getting married the day after tomorrow, Véra Pávlovna," said she, as she came in, "and tonight I'm bringing my sweetheart to see you."

"Undoubtedly it is Beaumont, over whom you have been mad so long."

"I? Mad? When all happened so simply?"

"I am willing to believe that you have acted simply with him, but with me nothing of the sort."

"Really? That is curious. But here is something more curious still: he loves both of you very much, but you, Véra Pávlovna, he loves even more than Alexánder Matvéich."

"What's there curious about that? If you have spoken to him of me with a particle of the enthusiasm with which you have spoken to me of him, it is needless to say."

"You think that he knows you through me? That's just the point; it is not through me, but through himself that he knows you, and much better than I do."

"That's news! How is that?"

"How? Since the first day of his arrival at St. Petersburg, he has wanted very much to see you, but it seemed to him that he would do better to postpone your acquaintance until he could come, not alone, but with his sweetheart or his wife. It seemed to him that it would be more agreeable to you to see him in this way. So you see that our marriage has arisen out of his desire to make your acquaintance."

"He's marrying you to make my acquaintance?"

"Who said that he is marrying me for your sake? Oh, no, it is not for love of you that we are to marry. But when he came to St. Petersburg, did either of us know of the other's existence? And if he hadn't come, how could we have known each other? Now, he came to St. Petersburg on your account. Do you begin to see?"

"He speaks Russian better than English, you say?" asked Véra Pavlovna, with emotion.

"Russian as well as I do, and English as well as I do."

"Kátenka, dear friend, how happy I am!"

Véra Pávlovna began to embrace her visitor.

"Sásha, come here! Quick! Quick!"

"What is the matter, Vérochka? How do you do, Katerína Vass . . ."

He had not time to pronounce her name before the visitor embraced him.

"It is Easter today, Sásha; so say to Kátenka: 'He is risen indeed.' " *

"But what is the matter with you?"

"Sit down, and she will tell us; I myself know almost nothing as yet. It is enough to embrace you,—and in my presence, too! Tell us, Kátenka."

: X X :

In the evening the excitement was certainly still greater. But, when order was restored, Beaumont, on the demand of his new acquaintances, told them the story of his life, beginning with his arrival in the United States. "As soon as I arrived," said he, "I was careful to do everything necessary to enable me to speedily become a citizen. To that end I had to join some party. But which one? The abolitionists, of course. I wrote some articles for the 'Tribune' on the influence of serfdom on the entire social organization of Russia. This was a new argument, of considerable value to the abolitionists, against slavery in the Southern States, and in consequence I became a citizen of Massachusetts.† Soon after my arrival, still through the influence of the abolitionists, I obtained a place in one of their few business houses in New York." Then came the story that we already know. This part of Beaumont's biography, then, is beyond doubt.

---

* During the Easter festivities the Orthodox, when they meet, embrace each other three times, one of them saying at the same time, "Christ is risen," whereupon the other responds, "He is risen indeed."

† Chernyshevsky's ideas of the method by which foreigners acquire American citizenship were erroneous.

: X X I :

It was agreed that the two families should look for two suites of rooms next to each other. Until convenient suites could be found and prepared, the Beaumonts lived in the factory, in which, in accordance with the orders of the house, a suite had been arranged for the manager. This retreat into the suburbs might be looked upon as corresponding to the trip which newly-married couples make, in accordance with an excellent English custom, which is now spreading throughout Europe.

When, six weeks later, two convenient suites next to each other had been found, the Kirsánovs went to live in one, the Beaumonts in the other, and the old Pólozov preferred to remain in the factory suite, the extent of which reminded him, if only feebly, of his past grandeur. It was agreeable to him to remain there for the additional reason that he was the most important personage for two or three miles around. Innumerable marks of consideration were shown him, not only by his own clerks and commissioners, but by those of the neighborhood and by the rest of the suburban population, some of whom were beneath and some slightly above the former in social position. And it was with immense pleasure that he received, after the manner of a patriarch, these marks of respectful consideration. The son-in-law came to the factory every morning, and Kátya came along with him almost always. In summer they went (as they still do) to live entirely in the factory, which thus serves as a country-house. During the rest of the year the old man, besides receiving every morning his daughter and his son-in-law (who does not cease to be a North American), has the pleasure of receiving once a week and oftener visitors coming to spend the evening with Katerína Vassílievna and her husband, or the Kirsánovs with some other young people, or an even more numerous company: the factory is made the object of frequent suburban excursions by the acquaintances of the Kirsánovs and the Beaumonts. Pólozov is delighted by all these visits, and how could it be otherwise? To him belongs the *rôle* of host, the patriarchal *rôle*.

: XXII :

Each of the two families lives after its own fashion, according to its own fancy. On ordinary days in one there is more stir, in the other tranquillity. They visit each other like relatives; one day more than ten times, but for one or two minutes at a time; another day one of the suites is empty almost all day, its inhabitants being in the other. There is no rule about this. Nor is there any rule when a number of visitors happen to come: now the door between the two suites remains closed (the door between the two parlors is generally closed, only the door between Véra Pávlovna's room and Katerína Vassílievna's being always open) —now, when the company is not numerous, the door connecting the reception rooms remains closed; at another time, when the number is greater, this door is open, and then the visitors do not realize where they are, whether at Véra Pávlovna's or at Katerína Vassílievna's, and the latter hardly know themselves.

What else? The workshops continue to exist and to work in closer concert; now there are three of them; Katerína Vassílievna organized hers long ago, and now very often acts as a substitute for Véra Pávlovna in the latter's shop; soon she will take her place entirely, for in the course of this year Véra Pávlovna—forgive her for it—will pass her medical examination, and then she will have no more time to give to the shop. "It is a pity that the development of these shops is impossible; how they would grow!" sometimes said Véra Pávlovna. Katerína Vassílievna made no answer; only her eyes flashed with hatred.

"How headstrong you are, Kátya! You are worse than I am," said Véra Pávlovna. "It is fortunate that your father has something left."

"Yes, Vérochka, one feels easier about her child." (Then she has a child.)

"But you have set me dreaming about I know not what. Our life will go on gently and tranquilly."

Katerína Vassílievna made no answer.

"Yes, why don't you say yes to me?"

Katerína Vassílievna smiled as she answered:

"It does not depend on my 'yes' or my 'no'; therefore to please you I will say, 'Yes, our life shall go on tranquilly.'"

And indeed they do live tranquilly. They live in harmony and amicably, in a gentle yet active fashion, in a joyous and reasonable fashion. But it does not at all follow from this that my story about them is finished; by no means. All four are still young and active, and, though their life is ordered as above described, it has not ceased on that account to be interesting; far from it. I still have much to tell you about them, and I guarantee that the sequel to my story will be much more interesting than anything that I have yet told you. They live gayly and as friends, working and resting, enjoying life and looking forward to the future, if not without anxiety, at least with the firm assurance that the farther we advance in life, the better it becomes.

April 4 (16) 1863.

ALEXANDRA KOLLONTAI: a biography
Cathy Porter

Brave, principled, beautiful, Alexandra Kollontai (1872-1952)
was the only woman in Lenin's government – and one of the most
famous women in Russian history. Passionate defender of the true
ideals of the revolution, she knew that revolution was not enough
– that real political change could only come with a transformation
in personal and family relationships. No one understood better the
conflict between love and work – her life, both personal and
political, was always stormy. She was a brilliant thinker, writer
and organiser, and intensely loyal to those she loved. Her ideas
are as important to day as they were in her own time. In this
magnificent and definitive biography, Cathy Porter offers a major
re-interpretation of an inspiring life.

'A valuable and admiring biography of this remarkable woman' –
E. J. Hobsbawm, *Guardian*

'Based on wide-ranging research and a firm grasp of political
issues . . . makes a very effective and important contribution' –
Dora Russell, *New Society*

'Carefully researched and sympathetic' – *New Statesman*

'Cathy Porter has made an important contribution to
contemporary understanding of this remarkable woman . . .
Her new book places Alexandra Kollontai's life properly in its
historical context' – *Financial Times*

LOVE OF WORKER BEES
Alexandra Kollontai
Translated and Introduced by Cathy Porter
Afterword by Sheila Rowbotham

Love of Worker Bees, written by one of the most famous and gifted Russian women of our century, was greeted on publication in 1923 as sexually too explicit. This new translation makes available – for the first time for over forty years – a remarkable work of fiction which is both a moving love story and a graphic and rare portrait of Russian life in the 1920s. Set in Russia after the October revolution and the Civil War, the heroine Vasya – one of the most-delightful in Russian literature – struggles to come to terms with her passionate need and love for her husband and the demands of the new world in which she lives. Her story unfolds against a backcloth of the 'ordinary' Russian people of the time – the Party workers, entrepreneurs, prostitutes, manipulators, idealists.

'Refreshingly transparent and yet unmistakeably honest, packed with detail, like a bright young woman's letters home to her best friend' – Alan Brien, *Sunday Times*

'An eloquent mixture of public and private themes' – Lorna Sage, *Observer*

If you would like to know more about Virago books, write to us at Ely House, 37 Dover Street, London W1X 4HS for a full catalogue.

Please send a stamped addressed envelope

Book Tokens

Give them
the pleasure of choosing
Book Tokens can be bought
and exchanged at most
bookshops